Stay With Me

SHAE RUBY

ISBN: 979-8-9905678-1-8

Cover Design & Interior Formatting by: Quirky Circe

Edited by: Julia at entirely bonkerz (@entirelybonkerz)

Lunar Rose Editing Services

Sensitivity Reader: Jay

Stay With Me

SHAE RUBY

For all my survivors

playlist

After Dark x Sweater Weather – *Daddy's Girl, Creamy & 11:11*

Past Lives – *Borns*

Arcade – *Duncan Laurence ft Fletcher*

Losing Game – *Gen Neo*

State Lines – *Novo Amor*

Die For You – *The Weeknd*

Face Down – *The Red Jumpsuit Apparatus*

Beautiful Things – *Benson Boone*

Your Guardian Angel – *The Red Jumpsuit*

Apparatus

Chemical – *Post Malone*

Teardrops – *Liam Payne*

Is It Really You? – *Sleep Token & Loathe*

Hopeless – *Too Close To Touch*

Trigger Warnings

Hello reader,

I write dark stories that can be disturbing to some. This book contains dark themes to include graphic sex scenes, rape (not by MMC), domestic violence, stabbing, murder, death, resuscitation, shooting of the FMC, nurse/patient hookup, unethical sex in the workplace (remember this is fiction, PLEASE), death of a sibling, grief. I may be missing some triggers, so instead, consider this a blanket trigger warning.

I trust you know your triggers before proceeding, and always remember to take care of your mental health.

For more things Shae Ruby,
visit **authorshaeruby.com**

PROLOGUE

There's shattered glass everywhere, the kind of shards that cut deeper than skin, and the ones that also shred the heart. And God, my heart is in tatters at the moment.

The other shoe has dropped.

I crawl over the crushed glass, tiny fragments digging into the palms of my hands and knees. The blood that trails under and behind me reminds me of the life I've led with Robert. A life full of pain, no less significant than my throbbing head from where he threw me against the kitchen cabinets.

The bloody knife gleams across the kitchen floor, and I don't even know how it got there. It's all a blur. But I still crawl over to it, slowly but surely, hoping he's slowed down. Maybe he thinks I'm done for, that this is how I go. *Did you really stab me, Rob?* It all feels like a dream. Except it must be real because the way my insides burn and the blood dripping down my side tell a different story than the one I want to convince myself of.

Right before I can reach the knife, just mere inches from my fingers, he kicks me in the side with his steel-toed boot. I wince, tensing as I brace myself for another hit on the only side of my body that seems to have any strength left. The crunch of my ribs is loud in my ears, and the pain is absolutely blinding. Blood, warm and sticky, is pooling under me, and I lie my cheek down on the kitchen tiles as I contemplate where I go from here. *How the hell do I get out of this?*

"You fucking slut!" He growls, gripping my hair in his fist as he removes me from the comfort of the cold floor. "I always knew there was something between y'all, you little liar."

"I swear there was nothing!"

Leave him.

Get out.

Run.

You don't need him.

You don't have to see him ever again.

I whimper again when he steps away from me, and the only reason I'm aware of it is from the crunch of his shoes on the shards of glass littering the tiled floor. He seems to be walking slow on purpose, and I count his steps.

One. Two. Three.

Pause.

And then the sound of the front door slamming behind him.

Full-body sobs take over me, making the pain worse, and I shift onto my hands and knees and crawl to the kitchen island. My ribs shift with every inch of space I cover, and I wheeze when I take hold of the edge of the counter and try to pull myself up.

With shaky, slippery, bloody hands, I grip the edge of the counter again, pulling myself up just for my knees to give out. A chuckle bursts past my lips, but it holds no humor. It's not lost on me that I've been told to leave him countless times.

He's ruining your life.

He's going to kill you one day, and I don't want to sit down and watch.

I worry about you.

He's dangerous.

I want him out of your life.

You just have to love yourself enough to leave.

You are stronger than he lets you think you are.

Cheyenne would say all of these things, and I didn't listen.

I didn't listen.

Now fucking look at me.

With one last cry, I manage to pull myself up from the ground. Immediately, I bend over, clutching at my side for dear life. I don't know how long I have before I bleed out, especially since he yanked the knife out. Everyone knows you should never take out the knife. Does he want me *dead?* Or just paralyzed for the rest of my life?

I shuffle over to the other side of the house, looking for my purse. Searching frantically in slow motion for the one thing I need to get out of here. I grab it with bloody fingers, finding my car keys inside of it, and slowly walk out of the house. Unlocking the car, I get in and reverse out of the driveway as fast as I can, barely managing to not hit the car parked behind me on the other side of the street.

I need to get out.

And little does Robert know, this is the last time he will ruin my life.

Or so I thought.

CHAPTER ONE

There's nothing like the adrenaline rush I get right before a game.

My heart thumps rapidly in my chest, and my hands sweat slightly from thinking about the crowd's noise—the one I can efficiently drown out as soon as I step onto the ice—and the fuzzy feeling in my head. It happens every single time, and even after twenty years of playing this game, it never gets old. The ice is my happy place, and playing with the team that became my family? I could never replace it.

I lace up my skates quickly, my hands taking over with muscle memory, and glance around at the boys putting on their base layers, chest protectors, and hockey pants. The hustle and bustle should give me a headache, but I find it strangely comforting. They're all talking but me. It's not that I'm a loner, I just have a little ritual that I don't break before every game. Going over plays from previous games, centering myself as much as possible. Focusing. Today's game is against Vancouver, a team that has left us in the dust before, and I refuse to let it happen in a home game.

The locker room goes suddenly quiet, and our captain, Noah, takes center stage. "Alright, boys," he begins his pregame speech, "I could give you all an inspirational speech or whatever the fuck." The guys snicker and smirk around the room. "Only I won't, because the only thing I want to say is that no one beats us at home. I expect excellence tonight, and I know it will be delivered. Now let's beat their asses!"

We all chant our agreement, "Sailors!" Hoping the crowd hears it, even though we know they won't.

Once we break apart, we single-file to the ice, and as soon as my skates touch the slippery surface, I can breathe again. I never noticed before how my shoulders are always tense, my neck stiff...until I come to the rink. As soon as I glide across the space and drop into a stretching position, I feel myself relax.

The lights of the arena bounce off the ice, painting it red and blue, and I breathe in deeply, exhaling slowly, drowning out the noise of the crowd. I stretch my groin, then my legs, then finally jump up and grab my stick.

As I make my way closer to our net, Jeremy skates up to me. "Wanna pass?" he asks me, his brown eyes crinkling. He sweeps his eyes over my face briefly, his strong nose wrinkling as he waits for my answer, and I nod.

"Let's do it."

Jeremy is a defenseman like me, my pair, and we spend a lot of time together during practice to perfect our plays. We're on the first line, along with Matthew, Noah, and Alex—who are loners despite getting along with everyone—and Oliver is our goalie.

These guys have been here for me through the highs and the lows for years now, and it's hard to imagine my life without them. When my little sister died of Leukemia, Jeremy moved in with me and took care of everything. I fell into a deep depression, not wanting to cook for myself or even clean my apartment. So he took it upon himself to do it all, and when I had no motivation to get out of bed and go to practice, he forced me to. He was my rock, and to this day, I'd say my bond is stronger with him than with the rest of the guys. He's my absolute best friend. Not to say that the other guys weren't there for me, though I couldn't have made it through without Jeremy by my side.

Either way, all of these guys have been a crucial part of my life for the past four years, as well as my journey in the NHL. Matthew is the extrovert in the group, right alongside Noah. If there was another pair of best friends, they'd be it. They're always the life of the party, and it's hard to be upset or down around them. Then there's Oliver, our goalie. He might be the funniest of the bunch and, surprisingly, a social butterfly.

Shaking myself out of my thoughts, I pay attention to Jeremy, who passes me the puck and lets it soar. It connects with my stick, flying towards the net. I'm more of an offensive defenseman, always seeking to score despite needing to protect the goalie. And Jeremy lives for that shit. I sink the puck into the net, and Oliver smirks as he slides the other way, letting me score. The asshole isn't even trying to practice.

After the twenty minutes, we all line up for the national anthem, hands over our hearts. Once that's done and the lights fully come on, we get into position. Matthew is taking the face-off this time, and once the referee drops the puck, it's fucking game time.

The energy in the arena is addictive, with the cheers, the oohs and ahs, and the clapping. But I don't let it distract me. Vancouver came to play today, and their offense is relentless, trying to score at all costs. Jeremy and I aren't letting them, though, hitting the puck to the other side of the rink and passing to our offense.

The left winger for Vancouver shoots it toward the net, and Jeremy soars for it, passing it to me. I pass to Noah, who is a couple of feet away, and he takes off with the puck across the other side of the rink. But it doesn't last long, seeing as the same guy who just tried to score, flies toward Noah and slams him into the boards, then steals it away.

It's almost time to switch lines when he comes flying toward us, taking a slap shot at the net. Only Oliver slaps it with his stick and then passes it to me. I pass it to Jeremy, who is then slammed by one of the guys from the opposite team, and he passes the puck right back to the asshole who tried to score. I get in front of the net and slap it away, but he comes back and hits it again, slamming my stick against his in the process. He throws himself into the crease, over my stick, and collides with Oliver.

I throw down my stick and yank him by the back of the jersey, taking off my helmet as we face off. With stick in hand, he shoves me back, and I do too.

"Don't mess with the fucking goalie, asshole!" I yell at him, but he just smirks.

"You fucking coward!" Jeremy yells out as everyone drops their helmets, and a fight breaks out.

I throw the first punch, connecting with his jaw since he still has a helmet on, the visor covering up to the bridge of his nose. His mouthguard falls out as I hear a crunch, and he groans. It doesn't stop him, though. He hits me square in the cheekbone, splitting my skin, and I hit him again, right over the same spot as before.

Instead of hitting me with his fist, he uses his hockey stick to smack me upside the head. I feel a crunch on the top of my head, and I fall on my ass. The rink becomes blurry, and I hear the refs whistle again. My spine begins to tingle, sweat rushes down my back, and right before I try to get up, I fall onto my back.

I blink once, trying to clear my blurry vision, but it doesn't work.

I'll always watch over you.

I hear Courtney's voice right before darkness engulfs me, swallowing me whole.

When my eyes open again, they're barely squinting, hurting from the bright lights ahead of me. I try to look around to see a white roof, except I'm moving. The rumble of an engine rocking my body side to side. The sound of sirens makes my head pound, and then my eyes connect with a man's blue ones from right beside me.

"It's okay," he assures me. "We're almost to the hospital."

Oh, that's right—asshole hit me with his hockey stick. Of fucking course. I think of replying to him, but instead just close my eyes briefly before the ambulance finally stops. That thing was making the headache worse with every bump of the road, and I bet anything that my life is about to suck even more.

"Up you go." The man says as another person helps him with the stretcher, taking me down from the ambulance and wheeling me into the entrance of the hospital.

I don't want to pay attention as one of the nurses shows up, in fact, I close my eyes. All I catch is the tail end of 'force blunt trauma to the head' and 'loss of consciousness'. I guess that does suck for me; if I have a concussion, I'm sitting out for the next few games. That won't bode well for Jeremy. I doubt any of the other guys can make a pair with him the way I do. He'll probably be stuck with one of the rookies.

They wheel me into a room and then leave, with the nurse staying behind. It's not lost on me that I'm still wearing all my hockey gear, and I'm burning up. My skates made it off my feet, at least, so I won't have sharp blades slicing anyone up around here. However, I'd like to see them try to take off my clothes to put me in one of those hospital gowns. That's the kind of stuff my friends would cackle over. Shit, I might too, at this point. Unless it hurts my head, then I'm holding it in.

"Hi, sweetheart," the nurse says as she stands next to the stretcher. "You got hit pretty good there, didn't ya?"

I groan, feeling the throbbing at the top of my head. "I guess so." Something tickles my cheek, and with a frown, I reach up to touch it. "What's this?" I rub the sticky liquid between my fingers, bringing them in front of my eyes as I squint to look at it. It's freaking blood.

Blood.

Oh, God.

"I think I'm gonna be sick," I blurt out, and the nurse produces a bag from her pocket and brings it to my face right before I hurl.

My stomach contracts, and I probably expelled everything I had to eat today, and more. My head is killing me the entire time, and with every heave, it feels like it's going to explode.

That asshole is going to pay for this—Meyers. I'm hunting him down the next time I play against him, and he's not making it out of that rink without his own concussion.

"It's okay," the nurse coos as I wipe my mouth with the back of my hand. She pulls the bag away and throws it in the nearest trash bin. "We're gonna get you all fixed up."

I look around the room for the first time since being wheeled in here. The walls are sterile white, there's a monitor that keeps beeping angrily, and there's a sink and another trash bin across the room. Oh, and hand sanitizer attached to the wall next to the door. I glance at the nurse, a lady older than me by at least thirty years, and see her kind brown eyes smiling up at me. She's trying to make me feel comfortable. Except there's nothing comfortable about this. I lost consciousness. I was hit in the head by a damn stick. What if I can't play anymore? What if I'm benched for the rest of the season?

"It hurts to open my eyes," I groan. "What's next?"

"Just a second." She replies softly, logging on to a computer next to me. The only reason I know it's because she's clacking on the keyboard so hard I'm afraid it's going to break. Oh, and it's hurting my head again. *Yay.* "The doctor ordered a CT scan, and then we will go from there. But if I'm correct, you're going to need stitches."

I'll definitely be needing stitches.

If my face is any indication, anyway. However, head injuries do bleed more. But I heard the crack. It doesn't take a genius to figure out something is *broken.* Just like my heart.

Hockey is my everything. I haven't done anything else since

I was five years old, and I always knew it was my future. Since I was a little kid, I have always dreamed of being an NHL player, and nothing was going to stop me from achieving that goal. Will this stop me now? Will this take my livelihood away? I can't help but be scared that this will literally take me out for the season, for life even. It feels like I'm failing my parents. After everything they sacrificed so I could be here, and now it could be taken away over a petty fight. My dad worked two jobs until I went to college on a full-ride scholarship. He worked so hard that I barely saw him, yet he still made time for my games. He didn't miss a single one. My parents both went through so much just so I could live out my dream, and the last thing I want to do is let them down.

My chest tightens painfully until it's hard to breathe, and I begin to sweat. Breathing is a chore, coming so hard and fast that I can't keep up. "Hey," The nurse says calmly, "It's okay. We're going to get you all fixed up. You're okay!"

I slow down my breaths as she mimics breathing exercises with me, and it actually works, relaxing me once more—as much as it's possible with a throbbing headache, nausea, and the inability to open my eyes fully. The light is really pissing me off, but nothing will ever piss me off more than if my hockey career ends here in this hospital bed. If I'm taken out of this game, I'll be ready for someone to take me out of this life, too.

"Hurts." I groan. "Really bad."

"I know, honey." The nurse touches my arm and her phone rings. "This is Stacey." The lady says, "Oh, you're ready? We'll be there in about ten minutes. God knows, I don't know how to take off hockey gear."

I smirk. "I don't know if I can help you either." I tell her honestly, "My head really fucking hurts."

"Well, you will try, big guy." She laughs, "How tall are you anyway?"

"Six-four." She gasps as I laugh, making my head throb more.

"Here, let's start with the pants, the socks, and the…oh my God." She frowns. "How many layers are you wearing?"

"A lot." I groan as she begins to pull off my socks. "I'll help, I swear."

Stacey makes quick work of removing my hockey pants, pads, and layers with the scissors. Just as my vision blurs and my head spins, there's another bag under my chin. It's like she's psychic, because I throw up again, and she pats my arm when I'm done.

"You poor thing." I do feel like a poor thing right now, not gonna lie. This royally sucks. "I'm going to remove your jersey and your top layers, and then we'll get you that CT scan, okay?"

"Alright," I grit out.

After cutting everything off, she gets me into a gown and wheels me over to radiology. It's still hard to open my eyes, but once they put me close to that dome and inject some dye into my IV, I try to relax. It's hard with the loud sound it makes, but I'm doing a pretty good job at staying still. It feels like I'm peeing myself though, with all the warmth rushing to my dick. What a strange feeling.

The radiology technician finishes up, wheeling my stretcher out to where my nurse is waiting for me, and Stacey takes me back out to the hallway with the bright lights. People pass me by, giving me looks full of pity, and I just know in my bones they probably recognize me. I hate that they pity me, mainly because it makes me think of the worst possible outcome.

Stacey opens the door to my room, pushing me in—I don't know how this small woman is wheeling me around—and hooks me back up to the monitors. The steady beep of them makes my headache worse, and I close my eyes as I try to block out as much of the light as possible. Thankfully, she walks out silently, leaving me to wait for the doctor.

After what feels like forever, there's a knock at the door, and a man in his—probably—sixties comes in. "Good evening, Mr.

Anderson." He looks me over quickly and sits on a short stool beside the stretcher. "How are you feeling?"

What a stupid question.

"Like shit," I reply with a grin. There's nothing funny about the situation, but since it feels like I'm getting bad news, I'm totally deflecting.

"Yes." He grimaces. "Though you do have a small brain bleed, which should dissolve fairly quickly judging by its size. And you have a really tiny skull fracture. Only about an inch."

Yep, bad news.

"Brain bleed?" I ask as my breathing speeds up again. All the possibilities run rampant in my head. "How long will I be benched?"

"Well, first, we want to keep you for monitoring until your brain bleed dissolves." He deadpans. "Just in case it gets worse."

"Worse?" My voice rises. *It can get worse?* "How long?"

"A week."

"And benched?"

"If everything goes smoothly and the brain bleed dissolves…" He trails off, looking at the CT scan results on the computer. "Probably a few more weeks after discharge. We have to take it day by day."

Fuck.

"Oh, okay." That is all I can say. Because, what choice do I have?

He continues to talk then, explaining all of the complications this can have and why he's keeping me in the hospital for a week. It all goes in one ear and out the other. All I can focus on is being here for a week, benched for at least a few weeks.

But what if it does get worse?

What if I'm benched for the season?

Bailey

CHAPTER TWO

December in Seattle is so much colder than December in Georgia. That's why I have the cheapest rug I could find just to put right next to my bed so I don't freeze my toes off when I step on the cheap linoleum that covers every square inch of my new-to-me studio apartment. Which, by the way—is falling apart.

The walls are weathered white and turning slightly yellow. They said it was water damage when I moved in. But I have no choice, as I'm paying for all the bills alone now and, quite frankly, struggling. I haven't even let Cheyenne, my best friend who lives ten minutes away, come over because I'm ashamed of my current living situation. That's why I'm working six days a week at the hospital—to try to make it better.

It's four p.m. now, and I have exactly two hours and forty-five minutes until I return to work. My body feels heavy with exhaustion, like I can barely move, so I get out of bed in search of coffee. Liquid courage. The only thing that pushes me to keep on moving, to keep on trucking along.

My feet touch the fluffy rug next to my bed, my toes sinking into it comfortingly, and I exhale roughly. Just another day in the life of Bailey Thomas—my new last name. I dip my hand under my oversized t-shirt, touching the scar on the side of my torso, the one where he sank the knife between my rib cage.

I'm lucky I'm alive. I'm damn lucky I even made it to a hospital before passing out, or dying, even. But I did, and I asked them to keep me in private status so Robert couldn't find me. And that's when Cheyenne told me it was 'the last fucking straw', bought me a one-way plane ticket, and now I'm here. In Seattle, Washington. With her.

I left everything behind, including my phone and car, not wanting to be tracked. Except sometimes, I wonder if it was all for nothing. Whether he'll find me no matter how far I run from him. He has a knack for chasing me, and I have one for running. Will I flee again if he comes to me? Or will I be strong and face him head-on? But I already know the answer to that. The fear that travels through my body—making me shiver—at the thought of seeing him again. Well, that answers all of my questions.

I can't face him again.

My body will freeze on the spot, a deer in headlights, and panic will take over until I can't breathe again. Maybe I *will* die after all.

Now I'm going to therapy weekly, thanks to him. What a fucking gift he's given me. The one that keeps on giving. I'm fairly certain I will never be able to trust a man again, no matter what my counselor Katherine has to say about it.

It's funny how different she and I are—night and day. Both of us are twenty-six, so I would've thought we'd have more in common. However, spending time with her only accentuates the fact that she's so put together, and I'm a mess. Maybe I'm wrong, and she has trauma hiding behind her Colgate smile, or perhaps she has the best relationship with both her mother and father and is lacking all the issues I have. It's hard to see eye to eye with someone like her, but at the same time she might be my only friend other than Cheyenne. And that's just sad. But I can't lie, she is kind to me. If it were up to that woman, I'd be healed by now. She'd do it with her bare hands if she could. Nevertheless, that's not how life works, and we both know it.

I am still paranoid everywhere I go, afraid that death will finally catch up to me. It's why I sprint to my car in the hospital parking lot. Always terrified he'll be waiting for me in the shadows of the awning right next to the employee's back door. The only thing protecting me, I hope, is that he needs a badge to get through those doors. That is, unless he enters this hospital as a patient. Or as a guest.

But I don't want to think about that.

I know I self-sabotage. That I'm a pessimist. A negative Nancy. But I can't help it, can I? How do I recover from this? All I see when I close my eyes are images of me crawling through glass. My knees and hands shredded, my heart torn to pieces. Blood trailing after me. A gash on my side.

And I can't unsee any of it.

I slowly pad across the space between my bed and the small kitchen, opening a cabinet above the stove since I don't have a pantry, and pull out the coffee. I fill the water compartment, replace the filter, and dump coffee in it. The fantastic aroma wafts through the air, filling my nostrils, and I take a deep breath. Sometimes, I think coffee is the only thing in my life that brings me joy. Even Cheyenne can't manage it most of the time, although I pretend she does. I don't want to hurt her feelings. So when she invites me over for wine, facials, and chocolate cake, I give her my best smile and pretend it makes me happy. The wine helps me pretend, if I'm being honest. It doesn't erase the fact that lately it's been hard to feel anything aside from despair.

Despair at the life I'm leading.

Starting over has been challenging. The past six months have been harder than I thought. Grueling, even. It takes all of my strength to put one foot in front of the other, especially when my future looks so bleak. I can't imagine a time when I won't be working six days a week, exhausting myself beyond repair, all because I could never let someone else in again. It's not that I don't have needs. It's just that I don't need a man to satisfy them. No. The toys in my nightstand are enough for me, and they will be for a long time to come.

I pour the coffee into a mug along with a shit load of creamer and sugar in it, because I'm that girl, and take a sip. The hot liquid rolls down my throat, instantly soothing me. I need to put on my big girl pants—or scrubs—and get my shit together. Despite hating my life, I do enjoy my job for the most part. I can get through it just fine as long as I don't talk much to my patients. However, some of them are persistent, to my chagrin. As long as no men grace me with their presence, I'm *mostly* fine.

It's just when there's a dick between their legs that I start feeling angsty and like I need to flee. I don't think that feeling will ever go away.

Getting my phone from the bedside table, I check it.

CHEY

We still on for five?

Fucccckkk.

I totally forgot I made plans to have breakfast for dinner with her, but I'm really not in the mood. It's one of those days. A day where cancelations are the only acceptable answer.

BAILEY

I'm soooo sorry. Still in bed. Feel dead. Rain check?

CHEY

You suck. I still love you, though. But fine… whatever. See you soon? Maybe you can come to learn to skate on your day off and fall on your face?

I smirk. I seem to do that a lot.

Cheyenne teaches skating lessons to toddlers and figure

skaters at the nearest Olympic arena, and she loves her job so much. Occasionally, I go watch her, jealously clutching my heart in a vice grip. I don't mean to feel that way; I just wish something brought me as much joy as teaching brings her. Nursing used to be that way for me once upon a time, until I had to uproot my entire life.

Sometimes I join Cheyenne at the rink and skate. I can't say I'm any good at it, but she's really good at teaching. I'm still marching, not quite ready to glide. Every time I try, my stomach dips, and I feel like I'm going to fall on my ass. Which is why I'm decked out with butt pads—I didn't know those were a thing—knee pads and a helmet. I look ridiculous. Yeah, she laughs every time. But I *am* getting better. At least, that's what I tell myself.

BAILEY

Saturday.

CHEY

You're not gonna sleep?

BAILEY

Do I ever? Fuck sleep. It's for the dead.

CHEY

That's the spirit. See ya there, babe.

I gulp my coffee down, because I'm taking forever, and when I look at the time, it's already five thirty p.m. So much for breakfast. I guess, an Uncrustable it is.

I brush my teeth, jump in the shower, and then get dressed. My hair is wet, but I still put it up in a ponytail, wearing a big scrunchie so my hair doesn't break—damn thin strands—and look at myself in the mirror. My sea-foam green eyes have dark bags underneath from lack of sleep, thanks to my nightmares, so I do my skincare and then correct them with plenty of concealer.

Next, I do the rest of my makeup because I look dead to the world without it. I don't even know why I bother. It's not like anyone freaking cares what I look like at work, except me. Although there's nothing orderly about my life, my appearance is the only thing I *can* control. Which is why I always try to look presentable. Being in control of something is crucial to my survival lately, especially when most of what I do feels so out of my norm.

By the time I'm all done getting ready, my Uncrustable is defrosted, and it's time to go. The drive to the hospital is thirty minutes one way, and I'm already pushing it on time. If I'm not careful, traffic will get the best of me and I'll be late.

With my food in hand and my work bag, I check that my bat is in its rightful place, then exit my studio apartment, locking the bolt on the way out. I look left and right before making my way to the stairs and running down them two at a time. Before I step down from them, I look around again, then sprint to my car when I deem it safe. I always park right in front of the stairs for a quick escape if it's ever needed. I don't even care if I look nervous and I won't ever deny it. But last time was the last time, and I will never put myself in a position again where I'm vulnerable enough to be abused once more.

I shut myself in the car and lock the doors, throwing my work bag to the passenger side of the vehicle and pulling out of the parking lot. It's six now, and I have forty-five minutes until I have to be there, clocked in and ready for report. So, I drive out of my apartment complex as fast as I can and onto the highway.

Thankfully, the drive to work is pretty uneventful, with barely any traffic. Yet when I pull into the hospital's parking lot and don't find a spot close to the entrance, my chest begins to feel tight with that fear all over again. Not today, *please*. Not today.

I end up having to park four rows away, officially at least a five-minute walk to the door, and my hands begin to shake. But I still grab my work bag and look around before getting out of my car. I lock it until I hear the beep and all but sprint toward the door. Maybe if I run fast enough I will make it there in half the time. It's freezing tonight, and I don't make my life any easier by not wearing a jacket. I totally forgot it, and I have long sleeves under my scrub top, but they're just not enough when I'm outside.

I make it to the door and scan my badge. Hearing the door's electric sound, I shut it behind me to prevent anyone from entering without their badge. Everyone is wearing their stethoscopes around their necks as we make our way to the elevator, and I grimace. I have mine safely tucked in my bag, refusing to put myself in a position where I could be choked with it.

God, I sound crazy sometimes.

Once in the elevator, we're so cramped I can barely breathe, and when we finally make it to the tenth floor, I all but run to the break room. Scanning my badge, I again hear that whirring sound that means the door is opening, and I step in. It's a big space, with lockers lining one of the walls, two long tables in the middle of the room surrounded by chairs, a television, and a sink. Posters cover every single wall, all about nursing skills and announcements. There are boxes of pizza on one of the tables and paper plates right next to it.

I go to my locker, put in the combination, and take my clipboard and stethoscope out of my bag. When I'm ready, I step out of the room and go to the nurse's station to get a report. There's a crowd already in the middle of it, and as always, I'm one of the last ones to get a turn. I guess I'm getting all my patients from the same nurse though, so that's reassuring since that means I don't have to wait for anyone else.

Nurse Linda, a pretty brunette with blue eyes who is

definitely younger than me, steps up to me with her own clipboard. "Ready?"

I nod, "As I'll ever be."

Linda walks me to one of the rooms, opening the door until we're both inside. "This is Mrs. Erin Jones. Seventy-five-year-old female presenting with Diabetic Ketoacidosis. Her last blood sugar was six hundred, and we've been trying to get it under control with an Insulin drip. Finger sticks every two hours…"

She goes on and on about lab work, and everything they've discussed. How Mrs. Jones has plenty of visitors per shift—*great*—even at night. Her husband sometimes stays the night when he feels well enough to do it and is sweet as pie.

"Hi, Mrs. Jones," I say with a fake smile, my lips almost refusing to tip up, my face tight from the strain. "My name is Bailey, and I will be taking care of you tonight. If you need anything at all, please press the call light. But I'll be in here quite a bit regardless."

"Oh, please, dear. Call me Erin."

I nod. "*Erin.*"

I feel relief as soon as I turn around, away from her prying eyes, to write my name and phone number on the board. Then I hurry out of the room with Linda on my heels. I can finally breathe again when I make it out to the hallway, and I gasp in some much-needed air. Ever since Rob—fuck, I hate thinking about him—I've had social anxiety. It affects my work. My hands and armpits get sweaty just from having a conversation with my patients. It brings me genuine physical pain.

I guess the only person I still let in is Cheyenne.

Linda closes Mrs. Jones' door and takes me to the next patient's room, rattling on and on as she clearly does. I follow the same ritual I always do: Introduce myself, put on a fake smile, write my name on the board, and leave the room. I do my best to maintain good bedside manners, but some days are harder than others.

The next and last patient is a male, apparently, but Linda stops me before I can go in the room. My heart is already beating fast as she grabs my elbow. "So, before we go in there, I must warn you. He's a hotshot NHL player. He's very *young*. All the nurses are after him, so you may have a lot—and I mean a *lot*—of help tonight."

Perfect.

The less I have to interact with him, the better.

She opens the door and we walk into the room, a cold gust of air hitting my face. I immediately stop in my tracks when the patient comes into view, and I narrow my eyes at him. I've never thought of a man as beautiful, especially not after everything I've been through, but I guess there's a first time for everything. And this man with his floppy brown hair and gorgeous blue eyes is heart-stopping. I've never seen an NHL player up close—I haven't even watched hockey, really—but he's all muscles and thick forearms. I can tell even through the gown. He is *hugging* it like a second skin.

Jesus.

Snap the fuck out of it, Bailey.

He's just another man.

"Theodore Anderson," Linda smirks. "He came in—"

"Theo, *please*," he groans, not even glancing my way. "You're making me feel old."

"With a skull fracture and a brain bleed." She rolls her eyes at him. "And he's apparently 'bored as fuck'. Yeah, I put that in the chart under nursing notes."

How amusing. I don't smile.

"Anyway," she continues when she realizes I don't find it funny, her face sobering. "He needs to stay until the brain bleed dissolves, which the doctor said could be a week. It's a tiny one."

"And how did he get the brain bleed?" I ask dryly. His eyes finally settle on me.

"Hockey stick to the head."

He and I both flinch at the same time.

"Oh…" I grimace. "That must have really hurt, Mr. Anderson."

"Theo."

"Mr. Anderson is just fine," I retort, moving to the board to write my name as Linda rattles on again. I swear, the girl never shuts the fuck up.

"And your name?" he asks me.

Right. "My name is Bailey." I give him my back as I write on the board, purposely neglecting to write my work phone number on it. He can call the nurses' station if he needs something. I'm sure everyone will be *oh so happy* to assist him.

"And tell me, sweet Bailey." I can hear the smile even though I can't see it. My spine goes ramrod straight at the nickname. "Are you always this happy? Or only on Tuesdays?"

I turn around and give him my tightest smile. "Oh, I'm never happy," I reply before heading for the door. I can hear him mumble *'I can tell'* under his breath, and it kind of pisses me off just a bit. But I ignore him. Guys are assholes. Maybe girls would work out better for me. "Now, if you'll excuse me, I have charting to do and medicine to distribute."

"Of course, of course." He smiles, a grin so bright it's freaking blinding. "Take your time. Can't wait to see you again."

Of course, you can't.

With a wink and a smile from him, I turn around and walk out of the room. I can feel my right eye twitching from that interaction, and I can tell I'm not going to like him at all.

"OMG," Linda says when she closes the door behind us. "Isn't he so cute?"

"Sure," I comment. "If you like jocks. They're mostly assholes, though."

Linda frowns, her lips tipping down. "He doesn't seem like an asshole…"

"Oh, come on, Linda." I roll my eyes as we walk to the

nurses' station. Personally I'm in search of a computer before they disappear. "You honestly think he's going to be an asshole right now? All eyes are on him."

"Maybe he's having the best attitude he can under these circumstances."

"Sure," I repeat.

She walks away from me, clearly tired of my shitty attitude. But I can't help it. I was really hoping tonight wasn't the night where I had a male patient. Yet here we are.

I grab the computer on wheels as well as a chair and open charts, going through them. I make sure to note lab values and any vital information about each patient, writing it down on my clipboard.

And then I get ready for the long shift ahead of me.

Theo

CHAPTER THREE

Tonight is my third night in this hospital, and if anything, I'm feeling worse by the minute. It's not just the boredom choking me, but the memories too. When I was in high school, my sister would be stuck in hospitals for months on end. Due to her Leukemia and fragile immune system from her treatments, she was always sick. It didn't matter what precautions we took to prevent it; it never seemed to help.

I was always by her side after school, wearing masks so that I could read to her. She loved it when I read Harry Potter books, especially when she was too weak to hold up heavy books. It was our thing—me reading to her while she looked at me with star-struck eyes. There was so much love and appreciation in them, and I knew right then and there that I could never let her down. That's why, despite my hatred of hospitals, I stuck around.

Now though, I have no desire to be here. Mainly because I'm now the one in a hospital bed. Maybe I'm naive since hockey is a contact sport, but I never expected to be hospitalized over an injury. I always thought I'd have something along the lines of a broken arm, not a cracked skull. I definitely would've never even dreamed of it being due to a petty fight I started.

Although, to be fair, you don't mess with the goalie. It's an unspoken rule in hockey, and Meyers knows that. *Everyone* knows that. He played dirty by hitting me with his hockey stick, and I hope he at least got suspended for a couple of games for it. *Fucking coward.*

I've been stuck here for three days now, and though I know I'm supposed to be out of here within a few more, I can't help but struggle to see the light at the end of the tunnel. I consider myself a carefree guy for the most part, but damn this sucks. There's really no way to be that happy when you're stuck in a room with nothing to do but watch TV, which I can't even do much of with this damn concussion. I've considered going to sleep, but I'm way too keyed up for it. I need to get out of here.

There's a knock at the door, and I rest my head back against the pillow and stare at the ceiling before letting out a soft breath. The door opens a crack, but then no one comes in. Instead, I hear arguing from the other side. One voice is heated while the other is placating, and my brows furrow in concentration as I strain my ears to try to hear what's going on.

"I don't need help!" Bailey growls. "I said I'm *fine*."

Bailey comes into the room, carrying a bunch of supplies in her hands and setting them on the bedside table. She starts opening wrappers, not once looking in my direction as she clearly fumes, her nostrils flaring slightly. Another nurse peeks her head in, grimacing for a second, then giving me a soft smile. She shakes her head and leaves.

"You don't have to be so rude, you know," I blurt out.

Bailey looks up at me, raising an eyebrow. "Why do you even care?" She opens a pack of something with a tourniquet, and I swallow hard. "It's none of your business."

I chuckle, and she stiffens. "If you didn't want me to make it my business, then you shouldn't have done it right outside my room where I could hear you."

Bailey's face blanches. Then she quickly shakes it off, pursing her lips. Even through her anger, she's beautiful. Her full lips are pursed, and there's a little wrinkle between her eyebrows as she frowns.

"I need to draw your blood, Mr. Anderson," she says softly, yet her frown hasn't disappeared. I can tell she's irritated, but I don't pry, especially not when she has a needle in her hand. "You ready?"

I gulp, nodding my head too quickly. It's not that I'm scared of needles. Not exactly. More apprehensive than anything. I just don't enjoy getting poked.

"I guess," I mumble.

"Extend your arm for me," she demands, and I narrow my eyes. Not even a *please*? However, I do as she says, giving her my arm and pumping my fist because it's not my first rodeo. They've been poking me every day since I got here. "There you go."

Bailey wraps the tourniquet around my arm, pressing on my veins, and then she cleans the area with an alcohol wipe. I wince from the cold wipe, but it's nothing compared to the way she shoves the needle into my arm. No warning, no gentleness to be found.

I groan because, holy fuck. What did I do to deserve this? Have I been mean to her? Or is she just this way with everyone? "Ow," I growl. "That *hurts*, Bailey."

Bailey looks up to make eye contact with me, then rolls her eyes. I drop mine to the tube that's filling up with my blood. And just when I think we're done, she replaces it with the next one. My head feels a little woozy, but I breathe in deeply through my nose and the feeling slightly dissipates.

"You'll be alright," she replies with a tight smile, letting go of the tourniquet and then pulling out the needle. You're kidding, right? "All done."

"That actually hurt."

"I'll be back later, Mr. Anderson."

I nod once. *Well, I won't be here.*

She gathers the trash, puts the needle in the sharps container, and then wordlessly exits the room. I look around for a moment, spotting my bag, then get out of bed. I can somehow feel how cold the floor is through my grippy socks, and I hurry up to get my sweatpants out of the bag Jeremy brought me yesterday. Being in this gown is not all it's cut out to be. Yeah, easy access for my care, but I refuse to show all my goods to the rest of the hospital.

Getting the sweatpants and a long-sleeve shirt from the bag, I dress myself as quickly as possible. My IV is in my hand, so I'm extra careful with it since I don't want a new one, and then I open the door silently. The lights are brighter than in my room, and it takes a moment for my eyes to adjust, but I slip out without a sound. There's not even one nurse or nurse assistant in the hallway, and I hurry toward the elevator. Thankfully, there's a sign with a directory for the hospital, and I press the eleventh-floor button that will take me to the cancer ward.

The elevator doors open, and silence greets me. It's eerie and lonely in here, and tears spring to my eyes from how sterile it feels and looks. I hate that these kids are stuck here, many times without anyone by their sides, just cruising through a life full of pain and heartache.

My sister would sob every time we had to leave her, especially since both of my parents had to work full time and I was too young to spend the night with her. I can't even imagine how alone she must have felt. No amount of reading to her or holding her hand could erase everything she lived on her own. The number of times she was poked and prodded, the MRIs, the PET scans, the surgeries, the chemo, radiation, and well, the never-ending pain all of that caused. And she had to go through it on her own, for the most part, as a teenager.

Her cancer journey was long and arduous, lasting many years. At first, she was very sick, but chemo started working, and she got better for a while. She even went into remission. But eventually, she relapsed again, and she had to do a bone marrow transplant. I had never seen her sicker than that. Not even when she was throwing up multiple times a day from the chemotherapy.

She had to be in the hospital for months on end, and her immune system was so deteriorated that she was constantly either sick or fighting some kind of infection in her body. After that, she went into the shortest remission ever, and when she eventually relapsed *again*, she did chemo and radiation one more time. It didn't work, and she started clinical trials.

Missing out on my childhood and my parents hurt really bad, although seeing her slowly dying, a walking corpse, hurt even worse. Many times not even moving, just perched on her bed, barely breathing. My best friend, the one who forced me to play Barbie dolls with her. The person who dressed me up in princess dresses and makeup and painted my nails. I let her do it because I loved her, because any ounce of her attention brought me joy.

And the day she died? It was the worst day of my life.

Courtney's breathing is shallow, strained. Her breaths are coming out in gasps, and her eyes can barely open. She looks skinnier than ever, gaunt. Her cheeks are hollowed, and her eyes are sunken in. It brings a sharp pain behind my ribcage, and I struggle to breathe too. This perfect girl, the one who has been my biggest cheerleader since we were little. The one who built snow castles with me and threw snowballs at my face. The one who held my hand before doing something scary and always told me everything would be alright.

I know I'm about to lose it all.

"Please don't leave me," I sob, holding Courtney's frail hand. It's all bones, and I'm being as gentle as possible, not wanting to hurt her. Except it's hard when all I want to do is hold on and never, ever, let go. "I'll give up hockey. Please, God, I'll do anything. Just don't take her from me."

Courtney's eyes open slightly, the blue peeking out through her lashes, and she gives my hand a gentle squeeze—barely there. She smiles through her pain, and this time I'm seeing double. Blurry. My vision is completely fucked up, but it's nothing compared to the pain in my heart. She coughs, a wet rattle coming from her lungs, and I flinch.

"Theo," she rasps, a wobbly smile on her pale and chapped lips. Her bottom lip splits slightly and blood bubbles up, making her flinch. She's on a lot of medications, and I can tell she's struggling to stick with me right now. They're trying to keep her comfortable, they said, to help her pass peacefully. Fuck that, I don't want her to go at all. I hold her hand tighter, and I know it's probably hurting her, but I don't let up and she doesn't complain. "I'm here, brother."

I sob, my shoulders shaking, "Don't leave me." I repeat. "Please, Court...I can't do this without you."

Tears stream down her face too, and she sniffles. "I love you." Her voice cracks, and I swear my chest splits down the middle. "I'll always watch over you."

"I wish you didn't have to go to Heaven," I sob. "I wish you could just keep being an angel on Earth."

Courtney sobs. "I know." Her hand shakes in mine. "Me too."

Her eyes close, and I panic, the beep from the machines becoming slower. I look up and see that her heart rate has dropped, and my chest begins to heave. "Wait—please."

"I'm so scared, T."

"I'm here, Court." I drape my body over the bed, trying not to crush her, but still hugging her to me all the same. Her head falls back on the pillow, her body so limp and bony. She can't even hold her weight up anymore. My body shakes with my sobs, and I hold her tightly. "I love you, I love you, I love you."

"I love—" she sighs, "You."

And then a flat line.

She was eighteen years old—too young. And at only twenty-two years old, I was ignorant of how much her death would impact my life. How grief would hurt me, change me. My parents tried to prepare me for the stages of grief, but no amount of preparation could possibly get me ready to face them.

Five nurses are at the nurse's station, and I lean on the counter slightly, giving them the brightest smile I can muster—one I don't feel like giving. But I do it all the same, because I'm here to bring light into these little kids' lives. My gift to them. A little bit of sunshine from my sister, if you will.

"Hey," I say softly to the nurse next to the call light phone. "Do you have a recreation center?"

She smiles back, "We do." Pointing me in the direction of the rec room, she nods. "But there's no one there at this time."

I get that, especially since it's nine p.m. Except I'm not leaving here until I see some kids. "I'd like to read to some of your kids—the ones that don't have any parents with them."

Malia—the nurse—nods slowly, and tears spring to her eyes. "O-okay." She clears her throat, then says, "I'll see what I can do. For now, you can go wait there."

I go in the direction she pointed me to and find a set of open glass double doors. The space is huge, with a big circle-time rug, a bunch of recliners, an art corner, and even a little nutrition area. I scoot a chair into the middle of the room, positioning the recliners all across from me, and sit and wait.

I miss you, Court.

Always.

Bailey

CHAPTER FOUR

Knocking on Mr. Anderson's room door, I'm met with silence. I frown and open it, only to find his room empty. The door to the bathroom is wide open, and it's also vacant.

No fucking way.

I know I was a little mean to him, but where the hell is he? There's no way the little shit left the hospital, right? That would just be the cherry on top of my shitty night. *Great.*

Returning to the nurse's station, I get the attention of the first person I see, "Hey, have you seen Theo Anderson? Big guy, muscles, blue eyes?"

"The hockey player?" Amanda's eyes light up. "I haven't seen him lately, but damn, he is hot."

I huff and roll my eyes because, of course, that's what all these women are focused on—how hot he is—not the fact that he's injured and could lose his career over this.

"Alright, thanks." For nothing.

Walking up and down all the halls in the unit—which is shaped like a rectangle—I find no trace of him. My hands begin to tremble and my breaths come out in hard pants. Oh my fuck, I'm going to lose my damn nursing license if he left this fucking hospital. How does a patient even go missing? Where the fuck did he go?

All the nurses are gathered at the nurse's station, talking in hushed tones amongst each other. My back begins to sweat under my long-sleeve shirt, and this is the first time this winter that I'm grateful I'm not wearing a jacket. Damn it, it's hot in here. The closer I get to them, the more they begin to look up and disperse. My hands slap on the countertop and I glance at Amanda once more, my chest heaving. I bet I look insane—I feel it.

"Nothing?" Amanda asks with a frown.

"Nope." I pop the *p*. "I'm gonna call it."

She nods slowly. "Veronica!" she calls out to the charge nurse. "Bailey needs you."

Veronica walks toward me with a smile—which immediately drops when she sees me wiping sweat from my forehead and my shaking hands. "What's happening?" Her lips turn down and she searches my gaze. She has never seen me this flustered. I'm not someone who gets shaken up easily at work. I pride myself on being able to handle even the toughest situations. But a missing patient? Who has a head injury? I don't think I'm cut out for this. "What's wrong?"

"Theo Anderson," I begin, then swallow hard, "is missing."

"Oh, hell," she mutters. "What did you do?"

I rear back as if she slapped me. What did *I* do? Why does it have to be my fault? *Because it is.* "I didn't do anything. I drew his blood, and then he wasn't in his room when I came back."

"Did you check the entire unit?" she asks.

"The hallways." I nod. "I think we should call it."

"Alright," she sighs. "Amanda and the rest of the girls will look in the rooms. But you need to get off this unit and search the hospital. I'll have it on lockdown. No one gets to leave until we find him."

I nod quickly again. "Alright." My hands tremble as I blow

out a steady breath, trying to calm down. If he doesn't turn up, I'm going to need my Xanax. "Okay."

"Go," Veronica says, then gives orders to the rest of the nurses.

As I run to the elevators, I see her heading to the nutrition room. Honestly, I don't even know where to start. But I guess I need to search everywhere. So I press the buttons to every floor below me, seeing as the ones above are for kids, and begin my search. Of course, no one has seen him, so I go down to the cafeteria, Starbucks, and the fast-food plaza. He's not here either. *Not here.*

Squatting down, I slide against the wall of the fast-food plaza, trying to take deep breaths. I'm sweating profusely at this point, and I can hear my heartbeat in my ears. It's thundering, beating so fast I'm afraid I'm going to pass out. But I focus on the thud, thud, thud—trying to take deep breaths.

A hand lands on my shoulder and I startle, but then relief makes me sag against the wall. Theo. Finally.

"Are you okay, miss?" an unfamiliar voice asks me, and I stiffen once more. "Do you need help?"

My hands begin to shake uncontrollably, and my breaths come out in gasps. "Don't. Touch. Me." I growl, and the man immediately removes his hand. I peer up at him, an older man with a white beard and white hair, and immediately feel bad. But no, he's a man just like any other. *Don't be stupid, Bailey.* Anyone could be like Robert. Old or not.

"Sorry," he says softly. "Do you need me to call someone?"

I shake my head quickly. "No." I grab onto my scrub pants, wiping my hands on them, trying to get them to stop shaking. "I'm okay. I'm okay." Maybe if I repeat it enough times my body will get with the program.

"Alright." He nods, then walks away.

Getting on my hands and knees, I force myself to get up slowly, letting my blood pressure adjust so I don't get dizzy. My phone rings, and I immediately answer. "Nurse Bailey."

"He's in the kid's cancer ward!" Veronica barks, and I frown. Kid's cancer ward? Why the hell would he be there? What is he even thinking?

"On my way," I reply, hanging up.

The trip to the cancer ward takes me back to the elevators, and I press the respective button. The whirring sound of it taking me up calms me slightly, and suddenly I'm grateful to whoever found him since I would've never imagined he'd be up here. It's the most ridiculous thing I've ever heard of. Why would he even come up here? I avoid it at all costs, not wanting to see how these little people suffer every minute of every day. It's just depressing to think about. Tiny humans dying before they even get to live.

It's sterile white in here, and some of the walls are covered in children's portraits that do nothing to give it life. I recognize Frozen and The Lion King, along with a variety of cartoon characters. The longest nurse's station I've ever seen is in the center, and I walk quickly toward it. It's freezing in here. Holy crap, these poor kids.

"Hey." I squint at the badge on the nurse's scrub top. "Rhonda."

"How can I help you?" Rhonda is actually very pretty with her light blonde hair, brown eyes, and full lips. I bet Theo was probably flirting with her for at least thirty minutes. Good for him. "Oh, wait. Are you here for the hockey player?"

I nod, biting my lip until I taste blood. Fucking hell, my nerves are frayed. "Yeah, I'm here for him."

"Oh my God," she whispers. He's the sweetest thing ever." I just bet he is.

"Please, tell me he's still here," I beg, and she nods with a small smile. "Oh, thank God. Can you take me to him?"

"Right this way," she replies, coming to my side and turning left into a long hallway.

A never-ending row of rooms is visible, and I shiver. "Have you ever heard of a thermostat? Those poor kids...it's freezing in here." I see her flinch, and her mouth turns down, though she doesn't say anything. I tell myself the shiver was due to the cold, but I know better. This place is desolate and sad.

"He's right through those doors." She points at a set of glass double doors that are wide open. "Really sweet guy."

I nod because I'm sure he is. I just don't care. "Thanks," I mutter.

Standing at the entryway, I don't make myself known. Mostly because I want to see what he's up to and why he'd come here in the first place. What I find is the most unexpected sight in all my life. Theo is sitting in the middle of the room, and there are six kids in recliners facing him. Some of them have their IV pumps with them, while others don't. There are some with neon bags that I know are chemotherapy, and my heart breaks a little in my chest. This is so freaking sad.

But the way he's reading to them animatedly brings a small smile to my face. "Mommy and Daddy say I'm clever," he reads to them with a huge smile on his face. "And that I'm the *best* big brother ever!"

All of the kids—and I mean all of them—gasp out raspy little laughs, clutching their bellies at the way he's reading to them. I can't see their faces, but I can only imagine the big smiles they must have on them.

"When baby sleeps, shhhh, no noise." Theo puts his index finger to his lips, then whispers, "I quietly play with all my toys."

I roll my eyes, but the kids simply laugh again.

Then the strangest thing happens. Theo's eyes meet mine from across the room, all shiny and watery, and my stomach flutters. I still scowl though, because he did leave his room without saying where he was going, which almost gave me a panic attack.

Be real, Bailey. You *had* a panic attack. Cancer ward or not, I'm pissed.

Theo stiffens immediately, and his eyes widen, probably

because I must be red in the face. I feel myself flushed from my anger, and I signal for him to come to me. He shakes his head, going back to the book. Oh, so now he's being stubborn. Just what I need.

"Show time's over, kiddos," I tell them, and awwww's ring out in unison. "Sorry, but this big guy needs to go back to his bed."

"No way!" a kid whines, and Theo smiles.

"Please, please stay!"

"No, don't go!"

I watch his face carefully, and he seems on the edge of a mental breakdown at the thought of leaving these kids. Only I don't have time to care right now. All that matters is that I found him, and he needs to come with me. I have other patients to worry about, and I can't look after him while he's playing with little kids.

"Let's go, Theo!" I bark, and he smiles.

"Finally," he calls out as I walk out of the room to wait for him. "You called me by my name!"

I don't reply, straining to hear what he's now saying to the kids.

"I'll be back tomorrow when the wicked witch is gone." They all giggle, and I smirk. Wicked witch, huh? That's just so freaking clever, Mr. Anderson. "Promise."

"Swear?" one of the kids demands.

"Cross my heart."

And then suddenly, he's at my side, and I feel warm all over.

"What," I growl, "were you thinking?"

"I was bored." He shrugs, and I narrow my eyes at him. "What? You try being stuck in bed all day for three days in a row. I'm going fucking insane in there."

"So you come to read to children?" Who the fuck would get out of their own bed and go find the children to read them a story just because they're bored?

"*Cancer* children," he snaps, "who don't have anyone here for them."

I roll my eyes, even though I know it's the last thing I should be doing. He was being nice to these kids, and here I am being mean to him. But I can't feel bad right now. He left without a word. He could've told me something. Not that I would've let him leave our floor. I wonder who's going to let him tomorrow. Just because he's pretty to look at, I bet he'll get away with whatever he wants. "Let's go back."

"A please would be nice," he replies dryly.

"And tell me," I laugh loudly. "Why in the world would I say please when you left without a word? I was worried sick." Literally.

Theo smirks. "All I'm hearing is that you were worried about me." A grin splits his face. "Did you miss me, sweet Bailey?"

"I missed my peace of mind."

"Of course you did." He winks, and my stomach flips.

Get it together, Bailey.

We walk back to the unit, and thankfully, he goes directly to his bed. Here, I thought I'd have to fight with him again to get him to comply. But no, he went willingly and seemed content that he had time away from his bed. Or maybe he's just happy to have spent time with little kids.

I can't even read him.

"Do us all a favor," I say calmly, though I feel anything but. "And stay in your damn bed."

"Yes, ma'am." He grins, and I frown.

"I don't want to see you for the rest of this damn shift." I sigh.

Then I leave the room and slump against his closed door.

What a fucking night.

CHAPTER FIVE

Being stuck in a hospital is much worse than I thought it would be, but being trapped in a bed? Nothing tops that. It's absolutely miserable. Going to the kid's cancer ward yesterday was a privilege and a gift I never thought I'd get, so I'm at least grateful for that. It's too bad my visit was cut short. I understand it must have been really stressful for Bailey to not find me in my room where I was supposed to be.

Either way, I thought the company of the nurses would make things better for me during my stay, except I got stuck with the cutest, grumpy little thing instead. So now I'm chained to this room, unhappy and without human contact, save for the times she comes in here throughout her shift—during which she mostly ignores my attempts to talk to her and makes me feel stupid for even trying. In fact, she wants nothing to do with me.

I've been pushing those feelings down though, and for the most part, it's been working. Maybe it's the fact that I'm doped up on pain meds for the skull fracture, but I've been in a slightly better mood the last few hours. At least that's what I show them when they come into the room. Other than that, I have been catastrophizing ever since I was admitted to the PCU. My career is on the line, and even my friends have been walking on eggshells around me.

No one has said it out loud, and the coach has been really supportive while I get through this. But it's an unspoken thing —if I don't get better soon, I won't just be benched for a few weeks. I could be benched for the season. Worse, if I'm unlucky.

However, I'm still trying to put one foot in front of the other and remain as positive as possible. Though I can't deny it's been really difficult. That's why I've been deflecting with humor, except tonight. I can tell it might be a miserable time if Nurse Bailey keeps being rude to me—or just plain ignoring me. Talking to her might make me feel better, if only she'd give in. I need the distraction...because if not, I'll just lie here and contemplate my failures—especially my career.

A knock sounds at the door and it opens a moment later, my friends strolling in with an armful of food. The smell of Dick's Drive-In is making my mouth water, and I groan. "That smells amazing," I tell them, my face scrunched up with the pain throbbing in my temples, but I brace it for the sake of not worrying them.

Jeremy comes in with five bags of burgers, Matthew has a cup holder, Oliver has snacks and an Icee, and Noah just brings a bright smile. I love my friends, now more than ever. They've been there for me through thick and thin. Especially when Angela broke up with me because this lifestyle was too much for her, including traveling and away games. And also through my little sister dying of Leukemia during my rookie year. That pain still hasn't left me, but it hurts a little less than it used to— at least most days. The anniversary of her death is still raw, fresh pain always accompanying it. That's yet another thing my ex-girlfriend could not handle—my journey with grief.

"How's our favorite D-man?" Oliver asks, grinning at me, waiting for Jeremy's retort. They always do this to press Jeremy's buttons, and it's entertaining for more reasons than one.

He doesn't disappoint. "Hey, what the hell?" He huffs, "What about me?"

We all laugh, and Noah says, "You're not the one in a hospital bed with a broken head."

"You're not wrong," Jer mumbles, his lips turning down. It's all an act, he knows they're just playing.

"As long as the other head is still intact," Matthew says. "It is, right?"

"Yes," I smirk. "Very much so."

The boys settle in some of the chairs Nurse Linda brought in, catering to me and all the people who have come to visit me, and Jeremy passes the burgers around. He also gets the snacks —Sour Patch Kids, cookies and cream Hershey's bar, Oreos— and sets them on the bedside table. My eyes bulge out of my head as he gives me the red Icee and my burger.

The first bite tastes like heaven, and so do the second and third. I wash it down with my Icee when I begin to feel choked up from how quickly I'm eating, and everyone stares at me with their eyes bugged out. "What? The food here is shit."

Jer laughs, "Did you think they were going to cater to the NHL star?"

"Sure would've been nice to have something other than bland mashed potatoes and chicken."

"Like what?" Oliver asks with a snicker.

"Oh, I don't know. Maybe loaded mashed potatoes. Or gravy. Anything with flavor, honestly." I sigh. "But seriously, thank you for having my back, Jer."

"No," Oliver interrupts. "Thank you both for having mine. That asshole deserved what he had coming."

"What do you mean?" I ask him with confusion.

"He got his teeth knocked out." He smirks. "Everyone lost their damn mind when you were wheeled out."

That should bring me a sense of satisfaction, but instead, I feel nothing. Because I'm still here in this fucking hospital bed. I'm pissed as fuck. Some teeth knocked out is not nearly enough punishment for what he did to me, and I very much plan on benching him for the rest of the season in our next game against each other.

If I'm back on, that is.

"He deserved it," is all I say, and all eyes land on me.

I know they can read me like a book, and they suspect—more like are aware—that I won't just stand there and let him play another game against us. He didn't deserve to have his teeth knocked out, he deserved to be in the hospital just like me.

"Hell yeah, he did," says Jer.

Our conversation is put to a stop by a knock at the door.

"Who's there?" I ask with a smirk.

"Bailey," she says as she begins to enter the room.

I fake furrow my brows. "Bailey, who?"

"Your nurse—" She looks at me with narrowed eyes. "I'm not falling for this."

With a smirk from all the guys in the room, she brings her computer to my bedside with a little syringe in her hand. *Fuuuuckkkk.* I guess it's that time again. It's a good thing I finished my burger. I hope I can keep it down. This medicine makes me nauseous.

"Falling for what?" I ask with feigned innocence. I love knock-knock jokes, so sue me.

Bailey turns her cute little nose up at me, her green eyes rolling to the back of her head. She seems to really dislike me. I don't know why. Maybe she doesn't like hockey players...or maybe it goes a little deeper than that.

"You know what."

"No, I don't—"

"Name and date of birth." She interrupts as she begins to scan medications.

"Theo Anderson," I say. "May fifteenth…"

"Alright, Mr. Anderson." She prepares the medicine for me, inserting a needle into a bottle and drawing up the Morphine. "On a scale of one to ten, how much pain are you in?"

My head begins to throb at her question, and I'd say a solid six. "Why, sweet Bailey?" She shakes her head and purses her lips at the nickname. "You gonna kiss it all better?"

Everyone in the room chuckles.

"You're insufferable, you know that?"

However a little smile tips up one side of her mouth, bringing me a deep sense of satisfaction. "That's a pretty smile you got there," I say, even though we both know it didn't bloom all the way. "You should try it more often."

"Smiling is overrated," she says seriously. "And you didn't answer the question."

"My pain is a six out of ten," I say with a tight smile.

"See? That wasn't so hard." She scrubs the IV port attached to the tubing and clamps it so it doesn't feed back into the Normal Saline bag. "You'll feel better soon."

"I will if you stay here with me."

"I have other patients," Bailey says, beginning to wheel her computer away. "But nice try."

"Oh, c'mon!" I put a hand to my chest as if wounded. "I'm the best patient you've ever had."

"Debatable, Mr. Anderson."

She heads for the door. "It's Theo!" I yell after her.

Silence descends upon the room when she leaves, then we all burst out laughing. My belly hurts and my head throbs, but I can't control it. There are tears in my eyes, for fuck's sake.

"*Dude*," Jer moans. "She is *hot*."

"I know," I reply.

"You were flirting with her," Oliver smirks. "Why?"

"Because I'm bored." Out of my damn mind.

"Nah." Jeremy rolls his eyes. "We all know that's not it."

"Why wouldn't I flirt?" I make eye contact with him and grin. "She's pretty, and she hates me."

I love the challenge.

But that's not the only reason. I just want to make her smile a little, even if she'd never give me a chance.

"He's right," Jeremy says. "I'd flirt with her too."

After we've all finished our burgers and I've dug into the snacks, Jeremy gathers all the trash and puts it in the big bin next to the door. "Alright, boys," I say. "I think I need my beauty sleep. My head is killing me."

Oliver snickers, Jeremy smirks, Noah rolls his eyes, and Matthew smiles at me knowingly. I may or may not want to be alone when Bailey comes back, and they all know it. So what if I want a few minutes alone with her to figure out what it is that's making her hate me without giving me a chance? I feel like there is so much I don't know about her, yet I *really* want to find out.

They exit the room single-file and shut the door quietly, giving me some much-needed peace. It's ten p.m. now, and I know it's around the time when she should be coming back to check on me, mostly to make sure my head is alright.

I have to admit it is feeling better after the morphine. I hate taking it, and I'm sure we will thankfully downgrade medications soon, but I can't lie and say it's not helping. And that's the scary part. I don't want to have to take it at all; it gives me anxiety to be in pain. I can't expect to not hurt after this type of injury, but it still sucks that I *am* injured in the first place.

The door opens suddenly, and Bailey strolls in, looking pretty as ever and with a little furrow in her brows. She clearly doesn't like the fact that she has to come in here, and if I didn't suspect there's a deeper reason for it, I'd honestly be slightly offended.

People tell me I'm basically a teddy bear in human form, so I really don't get it.

"Come back so soon?" I raise a brow, a smirk on my lips. "I knew you would."

Bailey doesn't even look at me as she talks, "Sit up for me. I have to take your blood pressure."

I roll my eyes and sit up for her, extending my arm so she can wrap the blood pressure cuff around it. She does, tightening it to the point it actually hurts. I narrow my eyes at her, but she doesn't even bother looking at me. I force a smile on my lips even though the cuff is tightening to the point where my fingertips are numb. I still can't help wincing when it gets to its tightest point.

Bailey moves behind me, adjusting my pillow by punching it a few times, and I smirk. What the hell is her problem? Why is she being so rude to me? And everyone else she talks to? I've heard her talking to other nurses, like Linda and another girl I don't know the name of. She's been really mean to them, as if she dislikes them deeply or is annoyed by them. I can tell from a mile away she doesn't want to be here, and that makes me kind of sad for her.

Her fingers are cold as she unwraps the blood pressure cuff from my arm, and I exhale roughly and flex my hand, trying to regain feeling in my fingers. They're asleep, and I groan at the tingling feeling. But instead of acknowledging me, she takes her stethoscope out of her scrubs pocket, popping a hip out and looking at me expectantly. I pretend I don't know what she's about to do.

"Can you lift your shirt, please?" She says with a huff, clearly exasperated.

"Usually, I go out to dinner first, but since you're asking so nicely," I reply with a grin.

She doesn't return it.

I lift my shirt for her, and her eyes widen like saucers as soon as she stares at my chest. She does a great job of hiding it after a second, but I've taken a picture of that face in my brain, and it will live there from now on. I just know it.

Her cold stethoscope meets my skin, making me shiver, and she puts a dainty hand on my chest as she leans over me to steady herself. I don't dare even breathe, scared she will pull away. My body feels hot from the inside out, the searing contact making me light-headed. Bailey is pretty. But up close? *She's Perfect.*

Her green eyes are cast down onto my chest, and she's breathing a little shallow, not daring to meet my gaze. It makes me want to smile, but then again, I don't know if she's affected by me or if she just dislikes me so much that she's uncomfortable. Either way, I stare at her features. Her heart-shaped face, light freckles dusted on her cheekbones, and long, dark lashes. A small, straight nose and full, kissable lips. Light brown hair that curls down her back.

"So why do you—"

"Be quiet," she chastises. "It hurts my ears if you talk."

God, she's so…snappy. But I oblige, if only because I really don't want to hurt her ears.

She moves on from my chest, letting go of it and trailing her stethoscope down to my abs. They clench out of instinct, mainly because it's cold, and she glares at me. Automatically, I try to relax, taking deep breaths. Leaning forward, I give her access to my back so she can listen to my lungs. Even if I want her to snap at me a little, I don't want to give her too much of a hard time.

"Thank you." She breathes, placing the stethoscope on my back, making me flinch. "Sorry, I know it's cold."

I rear back, surprised by her apology.

She removes the stethoscope from my skin, her hand trailing down my back for just a second before stepping away from me and then putting her stethoscope back in her pocket. "How come you don't wear it around your neck like everyone else?" I ask her, noticing how her hands shake slightly at my question. She doesn't wear any jewelry either, and that's weird in itself in comparison to the other women who work here.

"I just don't like things hanging around my neck."

I nod slowly.

But it still feels like a rehearsed answer. What is she hiding?

Seeming to be done with the conversation, she takes out a pen light and clicks it on, shining it in my eyes. I can sense her apprehension, and I don't want her to feel pressured.

"I'm sorry—I don't mean to make you uncomfortable. It was a dumb question."

"It wasn't," she blurts out. "I just don't like talking about it."

Okay, so that means the conversation is finished. Except now I'm wondering if it's a precaution or if something has already happened. Is she traumatized by something? She is uncomfortable. So *something* must have happened. I'm sure any other nurse on this floor would talk about it freely, but not her. She's guarded, keeping secrets.

"Can you look at the light?" I do as she points it at my eyes, and I can see her nodding out of my periphery. "Okay, now follow it."

I follow her directions again. "How am I?" I ask her nervously. "Everything okay?"

"You look good," she replies, then flushes when I look at her. "I meant—everything seems fine."

I smirk, even though she looks like she wants to hit me, so I stop my smile from blooming all the way. "Great." I sigh, feeling nervous. My whole future depends on this, and my hands shake slightly.

She frowns, "Are you okay?"

"Yes," I say quickly, like a reflex. I don't want to open up to anyone about it, but maybe I do need to talk about it with someone who's not on the team. These days, it seems like they're the only people I know.

Bailey puts the penlight away and touches my jaw, directing me so I can look down. She could've just said to do it, but I have a nagging suspicion she thinks I'm cute beneath that tough exterior.

She looks at the stitches on my hairline, pushing my hair back. Her hands on my skin feel so warm now, a contrast to how they felt only a few minutes ago. I close my eyes and take a deep breath, bracing myself.

"No." I tell her.

"No?"

"I am not okay," I whisper. "I'm far from okay."

Bailey steps back, hesitating. "Oh," she replies. "Well, that's refreshing to hear."

"Refreshing?" I ask with a frown, my lips tipping down.

"Yeah," she replies. "I hate when people pretend life isn't awful sometimes. I was starting to think you were one of them."

"How come?" I search her green eyes, and they slightly crinkle in the corners when her lips tip up into a small smile. I want to see more of them, but getting them out of her seems pretty difficult.

Bailey shrugs. "You smile a lot."

"Just because I smile doesn't mean I want to be here… Or that I am happy. But I am actually considerate of other people's feelings and hard work," I snap. "I don't need to be rude to you just because my life sucks."

Bailey flinches. "I—"

"You've been kind of mean to me, no offense." I breathe in deeply again. "I don't want to be worried about the possibility of getting worse, and I sure as hell don't want to be benched for weeks. It's too much for me and I don't know how to deal with it. I know you don't care." Her face drops, and she appears slightly guilty. "But I just want to go back to my team. Hockey is my life."

"Can't you do something other than hockey if this doesn't work out?"

My stomach drops. "Hockey is all I know. I have no other skills."

"Surely you went to college?"

"Yeah." I nod slowly. "For a degree in History. What the hell do I even do with that?"

She chuckles, "You could teach."

"Hell no." I laugh. "I can't do that. Coach, maybe. Except who wants to be coached by a failure?"

"You're *not* a failure."

"It feels like it right now. And what if my career ends, then what? Over a petty fight?" I shake my head grimly, my lips pursed, eyes downcast. "It wasn't worth it."

Bailey's face is sympathetic for once when I glance back up, and something stirs inside of me. I want to reach out and tuck her stray hair behind her ear. Although her hair is up in a ponytail, there are stray hairs hanging to the sides of her face. They must have slipped out of her scrunchie between rounds and assessments. I want to touch her face, trail my fingers down her jaw, and—

"Let's just focus on getting you better, okay?" she says gently. "Don't look too far into the future right now; live in the present a little. You're getting better right now."

"Is that what you do, Bailey?" I ask her, and she sucks in a sharp breath. "Do you like to live in the present?"

"Yes." She doesn't even hesitate as she says it, making me smile. I wish I could do that, but right now, I'm just living in the future.

"Why don't you like me?" I blurt, and she looks stricken—embarrassed even. For a tiny moment, I feel bad about asking her. I don't like confrontation in my personal life, which is ironic because it's the one thing that landed me here. I guess hockey doesn't count as confrontation, though. It's a contact sport.

"It's not…" Bailey takes a deep breath, her nostrils flaring, her dainty nose scrunching. "That I don't like you. I just—"

"Don't like anyone?"

She gasps. "Is that the impression I give?"

"Honestly," I smile gently, hoping to ease her, "Yes. You look like you hate being here, and everyone who talks to you."

"I'm just having a hard time getting used to my new life," she says with a question, as if she's not quite sure what she's feeling before putting it into words. "I'm new here. Well, I've been here for six months, but I'm not from here. This state."

"Ah," I say, understanding her a little more. "So you don't like Seattle?"

"I don't like anything." Bailey's eyes widen and she clasps a hand over her mouth. "I didn't mean that."

"Yes, you did." I frown. What could she possibly hate so much about her life? She's beautiful, has a career, and well...I guess I know nothing else. "And that's okay. New beginnings can be hard."

Bailey nods slowly, agreeing, and gazes into my eyes. "It's been difficult."

"Hey, if I can restart after embarrassing myself and almost losing my entire career, then so can you."

She returns my smile, dimples popping on each cheek. It makes her even more beautiful. *Wow.* "Maybe."

I'm not expecting her to take my advice, but maybe, just maybe, she will find something or someone who will make it worth her time.

And for whatever stupid reason, I hope it's me.

CHAPTER SIX

L ately, it feels like I'm racing toward my death, sprinting full force yet staying stagnant simultaneously. Another shift, another day down.

That's all I care about lately, for my days to fly by. I don't know why; there's nothing in particular that I want to do.

No matter how hard I try, I can't seem to move forward. My biggest wish is to get back to myself—the person I used to be, the one before him. But the further time slips from my grasp, the further I feel from accomplishing that. Shouldn't time heal all wounds? In a way, mine have, but the scars are there, still red and puckered. Literally. But I no longer miss him or cry over him as I fall asleep.

I'm no longer mourning the good times, the ones in between the mess and chaos, the ones that stood out more than the pain he inflicted. I see him as he is now, the act he was putting on just for me to fall for him. And God, did I fall hard as fuck.

I fell so hard I shattered pieces of myself on the way down.

Now, I'm trying to get used to a life without him, which doesn't make sense despite how much I don't miss him. In a way what I miss is the feeling of being loved, even if it was not real.

There's something terribly wrong with me though, a brokenness that I know will never let me trust another man. I gave and gave and gave until there was nothing left. The idea of never having anything left ever again to give to someone else terrifies me.

So, I live the only life I think I deserve. One in solitude, where I can't be broken again, hurt beyond repair. Because I bet if someone hurt me even in the slightest one more time, I wouldn't be able to put myself back together.

And that's why I work six days a week, keep myself as busy as possible, and only go out with Cheyenne occasionally. She doesn't pressure me; thankfully, she knows after six months, I'm still not ready for much. We go out to dinner or breakfast sometimes, or I go to the rink to watch her teach toddlers how to skate, and maybe, just maybe, I jump in and fall on my ass. Even so, it makes me feel alive for five minutes, and I forget about my problems. It makes me forget about the shit hole I live in that has black mold in the A/C. The water damage on the ceiling. The lack of furniture. I can forget I started over, and now I have *nothing*.

No boyfriend.

No love.

No home.

So I bury myself in my work, hoping to feel a sense of fulfillment. Only it never comes. *Ever*. And that's harder than not trying, because I'm *trying* so hard. I feel so isolated, it's painful. Yet I'm not willing to put myself out there to be taken advantage of yet again. I don't know what kind of man would be persistent enough—powerful enough—to get me out of my mind prison, but sometimes I wish for him. During my weakest moments, I wish for him with all my being.

I won't deny that I have needs, that it gets a little harder every day to not go and find someone to keep me warm for one night. Toys are friends, but nothing feels better than a body above yours, someone who can touch you. And man, I need to be touched desperately. But what if I'm dropped again, and more pieces shatter until there's nothing left?

I shake those thoughts out of my head and try to focus on my work. The computer screen becomes blurry as my eyes focus, and I shake my head, setting my mind to my charting. After I've recorded everyone's assessments in their medical records, I get up from my chair and make my way to the medication room with my computer, parking it right outside.

It's time to get Theo his pain medication, and we've downgraded him to Hydrocodone instead of Morphine. He seems to be adjusting well to the change but is still experiencing headaches. It might be a while before the headaches disappear, especially with his skull fracture, even if it's barely there.

Other than that, he had a CT scan earlier today, and it seems that his bleed is dissolving. It has gotten smaller. The doctors are saying he will probably be in the hospital for a few more days at the maximum. Which is great news, really.

Grabbing the medication, I make my way to his room. No matter how much I've tried to avoid it tonight, I haven't been able to. He and I had some sort of understanding yesterday, but now he thinks we're friends, so he keeps calling me. I don't want to say it's annoying—he's not. However, now he is getting in the way of me doing my job in the way I want—the way I promised myself I would.

Not to mention, he has so many friends here at night that it makes me feel suffocated. There's not enough room for five hockey players, and I feel a little cramped in there when I enter. But it's the way they look at me that makes me a little uncomfortable, as if they know something about me. Something they're not supposed to.

Or maybe I'm just paranoid.

I knock on the door but quickly open it before Theo can start with a new knock-knock joke. He seems to never run out of them.

"Who's there?" Theo sing-songs.

"Nope." I give him a small smile. "Not falling for it."

He smirks, "Maybe you'll fall for me instead."

"Okaayyyy," his friend says with a laugh. Jeremy, I think? There's so many of them. "That was corny, even for you."

I roll my eyes at them as I wheel my computer next to the bed, scanning the medication and putting it into a cup. After he tells me his name and date of birth, he glances at the small medicine cup and grimaces. He looks guilty for whatever reason, and I frown.

"What's wrong?" I ask him, and he shakes his head. But I know there is something, so instead I gently ask, "What's your pain level?"

"Six…" It's still a six on the pain scale every time. He's only been here for about five days, so I'm not surprised.

"Well, this will help you feel better," I assure him, bringing the medicine to his bedside. My legs touch the edge, and his fingers accidentally skim my thigh. I tense immediately, and he notices, pulling away. "Take it, *Theo*."

He smirks, loving that I've said his name instead of calling him Mr. Anderson, then pouts. "I'm tired of taking it. I feel so fucking useless just being here."

"Be a big boy and take the medicine, Theodore."

"Oh, he's a big boy—" Someone laughs from behind me.

"*Out*," I growl at them, maybe a little too aggressively. But I don't have time for this shit. After the last set of footsteps have faded and the door shuts quietly behind them, I look at him again. His eyebrows are drawn in, blue eyes staring at his lap, fingers fidgeting, floppy brown hair falling over his forehead.

I get even closer and lightly push the strands of hair back with my fingertips, and he freezes. It's a gentle touch, intimate, though I tell myself I'm only checking on his stitches as I move his hair away from his forehead and look at the laceration. What has gotten into me? Nothing has dissolved yet, but I didn't expect it to. It'll be at least two weeks before that happens. No redness, swelling, or warmth to the area.

His skin is so soft as I pull my fingers away and let his hair fall over his forehead again, and he grabs onto my wrist. "What are you doing, Bailey?"

"Looking at your wound, Mr. Anderson." I smirk, letting him hang on to my wrist for whatever stupid reason. I don't like male patients, but after yesterday, I feel...safe with him. How naive is that? "Now, tell me, who peed in your cereal?"

"Excuse me?" His brows furrow. "What do you mean?"

"Really?" I laugh, slowly pulling away from his grasp. His fingers trail up my arm, their warmth sending electricity all the way down to my toes. "It means what has your panties in a twist? Why are you upset now?"

"Upset *now*?" His eyes meet mine, narrowed. "As in, I'm always upset? Bailey, I am never as upset as you are."

"Then happily take your medication."

My thighs are still against the mattress, and my hand reaches for my stethoscope, waiting for his reply. He seems to contemplate it. "I will if you'll sit with me later," he replies.

"For what?"

"To talk to me." He rolls his eyes in a *duh* way that has me rolling mine back.

"About what?" I ask him, curious what else he wants to tell me.

"Everything," he says simply.

That feels very loaded, yet he looks at me with deep blue eyes that reach into my soul and I find myself nodding. "And if I don't?"

"Then I guess I'll be in pain, sweet Bailey."

I chuckle, "We can't have that now, can we?"

"Say you'll stay, then." He moves his hand toward mine, and I slide it away at the last moment. But his fingers still graze my own, making everything tingle. "Stay."

"I have other patients I need to tend to." I do have to go check on them soon too. "But I'll come back."

"Promise?"

I smile. "Pinky promise."

That makes him smile back, although I'd have to return to him regardless. He's my patient, and I have to take care of him. It's my job. I can't have him believing he's special now. Because he can't be. *Ever.* I don't want anyone else to be special to me.

Theo lies back on the pillow and stares at me, then opens his mouth, tongue out. I raise an eyebrow, and he waves his hand in a motion that tells me to get on with it. So I put the medicine on his tongue and hand him the water on his bedside table.

"Thanks," he tells me. "So nice."

"I'm not—"

"You *can* be."

Out of nowhere, a voice over the intercom snaps me out of the daze. "Rapid Response, Room ten-twenty-four, Rapid Response."

I feel the color drain from my face, and Theo's eyes roam it. "I—I have to go. *Now.*"

I all but run out of the room, going down the hall to find the nursing assistant taking my patient's vital signs. My patient is barely moving; her eyes are open but not responding either, and her breathing is slightly shallow. She looks *scared.*

"Erin," I tell her softly, except her eyes are still frozen forward. "Can you tell me where you are?" She says something unintelligible, her speech heavily slurred. I can't understand a word coming out of her mouth, even though she's still trying. "Smile for me, please." She tries, but one side droops. I lift her arms and one drops too.

Face, Arms, Speech, *Time.*

Time is brain.

Doctors begin to step into the room, as well as other nurses, and just as I'm explaining to them that she is having a stroke, I hear the heart monitor start to beep in a way that makes my stomach drop. I glance back to see her heart rate go from seventy to twenty to zero.

No.

Everything is a mess in the next moment. Nurses are opening the crash cart. I jump in and start compressions while others get ready for their own roles in the code. But it's no use. After forty-five minutes of trying to bring her back, nothing happens. So we call it. Time of death.

The doctor leaves the room to call the family and let them know what happened, as I go to the nurses' station and search for my computer. But it's no use; I left it in Theo's room. Because, of course, I did. It's like the universe wants me to go back in there every five minutes, and it's starting to get on my nerves. But it's not my fault I left it. I was in a hurry. I just hope he doesn't want to cash in now. I don't think I have time to talk to him yet.

I'm not usually emotional, but it's been a while since I had a patient pass away unexpectedly. She was here for her blood sugar, which we finally had under control, and now she's gone. Her family is going to be absolutely devastated. How do you tell someone that their mom was joking around thirty minutes ago, and now she's…gone?

With a lump in my throat, I go down the hall and enter Theo's room. I don't knock, and he doesn't try to joke. One look at my face has him furrowing his brows, and my breaths begin to come in a little faster. I hurry toward my computer, stumbling on the way and almost falling on all fours.

He's out of his bed in a heartbeat, dragging his IV pole toward me and reaching me with a steadying hand on my arm. "What is it?" He asks me, his concern lacing his voice. It's not the fake kind either, and that makes me nervous. "What's wrong?"

"I—" I take a deep breath, trying to keep the tears at bay, but when I blink they just tumble down like a row of dominoes. "She—*died*."

I choke on a sob as he pulls me into him by the back of my head, my face buried against his chest, and I drop my hands to my sides. "Shhhh," he says softly. "It's gonna be okay, B." My shoulders relax as his hands start to rub circles on my back slowly. "You're strong. You're resilient. You're a good person."

"How do you know?" I ask him, "I've treated you like shit."

"Shit?" He chuckles, "Nah."

"Stop…" A soft laugh escapes me. "I've been mean."

"Just a little," he replies softly, his hand roaming up to the back of my head and tugging on the hair at the nape of my neck. I tilt my head up so I can look at him. "But I can take it. Give me more, Bailey."

"Theo." I breathe.

"Break a little, B." No one has called me B since before my parents died. A gasp slips from between my lips, and he hugs me toward him, not soothing like before but demanding. "Break for me."

My hands shake as I consider his words, even as the answer is already on my tongue. I've been holding it all in since I stepped foot in this room, and I'm tired of being strong. I've been strong for six months. I haven't cried in three. I've told myself that if I'm strong enough, resilient enough, good enough, I will get over all of it. And in a way, I have, but there's something that lingers that I can't let go of. A nagging little pest in the back of my mind that tells me I'll never be whole again no matter what I do. And this feels like it's breaking me a little more.

What if I just let go for five minutes? What if I break and then put myself back together? I can do that, right?

The lump in my throat gets tighter, and it feels like I can't breathe. Warm tears flow down my cheeks quickly, and I bury my face into Theo's shirt. He smells like pine trees. Like freedom. Like all my camping dreams as a little girl. Images of me running through the woods scroll across my mind, my feet in the dirt, marshmallows on a stick. Suddenly, I'm on my daddy's shoulders, being walked around because I was scared of bugs and didn't want to get bitten by ants.

Theo feels safe.

So I turn my face until my cheek is against his chest and I let my tears fall faster. The problem with me crying is that I no longer know what I'm breaking for anymore. Was it the lady who passed away, or was she simply my breaking point? Is it Robert and all the pain he inflicted? No, that can't be. I'm over him, right? Or is it my new life? The one that I hate?

I'm not entirely sure what I hate so much about it. Sure, it's different from what I'm used to. I live in a shit hole and breathe for the sole purpose of clocking into work, but at least I'm safe now. At least I don't get beat up anymore. Stabbed. Humiliated. Hurt.

Theo pushes me away slightly, cupping my cheeks and rubbing his thumbs under my eyes, cleaning me up. Surprising me, he tugs at my ponytail, lets my hair loose, and then runs his hands through it slowly.

"What are you doing?" I stammer.

"I'm Putting you back together," he replies, and my heart somersaults. I try to take a step back, but he doesn't budge. He holds on to the back of my head and softly runs his fingers through my strands. "Let me, Bailey."

"No one can put me back together," I whisper, although I don't know if I'm trying to convince him or myself. "You might as well not even try."

He lets go of me and steps back, extending his arm to me and tapping at his IV. "What do you want?" I ask him, slightly confused.

"Take it off."

"I can't." I shake my head. "You're supposed to have it on."

"I need to use the bathroom," he smiles. You can put it back when I'm done."

I roll my eyes and step toward the machine, turning off the settings and then disconnecting him. He sighs in relief, except rather than going to the bathroom, he steps up to me, his front to my back, and surrounds me with his warmth.

And man, does he feel warm.

CHAPTER SEVEN

My front is pressed to Bailey's back, and I place a tentative hand on her hip, gripping her with my fingers. She feels so damn good against me, and my entire body is zapped with little electric shocks the longer we stay in this position.

Bailey's breathing picks up, and I can hear the exertion. "What are you doing?" It's a mix between a gasp and a whisper, and her back immediately tenses, going ramrod straight.

"Just being here for you."

Her sniffles are loud now, and her hand comes up to wipe under her nose. She takes a deep breath, and when it shudders out, I wait. "You happy now? You watched me break?"

I frown, "I could never be happy about that." I tug on her arm gently to turn her around, then cup her face with both hands. My stomach flutters as her eyes widen, and I give her a tentative smile. I can see the fear in her eyes from a mile away. Something happened to this girl that made her distrust everyone. "You have a tough job, Bailey, but you seem to be really good at it. You seem to care about it a lot." I tell her, wiping under her eye with my thumb.

"Not as much as I should." Her bottom lip trembles. "Not as much as I used to."

"So you're going through a rough patch. It happens." I try to reassure her. "You don't have to tell me what happened to make you this way, but you can tell me how to fix it."

"You can't." Her chin raises defiantly, shoulders squared, and her green eyes are narrowed to slits. "No one can help me fix anything. I can't even put my fucking self back together."

My hands flex on her cheeks, and she cowers, so I let them relax. "Then let someone else do it for you."

"Oh, you?" She scoffs, looking me up and down with disdain, but beneath it, there's a spark of something that looks a lot like longing after something you can't have. But she can have it. I'd give it to her right now, whatever it is.

"I can't think of anyone better," I smirk, hesitantly taking another step closer and dropping my hands to my sides. "You don't even know me. You won't ever have to worry about me again."

"Why do you even care?" I freeze at that, watching her heaving chest, the way heat blankets over her cheeks. "What does it matter to you?"

"It shouldn't," I acknowledge. "But I *do* care, and I can't even begin to explain why."

It happened as soon as I met her. I could see a brokenness in her, shadows of unhappiness under her eyes. I don't know what has her living this way, holding her breath through it all, but no one deserves it. She doesn't just look like she needs someone's hand to hold. She looks like she needs someone to put her world back together. Something tells me it's wholly destroyed; I can sense it.

"Theo—"

"Shhhh," I whisper, my nose brushing against hers. "Just let me help you."

"How?" she whispers back.

"However you need me to."

Bailey searches my eyes, and for a split second, I think she's going to back up and leave my room. Instead, she flings herself into my arms and buries her face into my chest as her body begins to shake with her sobs. She feels dainty in my hands, like a glass figurine that could be easily broken if I handle her too roughly. The smell of roses invades my senses, and I press my nose to her hair and take a deep breath in. It settles me, and I'd like to think that she's finding some comfort in my embrace.

"It's okay," I say softly. "Let it out."

After what feels like forever but is undoubtedly only a few minutes, Bailey pulls away from my embrace and takes a step back. Her face is blotchy and red, and she wipes under her eyes roughly as she gazes at me with parted lips. She looks like she regrets it, but doesn't say anything. Instead, she nods once and disappears from the room, leaving me behind.

The door slams on her way out, and I exhale roughly, going back to bed. There's a knock at the door, and just when my body relaxes—thinking she's back—a new nurse pokes her head in.

"Are you okay?" she asks me with a frown.

I nod. "Yes, I'm fine." I gesture for her to come in. "Thank you, though."

"What happened?" I don't want to get Bailey in trouble, so instead, I get ready to take the blame.

"Sorry." I shrug. "I may have been a little mean to her." She nods slowly, like she doesn't believe me, but doesn't say anything. On her way back to the door, I stop her. "Do you know what her problem is?"

The nurse glances back at me, her eyes gleaming like she has a juicy little secret, and walks back to my bedside. "Well, I've heard things."

I nod, my curiosity a living, breathing thing. "Like what?"

"Well, rumor has it…" She stops for dramatic effect, or my reaction—who knows. "That she was running away from something."

"Who?"

"No one knows." She shrugs, and I wonder why she thinks this rumor is so good. It's only speculation, but I listen intently regardless because I'm hungry for any scraps of information on Bailey. "But I think it's probably a person."

A person.

A man, more than likely.

That would make a lot of sense.

"Thank you," I look at her badge. "Savannah."

And with that, I let her walk out of the room, curious about the little rumor that keeps floating around, yet even more concerned. I bet they don't know the first of her truth—they don't know shit. But I plan to find out from *her*.

Bailey

CHAPTER EIGHT

It has been a few hours since Erin passed.

I've been busy taking care of her body, making sure she's all cleaned up and ready for transport. I take pride in my work, and I made sure she died with her dignity still intact. By the time I'm done with her, she is pristine. I've even braided her hair. It doesn't make me feel any better though, and I practically sob through the entire process. I think this is my wake-up call because while I wasn't mean to her, I also wasn't very nice.

I've hated working here for a while now, and I've been telling myself it's due to my circumstances. That may have something to do with it, but to be honest, I've been contemplating leaving this job. Working six days a week has me burned out, though I also think I need a change of scenery. A change of pace. I thought the problem was the nursing field, that I just didn't care anymore, only this has proved me wrong. I still have a heart. I still care. And somehow, that makes me feel a little better. Because I'm not cold and dead inside like I thought I was.

My hands tremble as I do the paperwork and make the phone call to report the death of my patient to the tissue and eye bank. I can't even believe I broke down in front of Theo—that I did it while he wrapped me up in his arms. I've never felt more safe in my life. But I know it's just an illusion, my mind playing tricks on me because I yearn for safety. So then why am I walking toward his room right now? Why do I feel the need to get back to him? There's no way he's safe. No man will ever be again.

I knock on the door once and enter, except Theo's lights are off with just the soft glow of the bathroom light illuminating the space. The door is halfway closed, giving the room enough brightness to see his peaceful face and the even rise and fall of his chest. His soft snores are the only sound in the room, and I shut the door behind me quietly, then hold my breath momentarily as I walk closer. I don't know what possesses me to do so, other than me wanting to get a better look at him. *Uninterrupted*. I realize I haven't had the time to *really* look at him for very long, always afraid to let my eyes linger. But it's okay right now. He doesn't know I'm doing it—no one does. I can allow myself to indulge for just a moment.

I stare at his perfect face. His long, dark lashes. His narrow, straight nose. His deep cupid's bow. The way his lips look pouty, dark pink, and totally kissable. The cleft in his chin. His square jaw—and the light stubble on his face. He looks all man, yet at the same so fucking pretty. It's unfair that he's this perfect.

As I get closer, my thighs graze the bed, and that pine smell invades my senses again. I breathe in deeply, closing my eyes for just a moment, my hand itching to touch him. Just one time. Really softly so he doesn't wake up. I don't know what takes over me, but I reach out and push the hair back from his forehead, letting my fingers linger in his strands. They're so soft and wavy, and I'm lost in the moment. Tears prick my eyes, mostly because I wish I could do this with someone. My someone. But that's not going to happen, unfortunately.

Theo's breath hitches, and I pull my hand back as if I've

been burned. "You came back." He whispers, his voice hoarse with sleep. I stiffen, and before stepping back, he grabs my hand in his large and very warm one. He gives me a slow smile, and his eyes crinkle in the corners. I can feel my hand trembling in his grasp, and he squeezes once—very gently. "Why?"

"I promised I would." Somehow I manage to keep my voice even, as if I wasn't just caught ogling him. "And I don't have any more patients." I grimace, feeling a stabbing pain in my heart. "So I'm all yours for the night."

"Yes, please." He grins lazily. "All mine for the night sounds good to me."

I feel the heat creeping up to my cheeks, cursing myself for the way I said that. "So, what do you want to talk about, Mr. Anderson?"

"Why do you make me feel so old when you call me that?" He rolls his eyes, and I smirk. "I can't be much older than you."

"You're younger." I smile, and this time it reaches my eyes. He must sense it because he smiles back and looks almost boyish. His floppy hair falling over his eyes makes him look younger than twenty-five. "By a year."

"Oh, please." He rolls his eyes at me. "I thought you were going to say by at least five more years. Which then I would've had to come up with something to make you give a young guy a chance."

I smirk. "Well, you're not trying very hard."

"You're not *that* old." He grins, and it makes me feel at ease. He's flirting with me. And I don't hate it. "If you were older, the effort would be higher."

"What I'm getting from this is that you like older women."

"Only by one year." He winks, and my insides heat. "So tell me something about yourself, sweet Bailey."

I grab a chair and sit on it right next to his bed, close enough for him to touch me. I don't know if it's a smart choice, but for some reason, I'm choosing to trust him right now—just for now, *just for tonight*.

He looks at me like I hung all the stars in his sky as we make eye contact, and my stomach does a weird little flutter. His eyes seem darker right now, a deeper shade of blue than when the light is illuminating them. And I don't hate it. In fact, for whatever stupid reason, I find myself getting lost in their depths. Like an ocean threatening to swallow me whole. I'm entranced.

"Bailey?"

I snap out of it and clear my throat, heat rising to my cheeks for being caught staring at him. "I don't really know what to say. I'm not much of a talker. And definitely not about myself."

"Okay, so how about I ask you questions, and you answer them?" His eyes glint with mischief. "You answer anything I want."

"That's not fair," I reply with a pout. A fucking pout I can't take back. "What about you?"

"I'll answer the same question I ask, after you answer it."

"Okay," I relent. "Shoot."

"Worst kindergarten teacher." He looks at me intently, as if his day depends on this answer, and I laugh.

"Seriously?" I ask him, but he just nods. "Ms. Alicia. Now tell me why we're doing this."

"To get to know each other, *obviously*." He rolls his eyes while giving me a little smirk. "These answers tell me more than you think. Anyway, my answer is Mrs. Garcia."

"Why was she the worst?" I ask him, genuinely curious about his answer. Who actually cares about why he hated a teacher? But I guess I want access to how he thinks.

"She had the most annoying voice ever." He pretends to shudder dramatically. "How about you?"

"Well, Ms. Alicia loved crafts." Theo raises an eyebrow at me. "And I hated them. With a passion. I still do, since I'm not creative at all."

"Makes sense." He chuckles. "Let me guess, you love math and science."

"Obviously," I reply dryly. "I'm a nurse."

Theo pretends to think for a moment. "Who was your first boyfriend?"

"John, first grade." I smirk, remembering how he would always bring me flowers. It was cute, and my mom loved it more than me. Though I secretly lived for it.

"Wow, you started out *young*, Bailey." He laughs.

"Hey." I shove his arm playfully. "I'll have you know he had the best presents. I loved painted rocks and chocolate."

"That's real cute." It was. I still remember rock painting together during recess and swapping by the end of it. He'd keep mine, and I'd keep his. "My first girlfriend was Delilah. Fifth grade. She was the worst kisser."

I choke on my saliva, coughing until I turn red—from laughter. "*You* say *I* started out young? Player."

"What?" he asks innocently. "She had *really* pretty blue eyes. And my dad said when you found the one, you had to kiss her to seal the deal."

"And was she the one?"

"Nah." He shakes his head with a grin. "Like I said, *worst* kisser."

"My first kiss was sloppy," I tell him, remembering Everett. "He tried to use his tongue on me and shoved it down my throat. Eighth grade."

"Gross." He laughs.

"Good times," I joke. "Okay. If you could eat one food for the rest of your life, what would it be?"

"Easy." His eyes light up. "Steak, medium. Loaded mashed potatoes and asparagus."

"That sounds healthy," I jab because I expected it to be a little more healthy. I guess at least he's eating his vegetables. "I could eat fish tacos forever, specifically mahi-mahi tacos."

"So you like seafood?"

"Love it." I smile, and I notice I feel at ease with him. I don't like it, but I can't bring myself to leave either. "You don't?"

"Just keep Salmon away from me, and all will be fine."

My work phone suddenly rings, and Theo's face falls. I give him a small smile as I answer it, to find out I have a new admission and our time is being cut short.

"Sorry." I touch his arm lightly, and he looks down at the contact. "I have to go."

"I'm here if you need me," he replies softly, though something has been bothering me, and I need to get it off my chest.

"I'm sorry," I blurt, feeling embarrassed about earlier. I can't let it go. It was inappropriate. It shouldn't have been a thing. He was sweet, but it can't happen again.

"For?" His brows furrow in confusion.

"For crying. I was out of line. You're my patient," I grimace. "I should've never let that happen."

"You don't have to apologize." He frowns, holding my hand and interlacing our fingers. "I wanted to be there for you."

"Thank you." I nod slowly. "But it can't happen again."

He's silent, but nods.

I gently remove my hand from his grasp and walk away, stopping at the door. I'm not sure why I do it, but I look back at him. He seems sad, suddenly, and I feel guilty for being the one to cause it.

"I'll be back later."

Without waiting for his answer, I shut the door behind me and go to see my new patient.

CHAPTER NINE

Today has been a long day. The only positive is that Bailey works again tonight. I had yet another CT scan to monitor my brain bleed, and thankfully the doctor was quick to come by with an update. The bleed is basically nonexistent at this point, and he's no longer worried about it.

Discharge is on the horizon, and yet I'm dreading it. What will happen when I leave this hospital? Will I ever see Bailey again? And why am I so invested?

Speak of the devil, and she will appear. Linda and Bailey walk into the room, talking amongst themselves. A grin stretches my face as she writes her name on the board, leaving out her work number. My smile falls as she walks away, opening the door to leave the room with the other nurse. Not even sparing me one glance.

I clear my throat. There's no way in hell I'm letting her walk out of this room right now. What the fuck happened between last night and tonight? Why is she acting like this? "Bailey," I call out, and she stops. Both she and Linda turn around to look at me. "Can I talk to you for a moment?"

Linda looks over at Bailey with a frown when she begins to

shake her head, and when she notices we have an audience, she sighs and says, "Sure, Mr. Anderson."

So we're back to that.

Square *fucking* one.

But even still, I force myself to smile until the other nurse leaves and we're alone again. "Where is the girl from last night?" I ask her, hurt in my voice.

"She doesn't exist." I search her gaze, even as she averts it, avoiding me. "It was a fluke."

"Bullshit," I growl, and when she flinches, I breathe in deeply. "She was right here. Why did she leave?"

Bailey sighs, and she looks like she's in physical pain. "I'm not a vulnerable person. I can't be that with you—or anyone else. I don't know what you want from me, but it's not happening."

I sit up in bed, shoving the blankets aside, my nostrils flaring with my anger, and then stand up. For just a moment, I'm rooted in place, but when she takes a step back, I follow her. Unable to stop myself. Apparently, I have no self-control when I'm around her. "Bailey—"

"Stop."

I don't. I keep moving forward until we're toe to toe. I lift my hand and she flinches, but I caress her cheek softly with my knuckles. Tears well up in her eyes, and I frown.

"Why won't you let me in?"

"I c-c-can't." Her voice trembles. "Last night can't happen again. I can't—"

Bailey takes another step backwards until she runs into the bathroom door, and she whimpers when I make it to her. I don't press myself against her, instead I stand in front of her and stay still. She sizes me up, her eyes traveling up and down my body like she's searching for something—and I want her to approve. Desperately, more than anything, I hope she finds whatever it is she's looking for.

"*Yes,* it can. Let me be there for you," I whisper, her wide eyes connecting with mine. "Just for a few minutes, if that's all I can get."

Bailey takes a deep breath and reaches behind her, opening the door. Slipping into the bathroom, she grabs my arm and all but drags me in there with her. My back meets the closed door, and I hold my breath, waiting for her to make the move. Only she doesn't, so I grab her hand and pull her into me, cupping the back of her head with my free one.

"I want you to know that I see you," I breathe against her lips, brushing mine against hers. "All of you." Bailey fists my shirt, pulling me impossibly closer as she closes her eyes. "And if you allow me, I want to see even more."

My fingers tighten in her hair, and I nuzzle my nose against hers.

"There's nothing else to see," she whispers.

"Liar," I call her out, and she smiles against my lips. "Let me help you feel something again."

She chuckles, "I don't want to feel more." My stomach sinks. "I want to feel less."

I spin us until she's against the door, then drop my hands. "I can make that happen."

Her wide eyes meet mine, her lips parted as she gazes up at me. She looks so dainty, so fragile. I don't want to break her. I want to put her back together. But damn it, I need her in my arms. Now.

"Theo—"

Fuck.

"Say my name again," I beg her as my nostrils flare. "Please."

"Theo," Bailey repeats in a breathy voice. Her eyes show her longing, and I'm powerless. I step up to her, questions in my own eyes. Can I touch you? Can I do this? Will you let me? She nods as if she knows exactly the words that are about to leave my lips. "*Yes*."

The cold tile meets my knees as I kneel in front of her, and my hand hovers, seeking direction. I know exactly where I want it, but I need her consent. I *have* to have it, otherwise I won't touch her. Bailey's lower lip trembles as I peer up at her, and she stares up at the ceiling instead. Just as I'm about to let my hand drop, she grabs my wrist and yanks. I don't give in, clenching my jaw as I await her words.

She drags my hand to her hip, nodding at me, and I purse my lips. "Words, Bailey," I tell her. "I need you to spell it out for me."

"Touch me," she whispers so low I barely hear it, and a groan travels up my throat as my fingers squeeze her hip. "*Please.*" She mouths, no sounds coming out.

"How?" I ask her, hooking my thumbs into her scrub pants and dragging them down slowly, waiting for her to back out. But she never does. She lets me. She *wants* this. I see her hands shaking from my periphery, and I don't want to make her nervous, but the truth is that, for some reason, I am, too. "I'll do whatever you want. Just tell me what to do."

Bailey licks her lips, a tear spilling free. She immediately wipes it away. "Lower my pants and underwear to my ankles." I exhale a shallow breath and do as I'm told. This is what she needs. *Control.* And I'm going to give it back to her.

I grab onto her lacy thong and drag it down to meet her scrub pants, lowering them all the way to her ankles, then helping her step out of them. My head tips back to look into her wide green eyes, and she seems like she wants to back out. But I don't want that now, although I'd do whatever she said at this point.

Surprising me, she strips off her scrubs shirt and drops it on the ground next to the rest of her clothes. We're in this bathroom—no lock on the door—where we could get caught at any moment, and the only thing keeping me from seeing all of her is a fucking bra. I want to take it off and run my hands all over her body, only I know I can't. Instead, a bright red scar catches my attention. It's on her ribs, puckered and angry. The only imperfection I see on her.

I lean in and kiss her scar, my lips lingering on it, and she gasps.

"And then?" I ask her, my voice husky. I've forced myself not to look at her cunt, but the scent of her arousal is driving me insane. I close my eyes and inhale, my nostrils flaring, and wait for instructions.

"Touch my—legs."

I begin to run my fingertips up her legs, all the way down from her ankles to the inside of her thighs, a slow torture even for me. I scoot closer on my knees, still refusing to look at her most intimate place. Because I know if I look, I will lose all control, and I need to keep myself in check for her. Especially right now.

I press my nose to the inside of her thigh and drag it up a little. "Is this okay?" I ask her, running my lips against her skin too.

"Mmm." She tries, and I stop. "*Yes. Keep going.*"

"Now…what?" I ask her through a breath, getting closer to that intoxicating scent: roses and *her*. My lips trail to her groin and I stop.

She huffs. "Now lick me."

I part my lips and take her skin between them, sucking the soft flesh of her upper thigh, and she growls at me. *Growls.* Her fingers come to the hair at the nape of my neck, and she tugs me off her with a popping sound. Before I can even think about what she's doing, she shoves me face first into her pelvis, then tilts her hips up.

My lips land on her pubic bone, and I smirk. "Here?"

"Lower."

"How about now?" I ask her, nipping at the flesh right above her bare pussy lips. "Here?"

"Theo," she groans, pulling my hair. It hurts like hell and I wince. "Oh, shit. Fuck, I'm sorry—"

"Don't apologize." I pull back and grab her thigh, putting her leg over my shoulder, and look at her. *Really* look at her. She squirms when my eyes linger on her cunt, memorizing the rosy hue of her lips, the way she's fucking dripping for me.

She's beautiful, perfect. I take a slow, tentative lick, her taste exploding on my tongue, and I hum. My tongue laps over her from entrance to clit once more, and she groans, her fingers tightening in my hair. God, my head is gonna hurt after this. "There?"

"More…"

So I do it again, swirling my tongue over her tight bud, and she moans. The sound sends a shiver down my spine and my stomach flips. Something about her makes me feel different. Like I'm new at this, and it's weird but also good at the same time. It's like this is *the* first time I'm hearing a woman moan all over again. And maybe it is—because none of them were her.

I'm vaguely aware of us being in a hospital bathroom, although thankfully, she's against the door, so if anyone were to try to come in, it'd give me at least a second or two to get my shit together.

Bailey moans when I circle my tongue against her clit, and I grip my cock over my underwear. "Shhh, baby," I groan. "We have to be really quiet."

I suck her clit into my mouth and slowly insert two fingers into her wet heat, giving her a chance to deny me, to tell me to stop. Instead, her smooth walls clamp around me and her fingers release my hair to find the skin of her thigh, where she claws at herself. After a moment of hesitation, I begin to move them in a come-here motion, rubbing her in a way that has her tightening her leg over my shoulder.

The sounds of her wetness echo in the small bathroom, and it makes me so hard it's painful. My dick is pressed against the waistband of my boxer briefs, straining to get free, and I breathe through it. It's not about me right now—not unless she wants it to be.

Letting go of her clit, I swirl my tongue over it and continue to fuck her with my fingers, slow but rough. "Oh, God." She moans, "Mmmm."

I feel her legs begin to shake, and I take that as my cue to suck on her clit—hard. Her breaths turn to pants quickly, and her moans pick up until it's all I hear. I look up at her to see her head thrown back against the door. Lips parted on a moan, her cheeks red, wholly flushed.

"Just like—" She groans, and I suck even harder. "*That*. Oh!"

With one more thrust of my fingers, she comes, and I don't close my eyes for one damn second because it's too beautiful of a sight to miss. Her hands both come to the back of my head as she shifts her hips, her fingers digging into my neck. I moan against her, which makes her fingers curl, and when she's done she doesn't push me away. No, she pulls me in harder, like she wants the sensitivity that comes after.

Oh, fuck.

Bailey pushes me away suddenly, and I remove my fingers from her, the wetness dripping down my knuckles. Making eye contact, I bring my fingers to my lips and take a tentative lick, then suck the wetness off them. She takes her bottom lip between her teeth and bites, letting it drag slowly until she lets go of it.

I take a deep breath and start to get up, but she shakes her head, so I stop. "What do you want, Bailey?"

"You." She breathes, her cheeks turning a deep shade of red. She's embarrassed. She wants something but doesn't know how to ask for it.

"You want me to fuck you?"

She shakes her head slowly and looks at the ground. "I want —" With a deep breath, she tries again. "*I* want to do it."

"You want to ride my dick, baby?" I ask her softly, and the fire flaring in her eyes is enough to have pre-cum leaking from me. Oh my God. "You want to be in control?" She nods, and I grab her hand, pulling her to me until she falls to her knees in front of me. "Look at me, Bailey. Whatever it is that you want, it's already yours. Just tell me, and I'll give it to you."

"Take off your underwear," Bailey demands softly, almost as a question, but I don't overthink it. I take them off, and then without even considering how cold it must be, I sit my ass on the freezing bathroom tiles against the door.

Bailey's eyes widen when they fall to my dick, and with one hand I grip it, giving it a slow tug that has my lips turning up when she can't look away. "What are you waiting for, baby?" I whisper. "Come sit on it."

Seeming to think about it, she pauses, but then I realize she's trying to hear if anyone is coming. If we get caught, she'd be so fucked. Except I can't even think about that right now. Not when she's crawling up to me and spreading her legs, sinking down onto my thighs.

Her firm ass leans on me, and she looks down at my dick as if in awe. Her hand reaches out tentatively, and she wraps her dainty fingers around me. As soon as she grips me, I let my head fall back to the door.

"So big, Theo." She looks at me as she says it, and I lower my chin to gaze into her eyes. "Don't make fun of me; it's been a long time."

"I would never." I grip her chin between my thumb and forefinger. "I could never make fun of you, Bailey. Go as fast or slow as you need to."

Her knees come to the ground beside my thighs as she lifts up from me and directs my dick to her entrance. At first contact, I notice two things: she's *so* wet and warm. When she sinks down on the first inch, my eyes literally roll to the back of my head. She wasn't joking. It's either been a long time, or she's a virgin because she's barely budging—even though her wetness is literally dripping down my shaft.

My hands fall to her hips, squeezing lightly. "Bounce," I tell her, and she does it slowly. "There you go, Bailey. Oh, *God*," I groan. "You're taking me so fucking well."

Bouncing her on my dick, she finally sinks all the way down, and we both moan together when I bottom out. Her hands fall to my chest, her thighs squeeze against mine, and when she pushes up and sinks back down, my head falls back against the door once more.

I close my eyes for a moment, wanting to savor the feeling of her cunt squeezing me, and when her breathy little moan reaches my ears, they fly open again. "Do that again, Bailey," I demand, grabbing her hips and helping her make that circular motion she just did that had her making that sound for me. "I love the sounds you make for me. Give me one more. Let me memorize it before you disappear from my life for good."

"Theo," she groans as I direct her hips so she's rubbing her clit against me, the slickness of her spreading over my lower abdomen and pelvis. "*Yes*."

She immediately changes the rhythm though, lifting off my dick slowly and then slamming down on it roughly. My eyes roll to the back of my head, my fingers gripping onto her hips, and her nails dig into my chest. I hear myself panting, my moans drowning my breathing every few seconds, and my balls drawing up into my body.

Goddamn.

Bailey feels unreal, and when my eyes are able to focus again, they trace all her features. Her beautiful hooded green eyes, small, straight nose, and full lips. Whatever she's doing, she loves because she bounces faster and harder, bracing herself on my shoulders. The door is creaking from how hard she's bouncing on my dick, but I can't seem to give a damn. It takes everything in me not to come right fucking now—I breathe in slowly through my nose, then exhale it even slower.

Her moans begin to crescendo, and I decide to help her out by pressing my thumb to her clit while I grip her with the rest of my hand. As soon as I begin to move it in circles, she whimpers. It's not long before she starts shaking on top of me—again. I love the sight, and even as my spine tingles and my balls draw up even more, I don't dare close my eyes. If I miss something, I might just die.

"*Yes*," I moan. "Ride my dick faster." She pants as she speeds up, moaning louder until I clamp my hand over her mouth, but even then she doesn't stop.

Bailey bites my hand as her cunt flutters, drawing blood, I'm sure, because it stings, and she squeezes me so hard my toes curl. After one more time of her slamming herself down on me, I'm coming inside of her.

Her forehead comes to rest against mine, both of our chests heaving, and I trail my hand from her hip all the way to her cheek and cup it. Our eyes meet, her green ones dilating as she stares into mine, and when I lean in to kiss her she pulls away from me completely.

"You're not that lucky, big guy," she says with a low chuckle, but the spell is broken, I can tell.

I frown, "So I can be inside you but not kiss you?"

"You are correct," she replies nonchalantly, getting off me and walking to her tangled scrubs and underwear.

"Can I at least help you clean up?" I ask her, noticing her hands are shaking. "Are you okay?"

"N-n-o." Bailey says through a shaky breath. "I'm not o-fucking-kay. I just had sex with a stranger—my *patient*—in the bathroom at work. Clearly, I've gone insane!"

"Lower your voice." I hiss, "You're not insane—this was amazing. But if you need to feel less guilty, consider me a charitable man. I seduced you, that's all."

"We both know—"

"Tell yourself…" I take a deep breath, my eyes stinging for whatever reason. I can't take her rejection right now. I just want her out. "Whatever you need to get through it. Just don't lie to yourself and say it didn't mean anything."

"It didn't—" She starts. "It was a mistake."

"Stop." I exhale roughly, getting up from my place in front of the door and pulling up my underwear. "Bailey, I can handle a lot, but not this. So if you're going to hurt my heart, please stop now. Just…leave."

We look at each other while she puts on her pants, me purposely keeping my eyes on her face, and she nods. "I'm gonna—go."

Of course, you are, sweet Bailey.

She's scared of something, I don't know what, but whatever it is, it's ruling her life. I want to make it better, so slap a Band-Aid on it. Or even better, help her scars fade…yet I have a nagging suspicion that she will never allow it. I know she enjoyed herself at least a little if the noises she was making were any indication. However, after everything was said and done, she thought it was a fucking mistake.

A mistake.

I was a mistake.

How am I supposed to get over that?

I felt so whole while it happened—everything felt better, even if for a short moment. But the instant gratification didn't pay off. Now, I just feel empty—even worse than I did initially.

Especially when she walks out the door and leaves me behind.

Bailey

CHAPTER TEN

There's messing up, and there's fucking up.

And I *fucked* up.

Big time.

I can't even believe I had sex with my patient in the hospital bathroom. Am I actually serious right now? What is wrong with me? What could have possibly possessed me to commit such an act?

Theo.

That's who.

Beautiful, blue-eyed, brown-haired, perfect fucking Theo.

God, I'm so stupid sometimes. Here, I promised myself I would not fall in love again, but then I jumped up on the dick of the first person who offered it. The difference is that he offered to do whatever I wanted to do. Men don't usually do that; they want to be the ones in control. But not here. I orchestrated every single move, and he delivered whatever I wanted him to. And it was amazing, he wasn't wrong about that. Except for the shameful feeling that washed over me after everything was said and done? No amount of sex-induced bliss can tamper with that.

I run from Theo's room and straight to the staff bathroom,

where I throw the door open and spill the contents of my stomach before properly closing the door. Someone pushes it, and I hear the creak, but as more bile rises in my throat, I decide it doesn't matter.

Stupid, stupid, stupid.

How am I supposed to go back to his room to take care of him? The night is still young; half of my shift is still left. I have sabotaged my own damn self at this point. This is the reason I don't trust myself to—

"Bailey," the charge nurse calls from the doorway. "Are you okay? Do you need to go home?"

Home?

That would be amazing.

Forget tonight and Theo.

"Uh." I wipe my face with the back of my hand and dry heave, trying to breathe in through my nose to make it stop. I'm not sick, not really. At least not in the regular sense. My nerves are just fried now. "Home would be..." Dry heave. "Safe."

"You only have Mr. Anderson left as a patient." Somehow, I haven't had any new admissions during this shift. "And I'm sure anyone in the unit would be willing to take him on." *I'm sure*. I'm also sure he'd be willing to fuck them with his big—

"Do your paperwork and go home."

"Okay." I get up from the toilet and flush, then head to the sink and turn on the cool water. "Thank you."

I walk back to my computer and chart the necessary information into Theo's medical record, all the while tensing at the fact that I have access to his stuff at this point. It feels too personal.

Once I've finished all my tasks, I give report to the new nurse taking on Theo. It all takes about an hour and a half, but I'm on my way down before I can remember that I parked my car really far from the staff entrance. I turn around, go to the nurse's station, and call security. Requesting a female to walk me down seems odd for many, but I don't feel safe around men anymore, so bringing a male officer down only makes me even more apprehensive.

Before long, a female officer is walking me to my car.

"You sure did park far, Bailey," the woman jokes. "How come you needed help tonight? You've never asked for an escort."

"Because I've never left in the middle of the night before." I smile tightly.

"You're right." She smiles back, but hers is genuine. "Us girls gotta stick together."

"Thank you," I reply, finding my vehicle, the beat-up white Honda Civic. "This is me."

"Have a good night," she says, turning around as soon as she sees that I'm okay with it.

I unlock the car and get in, immediately locking it, and release a big breath. My hands shake as I take my phone out of my work bag, but I can't go home like this. So I call the only person I know I can count on—Cheyenne.

The phone rings several times, so many that I almost think it's going to voicemail, but then she picks up. "Hello?" Her voice is sleepy from the other side, of course it is—it's one in the morning. "Are you okay, Bai?"

"Uh—" I clear my throat, "No." My voice cracks on the last word and I hear the covers rustle from her end of the call.

"Come over," she replies without hesitation. This is why she's my best friend. It doesn't matter the situation, the time, or the place; she's always there. She took me in when she didn't have to. She brought me here to live with her. Chey took me under her wing and nurtured me—and she's still doing it. "I'll be waiting with a glass of wine."

"Be there in ten," I tell her, my heart in my throat, then I hang up.

The drive to Cheyenne's apartment complex is a blur. It's actually closer to the hospital because she lives on the right side of town, the one where you don't have to worry about getting kidnapped. She doesn't know what side of town I'm living in because I refused to tell her—I know she would've forced me to stay. And I didn't want to. I need to be on my own. I'm too paranoid to not let it show. I don't want her to think I'm crazy, but I can't keep pretending every moment of every day. It's better this way, even if I hate where I live.

Pressing on the remote, I open the gate to the apartment complex and drive through, going right for my parking spot. Although Cheyenne is never lonely, she doesn't let anyone spend the night and there's an unspoken rule that the spare parking spot is mine. So no one is allowed to park there, instead they have to go on the visitor's side of the lot.

I grab my bag and step out of the car, the chill of the December air making me shiver. I practically run up the stairs to the second floor, locking my car from the top. I know it's safe here, that it's a gated community, and Robert would never be able to get in, but sometimes my mind plays tricks on me and convinces me that he will always find a way to make me pay for what I did to him.

Unlocking the door, I rush into the apartment. The lights are dimly lit, and my friend is perched on the three-piece sectional with a steaming mug of coffee. She must be really tired of me interrupting her sleep, though I can't even feel bad about it because I need her. I *need* her.

I sniff loudly, taking in the scent of her pumpkin spice candle, and take off my tennis shoes by the door. "Should I strip?"

"*Duh,*" Cheyenne says with an eye roll. "No one wants your germs on the couch, Bailey Bean."

Jelly beans were my favorite growing up, so she nicknamed me after them. Before I graduated from high school, we used to go to the mall every Saturday with my parents, and we would always buy jelly beans. Now, I haven't had one in seven years.

"Alright," I reply, stripping my clothes and leaving them on the ground right next to my shoes. "Is your fluffy robe still at the back of the bathroom door? If I'm going to be here, I'd rather be warm."

"Yeah." She nods, her nose wrinkling, blue eyes narrowing on my…underwear. "Bailey."

I freeze. "Yeah?"

"Why is there a wet spot on your underwear the size of my fucking hand?"

"Uh—"

"*No*. And you didn't tell me?" She shakes her head rapidly and her shrill shriek pierces my ears. "Get the robe. Hurry up, you have some explaining to do."

I grab the robe from the back of the bathroom door, then rush back to the living room, tying it as I walk. "I made a mistake."

"What happened?"

"I fucked my patient," I reply with shame, my face heating to a boil. I even feel hot when I inhale, the air singing my nostrils.

"You did *what*?" Cheyenne chokes on her coffee, sputtering until she turns red. I go to help her, but she holds up her hand. "Sit the fuck down, Bailey." I do, then grab her fluffy blanket and drape it over myself. Her cold toes touch my leg, and I jump, but I don't dare speak. "Tell me everything. *Now*."

"Where do I even start?"

"How about from the beginning? And tell me where you let him fuck you."

"Well…" I hesitate, fighting the urge to smirk. "I fucked *him*. He did whatever I wanted him to."

"Beginning."

I take a deep breath and tip my head back on the couch, resting it against the cushions, then close my eyes. I need to try to relax. But all I can see is Theo under me, gripping my hips, rubbing my clit. The man has some magic fingers, magic everything. I already feel myself wanting a repeat. But I won't do that—obviously. "Theo Anderson is my patient—the Sailors hockey player...and I'm sure you know what happened, so I don't have to fill you in."

"Oh?" I can hear the smirk in her voice. "Was he just too pretty to resist?"

With a roll of my eyes, I answer. "I mean, I'm sure you know his injuries; they must be all over the news."

"They are."

"Great." I nod, "Then I don't have to explain that part. Anyway, we had a moment...and—"

"Clearly," she interrupts sarcastically.

"Are you gonna let me fucking talk? Because you've always done this shit where you ask me to explain something, and then you keep interrupting me and—"

"Sorry, Bai. It's just a little hard to picture how your patient fell in your fucking *hole*." Cheyenne laughs. "Although with a face like that...it makes sense."

He does have a really pretty face. "Listen. We bonded, okay? And then my other patient died, and he was there, and—well... he offered to make it better. I didn't think he meant that—except then he told me to break for him and that he'd put me back together—"

"Some Wattpad shit."

"*And* he...did."

"I just bet he did, Bailey." Chey smirks, her whole face lighting up. She takes another sip of her coffee. "So you fucked a bangin' hot hockey player—which I want details *really* soon— but I'm failing to see why you look sick."

"*Okay.*" I laugh. "How about the fact that he's my patient, and it's against the law?" She raises an eyebrow at me and I look away. "Or, how about the fact that it was so good I almost passed out, and then I told him he was a mistake, and he told me to leave?"

"You said *what* to him?"

"Cheyenne." I huff in exasperation. "You know I'm emotionally unavailable, and this guy...he's *emotional*. I can tell this wasn't casual for him. And let's be real, he's all sunshine, and I'm a raging bitch."

"Maybe you need more sunshine in your life." She smiles, all teeth. "As for being casual or not, Bailey...I don't think you know how to do casual. Shit, you couldn't be *casual* if you tried."

"So what do you call a one-time thing?"

"*Not* a mistake, Bailey." She shakes her head in disappointment. "It's no wonder he told you to leave. He probably felt used. If what you're describing is true and he did everything your way, I'd be offended too."

I really messed up.

God.

"It was too much at once..."

"Why?" she asks me. "What did he do?"

"He didn't do anything." I throw the blanket off me and stand up, beginning to pace circles around the coffee table. "I told him step by step what to do. He was literally perfect. I didn't feel unsafe once, Chey. It was...amazing."

"So what's the problem?"

"The problem?" I laugh, "That *is* the problem. I felt safe and it was too good to be true, Cheyenne. There's nothing safe about life, especially not mine."

She pats the spot right next to her on the couch. "You deserve to be happy too. So if he felt safe, then maybe he is."

"No one is safe," I whisper, dropping down on the couch and resting my head on the pillow propped over her lap. "*I'm* not safe. I'll never be able to care for someone the way they deserve. I'm too..." My bottom lip wobbles as tears spring to my eyes. "Broken."

"You're not broken, Bailey." She assures me with a gentle mothering tone that I miss. I no longer have my mom or dad, so it's not like I can take advice from them. "You're amazing and stunning and special. So what if you can't trust someone at first? It'll come. Eventually, you'll be able to."

"I highly doubt that." Tears spill over, soaking the suede throw pillow. "He looked devastated. The worst part is that he's so nice. I actually enjoy his company, and now I've gone and messed that up. How do I even come back from it?"

"You apologize."

"And then what?" I chuckle. "Go back to the awkward nurse-patient relationship?"

"Is that what you want?"

Yes.

No.

"I don't know what I want. But I know I'm not ready for a relationship, if that's what you're asking."

"Do you want something from him? Sex?"

"No." I try to shake my head, but she pins it to the pillow, forcing me to think. "I don't want him just for sex. He could be a good friend, I guess."

"Being friends is better than nothing."

"I have to talk to him, don't I?"

"Yeah, babe," she tells me as she rubs my hair. "You do."

What the hell did I get myself into?

CHAPTER ELEVEN

Bailey left early yesterday and I'm thankful for it, especially after she called what we did a *mistake*. I've never seen a woman look more horrified after having sex with me, and it hurt me. Deeply. Not my ego, just…me. I'm not sure what it is about Bailey that makes her different, but if it were any other person, I frankly wouldn't have cared. Maybe I'm just emotional now and sensitive from everything happening to me.

Am I the problem?

Am I just being dramatic?

Whether I had a one-night stand with someone or a quickie in a bathroom, I'd never call them a mistake—to their face. That's just messed up in so many ways, and I guess she didn't even care about how I might take that.

There's a knock at the door, and someone comes in before I can object. It's time for a shift change, unfortunately. Which means Bailey is my nurse again. I'm not lucky enough for them to change that at this point.

Linda comes in with Bailey trailing after her, and they talk for a moment before she directs her attention to me. "Hey, Theo," Bailey says softly, sending butterflies erupting in my stomach at the way she says my name. "I'll be your nurse again tonight."

Great.

I want to say that out loud but refrain. Instead, I nod but don't reply. Linda, on the other hand, senses the vibes are off because she looks between the two of us with confusion.

Yeah, Linda, we fucked, and now she's acting like she didn't leave me behind in that bathroom just a few feet away from us. She left me like she didn't take a part of me with her, one I didn't willingly hand over. As if I didn't feel empty the instant she all but ran out of this room, seeming like she was sick— because I made her that way. Because that's how much she hated it. So yeah, *great.* I love that I'll be subjected to more cruel and unusual punishment during my hospital stay. As if I don't have enough shit bringing me down, like I'm not unhappy enough already.

"How are you feeling tonight?" Bailey asks with a small smile, an apologetic one. Does she feel guilty? She should. "How's your head?"

Which one? I want to be immature and ask, but I won't joke with her. Not now.

"Fine," is all I give her.

She nods quickly, her bottom lip quivering before she clamps it down between her teeth, and her face turns red. "Okay. I'll stay and do your assessment as soon as Linda is done with me."

"Oh, I'm done," Linda says and walks away. Only before she leaves, she tells me, "It was nice taking care of you, Theo. I hope you're out of here before I get back. You look like you want to go home."

"I do, Linda." I smile at her, knowing she notices how forced it is. "Thank you for everything."

"Of course." With another smile, one that reaches her eyes, she exits the room.

An awkward silence descends, and I want to break it. I want

to joke and flirt with Bailey again. I want to go back in time to before I fucked up and offered myself on a silver platter. Fuck me for always trying to be nice. But it was more than that. I was actually beginning to think there was a spark between us, that it was more than just her being nice to a patient for a few minutes at a time. Clearly, I was right to some degree if her riding my dick like I was the only man on this planet for her was any indication.

"Can you lift your shirt, please?" Bailey asks me, stepping up to the bed until her thighs are against the mattress. She takes the stethoscope out of her pocket, and for some reason, I recall what she said about not liking it around her neck. She's always paranoid, watching out for herself. Is that why she ran out? Did I scare her? "I need to listen to your heart."

Fantastic.

Now she'll be able to tell how nervous I feel around her. And also hurt. Mostly because she treated me like I didn't matter. I'd never treat anyone that way—but especially not her. Maybe she makes a habit of having sex and discarding people. Then again, that would require a level of trust that she doesn't have. It makes me wonder how true the rumors are about her.

What are you running from, Bailey?

"Sure," I tell her, lifting my shirt above my chest and holding it there.

She listens to my heart, lingering, her hand on my chest. It feels like it's searing my skin, sending little electric shocks through my body. I don't dare make eye contact with her, and it's a good thing since my eyes are beginning to sting with unshed tears. I just want her out of here. I want to leave this stupid hospital and never see her again.

"Your heart is beating really fast," Bailey whispers, her fingers tracing my chest for a moment before she lets her hand drop. Her eyes flick to my face. I can feel them, but I don't look up. "I'm really sorry, Theo. I fucked up. I don't know why I said we were a mistake. It just…scared me. I hadn't had sex in a long time, and I didn't expect it to be with a patient, in the middle of my workday…at my job."

"I understand." I nod once. And in a way, I do. What she's saying makes sense, but being left that way without explanation still hurts.

"Look at me," she demands, and I do, my eyes coming to her face and slowly drifting up to meet her gaze. "Where did happy Theo go? I don't like seeing you this way."

I stare into space, not answering her question.

"Well, I still wanted to apologize." She murmurs, moving down to my abs to listen to my stomach. "Can you please forgive me?"

"And then what, Bailey?" *Never see each other again? Live my whole existence wondering what if?* The words hang in the air, and she looks like she's going to cry.

"We can be friends."

My heart nearly stops, then doubles in rhythm. "Like… outside of the hospital?"

"Why not?" She smiles, looking at me after she removes the stethoscope from my skin. "You're nice."

I shake my head and look away.

"Give me your phone," she orders, and my brows furrow. "As soon as you're out of the hospital, call me, and we can hang out."

Hope swells in my chest, and I reach for the bedside table and hand her my phone. She quickly types, saving her phone number to my contacts list. Relief hits me, and maybe a small part hopes she will eventually give me a chance. She's made it more than clear that she's not ready, though. But I can still dream.

"Just a few more days." I smile, and this time it is genuine. It stretches my face, hurting my cheeks, and her dimples pop as she returns it. "Then I'm all yours."

"What do you want to do?" She asks me, "When we hang out?"

"Maybe we can have dinner." *It's not a date, Theo.* "Go somewhere public so you feel comfortable."

"That sounds nice."

"Or breakfast, considering your schedule."

The door barges open, and in comes Jeremy, holding up a bag of McDonald's. I love that place, but damn, his timing could not be more off. I thought Bailey and I were having another moment, but as soon as he strolls in and sits down, she stiffens. I pull my shirt down, and her gaze drags down my body as I do. It reminds me of her riding me, the way I touched her, the look in her eyes as she came. Her mouth wide open on a moan, her eyes rolling to the back of her head as pleasure consumed her and—

"I'll be back later to give you pain meds," she tells me before walking away, not even looking back as she exits the room.

I don't dare look at Jeremy when she leaves. Immediately, he notices something is up because he clears his throat.

"Well, I feel like I just walked in on something." I snap my eyes up to his, and he smirks. "Did I?"

"You have the worst fucking timing, you know that?" The exasperation in my voice is evident because his smirk drops, and instead, he furrows his eyebrows. "We were talking."

"Oh?" One eyebrow quirks. "Be honest with me, did you fuck her?"

After a brief moment of silence, I relent, mostly because we've never kept secrets from each other. "Yes, and it was the best sex of my life."

"So what's wrong, then?"

"She...ran away." I sigh, "She was just apologizing and saying we should be *friends*."

"*Ouch.*" Jeremy winces. "She already friend-zoned you? Brutal."

"I'm not giving up," I tell him honestly. "I'll wait it out."

"What made you suddenly so interested, Theo?" Beats me, but I am. She has layers I want to uncover, and I'm determined not to give up. "You've never been so interested in anyone to the point of taking a spot in the friend zone."

"Bailey is different, man." And she is. "I want to get to know her."

"And you're saying this after only a few days of being here?" He narrows his eyes on my face. "You haven't even been here for a week."

"Don't judge me, okay?" He rolls his eyes at that. "But we connected, and I don't get that often. It felt real for once."

"Is your brain misfiring?"

I laugh, loudly. "Maybe."

"Clearly, bro." It's not just about sex. I know that, and she knows that. "It's too early to be pussy whipped, though. So you need to chill."

"I'm chill as fuck, dude." Lies, there's nothing chill about me right now. Not when it comes to Bailey, not after everything that happened between us. But she agreed to go out with me, even if it's just as friends. That right there is enough to have me feeling relieved. "Anyway, thanks for Mickey D's."

"Of course," Jeremy says as I open the bag, pulling out a million chicken nuggets with BBQ sauce. "Anything for my D-man."

"You're just so…" I stuff my mouth and speak through a mouthful of food. He grimaces. "*Sweet.*"

"When will you be out of here, Anderson?"

"I think within the next few days if everything goes as planned," I reply, my stomach dropping at the possibility that it won't. "And then Bailey and I have *not a date*. Well, a *friend* date."

"Oh my God." Jer shakes his head. "Are you sure you're gonna be able to change her mind? You're friend-zoned as fuck."

"She'll change her mind." I shrug with a nonchalance I don't feel. One way or another, I'll make her change her mind.

"If you say so."

We finish our food in silence, him occasionally looking at me like I'm crazy, and then he takes the bag and discards it. I know he's going to get going before he even says it. We've been friends long enough for me to know how he thinks and to recognize his body language, too. And I'm fine with it, truly. Maybe I need some alone time before Bailey comes back in. I really need to think about how I'm going to keep myself in check when we're hanging out. Because all I want to do is make her mine.

"Alright." Jeremy breaks the silence, his lips tipping up in a small smirk. "Time to go."

"Drive safe."

"I'm glad you'll be out of here soon," he replies. "I miss you on the ice."

I miss the ice myself, but I'm trying not to think about it often. It seems there are some hurdles I need to overcome before I'm allowed to play, and quite honestly, I don't want my mood to plummet again. Maybe fucking Bailey was about me as much as her, especially since I can't deny that I felt so much better while it was happening. Nothing else mattered except her, and it was a nice change to have a break from all the thoughts running rampant in my brain at all hours of the day and night.

"Soon," I lie, knowing damn well it'll be weeks before I can go back on the ice.

Jeremy heads to the door and glances back at me, giving me a soft smile, then exits the room without another word. The sudden silence makes me feel cold and empty. *Lonely*. But that's how I've been feeling for days now like I have no one to lean on, even though I know I do. They couldn't possibly understand what I've been going through, and there's only one person I've actually talked to about it. And that's Bailey.

I want to tell her more—more than just my worst

kindergarten teacher or my first kiss. I want to tell her about my sister. I want to give her a glimpse of everything that makes me, *me*. That's what friends do, after all, but something is stopping me. I just can't put my finger on it. I think I just don't want to scare her away. What if she thinks this is getting too deep and that's not what she wants? Or what if I cross a boundary I didn't even know she set?

After a while, I think I fall asleep. My head is nodding without my consent, and my fingers are twitching. But something wakes me all the way; a commotion in the hallway, right outside my room. I get out of bed and press my ear to the door, not wanting to interrupt whatever is happening. The voices are loud, and there's clearly an argument happening.

"Did you think you could just run away and I wouldn't find you, Bailey?" The voice rises even more. "You fucking slut."

I flinch, and when a sob breaks from the other side and something thumps against my door, I run to the phone at my bedside and call security.

"Security." The man on the phone answers.

"Yes, sir. I'm calling because there's a nurse being attacked in the hallway right in front of my room." My voice is raspy, and I clear it. "Tenth floor. Room 1008."

"Be right there."

But I can't just stand here and listen to whatever that prick is saying to Bailey, so I open the door.

There's a man with dark hair and midnight eyes standing outside of the door, getting in Bailey's face. He looks enraged, but what bothers me is the grip he has on her arm. "Is there a problem here?" I ask, looking at the girl with tears trailing down her face. "Bailey?"

"Oh, this is rich." He spits, tightening his grip on her arm until his knuckles turn white. "Is this your new knight in shining armor? I knew you wouldn't stop being the same fucking whore you've always been. But don't sweat it, Bailey, because I forgive you, babe. And you're coming home with me."

"Let go," she whispers. "I'm not going anywhere with you."

"The fuck you're not," he growls, spit flying from his mouth as he steps even closer to her.

I shove him away, "You heard the lady."

"Theo, go back to your room," Bailey tells me with furrowed brows. "This isn't your business."

"Damn right, it's not," the man replies.

"Robert." She hisses. "This is my work. You need to leave."

"I'm not going anywhere without you." He advances on her again, shoving her against the wall and grabbing her by the hair, yanking back roughly. "And if you don't come with me, I will fuck you up like I did the last time."

Bailey whimpers, and I take a step forward.

"Robert, please," Bailey tries to placate him. "I can't go with you right now. I'll lose my license for abandoning my patients."

"You're not fucking working again." He laughs, "So it doesn't matter."

"Bailey—" I whisper, looking to either side of the hallway, hoping security shows up.

"You need to shut the fuck up," Robert growls at me. "Go back to your room, pretty boy. Stay the fuck out of our business."

My fists clench at my sides, but when he grabs Bailey by the neck, I snap. I mirror what he just did to her, gripping his neck and shoving him to the opposite wall. "Touch her again, and I'll set you on fire, motherfucker."

"Theo." Bailey all but growls, coming to grip my arms as I choke him and cage him in simultaneously. "Stop, please."

"No, Bailey," I tell her as I see his face turning red, his eyes bulging out of his head. "Someone needs to teach him to keep his hands to himself."

I hear a commotion down the hall as the elevators open, and in strolls security. Just when I think I have everything under control though and loosen my grip on his neck, Robert gets out of my choke hold and begins to run. Security goes after him, not even stopping to ask any questions, to see if it's the right guy. He pretty much told on himself the second he ran. I hope they catch him and send him to jail tonight. That's what he deserves.

I turn around to face the girl with my heart in a vice grip. "Are you okay?"

She sniffles, grabs my arm, and all but shoves me back into my room. I let her push me against the wall, her small hands on my chest hot. "You had no right, Theo."

I flinch, feeling like I'm in trouble. "I had every right, B. He put his hands on you."

"I'm not your girl," she growls. *The fuck you're not.* "You don't have to rescue me."

"I would've done it for anyone, Bailey," I tell her honestly, because I would've. There's nothing that pisses me off more than a man putting his hands on a woman. *Coward.* "Now tell me who the hell he is."

Bailey raises her chin defiantly, "It's none of your business. And if you ever pull shit like this again, I'm going to revoke your friend card."

"Do what you need to do," I scoff. "Just know that I'd rather have that happen than you getting hurt."

"I've been hurt way worse than that," she tells me gently, her hand trailing down my chest slightly until her hand is on my abs. It makes me tense the way she feels so comfortable touching me. As if she didn't just ask to be friends. Friends don't touch each other this way, and they certainly don't fuck either. "Trust me, I'm okay."

"If you say so, baby." Her eyes flare at the word, but then she looks down. "But I'm not going to stand by and let it happen."

"Right," She rolls her eyes. "Because you have to be my knight in shining armor."

"Fuck that," I reply, grabbing her wrist to keep her hand on me. I want to be more than her knight in shining armor. Way more. "I'm not your knight in shining armor. I'm your friend, right? Friends don't stand by to watch each other get hurt."

"Fine." She huffs. "Just don't do that again."

"I make no promises."

And I don't because I know if I ever see anyone hurt her again, I might just kill them.

CHAPTER TWELVE

The shower floor feels cold and hard under my shoulder blades, the tiles scraping my back with every shove. Robert straddles me, pinning my hips in place, and I slap at him as much as I can until he pins my wrists down, that is. Cold water falls over my face, the droplets stinging my cheeks as they land hard and fast, some of it getting in my mouth and making me feel like I'm about to drown. And maybe I am. This might just be what I deserve. Discipline.

"What the fuck don't you understand, Bells?" I cringe at the nickname, beginning to hate it. Hating everything about him. I close my eyes, but he tightens his grip on my wrists to a painful degree, forcing my eyes back open. "You don't talk to any men. None. I'm the only man you're allowed to talk to."

"He's my coworker, Rob." I cry out, tears streaming down my face now because I'm weak. I wish I wasn't, that I could be strong like Cheyenne and leave him already. But I can't. I love him, so fucking much. "I'm sorry, babe. I couldn't help it. It wasn't my choice…"

He lets go of my wrists and slaps me across the face. My cheek stings, but I should've seen it coming. I need to watch my mouth. "There's always a choice, Bells."

Robert gets off me, and I breathe a sigh of relief. But the look in his *eyes is crazed, and my heart beats a little faster. However, it's nothing compared to the pounding in my chest when he shoves my legs up to my chest and settles his cock against my entrance. "No." I shake my head, "Please don't, Rob. This isn't you, babe, please don't do this."*

"This is my choice, Bells." He grins as he shoves his way into me. Roughly, violently. It stings so bad I'm sure something ripped, and I cry out, sobs breaking free from deep within my chest. "Now shut the fuck up and take it."

And I do.

I always do.

My phone's alarm blares through the silence of my little studio, effectively waking me up. I sit up in bed with a start, mostly from the stupid nightmares that invade my sleeping moments—memories. Not always, but occasionally they sneak their way into my mind, unbidden and not welcomed. I figured after six months they'd stop, that Robert would have no control over me, but ever since I saw him four days ago, the nightmares came back.

A ding sounds from my phone, again and again and again. I forgot to put it on silent mode, shit I forgot to put it on Do Not Disturb. I usually do so, so none of the spam calls wake me up. Stupid extended warranty bullshit. OnStar crap too. Student loans that I still need to pay but I'm too broke to do it. It's probably Cheyenne though, since I promised her I'd go ice skating today considering it's my day off. Fucking finally.

I know it's a distraction from my life—working—but ever since Rob showed up, I have felt unsafe in Seattle. He knows where I work. Does he know where I live? My new last name? It would be so easy to track me down. Apparently, it already was. I don't know how he achieved it, but the reach he has is scary. Fear inducing. He has me in a chokehold—the kind where I can't live my life in peace. All I know is distress, heart-stopping fear. And he brought all those feelings back with one visit.

I know I talked shit to Theo for defending me, but the truth is, I don't know what would've happened if he had not done it.

If he hadn't called security…I can't even imagine the kind of mess I'd be in. Probably fired from him throwing a fit at the nurse's station. Or even dead. I bet he *does* want to kill me. So, while I'm irritated that Theo intervened because I can fight my own battles—I think—I'm also so grateful that he stepped in.

I pick up my phone from my bedside table, the second-hand one that has chips in the paint, barely holding itself together. But beggars can't be choosers, and I couldn't afford anything better. Hell, I bought the ninety-nine-cent plates and cups at Target. Only one of each. Plastic forks too, so I could save some money. The only decent things I have are new clothes and shoes.

Cheyenne was kind enough to give me some of the clothes in her closet that she hadn't used in a while. The ones she said she hadn't even looked at in a year, though they still had the tags on them. Must be nice to have the luxury to do that. However, I can't complain anymore, even if I'm only shopping at Forever 21 and Old Navy. But fuck it, my clothes don't have to be expensive to be cute. I'm lucky I even have a friend like her, and I don't take it for granted. I'm so grateful.

I stare at my screen, only to see I have three text messages.

> **UNKNOWN**
>
> Good morning, or should I say good afternoon? Evening?

> **UNKNOWN**
>
> Bailey? Are you there?

> **UNKNOWN**
>
> I know it's your day off. I checked.

My stomach drops at that, since who could possibly have my schedule memorized? Thoughts of it being Robert freeze me on the spot, but even with shaking hands I manage to unlock the screen and enter the chat.

BAILEY

Who is this?

UNKNOWN

It's your friend Theo.

Butterflies invade my stomach for some unknown reason, but I smile, an ache in my cheeks that's completely unfamiliar. I can feel my dimples popping, but I choose not to think about what that means. We're just friends, and it's staying that way. Friends who fucked…and it was amazing. He is amazing.

BAILEY

Oh, hi! I totally forgot you had my number.

Liar.

You were hoping he'd text you much sooner than this, Bailey. Although I did tell him to contact me after he was out of the hospital. I guess that's now.

THEO

Well now you remember. And since it's your day off I thought maybe we could meet up. For that dinner we talked about, remember?

Oh, shit.

How did I make plans with two people at once? My brain really needs to start working again. But I've been distracted lately with Robert's appearance, and I haven't even told Chey about it. She's going to kill me. Maybe if I tell her I'm going out with Theo, she will forgive me. Or I could stop by the rink after I'm done with him, whenever that is.

Either way, she has *'learn to skate'* classes for toddlers at six p.m. and then figure skating at eight p.m. Realistically, I should be able to make it to figure skating.

I look for Chey in my contacts list, then hit call. The phone rings *once*, and she picks up. I love her. "Oh my God, bitch." I laugh. "Were you waiting by your phone this whole time?"

"Of course I was," she replies with what I know is a smirk. "We have plans today."

"Uh." I fidget. "About that…"

"No," she growls. "You better not cancel on me."

"I'm not." I'm quick to assure her. "But can I come to the figure skating lesson instead?"

"Bai." She laughs. "Baby, no offense, but I don't think you're on that level yet."

"Yeah, yeah." I laugh too. "I know I'm at the *toddler* level, no need to remind me. It's just that Theo asked me out to dinner." I almost slap myself from how that sounds. "As friends. Not a date."

"Mhmm. Sure," Chey replies, chuckling under her breath like she doesn't believe me. Which I know she doesn't. I don't even know if I believe myself. But it can only be a friendship; I was clear about that.

"Go get that dick."

I groan, "No dick for me, you little slut." She laughs at my jab. "See you at eight."

"See ya."

I hang up on her, immediately going back to my text messages.

BAILEY

Six p.m.?

THEO

That's in one hour, you know that, right?

BAILEY

Is that a no?

My stomach does a little flip when the dots appear and he's

typing, then they stop. It happens three times before a text comes through.

THEO

I'll be there. Where would you like to eat?

BAILEY

I'm not picky. Just tell me where to go.

THEO

I can pick you up.

BAILEY

No, thanks. See you there.

I put my phone down before he can reply and go to the bathroom to get ready. After doing my makeup—a simple look with tinted sunscreen and a little blush and mascara—I put my best high-waisted jeans on and a black long-sleeve sweatshirt that says the name of the rink where Chey works. I lace up my pink Chucks, curl my hair, and call it a day. I can't even deny I look cute yet casual. Nothing that screams *first date*. I don't want to give him the wrong idea.

Grabbing my wallet, I put it in my purse and head out to get in my car. I didn't grab a jacket, so I'm really hoping that it's not too cold by the time I have to go to the rink. But then again, the sweatshirt should keep me slightly warm, at the very least.

Once in my car, I crank up the heat and pull out of the parking lot. My message says we're going to a pizzeria and brewery. It's a reasonably short drive to the restaurant, and when I park, Theo is already waiting for me right in front of the restaurant doors. He's wearing jeans and Chucks just like me, as well as a blue shirt with an open North Face jacket over the top. The shirt makes his eyes look more blue even from a distance, and I can't deny he is *so* beautiful.

When Theo comes to open my door, I unlock it for him. A

gust of cold air comes into my car, and I shiver as I remove the key from the ignition. I just want to hurry up and go in before I freeze.

"Hey," Theo says with a soft voice. "It's good to see you again."

I smile shyly. "Hey, Theo."

"Let's go inside before you freeze, B." He closes the door to my car, gently grabbing me by the arm and steering me toward the restaurant doors. Ever the gentleman, he opens the door for me again and we step into the hostess area. "What were you thinking, not wearing a jacket? It's twenty-five degrees out."

"Yeah, so I'm bad at that." I smirk. "I usually always forget my jacket."

"That's okay," he replies with a frown. "I'll be setting reminders for you."

I chuckle. "You don't have to do that, Theo."

"Someone has to." He smiles, gazing into my eyes. His are so light blue that they look transparent, and they slightly dilate as he looks at me. "I can't have you getting sick."

"Table for two?" The hostess asks, interrupting the little moment we were sharing. I should be grateful because it felt a little too intimate, but instead, I'm annoyed. Theo nods, looking like he could strangle her, and she says, "Right this way."

We walk to the booth and she sets two menus on it, then tells us our server will be with us shortly. I get in, but instead of Theo sitting across from me he slides into the booth with me. There's an awkward silence at first, but then he smiles and I laugh.

"What are you doing?" I ask him, amusement in my voice.

"I want to get to know you..." Butterflies rage in my stomach, and I shift slightly to get more space between us. He slightly frowns but drops it. "Yelling from across the table doesn't sound very appealing right now."

"Fine." I chuckle. "Just this once. And only because it's our first time going out, and I do want to hear what you have to say."

Theo grins, straight, white teeth on full display. I swear there's not one part of this man that isn't beautiful. It's truly unfair. "Do you like pizza?"

I hesitate, "I do, but I just had some yesterday at work, so I'll be getting something else."

"That makes sense." He replies, "They have a big variety here. Lots of good food. I'm sure you will find something."

I look through the menu and find a calzone, which is just what I want to eat. "Do you love pizza? Is that why you picked this place?"

"Guilty as charged." He laughs, "But we don't have to love the same things to get along."

"Hey, I like pizza." I bump his arm with my shoulder. He's so damn tall. "Just probably not as much as you do."

"To be fair, I don't get a cheat meal that often." He replies, "But I'll choose a seafood spot next time. I mean, if you want to go out again."

He seems a little flustered, and I smirk. "I don't know." I shrug exaggeratedly. "You have a lot of tests to pass today to move on to the next level."

"Our friendship has levels?" He smiles as he looks into my eyes, and his hand is so close to mine that I can feel the heat of it. "How many do I need to unlock?"

"Three if you want to make it to best friends." I grin and wink. "But you're going to have to take me to eat seafood. Sorry about your cheat meals."

"Eh." He shrugs, "I've had a very long time to get used to it."

I look down at his hand for a short moment, noticing how our pinkies are almost touching. Centimeters apart. "How long have you been playing?"

"Well, I started skating when I was three," Theo replies and my jaw drops. "Hockey since I was five."

"Oh my God." He's been skating for over twenty years. "Your whole life, pretty much."

"That's why I said I don't know what else to do with my life. When I told you hockey is the only thing I know how to do, I wasn't joking."

"Did you play any other sports growing up?" I don't even know what's prompting me to ask all these questions. But if we're going to be friends, I guess we might as well get to know each other. At least, that's what I keep telling myself, rather than admitting that I'm hung up on his every word and that I don't want him to stop talking, don't want to stop listening to the soft, deep cadence of his voice.

"Baseball." He smiles. "And soccer. But hockey was the only one that stuck once I turned eight. My parents didn't have a lot of money, and they told me to choose. Of course, I chose the most expensive sport out of the three, but I didn't know that at the time, and they never said anything. It's not until high school that I realized they were paying thousands of dollars a season so I could live out my dreams. At least I had a full scholarship to college…that helped them a lot."

"It really paid off." I smile, "Look at you now, a professional athlete."

"Yeah." He looks down with a frown. "I'm living the dream."

Instead of looking happy as he says that, he seems upset. "What's wrong, Theo?"

"Oh, nothing." He shakes his head. "Just the fact that I don't know how my career is about to play out. I'll be benched for a couple more weeks and then what? I'll have an MRI and they will determine if I can play this season or not. I feel like I can't even breathe just thinking about it."

"It's going to be okay." I touch his hand for a millisecond and then let it drop, but it's long enough to feel the warmth of his skin against mine—again—and it's enough to take me back to that bathroom floor, where I was looking at his face as he came. His parted lips, the gasps escaping his lips, the way his eyes flared as he looked at me and—

Theo jolts. "I sure hope so." He smiles, but it's sad. "What about you? Did you play any sports?"

"I cheered and danced." I smirk, trying to make him smile for a second, but a genuine one. "Does that count?"

"Absolutely." He nods quickly, like he doesn't believe it.

I sigh, "I loved every second of it." And I loved every second of high school too, even if that's where I met my biggest nightmare.

"Can I ask you something?" I raise an eyebrow at him, and he smiles reassuringly. "But please don't take it the wrong way."

"Just spit it out, Theo." I roll my eyes, but the truth is I'm already nervous. Nothing good comes from asking if you can ask a question. Is this about Robert? Because I'm sure as hell not ready to talk about him.

"Do you enjoy being a nurse?" he asks softly. "Is it everything you thought it would be?"

My shoulders relax, and I hadn't even noticed I was tense. He must think I'm crazy, always on my guard, never dropping it for anyone or any reason. "I used to." I admit, "But now... well, it was ruined for me, and I'm just scared instead."

"Of what?"

"For my safety." I scoff, "I know it sounds really stupid, and I don't blame you if you think I'm crazy, but I just feel like I can't relax around men anymore and it makes me nervous all the time when I have a male patient. I know I should get over —" I fall silent, trying to make the elephant in the room disappear.

"Because of Robert?" I purse my lips and don't answer him. "I heard him. When he said, you couldn't escape him. Now, I'm not going to pressure you into telling me what he did. But is he the reason you're scared?"

I nod. "Yes."

"I'm sure security took care of him, and he won't be bothering you anymore."

Yeah, that's what I've been hoping for, but at the same time I know I shouldn't. Because he always finds a way back to me, and I think nothing short of death will stop him from finding me.

"You're right." I force myself to say, even if I don't believe one word of that statement.

The waitress appears with water then, and asks us if we're ready to order. And we are. Theo starts with an appetizer, getting fried shrimp and fried pickles, just in case he says. He also orders a meat lovers large pizza, and I get a three-cheese calzone. The boy can clearly eat.

"That's a lot of food, Theo." I point out, and we both laugh.

"And I'll be eating it all." He grins. "Consider it my cheat meal."

"I love that for you." Theo looks at me with soft eyes, and I can't decipher his thoughts. However, I want to know. So I ask him, "What are you thinking?"

"About everything," he says, and I roll my eyes, which makes him smile at me. "You. Our friendship."

I'm thinking about you too.

"Oh." I can feel myself blushing. How embarrassing.

"So...a skating shirt, huh?" He smirks, "Wanna go sometime?"

I almost cackle. "Only if you want to pick me up from the ground every two minutes." He laughs at me too, "I'm with the *toddler* class. Snowplow Sam 2."

"*Stop.*" His shoulders shake from how hard he's laughing and making a wheezing sound. "But if I hold your hand...well, I won't let you fall. Too much."

"Ah." I smile. "I've gotten better, okay? No need to laugh at me."

"I guess two minutes is better than thirty seconds."

"You're not wrong."

When the food arrives, he immediately digs in, staying quiet until we're done with the appetizer. But even now, it's not awkward; instead, it's a comfortable silence that I could get used to.

Is this really a friendship now?

I enter the arena and immediately shiver, but thankfully, I won't be here for a long time because the figure skating lessons only last forty-five minutes a few times a week. It's younger kids, and yet they're so much more advanced than me. It honestly makes me want to giggle at how bad I am at ice skating. Theo said he wants to take me some time. I'm going to make a fool of myself.

The date—wait, the *non-date*—went really well. Way better than I expected, if I'm being honest. I thought there would be awkwardness since we had never seen each other outside of the hospital, but it turns out he and I could talk for hours without a problem. I'm quite surprised because I can't even speak to Cheyenne for that long.

In the short amount of time that we were at the restaurant— two hours—we talked so much it almost feels like we've caught up on our entire lives. That might be a bit of an exaggeration but we really did talk for hours. About nothing and everything. And the best part is that he listens…*really* listens. He's not pretending to or trying to make me feel better by paying attention. It's as if he's genuinely interested in every word coming out of my mouth. It was exhilarating, the way he looked at me, and it made me want to keep talking all night just so he wouldn't take those pretty blue eyes off my face.

Navigating the Ice Hall arena is like going through a maze, but I finally find Cheyenne on the ice. I'm not skating today; I'm too tired, but I'm willing to stand here and talk however long she wants me to. It's not that talking to Theo made me tired, although I did go over the time limit with him and now I'm late to see Chey, but it's the fact that I've been working non-stop six days a week for months at a time. I'm starting to wonder if the extra money is worth it in exchange for my mental health. But I know it's not—at least, my therapist doesn't seem to think so.

"Chey!" I call out.

She skates right to me and narrows her eyes. "You're late, but if you got some dick I'll forgive you."

"I did not get dick."

"Then you're in time out, babe." She smirks. "You gonna lace up and get out here?"

Yawning, I cover my mouth. "Not tonight." Her jaw drops. "But I'll be back, I promise. Maybe I'll even start taking more days off…"

"Really?" Her voice is incredulous. "Why the change of heart?"

"Maybe I'm missing out on life a little bit by drowning in work. Plus, I fucking hate it there." And Robert showed up and about ruined my life.

"It's probably because you don't take a break." I nod, "I think that's a great idea, Bai. You'll have more time for you, me, and *Theo*."

"And what makes you think I'll be hanging out with him?"

"Oh, bitch, please." She rolls her eyes. "I can read you better than a book."

We both laugh at that because she's not wrong. She has always been able to tell me what I think and even predict my next move. About everything, every single time, I'm going to make a decision. That's one of the reasons I got a plane ticket so fast after Robert—well, the *incident*. It's because she was saving all her air miles for me, and as soon as I called her in my crisis, she bit the bullet and had me out of Georgia before I could say the word peach.

"Okay, so maybe I'll give him a chance." I smile, and hers

turns into a full grin. "But just because I enjoyed hanging out with him…and he's a good *friend*."

"Spill, baby." She shakes her head at me, looking back at the skaters on the ice and yelling at them to practice their twizzles. "Did he look hot for the date? What was he wearing? Where did you go? Was it awkward? Did he kiss you? What did it taste like? Good? Bad?"

"Chill." I huff, watching a ten-year-old fall on her butt, attempting to spin. I can relate *so* hard, my girl. "You know he looked hot. Jeans, Chucks, a shirt that made his eyes bluer than they already are, if that even makes sense…"

"Oh, totally." Chey chuckles. "Blue eyes are so dreamy; just look at mine."

"God, you are so annoying." I laugh. "We went to a pizzeria and I ate a calzone. Everything was great, honestly. I just lost track of time because we wouldn't shut up." She smirks at that. "He might just replace you in the bestie category."

"Don't you dare," Cheyenne growls playfully, giving me a shove. "So, did he kiss you? Or are you just ignoring that question?"

"Uh. No kiss." I didn't want a damn kiss! "I'm sure he's scared after I rejected him."

"Rejected him?"

I scratch my head and look away from her. "Yeah. I had sex with him, but when he tried to kiss me, I told him no." Cheyenne's jaw drops, "It just felt too intimate, okay?"

"And *sex* didn't?"

"You have a point, but none of it was planned, and I freaked out." I wave my hands in front of my face while I explain, then lower them when I realize she's watching how flustered I am. "So maybe I should've let him. Because now I think about what it would be like to kiss him, and I'm not allowed."

"Why the fuck not?" Cheyenne raises an eyebrow, her blue eyes widening. "If you want a kiss, take it."

"We're supposed to be friends, Chey. Friends do not kiss, remember?"

"It's honestly criminal to have the chance to kiss Theo fucking Anderson and not do it." She smirks. "However if you don't, I will."

"Fuck you." I sniff, turning my nose up in the air. "You wouldn't do that to me."

"Why not?" Cheyenne chuckles. "Forget girl code. You don't even want him."

"Chey," I warn. "It's not that I don't want him, I just think he deserves better than me."

"I swear to God, Bai." She looks down with a sad face, her brows furrowed and her mouth turning down slightly. "You self-sabotage more than anyone I have ever met."

That's because of Robert. He ruined me, my life, my heart. I can't trust anyone or let them in. I have issues now, which won't even be resolved with therapy for the next few years if ever. And now he's back to taunt me, and I don't even know if he was taken by security or if he was able to ditch them.

My stomach churns, "Maybe. But at least I'm honest."

"Then be less honest and try being happier instead." Chey grabs my hand and squeezes it once, then lets go. "Now chin up and smile, you're ruining my vibe."

One of the girls comes up to us, stepping off the ice. "I just need some water." She tells us, then walks past us to her bag sitting on the floor behind me.

Cheyenne nods once, and steps on the ice. "Be right back!" She yells to me, then skates up to a girl that keeps falling down. "Amy! Don't stick out your butt so much, it's no wonder you keep falling!"

I snicker, because that would be me too. Poor, sweet, summer child. Amy has no idea what she's in for—she's new—and Chey is strict with her kiddos. The look of regret on Amy's face is evident, and I have to hide my laugh because Cheyenne expects it at the same moment as she turns, raising an eyebrow. She really does read me like a book.

How annoying.

For even after everyone has cleared out and there's no children left on the ice, I still can't take my mind off Theo. Even as Cheyenne cleans up, taking the cones with her, and even after the Zamboni comes to make the ice flawless again, I *still* can't take my mind off Theo.

And the sad part is that it's not even about the sex; no, it's deeper than that. If it were only about the sex it wouldn't even bother me too much. But the red flag is that I know I'm starting to actually like him for who he is, and that's scarier than sleeping with him.

"Wine and charcuterie board?" Cheyenne asks me as she picks up her bag from the floor and sits on the bleachers to take off her skates. "You down?"

"You're telling me that you already have a charcuterie board ready at the apartment? At nine p.m.?"

"Obviously not." She rolls her eyes. "But I can whip one up in five minutes. Everything is already in Ziplock bags waiting for us."

I chuckle, because it's literally the same thing. This neurotic, funny woman always makes me laugh. And it's my favorite thing about her. "Alright, but white wine tonight. I'm too cool for that dry shit you fed me last time."

"Cabernet Sauvignon is amazing, bitch."

I make a disgusted face at her, "If you say so."

After she puts her skates in her bag and we make our way out of the maze, I follow her home in my car. Maybe now she will help me figure out what's going on in my head. She's better at dissecting me than I am. But now I wonder if I should see Theo again because friends don't have crushes on friends. And this is bound to end badly.

The last thing I want to do is hurt him.

Theo

CHAPTER THIRTEEN

J er, Matt, Oliver, and Noah are all sitting around my coffee table playing Uno—which is my favorite card game—while I grill some steaks. Yeah, it's twenty-eight degrees outside at five p.m., but I'm not letting a little cold stop me from living my best life. That's what jackets are for.

Speaking of jackets, I can't help but remember the fact that Bailey wasn't wearing one in this weather. She's absolutely insane for it, and I'm determined to remind her, even if she probably took it as a joke. It wasn't one. Thankfully, the restaurant was warm, even if all I wanted was to snuggle her in close instead of relying on the heater, yet even I have to admit that wasn't a possibility.

Instead, I had to watch our hands—our fucking pinkies—almost touch multiple times. I had to feel the heat of her body close to mine, and it was driving me insane. I'm not sure that I'm strong enough to just be her friend, not after hanging out with her. There's too much between us—I'm *feeling* too much. All I can think about is kissing her, probably because she stole that from me. I want to snuggle her close and talk about our entire lives. I want to find her missing pieces and put them back together. I want—

A lot of things.

And all of them with her.

But I know she's not going to give them to me, and that's why I'm questioning why I'm putting myself through all of this torture. But if friendship is all she will let me have, I'll gladly take it because I'm selfish and don't want her out of my life forever. Not after I've had a taste of her, not without trying to win this girl's heart first. And if I try and fail, at least I'll know I gave it my best shot.

I still can't help but think of that Robert guy, how Bailey said he's the reason for her fear all the time. That she's scared of him, of men in general. What did he do to her? He mentioned she ran away and that he fucked her up, so it must have been very serious. The way she outright rejected the idea of being civilized with me when I was assigned to her as a patient is concerning. And for some odd reason, she loosened up a bit, started trusting me slightly, and I went and ruined all of it by putting my dick inside her.

I'm a world-class prick. However, now there's no going back, so I just have to show her that I don't usually behave that way. I don't know what came over me that day. Maybe it was the fact that we were both feeling vulnerable, and I wanted to help her—us—feel better. Although I never should've done it. I think I scared her away, and all my chances of *more* are now out the window. But at the same time, I let her be in control. I wanted her to feel empowered, strong, safe. Even though, at the time, I had no idea why she needed it, I could tell that she did.

I flip the steaks and open the sliding glass door, peeking inside at the boys. "You all good in here?"

"Close the dooooooor!" Noah yells, and everyone chuckles.

"Noah, you realize you spend your days in low temperatures? It's your job," I tell him as I grin, opening the door wider.

"Yeah, well, I'm not working right now."

"Fair." I nod, closing the door behind me. "Steaks are almost done. Who's making the salad?"

Jeremy stands up, a smile on his face. "I'll do it. Just please don't overcook my steak, for the love of God."

"I'd never do you like that, bro," I reply, making my way back to the balcony with a plate and a pair of tongs.

Once the boys and I are settled at the long dining room table —which I bought just for them because I host a lot—we begin serving ourselves. There's a bowl of garlic mashed potatoes, Caesar salad, and asparagus, as well as the rib-eyes. A feast, really. One I wish I could share with the girl who won't stop invading my thoughts. But maybe soon she'll let me bring her here without getting the wrong impression.

"So, Theo," Jer says between chews. I look at him pointedly, and he waits until he's done swallowing. "Have you talked to coach yet?"

"Uh." I swallow hard, "Not yet. But I have a meeting with him tomorrow."

Noah smiles at me, but it's hard to return it, so instead, I make a half-assed attempt, and they notice. "Hey, everything is going to be okay," Noah reassures me. "You'll be back on the ice in no time."

My stomach drops, because he's just saying that to make me feel better. I don't even know if that's true and it's my body. "Sure." I nod. "I'll know more after the MRI."

"How long will it be until you have it?"

"Another ten days."

Everyone nods quietly. It's an awkward silence—the kind where people don't want to acknowledge something, no matter how obvious it is. And just like that, my good mood is gone, and I want them out. I can't very well say that though, especially because this night has been planned since I was in the hospital. Now we can either play UNO and forget about this, or play video games. Probably the latter, so we don't have to talk to each other.

After about an hour of talking shit at the table, we move to my three-piece sectional. Again, I bought it with the boys in mind, but I don't regret it at all. My living room is spacious enough that it doesn't look crowded with it, and it's great when I fall asleep watching TV. The only thing that's missing is a certain someone to cuddle with—Bailey.

It's so sad that all I've been thinking of ever since I met her is —her. From the moment she walked into my hospital room, I knew. She made my heart race and my palms sweat. I thought I was going to die just from her proximity. But now? I think I'll die without it. Because one taste of her wasn't enough, and I want more. But I also want so much more than what she thinks I must want her for. And this isn't even something I've thought of before. I would give her a relationship. I'd try for her. Who am I kidding? I'd do whatever she wanted. Anything for the smallest scrap of her.

Jeremy and Oliver turn on Call of Duty on the PS5 and get to work. Meanwhile, Noah and Matt sit on the other side of the couch, giving me the space I obviously need. Except not completely, because as soon as I'm about to unlock my phone Matt clears his throat.

"Soooo," he draws the word out. "Did that cute nurse ever stop being mean to you?"

Butterflies fill my stomach at the mention of her. *Pathetic.* "Um, yeah. She was really nice by the end." I say sarcastically, even though she was.

Jeremy shoots me a knowing look, like he can see right through me, but doesn't say anything.

"Cool, cool," Matt replies. "Are you gonna ask her out or what? You looked like you had a huge crush on her."

I did.

I *do.*

"Yeah, well, I'm her patient. Or was. But I doubt she'll go

out with me." Lies, she already did. But for some reason I don't want to tell them about it. Maybe if I keep it a secret right now, the bubble I find myself living in won't pop just yet. "It's all good. I'm over it."

"Sure." Jeremy adds, "And I'm the queen of England."

"All Hail the Queen, Jeremy."

"We all know you wanted a piece of that," he replies with a grin, glancing away from the TV long enough to get killed. *I already had a piece of that, and now I want the whole cake.* "Quit lying. When are you gonna see her?"

"Maybe I'll pay her a visit at work and find out." I smirk, knowing I only have to call her at this point. But I'm not telling them shit, nothing of substance.

"You do that, bud." He grins, restarting the game at level one. "And then be a good boy and tell us all about it."

Over my dead body. "Sure."

A few hours later, Jeremy and Oliver are asleep on the floor with my throw pillows, and Matt and Noah have taken over the couch. Quite literally, because I don't even have space to join the sleepover, and my couch is enormous. Just as I'm heading to my room, I stop in my tracks as my phone dings, and I see it's from the last person I expected—Bailey. She hadn't texted me in days, since our non-date. But now that she has, my heart starts galloping faster in my chest, making it hard to breathe.

BAILEY

Can I call you?

THEO

Sure! You don't ever have to ask.

I look at the time—two in the morning. She's probably on a short break… and she's choosing to talk to me? My heart does a weird little flutter, and I clutch my chest as the phone begins to ring in my hand. I answer it quickly to not wake anyone up.

"Hey, B." She chuckles and I smile. Her breathy little laugh lights up my insides. "How's work?"

"Boring now that you're not here."

I want to say it's because you're not having sex in bathrooms, but I think it's too early to joke about it. Yeah, definitely too early. "Yeah, I know I'm the life of the party. You don't need to give me a bigger head."

"I don't think that's possible, Theo," Bailey says in a flirty tone, and now I wonder if there is a double meaning behind it. "What have you been up to?"

"*Not* playing hockey," I reply, then slap a hand to my forehead. How fucking grim. "I've been hanging out with my friends. They're actually sleeping on my couch."

"Wow." She laughs, "That must be a big couch to fit all those hockey players."

"Some took the floor, but uh, yeah—" I scratch the back of my head. "It's a big couch." And I want you on it, with me— cuddled up while I rub your back. "But I'm actually going to my bed."

"Oh—" she half yells. "Of course! I'll, uh, let you go."

Hell no. "I didn't mean to sleep, silly."

"Oh," Bailey replies with an awkward laugh, which I join her in. "Okay. Well, I was calling to ask if you want to—do it again?"

Do what again? That could mean so many things right now. "Umm…do what?"

"Hang out?" I wait for her to catch up, "Oh my God. *Please* tell me that didn't sound like I was propositioning you."

"I know you're not." I chuckle. "I remember what you sound like when you are."

"And there you go, making it worse!" But instead of it being awkward, we both laugh about it. "You don't have to see me again, you know. If I'm a boring friend…or whatever."

"I want to see you again," I say quickly, too quickly. Eagerly.

"Are you lying?" I can almost see the little frown on her

face. The way her perfectly shaped eyebrows draw in, and her mouth turns slightly down, making dimples on her chin appear.

"Why would I lie, Bailey? I'd never lie to you." There's a moment of silence that she doesn't fill, so I continue. "So what do you want to do?"

"You could watch me make a fool of myself." She laughs, but I think it's forced. "Come watch me take a skating class?"

"You want me to come watch you skate with *toddlers*?" I laugh and she groans, "Fine, but only if we can skate together after."

"I think that can be arranged." She says with what I'm one hundred percent sure is a smile. Even if I can't see it. I think I'm starting to get to know her. "Cheyenne will have a blast seeing me on my ass the whole night. After the toddler class, we can have the rink to ourselves for about thirty minutes before the Zamboni ruins it all for us."

"Sad." I chuckle. "I love skating on fresh ice."

"I don't," she replies quickly. "Something about that wet ice makes me fall even more."

I laugh outright. "You'll get better, B. I'm going to teach you all my tricks."

"Doubtful, Mr. I've been skating for twenty-two years."

"Oh." My lips twitch. "Counting now, are we? I love that you remember."

"I remember everything about you—even medically." We both laugh at that because of course she probably memorized every detail about me. "But I bet you do have a lot of tricks up your sleeve. Please feel free to share them."

"I'll share everything with you," I tell her, and she chokes on something, but I just keep going. "But how about you tell me more about you? Ms. I Don't Have Your Medical Chart To Stalk You. It's unfair."

"Excuse me?" She cackles. "I've never *stalked* you, just did my job."

"But you definitely have the advantage now." I point out, "And you can't even deny it."

"Fine. I broke my arm when I was four, got stitches on my hairline when I was seven, and chipped my tooth when I was fifteen. Cheerleading was brutal." She sighs. "Does that make you feel better?"

"Tell me more about that chipped tooth, Bailey," I tease.

Bailey laughs and I just know she's rolling her eyes. "That's what you want to know about? Oh my God, Theo. Yeah, I chipped one of my front teeth when I fell off a pyramid. Happy? It's all fixed now, no one but you will know better."

"I just had to find something *not* perfect about you."

"There's a lot to unpack there, Theo." She chuckles. "I'll have you know there's plenty not perfect about me. It's actually a little scary, and I bet you scare easily."

"Not when it comes to you, sweet Bailey." I tell her honestly, "I want to know more."

"Maybe another time, Theo." I groan, knowing she has to hang up. "Gotta go back to work now. But we can go to the rink tomorrow if you want?"

"I want anything you want."

She's silent for a second. "It's settled then. See you soon."

"See you soon," I whisper as she hangs up.

I get comfortable in bed, fluffing my pillow and putting the cold side against my cheek. There's something about her that has me so fixated, and nothing other than hockey has held my interest for this long. All I want to do is see her again, spend time with her.

But mostly, I just want to stop wanting those things because something tells me it will hurt so bad in the end.

It's cold at the arena, and something like nostalgia hits me square in the chest. Not being here for the past week and a half has been possibly the hardest thing ever, but hey, I've made it without a mental breakdown—so far. I don't consider myself lucky because I know I'm on the precipice of one. It's right there, almost within reach. All I'd have to do is stretch my hand slightly and—

"Anderson!" my coach barks. "Office, now."

Okay, so I was a little late. I'm just nervous, but he's not going to care about that, so I just mumble, "Yes, Coach O."

I go into his office, a large space with light hardwood floors and a mahogany desk in the middle of the room. There are bookshelves all around housing trophies. It's a sight to see, one that I wish for my future. Which is exactly why we're here, to talk about it. So I take one of the chairs across from his desk and sit down—a really comfortable leather, by the way.

"How you feelin' son?"

My shoulders drop, and I instantly relax. "I feel great." Not a lie, actually. "I'm ready to come back. Put me in, coach."

Coach Oelschlaeger chuckles, "I know you want to be back on the ice, but right now, you're the biggest priority. We want you to heal before you can come back so that you can be at your very best."

"And when will that be?"

"You have one more week on the bench, and then you get your MRI on the last day. So, depending on the results, we will decide whether you're benched for longer or if we put you back in."

The little flip my stomach does is scary. I can't decipher if it's from fear or excitement. Maybe both. I nod, "Got it."

"It'll be okay, Anderson." He says, something like sympathy in his eyes.

"Right." I fake a smile, "Am I good to go?" The last thing I want to do is spend more time here without working. It's been hard to even show up for this meeting as it is, seeing all my friends have ice time before the game tonight. A game I'm going to miss, one of the few I already have. And I hate that the prick who put me in the hospital has power over me right now. He's probably laughing at me all the way from fucking Vancouver.

"Yeah." Coach O nods, his gray brows furrowing. "Don't worry about anything. You'll be just fine."

With his last word, I get up from the chair and exit the office, immediately hitting the cold arena air as I try to leave as quickly as possible and without anyone spotting me. I'm sure they're going to hear about the meeting from someone, but I just don't want to stop and chat. No, I want to get the hell out of here. It's been three days since I've seen Bailey, and our date is tonight—our *friend* date. Either way, I'm excited about it, and even though she warned me she sucks at skating, I don't even care.

I just want to spend time with her.

Bailey

CHAPTER FOURTEEN

By the time Theo makes it to the ice hall, I have my rental skates in hand. He is already wearing his skates as he steps up to the bleachers where I'm sitting. The smile he gives me is quite literally heart-stopping. I can hear my pulse drumming in my ears now, and the closer he gets to me, the faster it beats.

I'll never get over how beautiful he is with his dark, floppy hair hanging over his eyes and those blue orbs that make me weak in the knees. But it's not just that. He's also kind, sweet, and funny. He's empathetic and considerate. He *cares*. And only a dumb bitch like me would pass him up.

"Here," Theo says as he kneels in front of me, making my heart flutter all over again. If I didn't know better, I'd say he's going to kill me from high blood pressure or tachycardia. His fingers are warm as they touch my leg, and I can feel them searing through the material of my wool leggings. But it's when he takes my foot and begins to lace up one of my skates that my eyes tear up.

What is wrong with me? Why am I so emotional right now?

When he finishes up the second skate, he smiles and looks

into my eyes, then frowns when he realizes something is up. "What happened?"

"Oh, nothing." I peer up, willing the moisture to dry up from my eyes before looking down at him again. "You're just so...sweet. I can't remember the last time someone treated me this way."

"I'll treat you even better if you let me." Theo smiles softly.

I deflect, "Let's go meet Chey."

He looks disappointed for a second but then masks it quickly, probably not wanting to show me just how much that affected him. But honestly, it's affecting me too. Is this little crush that I have on him growing? Why am I feeling like I can't breathe around him? Or without him?

I spot Cheyenne easily since I knew exactly where she'd be. The toddlers are gathered around her and she's taking roll-call. Once they're all on the ice, another instructor appears to help Chey, and I take the opportunity to grab Theo's jacket sleeve to pull him with me. I could have grabbed his hand, I'm sure, but not only do I not want to give him the wrong impression—or myself, for that matter. Only I'm scared that if I touch him, I'm going to cave.

"Cheyenne," I call out, and she turns around, her eyes widening. Her grin stretches her face immediately. "This is Theo." I look over at him, who glances at Chey briefly then at me. "Theo, this is Chey."

Theo nods once with a polite smile. "Nice to meet you, Cheyenne."

"It's about damn time you brought hot stuff with you," she chides. "I've been waiting for this moment, you know?"

"Sure," I say with a smirk, walking toward the ice.

"If she won't have you, I'll take you." Cheyenne winks at Theo and he blanches. "Just putting it out there."

It would be funnier if there wasn't a little green monster inside of me that wanted to choke her the fuck out. I narrow my eyes on her and her smile grows. "Slut," is all I say before following the toddlers.

When I look back, Theo and Cheyenne are lost in conversation. He's laughing at something she's saying, and a little—okay, huge—fire ignites in my belly. Something that closely resembles jealousy, yet if I didn't know better I'd call it rage.

Why am I so upset? It's Cheyenne. She jokes a lot, though she'd never do anything to hurt me. Right? Then again, why would it hurt? We're nothing. Just friends...but still. *Girl code.* I had sex with him, for fuck's sake. That has to mean something. But does it? He could be free game if I don't claim him.

Focus.

One wrong step, and I'm on my ass.

Fuck that hurts.

I groan as I get on all fours and push myself up like I've been taught. Except I'm about one hundred pounds heavier than these toddlers, so it's harder for me. Sometimes I envy how flexible and resilient the little shits are. It makes me wish I had learned how to skate all those years ago. But it's too late for me. And I forgot to bring my butt pads. Okay—I didn't bring them because I didn't want to look ridiculous in front of Theo.

Speak of the devil; he's skating up to me now, and as I get on my feet, he smiles. "You good?"

My face turns red the bigger his smile grows until his shoulders begin to shake, and he starts cackling. "Oh? I'm so glad you find this funny, you asshole. I told you I'd be on my ass every two minutes."

"That was like thirty seconds, B. Which you said wouldn't happen."

"That was before you were making eyes at my best friend." I snap, clamping my mouth shut as his smile falls and a frown replaces it. "Sorry—that's none of my business."

"I was trying to be nice, Bailey," he replies softly. "I know she means a lot to you. If I gave that impression, I'm sorry. I'm here for *you*."

"So you don't want to ask her out?" My voice softens.

"Ask her out?" His jaw drops, and he brushes a stray hair away from my face, his thumb brushing my cheek. "Bailey, I only want *you*."

Butterflies rage in my stomach at his words, and I look down, my eyes stinging again. No one has ever told me that before, chose me in such a blatant way. Yeah, Rob used to tell me how much he wanted me, but always in toxic ways. In ways that took from me. But Theo? He's giving, not taking. He's a *giver*.

"Look at me, B," he whispers, using his thumb to tilt my chin up so I can stare into his eyes. "Are you jealous?"

"Never," I reply quickly, shaking my head. "I just—" Just what? You *are* jealous, twat. "We're just friends, Theo."

He looks down at our skates, his lips pursing. But I see the way his eyes crinkle in the corners, his mouth turning down. "Yeah, *friends*." But then he shakes his head, "Wanna skate with me and ditch these semen demons?"

I cackle at that, the tension inside of me easing. "Semen demons? I'm going to use that from now on."

Theo holds his hand out to me, and I take it. My hands are gloved, but his aren't, and he still doesn't even feel cold. He must be used to it. I mean, of course he is. It's his job, Bailey.

He begins to glide backwards slowly, grabbing both my hands and taking me with him. It's like I'm on a ride, not putting in any effort. "This okay?"

I nod with a grin. "Perfect." I gaze down at our skates, at the way he so easily works his feet without any effort. "What about those tricks we talked about?"

"Okay, show me how you get around."

I smirk, my face heating up, and I begin to march. His lips twitch, but he can't contain his laughter, and soon it erupts from deep within his chest. "Oh, stop, Theo. You're making me self-conscious."

"Don't be," he says quickly. "Don't take me seriously." My heart pounds at that one little word. "It's all in good fun."

"So what do I do?"

"You need to learn how to glide. Push with one foot and slide." I do it, almost falling on my face. "Here, hold my hand."

Holding his hand, he glides with me, pulling me with him so that I am doing it. It's easy this way, being forced to do it and putting in minimal effort, but I think I'm getting the gist of it.

I'm gliding.

I glance back at the toddlers and grin, watching them fall, and just when I think I'm in the clear, I lose my balance. I should really focus on what I'm doing, but for some reason I can't with Theo by my side. He catches me easily by the waist and chuckles against my ear, sending shivers down my spine.

His lips brush against my ear, and I tighten my fists to avoid touching him. "Cute."

"Ridiculous."

We both laugh. "How about we do some head, shoulders, knees, and toes?" he asks, and I all but choke.

"*What?*"

"I used to be a toddler too." He winks, "And my teacher would make us do that for balance and learn how to squat on skates."

"I don't want to squat, Theo." I roll my eyes. "I want to skate."

"We all have to start somewhere, my little sour patch kid." He grabs my hand and pulls me into his chest. "Now humor me."

I step back, touching my head, shoulders, then knees and toes. "Ya happy?"

"No," Theo says playfully. "Let's do it together."

And we do, making a fool of ourselves for the next twenty minutes until class is over. There's something so easygoing about him that draws me in, and I can't hold back when I'm around him. I want to let myself go, just be.

Forget all about how I've sworn off relationships, because the truth is when I'm with him, I do forget, even if only momentarily. But I know it could be different with him—it already is. He's so easy to like, to love, even. And that scares me, because falling is dangerous, and no one has ever caught me. Something tells me he'd be there waiting for me, though. But will I catch him? Or will he slip through my grasp? Am I ready to give him everything? Absolutely not.

After we both take off our skates, we begin walking toward the doors of the rink to go back to the main area.

"Hey, Bailey?" he starts, and I peer up at him. "I saw this little coffee shop at the front. Wanna go?"

"Um." I've never been there before, and I'm always too broke to consider it, but I just got paid, so I nod. "Sure."

"What do you want to get?" he asks, walking next to me, shortening his strides for me.

"Hmmm." I pretend to think. "Hot chocolate."

"Oh, that sounds so good." He grins, and when we get to the shop, he turns to me. "Go find us a little table."

"Here—" I dig through my purse, pulling out some cash for my hot chocolate. "For my—"

"Hell, no." Theo shakes his head. "Don't offend me that way, Bailey."

"I'm not," I assure him. "I'm just paying for myself."

"I invited you." He shakes his head again. "I'm paying. So put your money away and never pull that shit again."

With that, he turns his back on me, clearly irritated, so I go to find us a table in the furthest corner away from everyone. The last thing I need is to be seen out with a famous hockey player and then have my face plastered all over every magazine in this stupid town.

Theo finishes up and heads my way with a bag hanging from his arm and two cups in his hands. The smile that breaks free when he spots me is *everything*, and I never want to stop seeing it. Please, please, keep smiling at me.

"Hot chocolate for my Bailey." *My Bailey.* "And hot chocolate for me." He grins again as he sits down, and my heart thumps a little faster in my chest. I'm sweating just watching him sit across from me. "You're lucky this isn't a booth, or I'd be sitting next to you."

"We agreed that was a one-time thing, Theo." I roll my eyes playfully. "Now, what's in the bag?" I wag my eyebrows, waiting for him to pull out the contents.

"Cheese Danish, cake pops, and uh—" He digs through it. "Blueberry muffin. Take your pick."

"Blueberry muffin, duh." Not that he'd know that, but he chuckles anyway, handing it over.

"Can I have a bite?" He asks me with puppy dog eyes.

"Absolutely not," I reply, taking the biggest bite of my life. The taste of the blueberries and the sugar on top burst on my tastebuds. Ugh, fine." I pass it to him, and he takes the smallest bite possible—like a gentleman.

"Here, have some of my hot chocolate," he tells me after taking a sip.

"Why? It's the same, isn't it?"

"Nope." He pops the *p*. "Mine is mint hot chocolate."

"That sounds pretty good," I admit as he passes the drink over to me, and I take a sip. I savor it, loving how the taste is similar to a Peppermint mocha from Starbucks. "It *is* good. Wow, you have good taste, who knew?"

Theo smiles, "Yes, I do." Again, with that smile that makes my insides melt. "Does that mean we just kissed?"

My eyebrows turn down in confusion. "What do you mean?"

"Our lips touched on the cup."

"Oh my God." I gasp. "You're not even a little funny, Theo. Cut it out."

"It was cute, and you know it."

I mean, it's a little corny, but he is cute. "Whatever." Only now that we're sitting here with nothing except time to talk—that is, before they close in fifteen minutes—I want to know what was making him smile so much with Cheyenne. So I don't even care how it sounds when I ask, "So what were you and Chey talking about?"

Theo looks at me for a long moment, pursing his lips. I motion with my hand to urge him on, and he smiles softly. "You."

"Oh, no way!" I reply sarcastically. "Please elaborate."

"Someone's saltier than a Ritz cracker today."

I choke on my hot chocolate. "Excuse me?"

"You're a grump sometimes, Bailey." He affirms. "Who peed in your cereal?"

I grin, remembering I asked him that exact question before. "Wow, that bad?"

Theo smiles, then grimaces. Okay, then. "She was telling me you like me." As in like him, like him? She's a fucking traitor, and we're going to have words. "Oh, and she said if you care about me even a little bit, you'd gift me a plant. Whatever that means."

I laugh, "Yeah, she makes fun of me for being a plant mom."

"A plant *mom*?"

"Yeah, you know. I have a lot of plants. Kinda like a cat lady but with lots of plants."

"How many are we talking?" His eyes sparkle at the question and I chuckle.

"Ummm." I pretend to think. "Fifteen, give or take?"

"Like, outside, right?"

"No," I reply, then take a sip of hot chocolate. "I don't have a yard. I live in a studio." Wow, how embarrassing. From the looks of him, he probably owns a house with ten bedrooms. He makes millions of dollars per year, and here he is dressed like a commoner. What does he do with this money? He probably buys a huge mansion.

"Wow, Bailey." He laughs, "I guess you really are a plant mom. Are they hard to take care of?"

"Nope." I admit, "I have an app that tells me when to water them."

What the fuck? What is it about this man that makes me tell him everything about myself?

"Sorry to interrupt," a girl a couple of years younger than us says. "I just wanted to let you know we close in five minutes."

I nod at her, "Thanks." And when I glance up, Theo's eyes are still on me.

Beginning to chug my hot chocolate, I feel the burn on my tongue and wince. "You don't have to do that," says Theo. "We can go to my house and hang out. You're gonna be up all night anyway, right? I can stay up too."

"I can't."

"You don't have to be alone tonight," he replies softly. "I'll keep you company."

"Oh, I'm not alone." I smile, "I have Callie and Christina."

"Are those like your roommates?" His brows furrow. "I thought you said you live in a studio?"

"You could say that." I nod, knowing damn well I don't have roommates, but I'm waiting for him to catch up. "Except they don't talk to me. It's great."

"Oh my God, please tell me I'm wrong." His eyes widen and he puts his hand against his heart, clearly playing around. "Please tell me you don't name your plants."

"If I said no, it would be a lie." We both laugh.

"So tell me. You said they don't talk to you, but since they're your roommates," he pauses. "Do you talk to *them*?"

"Would it be crazy if I did?"

"A little." He grins, "But I like a little crazy."

"Fine," I admit, "But only when I feel lonely."

Theo frowns, gripping his cup tighter and bringing it to his lips. Great, now I made it awkward. I'm about to backtrack and tell him I'm just playing when he sets his cup on the table and says, "You don't have to feel lonely anymore." He gazes into my eyes, the blue of his a little stormier as he looks at me. "I'm here now."

I deflect again, "You're just keeping me here, aren't you?"

His smile slips, but he recovers quickly. "Busted," he whispers. "Did it work?"

"Only a little bit," I admit.

Just then, we're interrupted again by the same girl who works here. "Alright, love birds, time to go." A little smirk tips up her thin lips, and I smile at her briefly before my cheeks heat. Love birds, my ass.

I grab my trash and put it in the bin, and he does the same. He is waiting for me by the door leading to the parking lot. My steps falter as I reach him, and I notice how his eyes stare into mine, making me bite my bottom lip.

"Let me walk you to your car." Great, now he's going to see the piece of trash I drive around every day because I couldn't afford anything better.

I don't reply. Instead, I head to my car without a glance back, not wanting him to see how affected I am by this. It's harder because I probably wouldn't be as embarrassed if it were just a regular man. But it's Theo Anderson—star hockey player—and he probably owns five cars. I feel judged.

But when I unlock my car and turn around, his expression doesn't even change as he looks at me and the vehicle. He's unfazed, completely. "What?" I ask him. "No snarky remark about my car?" I know I'm a bitch, but this is my way of protecting myself before the blow comes.

"Why would there be a snarky remark?" He asks, clearly confused.

I frown, "Because it's a piece of shit."

"You act like I'm a spoiled brat, Bailey." Theo sighs, running a hand through his stupidly perfect hair. "I didn't come from money. Just so you know."

"But you have it now."

"And I only use it on things that matter to me."

"Like what?" I snap.

"This feels like a conversation for another time," Theo replies, "Why are you picking a fight?"

I don't answer, and he presses me against my car door and cages me in.

"Are you scared of me?" His nose brushes against mine, and my lower lip trembles. I don't speak. "Are you trying to ruin this between us? Because I won't let you."

I stay silent, contemplating my options. It doesn't feel like I have many, and this thing between us? I think I'm starting to like him more than I should. I mean, I spoke to him about naming my fucking plants. I've never even said that to anyone but Cheyenne. Cutting this off at the roots feels like the smartest thing to do.

"Cat got your tongue, baby?" Theo breathes against my cheek, then presses his lips to my skin. They're so soft and full I literally groan at the contact. "Stop pushing me away. I don't give up when I want something, Bailey."

"There's nothing to give up on." I reply coldly, "We have nothing."

"You're a liar." He smiles, entirely at odds with the conversation. "You're a puddle every time I look at you. Quit lying to yourself and see what's right in front of you."

"And what's that?"

"*Me.*" Theo pulls away and fixes my jacket. "Anyway, I'm glad to see you're wearing a jacket this time." He tells me, changing the subject drastically. I have a feeling he wants to put me at ease, but it only serves to make me more nervous.

"Yeah," I clear my throat. "I'm warm for once."

"I bet you are," he murmurs, sending tingles all the way down my body. "Are we still on for two days from now?"

"Uh, yeah." I reply, "Sure."

"Good."

"See you soon, then?" I ask him, almost slapping my hand

against my forehead. Obviously, I'm seeing him soon—in two days.

But he just grins, opening my car door and holding it in place until I get in. "See you soon, Bailey."

And then he closes the door, leaving me to contemplate my life. My choices.

My feelings.

Theo

CHAPTER FIFTEEN

I've been pacing my condo for the last thirty minutes, nervously picking at my nails whenever I think about Bailey being on her way over. I've fluffed the pillows again, wiped the kitchen countertops, lit a vanilla candle, and vacuumed. But the place still doesn't look good enough. Something is missing—and I don't know what.

I head to my linen closet and pull out a soft, red plaid throw blanket that I put on top of my couch and call it a day, with the hope she likes it, seeing as we will probably spend most of our time watching movies. I invited her over at the last minute, wanting to do something new instead of going out to eat again. After the other night, I thought she was going to reject me, but she surprisingly said yes. That's the only word I've been wanting to hear from her all this time.

There's a soft knock at the door—three raps—and my spine stiffens. With shaking hands, I go to open it. I don't know why she makes me so nervous, but I am. My hands are freaking sweating just thinking of sitting next to her for the next few hours without touching her. And my God, I want to touch her so bad. I want to wrap my arms around her, cuddle her, and rub her back.

I yank the door open a little more forcefully than intended, and Bailey's eyes widen. "Sorry." I chuckle awkwardly. "Don't know my strength sometimes." At least, I hope she believes that because it's way less embarrassing than admitting how much she affects me.

Bailey clears her throat, looking around at my condo. "It's very…masculine."

My heart drops. "What does that mean, B? You don't like it?" Damn it, I tried so hard too.

"There's just no…plants."

I chuckle at her jab, "Not everyone can have a green thumb, Bailey." I lead her inside by her arm, and she drops a bag on the couch. I raise an eyebrow. "Staying?"

"Nah." She shakes her head with a smile. "Going to Chey's after."

I shake my head in disappointment, "And here I thought I was your new bestie."

"*Anyway*." She grins, deflecting again. When will she stop doing that and just let me in? "Do you have any pets? Or is it just you in here?"

"Uh, no." I scratch my head, slightly embarrassed. "I've never had a pet before."

"*What?*" she asks, outrage in her voice. "Never?"

I give her a tight smile, "No." I've never had the time for a pet. I'm always gone. I've never even had time for a girl, but for her, I'd make time. "Do you have pets?"

"Well, I used to have a pet goldfish." She smirks, then shrugs. "I killed it in a week."

"And you're judging *me*?" I ask her incredulously. "How do you kill a goldfish when you have a million plants?"

She narrows her eyes. "I guess the only thing I have going for me is my green thumb."

I grin. "Nah." Getting all up in her space, I pull her in for a hug and she lets me. "You've got a lot more than that going for you."

"What?"

"Your shining personality," I reply, and she pushes me away forcefully, grabbing a pillow from the couch—fairly quickly, actually—and hitting me with it. "*Ow.*"

"I'm kind of a jerk." Bailey shrugs and I laugh.

"You said it, not me."

There's a moment of silence as we look at each other. Bailey is a foot apart from me, and I look down at her body. She dressed comfortably today. Sweats that look baggy, a t-shirt from her hospital, and slippers on her feet. Her attire makes me smile, but then I look at her face and it drops. Bailey watches me intently, green eyes widening when I meet her gaze, but her lips tip up in the slightest smile. Even though it's barely there— it goes straight to my heart. What am I going to do with myself for the next few hours? I see her, and I just want to pull her in, kiss her senseless, and not let her go. Is that actually insane?

Bailey breaks the silence first, "How about a tour, then?"

"You wanna see the whole place?"

"Is it big?" She asks quietly, a little closed off. "Do you have like five bedrooms?"

"It's nothing crazy, Bailey," I tell her, ready to snuggle her on the couch and cut the bullshit already. She's stalling. Or maybe she really is interested in getting to know my space. I don't even know anymore. "Two bedrooms, two bathrooms."

"That's it?" she asks, her jaw dropping.

I put my fingers under her chin and close her mouth back up. "I'm only one person. I don't splurge."

"So what do you do with all that money, then?"

"Save up." I smile. "Help my parents. Like I said, I didn't come from money, and they sacrificed a lot for me. I wanted to return the favor."

Bailey's eyes widen. "That's actually very kind of you."

I guess I don't do well with too much praise, which is… surprising. I swallow hard, "Yeah. I guess." She smiles at me, and I return it. "Okay, so as you already know, this is the living room." I point at the three-piece sectional couch with the wooden coffee table in front of it. She stares at it for a long time, then directs her eyes toward the flat-screen TV mounted on the wall.

"This is where we'll be tonight?" she asks me with awe in her voice.

"Yeah," I reply, grabbing her by the t-shirt and pulling her toward the kitchen. "Now, obviously, you know what this place is." Although I still open the fridge and show it to her, "You can take whatever you want from here. Any time you want, no need to ask." Bailey peers down at the ground, refusing to meet my eyes. "My stove, my island." The one I want to fuck her on. "And yeah, the dishwasher. Any questions?"

There's a hint of a smile. "Do you leave your clean stuff in the dishwasher?"

"Sometimes."

"Sounds convenient." She nods, opening it. "I don't have one of these."

"*What*?" I all but shout. "That's a literal crime. You wash your dishes by hand?"

"Mhmm." She smiles, but it doesn't reach her eyes. "Fuckin' rich people."

I grab her hand. "That just means that you can come here more often and use my dishwasher."

Bailey laughs. "You freaking wish."

I do, though I'm not saying it and scaring her away. "So this way," I grab her t-shirt again. "Is the guest bathroom, and there's the guest room down that hall."

She walks down the hall, opens the guest room door, and whistles, "Pretty." Then she looks at me expectantly, "Where's your room?"

"Oh, you want me to show you my room?" I raise an eyebrow.

"For research, of course." She's quick to reply. "A bedroom says a lot about a person."

"This way." I point to the opposite end of the hall, and she walks ahead of me. "You can just open the door and make yourself comfy."

"Wow," she breathes. "It's beautiful, Theo."

"So, what do you think?" I ask her. "What does my room say about me?"

"You're a neat freak."

I laugh. "That's it?"

"Yeah." Bailey bites her bottom lip, pulling it slightly into her mouth. It sends tingles all the way to my dick. "The other things are inappropriate."

"Oh?" I just bet they are. "What are those things?"

Bailey chuckles, "Not a chance, big boy."

"Right," I reply. "Well, since there's no chance you're telling me, let's go watch TV. What movie do you want to watch?" I walk ahead of her. "Wait, what's your favorite movie?"

"I don't have one," she replies without hesitation.

"Excuse me?" I stop in my tracks, twisting toward her. She runs into my chest and stumbles backward. With an apologetic smile, I help right her. "What do you mean you don't have a *favorite* movie?" She has to, right? "Everyone has one."

"I mean, I guess if you pull my arm, I'd say *How to Lose a Guy in 10 Days*."

Okay. I've never seen that. "Wanna watch it?"

Bailey smirks, "What's yours?"

"*Jurassic Park*," I blurt.

"Oh, lord, you're *that* guy."

"What guy?" I ask her defensively.

"The one who knows every dinosaur species known to mankind," she jabs, pushing my shoulder with her dainty hand and walking past me.

"So?" I call out. "I bet you know the same shit about every plant under the sun."

Bailey stops and chuckles, then drops onto the couch,

grabbing the throw blanket immediately and draping it over her legs. *Score.* "You're not funny, Theo."

"I wasn't trying to be," I mumble.

She puts her hand out to me, and I give her the remote. "So, this is how it's going to go, big boy." I raise an eyebrow at her as I watch her face. Her green eyes are shining. Her smile is wide, and her dimples are popping. Her hair is in a messy bun at the top of her head, and she's never looked more beautiful. I'm mesmerized. "You're going to sit here and rub my feet," I open my mouth, but she puts a little finger up in the air. So bossy. "And watch *The Summer I Turned Pretty* with me."

"The what now?"

"It's a show, Theodore."

"Yeah," I huff, "I gathered it was something on TV. But what the hell is it?"

"Okay." She grins as I sit next to her, and she turns her body to me and drapes her feet over my lap. Sighing, she leans back. "It's about a girl who falls in love with not one—but *two* boys."

"*Stop,*" I groan, shaking my head. "Is there cheating involved?"

"I don't want to spoil anything." She rolls her eyes as I take off her socks and look at her pretty, bubblegum pink, painted toenails. She's that kind of girl—the one who doesn't look that girly yet is beneath it all. "It's so good."

"Just why, Bailey?"

"I *love* a good love triangle, Theo." She grins. "So sue me. You're watching with me."

"I don't know." I shake my head, "You better not be getting any crazy ideas. I don't do well with sharing."

"Your parents didn't teach you how?" she jokes. At least, I think it's a joke.

"Nope."

Bailey plays the first episode, and I swear my balls shrivel on the spot. This girl—Belly, apparently. Who the fuck nicknames a girl Belly?—gets to a beach house, and the blond guy comes and hugs her, lifting her up off the ground. Then, a brooding, dark-haired one comes to say hi too. I see where this is going—and I don't like it, at all.

Still, I rub Bailey's feet, making her groan, which then causes my dick to twitch. She must feel it because she glances at me and raises her little foot, kicking me right on the arm. I laugh about it, but then again, is that even surprising? She makes me laugh *a lot*.

I breathe in slowly, willing the erection away, and keep watching. After about three episodes, she pauses the show. "So, what do you think?"

I'm about to ask her what the hell she was thinking by making me watch this, but instead all that comes out is, "Why the fuck is Belly being a hoe? You think Conrad is a fuck boy? Just look at Belly—she's a fuck girl. And what about Jeremiah, huh? He's hooking up with literally everyone. I'm not convinced."

"That's kind of the point," she says, her eyes shining. You have to pick a team."

"I *cannot* do that." I shake my head. No. Fucking. Way.

"Please, Theo." She pouts, "*Please*."

"Bailey," I tell her softly, shifting my body toward her and pinching her chin between my fingers. "There's no fucking way I can pick between two assholes."

"Well, I disagree," Bailey huffs. "I think Jeremiah is the better option."

I scoff. "Does he even like her? He literally kisses *everyone*, B."

"They are *end game*," she says pointedly, narrowing her eyes at me. "Team Jellyfish *forever*."

Oh. My. God.

"Please be joking," I whisper.

"There's nothing funny about this, Theo." Bailey rolls her eyes. "But you'll come around, don't you worry."

"I highly doubt that," I mumble.

Just like that, we go back to watching the show. I rub her feet, kneading the bottom as she sighs softly. I know I should be paying attention, except instead, I'm hypnotized by her—the way her green eyes widen when Jeremiah appears on screen. The little smiles that tip up her full lips when something cute happens, and even the way she seems to be twisting her fingers with anxiety from my proximity.

After another hour, Bailey pauses the show again, and I realize we've binged almost the entire series.

What the hell.

"What about now?" she asks softly, and I shift my head to rest my cheek on the couch to look at her. "What do you think?"

"Honestly, I'm having some seriously intense feelings right now, Bailey," I start. "Like, why is Jeremiah looking at Belly like that? That's Connie's brother. *Bro code.* You don't do that."

Bailey smirks, "What else?"

"This show is pissing me off."

She laughs, "It has that effect on some people."

"Ugh." I groan, grabbing the nearest throw pillow and hitting her head with it. "Why'd you do this to me? I can't watch the second season by myself, but now I need to know what happens. So you're coming back, right?"

"Ummm." Bailey bites her bottom lip again. "Can I actually stay?" She pauses to gauge my reaction, and when I don't reply, she rattles on. "I don't have to—I mean, it's just raining outside, that's all, and I don't like driving in the rain when it's dark and—"

"Bailey," I say softly, interrupting her. "You can stay whenever you want."

"I'll sleep on the couch."

"There's another bed..."

"Oh," she mumbles. "True."

"Are we done for tonight?" I ask her, "Are you tired?"

I look at my phone, and it's three in the morning. "Not really, but you can lie down."

"I don't want to go to sleep without you. I mean, if you're not going to bed." I amend. "But I just need to shower real quick, and I'll be back?"

"Alright," She replies. "But don't take too long."

"Come with me," I tell her as I get up from the couch and walk to my bedroom.

"Theo—I don't think that's a good idea."

"Relax, B." I chuckle. "I'm just gonna give you something."

I go to my closet, pull out one of my soft, oversized shirts, and give it to her. She looks between the shirt and my hand. "I'm already wearing pajamas."

"Eh," I take a good look at her, hating all the layers of clothing on her. She'd look so good in just my T-shirt. My dick wakes up again—and it really needs to stop. "Just in case, though."

"Thank you." She whispers.

My shower is relatively short, especially because I don't want to miss any more time with her. But as I open the door and the light from inside the bathroom shines in front of my bed, I realize there's a small body curled up on the floor—Bailey.

What is she doing?

Bailey's shoulders shake slightly, and she sniffles, draping an arm over her face so it's not visible—so I can't see her tears. "Bailey," I call out softly, kneeling next to her. I scoop her up in my arms and carry her to the bed. "What's wrong?"

She sniffles, "Sorry, it's stupid."

"Try again." My heart squeezes in my chest at her words, "Nothing you do is stupid."

"I—uh." She pauses and restarts. "Sleep on the floor when it's storming out…"

Trying to understand, I ask, "Why?"

"Because I'm scared," she whispers.

"Do you want to go back to the floor, Bailey?"

"*Please*."

One word makes me feel like my heart is cracking down the

middle, but I still grab all the six pillows on my bed and arrange them on the floor for her. Scooping her up, I put her back where I found her and drape my blankets over her. Just as I turn off the bathroom light, she whispers again.

"Theo?"

I kneel next to her, caressing her cheek with my thumb and pushing her hair away from her face. "I'm right here."

"Please hold me."

My heart beats a little faster as I lie down next to her, pulling her body into me until she's resting her cheek on my chest, and nothing has ever felt more perfect. The way she smells—like roses—permeates my senses, making me dizzy. Everything about her is too much and just enough. "Whatever you want, B. Just ask, and I'll do it."

There's a moment of silence, and then her tears soak my chest. I'm not wearing a shirt, so it's smearing under her cheek as she pulls away to wipe her face. "I'm sorry."

"Don't you dare apologize," I reply, being as gentle as possible. "Can you tell me what happened?"

"Robert…" she replies softly, barely audible.

I tense, and reply through gritted teeth. "Yes…" I trail off so she feels comfortable enough to fill in the silence—hopefully.

"He used to always drink when it was raining." She scoffs. "Something about how it brought bad memories."

I stay silent.

"He'd always fight with me when he was drunk…and he'd always end up hitting me." My arms wrap tightly around her small form, and I'm so stiff I feel like a fucking board. But I don't know what to do or say—so I stay silent. Because I want her to feel safe enough to tell me whatever she needs to get off her chest. I have a feeling that if I speak, she'll shut her mouth instead.

"He would force me to sleep on the floor when we had fights—after he beat the shit out of me." Bailey chuckles. "I guess it stuck. I know…I'm stupid. One night, he got home from work and started drinking. He asked why I was talking to my male coworker at work. Said I wasn't allowed to anymore. I didn't stay quiet; I fought back that time, and he hit me even harder. Then he r-r-raped me. He'd do that a lot. I guess it made him feel like he could control me that way. That I'd do whatever he wanted, so he wouldn't keep doing it."

There's a tense moment of silence before she wiggles in my hold, and I try to relax my arms slightly so she doesn't feel like I'm smothering her. "Fuck, Bailey," I whisper. "You're safe now. With me, you'll always be safe."

"If you're my safe place, who's going to be yours?" she whispers back.

I grimace, tipping my head up at the ceiling and closing my eyes. I try not to let her question get to me, but it doesn't work. My eyes are stinging, a lone tear trying to work itself out from behind my eyes. "She's not here anymore."

Bailey stiffens, "Oh?"

"That came out wrong." I chuckle. "My sister—she's dead." I think of the young brunette with blue eyes, the ones whose pictures I keep in my nightstand drawer. I look at them every time I feel myself forgetting her. The way her eyes squinted when she smiled, or how she always closed her eyes for every picture, hiding the pretty blue.

"She had Leukemia. She was my best friend, my everything. The day she died, it was the worst day of my life. She was stuck in the hospital a lot." My voice breaks, and I clear my throat. "That's why I went to read to the kids in the cancer ward. So they wouldn't feel as lonely as she did. Back when she was alive, I was too focused on school and hockey, and I didn't have much time to give her, so she was alone a lot."

"Oh, God, Theo." Fresh tears soak my skin, and she brings her hand to my face and pulls me in. "I'm sorry."

My chest tightens to the point where I can't even breathe. "Thank you," I tell her, then kiss the tip of her nose. "It's slowly getting easier."

"I can be your safe space, too," Bailey murmurs. "If you want me to be."

I wish you could be so much more than that.

"It's a start," I tell her softly, holding her tighter again.

"The start of what?" She asks me, her breath hitching.

"*Us*," I whisper. "Whatever you want us to be."

Bailey caresses my cheek with her soft fingertips, dragging them down my jaw and up again, making me close my eyes in distress. Her proximity has my body coiled, ready to strike. There's not one part of me that's calm. No, there's a little devil on my shoulder telling me to throw caution to the wind and take what I want, even when I know I shouldn't. And damn it, *damn it,* it's getting harder by the second.

"Bailey," I groan, halting her hand with my own. "*Fuck.*"

"What?"

"You're driving me crazy," I say softly. "I want you so bad I can't even think straight. You're on my mind all day. And when you're not, it's because you're right next to me. All I see is you, B. Everywhere. *You,* and only *you.*"

She gets even closer, her nose against mine, and when she angles her head and hovers over my lips...I know I've lost. "Theo," She breathes, and my cock thickens.

"I'm right here, baby."

"No." She shakes her head, brushing our noses against each other, our lips touching for a split second. "I just—I can never have what I want."

"You can have me, Bailey," I assure her, this time cupping her face and bringing her closer until our breaths mingle. The scent of vanilla fills my nostrils from the soda she was just drinking, and I close my eyes. "Take me."

"Tell me to stop, Theo."

"No." I shake my head, licking my lips, my tongue brushing against her bottom lip. "I won't do that."

Bailey groans, then presses her lips against mine. They're so fucking soft, and I think I've died, because there's no way I'm kissing her. There's no way she's letting me. *Finally*. But if this is the only chance I get, then I'm going to make it memorable. I'm going to give her fireworks.

I flip her onto her back and spread her legs, settling between them and yanking her head back with my fist wrapped around her hair. She moans when I brush my lips against hers again, and I take her bottom lip between mine and suck. Bailey returns the kiss greedily, shoving her tongue into my mouth roughly, shifting her hips ever so slightly until my hard dick presses against her center.

Electricity zaps down my spine the longer we kiss, and when she takes my bottom lip between her teeth and bites, I almost growl at her. There's so much pent-up energy inside of me, and I want to take it all out on her. I want to make her feel good—the best she's ever felt in her life. But goddamn it, she's not ready.

"You're so beautiful," I whisper, kissing her softly. "So strong." Another kiss. "Resilient." And another. "*Amazing*."

"Theo," she chokes, sniffling again.

"Do you see me, Bailey?" I ask her, my hand shaking uncontrollably as I brush my thumb over her bottom lip. "I'm right here."

"I see you."

And with those three words, she's put my whole world back together.

CHAPTER SIXTEEN

Sweat coats my skin, and it feels like I'm being blasted with a space heater, but as I open my eyes and come face to face with Theo…I realize—it's his body heat. First of all, holy shit, he runs hot. Secondly, what the fuck have I done?

His eyes are closed, and his breathing is heavy, which tells me he's clearly sleeping. Even through my racing heart and shaking hands, I admire the way his thick, black eyelashes caress his cheekbones. His nostrils slightly flaring as he breathes. Full lips pursing, making me want to kiss him all over again.

And oh my God.

That kiss.

It's honestly criminal how good it was. I can't even believe it happened—or that I let it. And that's the biggest problem of all. I should've known better than to get involved to this degree. But I still remember the way his hand tangled in my hair, tilting my face up to his. And his tongue pushing through my lips, tangling with mine. But mostly, I remember the way my body was lit on fire the moment he flipped me onto my back. My hips had a mind of their own—and so did my lips, my hands, all of me. This whole mind-body connection I've always been in control of...poof—freaking gone.

I was no longer in control of my body, my thoughts, or my feelings. I'm still confused because my brain tells me I need to get the hell out of here and never come back. But my heart tells me to stay and admire him some more. Possibly repeat last night for the rest of my life, because even I can admit to myself that I have never felt this way with anyone, and definitely not over a simple kiss.

That's the thing, though; there was nothing simple about it. It was the single most erotic thing I've ever experienced. And now I want to know what it feels like to be under him instead of on top, to give him the reins and let him play me like an instrument. I want him all over me. Lips, tongue, hands, *teeth*. But I'll probably never know how any of it feels...because I can't do that to him.

So, as much as it pains me, I untangle our limbs and hold my breath, dreading the wait. Hoping his eyelashes flutter open so I can't escape, while also begging whatever superior being that watches over me to please not let him wake up. To my chagrin, he stirs but doesn't wake, and I use that as a sign from the universe that this choice is the right one.

I quietly get up from the ground, my hips screaming in protest, and tiptoe all the way to the living room, where my bag and shoes are. Not even bothering to change or caring that I'm only wearing his oversized T-shirt, I grab my things and slip out of the apartment like a mouse in the night. I don't even know how I managed not to wake him, but now is not the time to overthink.

Once in the car, I look at the time on my phone, which was in my bag thankfully. It's almost noon—which means I have forty-five minutes to make it to my therapy appointment. By some miracle, I brought a change of clothes with me since I was going to spend the night at Cheyenne's...which brings me to now—a million text messages from her littering my inbox.

CHEY

Hey, where are you? I thought you were coming over.

CHEY

Call me. I'm getting worried.

CHEY

Do I need to call the cops?

CHEY

Seriously, Bai. Stop playing fucking games.

CHEY

What the actual fuck, Bailey? TELL ME WHERE YOU ARE.

CHEY

ANSWER ME. NOW.

CHEY

That's it, bitch. I'm calling the cops.

I dial her number, my hands shaking, and put her on speaker as I put pants on and get out of this shirt that smells just like Theo. Like a freaking forest.

"You have got to be joking with me right now," Chey mutters after only letting the phone ring twice. "Where are you? I filed a missing person's report."

"You did *what*?" I screech.

"Yeah, well, I didn't know if Robert took you." My stomach drops at that suggestion, not liking that I'm keeping secrets from her but also not willing to talk about them. "Can you honestly blame me? You have never disappeared on me or not answered the phone. And in the literal fifteen years we've been best friends, you have *never* ditched me."

"First of all. Please tell the police you found me." I sigh, smoothing my hair down while looking in the mirror. I should've brushed my teeth and maybe washed my face too. Now I have to go see my therapist, looking like the hot mess I am. "And I am so fucking sorry, Chey." Tears prick my eyes, and I let them fall. With a choked-up voice, I continue, "I lost track of time, and I fell asleep and—I was with Theo."

"Ah." She sighs. "That explains a lot."

"What does it explain?"

"That you like him, Bailey." It's not an accusation. She's so matter-of-fact about it that it's scary. Because if she has noticed, then he probably has, too. And I can't have him believing we have a chance. "You should probably tell him."

"After last night…he knows." He more than knows. And I'm the worst person ever to leave him in that room all alone. To wake up without me, wondering what he did wrong. The answer is nothing at all and simultaneously everything. "We kissed."

"Oh my fucking God!" she squeals, and I can just imagine her jumping off her couch to bounce on her feet up and down. "Tell me everything."

I clear my throat, trying to get the lump out of it, to no avail. "It was storming out…and you know how much that scares me. So I laid down on the floor next to his bed while he was showering. But he came out and put all the pillows on the floor for me, along with his blankets. Then stayed, Chey." I sob, "He stayed. And then he kissed me—and it was the most amazing kiss of my entire life."

"And then?"

"Then I left him." Tears fall faster down my face, and I look back at the parking garage elevators. I could go back—it's not too late. I could say I left something in my car. I could make up an excuse. Anything, and he would believe it. "I left him all alone, sleeping."

"What the hell is wrong with you, Bailey Russell?"

"Thomas now," I mutter.

"Don't deflect." She growls. "Not with me. You know fucking better. And let me tell you something, dumbass. That right there was the biggest mistake of your life, and I want you to never forget these words. You will regret this until the day you die. If you never see him again the way I know you plan to do…a part of you will never be whole again. That man is crazy about you. Why are you letting him go? Are you stupid?"

I. Am. *So*. Stupid.

"Yes, I am. But Cheyenne, I can't give him what he wants." I shake my head, catching my tears and snot with the back of my hand. "What he deserves. He needs more than I can offer him. He doesn't deserve someone who runs away in the morning, who won't be there to catch him."

"He knows that now." Cheyenne scoffs, "Clearly. He's probably broken, Bailey. You're breaking him."

"I can't be the one to put him back together."

"I love you, Bailey." She sighs, "But sometimes you are one dumb bitch. And if he comes to the rink to ask about you? What do I even say? Oh, she's fine. She just doesn't care about you?"

"I care!" I yell out, "That is why I'm doing this."

"Don't involve me, Bai." I can just imagine her shaking her head, pursing her lips. Her stubbornness is so potent I can feel it through the phone. "I won't lie to him."

"You're *my* best friend," I argue.

"I don't care." She yells, "You should give him a chance, and I won't be the one to get in the way of that. If he wants to go after you, I'll let him."

"Fucking traitor," I mutter, then hang up and toss the phone to the floor on the passenger side of the car. "Give him a chance." I mock, pulling on a new shirt, then out of the parking spot.

I drive fast, so fast I'm surprised I don't get pulled over before arriving at my destination. I take the first parking spot right in front of the clinic, ready to wait a few minutes before going in. I don't enjoy being in a waiting room; it makes me anxious. At least my therapist knows that and lets it slide, so as long as I park here, the receptionist sees my car and checks me in. I walk in right at the time of my appointment, since Katherine is always ready on time.

I started coming to therapy after a month of being in Seattle. I couldn't sleep, couldn't eat, couldn't even get a job. The way I was living my life wasn't what I wanted for myself, and although Cheyenne was being super patient with me, I didn't want that anymore. It's embarrassing to admit that one of the reasons I even got a job was for the health insurance—to pay for this and my anti-depressants.

But here I am, feeling astronomically better than I did seven months ago…even if more confused than ever.

My phone alarm rings, and I hit stop and get out of my car. The gravel crunches under my slippers, and I silently curse, just now realizing I have no other shoes. Oh well, I guess I'm doing the walk of shame all the way into Katherine's office. At least she won't judge me—too much. I bypass the reception desk and go directly to the back, where she is already waiting for me.

"Oh." Katherine frowns. "I'd ask you how you're doing—but you look like you're not well."

"You can say it." I grin at her, loving how friendly she is with me, and how I don't even mind her pointing this out. It's pathetic that she's my only friend besides Cheyenne and Theo. Not that Theo will want anything to do with me after this. "I look like shit."

"You said it, not me." She shrugs. "Sit, please."

I take a seat across from her and get comfortable on the loveseat. "I *feel* like shit." I sigh, "I did something really bad."

Katherine's eyebrows jump to her hairline. "Are you sure? We're talking about you." I chuckle, not missing her point. I don't take risks. Ever. "Not Cheyenne?"

"Definitely me." I sigh.

"Sooooo," she prompts. "What did you do?"

The thing I love about Katherine is that she's my age—

twenty-six—and we have connected deeper than I thought we would. Which is why I don't feel shame when I say, "I stayed over at a guy's house last night, for the first time since Robert." I gulp, and she nods encouragingly. "It's different with him...I—it doesn't matter. I left before he woke up."

She visibly winces. "Ouch, my girl." She laughs, trying to lighten the mood. I'm grateful for it. "Heartless."

"No." I shake my head. "It hurts so bad, Kat." Then the dam breaks, tears bursting from my eyes at high velocity, soaking my cheeks and trailing down my chest. I'm a freaking mess. "I *want* him."

"So why are you crying?" She frowns. "Why did you leave him?"

"I'm broken." I smile through the tears, feeling that statement in my soul. "I can't even leave my house without being paranoid. With good fucking reason—Robert showed up at my work last week."

"And how did that make you feel, Bailey?"

I chuckle at her shrink question. "Don't shrink me now, Katherine. Of course, I'm freaking the hell out. He was hurting me, and the guy I like—*Theo*—stepped in. He choked him and called security."

"So the threat is gone." She nods once. "More than likely, he's in jail now. What I want to know more about is this Theo guy."

"He's, uh—Theo Anderson. The hockey player."

"Oh my, my, my." She laughs, clapping her hands together. "Go big or go home, yeah?"

"I guess so," I mutter. "I went so big I fucked him in the bathroom at work."

"Oh, shit," she whispers.

"That can't go in my chart, please."

"Fuck," she mutters. "You know I got you."

"Oh, thank God," I whisper. "Let's just say I couldn't think straight when it happened. He affects me so much. But then we decided to be friends, and I felt fine. Let me let you in on a little secret."

"What?" she asks, zipping her lips closed.

"I don't think it's working out."

She chuckles. "You don't say?"

"Nope." I wipe my tears again. "Because friends don't kiss the way we did last night, and friends *definitely* don't wake up tangled up with their faces against each other. He's scaring me. I know I can't give him what he needs."

"You can," she affirms. "You're just too scared to."

"He deserves better."

Katherine's face hardens as she sits up taller, smacking her hands on the top of the desk. "You are enough for him. He deserves *you*."

I sigh, long and loud. "I don't think I can do it."

"Think about a trial phase," she murmurs, and my ears perk up. "Maybe something casual with him—laying down some rules. Do you want just sex?"

"No." I shake my head. "I still want to be his friend."

"What about friends with benefits?"

"That sounds—so high school, Katherine."

"Yeah." She nods. "So what? If it works for you, then it works."

"Except there's nothing casual about fucking a friend," I point out, knowing he'll be hurt in the end. "It'll all be a mess in the end, especially when I cut things off."

"It's a risk you must ask yourself if you're willing to take. Being that I think if you like him, you should give him a chance."

"I do." More tears fall down my face. "He's a great guy."

She stays silent, letting me finish.

"Just not *my* guy."

CHAPTER SEVENTEEN

I haven't seen Bailey in weeks, not since the night of our kiss. The next morning, she was nowhere to be found, and when I woke up alone on that stupid floor with the pillows and blankets I laid out for her, all I felt was empty. And I still do—the emptiness is more present than ever as I've tried contacting her with no luck. She either has blocked my number or is ignoring me. Considering my calls go straight to voicemail, I will go with the former. Which I guess also means she's ignoring me as well, but to-ma-to, to-mah-to.

My lowest point was seeking out her best friend, Cheyenne, in hopes of getting more information. However, she said Bailey was a very private person and didn't give her a home address, and that she's also been taking on more shifts at work again. Oh, and they're not on speaking terms right now. I asked her why, and she wouldn't tell me. She said Bailey wouldn't like it if she talked about it. So, at least she's loyal. Just when I need her to *not* be.

The only positive thing in my life right now is hockey. I passed the test; the MRI came back clear. My skull fracture is healed, so I'm no longer benched. I should be happy, really. Ecstatic, even. Yet all I can think about is her. The way her lips felt against mine, how her hips shifted when I bit her lip, how she tangled her tongue with mine.

Her scent.

Everything about her.

I'm going crazier than ever, feeling abandoned. I know the feelings aren't one-sided. She fucking likes me, so why is she acting this way? Was she not ready for that kiss? She was the one who initiated it, after all. She asked me to stop her, and now, looking back, maybe I should've. It would have saved me a bunch of heartache.

Though I'm not sure why I'm feeling this sad over a silly kiss. Except nothing about it was silly. That single act touched my soul in a way I won't be forgetting any time soon—if ever. Will I see her again? Hear her voice? Caress her skin? I don't know. But I can confidently say that I'm not done with Bailey, and I'm going to do whatever it takes to get her back in my arms. Even if that makes me look insane.

She's not a bad person, just scared. I can practically taste the fear emanating from her pores whenever we spend time together, and I really don't know how to put her at ease. If she were to give me a chance, regardless of how minuscule it is, I'd play by her rules.

"T!" Jeremy yells, skating up to me. "You ready to crush them?"

"Absolutely." I grin, feeling more than ready. There's something to be said about the way my chest tightens from happiness at the opportunity of being here today. Seeing as I'm not benched anymore, and my career isn't over, I'm so damn lucky.

"Let's do this, boys!" Yells Oliver, taking his position in front of the net.

The adrenaline lasts me all the way from the first period to the third—where we're leading by three goals. Three to zero, to be exact. With only two minutes left in the game, I'm more ready than ever to protect Oliver, our goalie. So just as the

Colorado offense comes barging toward us, more than determined to sink one in, I intercept the puck from the opponent and take off.

I go the opposite way, flying through the rink with one objective: scoring a goal. I could pass it to our left winger right now, in fact, I could pass it to just about everyone. But since I'm practically flying through the ice, I keep my eyes on the net. Three Colorado players come after me, trying to barrel me into the boards, but I don't slow down, and they miss me.

I can see Jeremy, Matt, and Noah skating my way, trying to clear the way and ready themselves for a pass that never comes. As soon as I find my chance, I rear back and slap the puck into the net, skating away with a grin on my face. With one knee on the ground and my other skate on the ice, I glide while pretending to play a guitar, then my teammates come rushing toward me to hug and tap my helmet.

Just like that, the buzzer goes off, and we win.

We step off the ice and make our way to the locker room, high-fiving some fans on the way through the tunnel. The high of the win doesn't feel as good as usual, and I know exactly what's dimming my good mood—and I can't ignore it anymore.

Finally, in the locker room, we take off our nasty gear. Many stand around in base layers, while others are already naked and getting in the showers. I, on the other hand, am checking my phone like a thirteen-year-old girl, waiting for her crush to text her. But the problem is, there's never a text, and I'm starting to feel sad instead of just disappointed. Did I mean that little to her?

I take out my phone and read over the messages that I've sent her over the past few weeks, like the love-sick puppy I am.

THEO

Bailey, please. I need to see you.

THEO

We need to talk.

THEO

Please answer me.

THEO

Baby. Please.

THEO

Did I do something wrong? Did I hurt you? Did I misread the room?

THEO

Five minutes. That's all I'm asking for.

God, I know I am pathetic. Even still, I type again, sending one more message—one I hope she replies to but probably won't.

THEO

I'm really so sorry. I don't know what I did wrong. I thought you wanted me to. It doesn't matter what I thought. I swear it won't happen again if you don't want it to. Just come back to me. I miss you.

The strangest thing happens after that.

Bubbles.

As in typing bubbles.

They appear and disappear repeatedly, and just when I think she's about to reply, they disappear again. Poof, gone. Goodbye.

My heart sinks in my chest and I put my phone away, taking off my base layers and going in search of an empty shower stall. Once I find one, I set the water to the hottest temperature I can handle and get in. Maybe I can drown myself in it for a little while so my brain stops overthinking. Only that's what happens when you're going insane over someone, and it's unrequited.

Am I a masochist? Is that what this is? Do I just love the pain of rejection? I know I should be moving on without a glance back. I could have any woman I wanted, even if I'd never be sure if it was for me or my money. Instead, I'm hung up on the only one who wants nothing to do with me, and make no mistake: she wants *nothing* to do with me. She left me behind, discarded me, and now she won't even answer my messages. So why do I want to seek her out? Why am I wondering if she's the one who isn't okay?

I lean my forehead onto the shower tiles and bang my head softly against it. "Don't give yourself another brain bleed, T," Jeremy jokes, taking a shower stall next to mine. "Or crack your skull open any more than it already is. We need you out there, man."

"Oh." I chuckle. "I know. I'm just…thinking."

"Thinking real hard there, dude." I don't look at him even though I can feel his eyes blasting my face with heat. "Wouldn't happen to be about a sexy nurse we all know and care about?"

"You don't care about her," I spit, realizing my mistake before I've even finished my sentence. That was his plan all along, to rile me up and get me to talk since I haven't been saying anything to them. They don't even know she came over.

"Ah," Jeremy replies. "So it is about, what's her face again? Bailey?"

"You know her name," I say coldly, getting soap and lathering myself up with it.

"You're so touchy." He smirks, "Now tell me what happened."

"Nothing happened."

A laugh erupts from him, loud and quick. "You're a freaking liar, T. Just look at you—like a puppy whose treat was taken away. Now tell me what has a stick up your ass all of a sudden."

"I was seeing her," I blurt, glancing at Jeremy, whose brown eyes widen. A grin takes over his face immediately, but I want it gone, so I look away and keep talking. "Went out together a few times. A couple of weeks ago, she came over, and we watched TV, and one thing led to another and—"

"Oh my *fucking* God." Jeremy gasps. "You had sex with her?"

I want to say I already did that–which he knows–but I refrain.

"She kissed me. We fell asleep. She left me without saying goodbye." I swallow and look at him. He drops his eyes to the shower floor and busies himself by lathering soap on his own body. "Now, she's not answering any of my calls or texts."

"Ouch, bro." Jeremy winces. "Maybe it's time to move on."

"Maybe," I agree, knowing damn well I'm going after her regardless. "Or maybe she just needs someone to fight for her."

"Whatever." He shakes his head, "You're a fixer, T. But you can't fix everyone."

"I know," I sadly whisper, "But maybe I can fix whatever happened between us to make her run."

"Don't get your hopes up," he says, but my hopes are crushed already, so there's no problem in that department. "Some people just can't be put back together."

"My hopes are nonexistent," I affirm. "Don't worry about me."

"I'll always worry about you." He laughs, "You're my brother. Now let's go get some pizza and beer."

"Alright."

I go back to showering, trying to finish up as quickly as possible, but I can't help thinking of Bailey. Everyone has already cleared out, and I'm tense as fuck. I need to—I don't even know what I need. But the longer I stand here, the more I realize it's something I can't have. And the next best thing is in my memories.

Bailey's lips against mine. Her tongue in my mouth. Her hips shifting under me, seeking me, her release. My hand in her hair, fingers gripping the soft strands. The sounds she made as I kissed her.

My dick hardens immediately, and I look around to make sure I'm alone. And I am. If I don't take care of this, I won't be able to leave here. I'm so hard it's actually painful, and when I wrap my fist around my dick, I think of her.

With every tug, I think of her.

My hand picks up speed, fisting myself and tugging harder. I moan lowly, trying not to have anyone hear me as pleasure skates down my spine. With every brush over the head, I think of her, and when my thumb touches the little nerve under the head, my stomach flips. Then, when I'm finally coming down the drain, I think of her, too. My palm slaps against the tiles as I groan loudly, unable to control myself now.

Fuck.

I want her back.

No, I *need* her back.

So I get out of the shower and get dressed. Sitting on one of the benches in the locker room, I get my phone out of my bag. I do the only logical thing: I get a plane ticket home instead of waiting to fly back with the team tomorrow. I text my coach to let him know, then grab all my stuff from the hotel room, and bounce.

Thankfully, Jeremy is not in the hotel room when I come in, so I'm able to slip out undetected. I feel kind of bad because they invited me out to dinner, and now I'm ghosting them without an explanation, but I have business to take care of. I need to fix whatever I did, even if I don't know how.

After almost eight hours of flying, driving, and overthinking, I'm sitting in my car outside the hospital. It's nearly time for Bailey to be off work, so I take off my seatbelt and enter the building through the ER doors. No one questions me as I navigate the halls that lead into the inpatient area, and I'm grateful that I remember exactly where I'm going.

Except once there, I don't know what I'm going to do.

I don't have to think about it long though, because as soon as I step onto the floor and walk toward the nurse's station, I see Bailey. She freezes on the spot, just a few feet away from me, and without hesitation, I grab her arm and haul her into an empty room, closing the door behind us.

Bailey is shaking, and it's so noticeable that even her teeth chatter. Now I'm wondering if this was a good idea. But when she whispers, "*Theo*—" my composure breaks, and I cage her against the wall.

"I told you I wouldn't let you ruin this thing between us."

Then I slam my lips against hers.

Bailey

CHAPTER EIGHTEEN

Electricity courses through my body when his lips meet mine, threatening to shock everything that comes into contact with me. Except it's him—the one who is searing my skin with every touch—and it feels like I'm having the same effect on him.

Lips mold against mine, nipping, licking, sucking. But then he pulls away just as quickly, chest heaving at the same pace as mine. I reach for my heart, holding it where it pounds, and I think about how much I must have hurt him. I also think about what my therapist said—*friends with benefits*. I don't want to lose him, but I also can't give him what he wants from me. What if we can meet in the middle?

In one frenzied movement, I close the space between us once more, and he bends at the waist to pick me up. He pushes me against the wall, my back meeting it with a hard thud, and I grab the back of his neck to pull his face toward mine. Our lips meet again, this time faster, harder, rougher. Tongues war with each other, teeth nip at lips, and when I suck his bottom lip into my mouth, he *moans* for me. My hips move over his abs of their own accord, rubbing myself on him. And I swear it's like someone's set my clit on fire because it's pulsing, pounding to the beat of my heart—and I need relief.

"Suck on my tongue, baby." He groans as he pulls away, and then suddenly, his bottom lip is caught between my teeth again, and I pull on it slowly. "Bailey," he whispers, "I will fuck you right here if you don't stop biting me like that."

I inhale sharply, but then angle my face up to his. Theo takes the hint, lowering his face toward mine and letting me into his mouth. After a slow kiss, his tongue brushes against my lips, and I open up, sucking on his tongue.

"Mmmm," he moans again, and I bury my fingers in his hair and pull on the strands softly.

Theo's mouth descends, trailing a path from my jaw down to my neck. I tilt my head at an angle, giving him access to nip and lick as he wants, and I can tell he's warring with his feelings. We're caught in a state of desperation, although I can feel the anger coming off him in waves. He's pissed that I left him, ghosted him, and I can't even blame him for it. I'm angry with my own damn self.

"We have to stop meeting like this," I tell him softly as I pull away.

"How?"

I give him an accusatory look, knowing he doesn't care. "In hospitals."

"Then let's meet at my place." I open my mouth to object, even as he gives me a quick kiss to shut me up. "Hear me out. You're about to be off work. So do what you need to do and come home with me."

Home.

My studio doesn't feel like home, though he says it like calling a place *home* is the most natural thing in the world. "Why would I do that?"

"Because we need to talk, and you know it." Theo sighs, letting me down and putting me on my feet. "You left me—over a fucking kiss, Bailey. Do you know how much that hurt? The least you can do is come home with me and fix this ache in my chest."

"I don't know how to do that," I reply, my voice hoarse and cracking.

"All you have to do is be there," he whispers, crowding me again, his thumb meeting my bottom lip. "Please."

"Alright," I relent. "Wait for me in the waiting room, and I'll be there in about twenty minutes. I have to give report on two patients, so it should be fairly quick."

"I'll wait however long you need me to wait, Bailey."

My heart somersaults in my chest at his words, but all I can do is nod and walk out of the room, leaving the door open behind me. No one pays me any attention as I return to the nurse's station, although I'm sure when they spot Theo waiting for me they will have a million questions. Like, are you fucking your patient? Ex-patient? Does it matter if I'm no longer taking care of him? Is it unethical? I don't even fucking know. But there's a strong attraction between us, chemistry. Spending time together is easy. These are all things I've never experienced before. And I plan on exploring all of that.

The next twenty minutes are some of the longest of my life, and of course, I have Linda again, who just loves to talk. Unfortunately, I don't feel the same about her. That may sound a little cruel, but I'm not one for small talk. I guess unless it's with Theo. Sometimes, I think that everything that comes out of each other's mouths during the time we spend together is meaningful.

Once I am done with report, I clock out, get my bag from the break room, and go to the waiting room where he's meeting me. I follow him all the way to the ER entrance in silence, but when we get to his black Audi R8, I audibly gasp. I don't know how he's not judging the piece of shit I drive. He just opens the door instead, and I get in.

The scent of leather meets my nostrils as I sit down. He closes the door behind me, and suddenly, I feel very self-conscious about my scrubs. It feels criminal to have spent an entire night in the hospital and then put my filthy scrubs on his beautiful leather seats.

"Nice car," I murmur as soon as he gets in. "I feel dirty just being in it."

Theo chuckles, "It's okay. I'll clean it later."

"So you admit I'm dirty?"

"Yes," he says without hesitation. "Who even knows where those scrubs have been all night."

"And you're okay with me being here? Dirtying up your car?"

"Bailey," he sighs, "I'd let you dirty up whatever you want."

Images of me dirtying him up come to mind. Me riding his dick. Him holding me and pushing me against the wall. The feel of his lip between my teeth, the way I sucked on his tongue.

Fuck.

I need to get it together.

I don't say anything for the rest of the ride, bouncing my leg as I pray for us to make it to the condo quickly. The air is thick in the car—the silence all but audible. Sadly, The traffic is not helping matters either, and I focus on the bumps in the road as a distraction until we arrive at the condo and get out of his car.

I don't know what to expect when we get inside. Is it going to be awkward? Or is he going to try to maul me again? Do I want him to? The answer is yes, but I know we need to talk first and that's the problem. I don't want to. If things could just progress naturally until we decide to give this friends-with-benefits thing a shot—which he doesn't even know I want—that would be amazing. But he deserves better than that, and I have to give it to him.

Once inside, I drop my bag by the front door and take off my shoes as well. "Can I take a shower?" I ask him.

I didn't bring spare clothes, but I'm not above wearing a T-shirt at home, even in the cold weather. I'm sure he'd lend me a pair of sweatpants if it came down to it. Let's just hope they have drawstrings because I'm tiny compared to him.

"Sure," he says softly. "Do you have spare clothes?"

"No." My lips tip up slightly. "Do you mind lending me a shirt?"

Theo pushes my shoulder playfully, closing the door behind him. "I'd never mind seeing you in my clothes."

My stomach fills with butterflies, though I ignore the feeling. "Where's your laundry room?"

"I'll take you."

Theo takes me into the kitchen and through a door next to the fridge. A spacious laundry room comes into sight, light and airy with its bright white walls and decorative shelves. The floors are checkered tile, and there's a sign that says *in this kitchen, we dance.*

I smirk, "This isn't even the kitchen, Theo." I point at the sign. "Or am I missing something?"

"I just like it, okay?" Theo shrugs. "I will dance anywhere." He clears his throat. "Clean laundry is in the dryer, so you can just grab whatever shirt you want from there."

"Thank you," I reply, looking up at him and making eye contact. His blue eyes widen slightly, and he licks his lips and then looks away. It's endearing how shy he just became. I wonder how shy he'll be at my proposition. "Can you stay in the living room until I'm done with my shower? My scrubs are dirty so I need to put them in your washer and then go to the bathroom."

"Naked?" Theo gulps.

"Yeah." I nod with a smile.

"Right." He runs a hand through his floppy brown hair. "Of course."

With that, he leaves me alone to get out of my clothes, and I immediately start the wash and grab a shirt from the dryer. I pad across the condo quietly, get in the shower, and admire it. It has white subway tiles from floor to ceiling, double shower heads, and even a bench. The shower has glass double doors, but I can't see the bathroom anymore due to the steam.

Getting under the stream of water, I close my eyes and use Theo's shampoo and body wash, loving that I'll be smelling like him for the rest of the day. Like pine trees. I never found the smell appealing before, but it's quickly becoming a favorite of mine now.

Done with the shower, I dry off and put the t-shirt on. It's going to be cold out there, I already know, and the one thing I want the most is to lie down on his bed and sleep. But again, we have to talk before any of that happens, and I wonder if he'll even let me stay after what I have to say. I know I hurt him, but how much does he actually like me? Will he forgive that? Something tells me if I'm here, then he must be willing to.

Opening the bathroom door, I take a deep breath and make my way to the living room. There sits Theo, paying attention to his phone, his foot propped up on the couch. He looks so comfortable, so at ease, something I never am. It's a sight to behold how beautiful he is. He's now wearing gray sweatpants slung low on his hips, and he's shirtless, showing off his sculpted chest and cut shoulders, huge biceps, and corded forearms. An athlete through and through. My mouth waters, and I swallow hard.

With my next step, he looks up from his phone. "Hey, Bailey." His voice is rough, low. It does things to my insides that I can't even ignore anymore. "Come sit."

"Okay." I sit next to him, making sure to pull the shirt down slightly and close my legs so as not to flash him since I'm not wearing any underwear. Damn it, I really didn't think this through. "I just want to say—"

"Why?" Theo interrupts, his voice cracking on the word. His face is anguished, and I know right now that I truly hurt him— more than hurt him, even. "Why would you leave me that way, Bailey?" I inhale slowly, trying to calm the erratic beat of my heart. You said we were a mistake, and I forgave that, but leaving me like that after we shared a moment? How could you do that to me?"

My eyes sting as I try to blink the tears back, yet one traitorous one escapes. He closes the distance between us and brushes it away with his thumb. "I was just scared."

"You know what I was scared of?" he asks, and I shake my head. "Never seeing you again. When you didn't reply to any of my messages, I was going fucking insane, Bailey."

"I'm sorry."

"What was that?"

"I'm so sorry, Theo," I whisper. "You don't understand how hard it is for me to let anyone in."

"Then explain."

"I blocked you *because* I like you. I like you… and I don't want to, because all I can do is hurt you in the end, Theo. And I don't want to do that."

"Why is it so hard for you to give us a chance?"

"Because of Robert!" I exclaim, getting up from the couch and pacing circles around the living room. "Theo…I ran away because he almost killed me. I don't trust anyone anymore. I *can't.*"

"You can trust me," he pleads. "I promise."

"It's not about you," I reply, "You're a great guy—you really are. It's not personal. But I know I can't be the person you need me to be. I can't catch you if you fall."

"You're just saying that because no one's ever caught *you* before."

"Maybe." I chuckle, holding on to the last thread of my sanity. I don't want to relive what happened seven months ago, but he needs to understand why I am the way I am. "He thought I was cheating on him…and he beat me…*stabbed* me. Then he left me for dead." I pause and stare into his eyes. "I ran as soon as I was out of the hospital and never looked back. Cheyenne has been the only person I've let in…" I gulp, hating that I haven't talked to her since she told me she wouldn't cover my ass with Theo. "I came here to start over, and none of that involved *you*."

"Maybe not at first," Theo says slowly. "Except now it does. I want it to involve me."

"The thing is, Theo." I sigh, loud and long. "I'm emotionally unavailable."

"Bailey, if you let me, I'll show you what your life is supposed to look like."

"I want to keep seeing you," I blurt, and he rears back, a smile widening on his face quickly. "But it needs to be *casual*."

That pretty smile drops just as quickly as it came. "Casual, how?"

"Friends," I tell him. "With benefits."

Theo raises an eyebrow. "And what's in it for me, Bailey? Besides the pleasure of your company."

"What do you want?" I ask him with furrowed brows.

"I want some relationship perks." My eyes widen. "The benefits part of the deal."

"That's called sex, Theo."

He just shakes his head. "No. I want *more* than sex." My stomach drops, and it's my turn to shake my head. "You go to parties with me, come to my games. We spend time together. Sleepovers."

"That's a *relationship,* Theodore."

He smiles now. "Those are the terms." I stare at him wide-eyed, unable to reply. I want your friendship, and friends do those things with each other."

I know they do. I fucking know, but I also know that if I did all of that with him, it would be hard not to fall in love with him. "On one condition," I add. "If you fall in love with me, you have to promise we end this between us. No hard feelings."

"That's it?" he asks with a straight face that is totally unreadable. "Those are your terms?"

"Simple." I shrug. "Don't fall in love with me, and we can have sex all you want."

"I don't just have sex with people," Theo counters. "I'm taking my time with you."

"Oh?" I ask with disappointment. "You don't want to have sex with me?"

Theo grabs me by the waist, yanking me toward him until I'm on his lap. "Baby, I want to *fuck* you," he whispers against my lips. "I want to make you cry with how good you feel." He trails his fingers slowly over my cheek. "I want your face soaked with tears, the same way I want your cum all over my dick."

My hips give a little rock against his, feeling his erection thickening underneath my bare pussy. A little zap goes straight to my clit when he grabs my ass cheeks with both hands and squeezes. Oh *God*. I think my brain is short-circuiting.

"Monogamous," I gasp when his hand comes between us and he begins to rub my clit. "Oh my God, Theo."

"Right there, baby?"

"*Yes*," I grit my teeth. "*Only* me."

"Only you," He agrees. "Only ever you."

His fingers come to my entrance and hook into me, his palm against my clit. He thrusts in and out at a torturous pace, his hand rubbing against my clit with perfect timing, and my eyes roll to the back of my head. "*There.*"

I cup his face and bring his lips to mine, letting him finger me while I suck on his tongue, and he moans. It makes my stomach flip, every groan coming from him. Every sound he makes turns me on even more.

He hits a spot inside of me that makes me see black, and I begin to rock my hips to the rhythm of his thrusts. "*Theo.*" I moan, "Fuck."

"That's right, baby," he groans, going faster. "Fuck yourself on my fingers. Come for me."

I pick up the pace, rubbing my clit against his hand, seeking the friction. It feels like I'm going to detonate any moment, the way my spine tingles. Though I'm feeling it all the way down to my toes. And when my legs lock up and my pussy tightens, I know it's over.

My head begins to spin at the exact moment my legs begin to shake, but I don't stop. If anything, I go faster, and Theo yanks my head back and bites on my neck—hard. It sends a shiver down my spine, getting me closer, closer—

And then I fall off the edge.

"I know, baby," he whispers against the shell of my ear. "Look at how perfect you are with your pretty pussy wrapped around my fingers."

"Oh, God."

"*Yes*." He groans, "Fuck, Bailey. You're soaking me."

And just like that, I know this arrangement we made is the best thing that's ever going to happen to me. Because the sweet Theo who opens my doors and cuddles me during thunderstorms is not the same man who just finger fucked me.

And I can't wait to unwrap even more of his layers.

CHAPTER NINETEEN

C hristmas Eve is usually the same each year. I throw a party at my condo, with all my closest friends and their girls coming over. It's a potluck-style ordeal where each of them brings food, and I have a couple of dishes for them as well. This year is different, though. Not only did I cancel the party because I knew Bailey wasn't ready for a gathering where she would be forced to interact with my friends, but I changed the plans for all of us to go to a fair. In the middle of winter.

Because I knew my girl would like that.

They have no idea that I've invited her and her friend. When they realize Bailey is coming here after how unimpressed she was back when I was her patient, they're going to lose their fucking minds. Only I don't care; I don't owe them an explanation, though I'm probably still going to give it to them once we're alone.

Now that Bailey and I are friends with benefits, I know she's going to let herself be…well, herself. I don't know why I feel that way, but something tells me that she's allergic to commitment at the moment, that it gives her a damn rash. Eventually, I'll change that, even if it's the last thing I ever do.

She told me if I started developing feelings for her that I needed to speak up so we could break it off. The biggest problem is that I agreed knowing that I'd already *developed* feelings for her.

That's why I asked for conditions because I want her with me as much as possible, not just to be used as a sex toy. Not that I think she has it in her to do that to me. Regardless of her tough girl act, she's a good person, and she cares about my feelings. Which is a step in the right direction for 'Operation Relationship'. She just doesn't know it yet.

Jeremy and I are waiting in the parking lot for the girls, and the rest of the group is already inside, waiting by the entrance for introductions. I hope this doesn't overwhelm Bailey, but she was happy when I suggested we do this. She said she hadn't been to a fair since she was a little girl, and something about kissing at the top of the Ferris wheel had me jumping at the chance. Call me romantic, but it would be perfect.

Footsteps crunch behind us, and we turn around. My eyes collide with Bailey's, and she smiles, yet I hear a gasp from my side. Jeremy is looking at them wide-eyed and with a gaping mouth, which makes me frown. Before I can ask him what's happening, they begin to walk faster.

"No fucking way," Jeremy mutters under his breath, and I raise an eyebrow at him.

What now?

I look down Bailey's body slowly, my eyes traveling the entire length of her, and I tighten my fists at my sides. I want to run to her, lift her up into my arms, and kiss the hell out of her. Except I'm also not sure of the rules, so I stay rooted to the spot. I let myself admire her beauty. She's dressed in bell-bottom jeans, a pink crop top, and—finally—a black bomber jacket. I want to peel those clothes off her body and put her in mine, which I'll be convincing her of later when I bring up that sleepovers start today.

My lips tip up until a full grin breaks out. She returns it, dimples popping in such an endearing way that I want to poke them. Surprisingly, she closes the distance between us with a cute little run, throwing herself into my arms. When our lips meet, fireworks explode inside me, instantly making me hot. Her fingers reach the back of my neck and get lost in my hair, and I hold her tighter to me. My tongue thrusts into her mouth, and she sucks on it like I asked her to that one time, which makes me groan and—

"For fuck's sake," Cheyenne growls from behind Bailey. "Can we get a move on it?"

Bailey and I both chuckle as a chorus of *what the fucks* come from behind us, and I guess that means the rest of my friends came to see what was taking so long. Questions such as *Isn't that the hot nurse? Didn't she hate him? Ain't no fucking way she fell for his shit.*

"You made up," I point out to Cheyenne. "Glad to see it."

"Yeah, well," Bailey starts. "I'm pretty irresistible."

"More like good at groveling," Cheyenne mutters under her breath.

Bailey and I begin to turn around so I can make introductions, when Cheyenne gasps. She immediately freezes on the spot as she looks at Jeremy, who is sizing her up the exact same way. His eyes roam from her petite made-up face, to her gray sweatshirt that says 'skate, shoot, score' with hockey pucks around the letters, down to her jean-clad legs and her black sparkly Authentic Vans. Clearly, she's understood the assignment because a grin breaks out on his face, and she huffs, rolling her eyes.

"She likes him," Bailey whispers.

"In his fucking dreams," Cheyenne mutters. "Unlike you, I don't date hockey players."

"Hey, what do you have against us?" I complain, and at the same time, Bailey says, "We're not dating, just friends." For whatever reason, that hurts more than if she had said we're fucking, but I don't have much time to think about it when Cheyenne is already replying.

"I have nothing against you all," Chey says, pointing at her sweatshirt. "I love hockey, just not the fuck boys who play it."

"I'm offended." I touch my heart in mockery, knowing damn well she's not affecting me in the slightest. "Not all of us are fuck boys."

"Says the one who is literally fucking my best friend." She smiles sweetly, in a fake way. So, unlike how she acted at the rink, it makes me wonder what has gotten into her.

"Not just yet." I grin, and she goes directly to Jeremy.

"Jeremy." She nods once and keeps walking toward the rest of my friends, where she gives him her back.

"*Honeybun.*" Jeremy grins.

"There's nothing sweet about me when it comes to you," Chey mutters.

"Oh, I know." But Jeremy's grin just grows impossibly wider.

What the fuck is going on, and how do they know each other? Something must have happened since Cheyenne goes right back to ignoring him, then introduces herself to the rest of the friend group, not casting one more glance in Jeremy's direction.

"What the fuck?" I mouth at him.

Jeremy shrugs, "Hell if I know."

"Liar," I whisper-yell.

But whatever, I don't care enough to dissect their interaction today. Grabbing Bailey's hand, I pull her toward the entrance, then slip my arm around her waist and pull her in.

"Noah, Oliver, Matt, Jeremy," I start. "This is Bailey."

"Oh, we know," Oliver says with a grin, his green eyes twinkling, which earns him an elbow to the ribs from his girlfriend, Alejandra.

"How did we get here?" Matt asks.

"What were you thinking?" Noah asks.

"You're gonna regret this," Jeremy says, running a hand through his light brown hair, and I shoot him a murderous look.

"Everyone calm down." I roll my eyes. "She's my friend."

"Sure she is." Alicia—Noah's wife—says with a grin, and Alejandra shoots Bailey a small smile. She's the shiest of the group, never talking much, which is perfect because Bailey isn't much of a talker with strangers either.

"Let's go inside," I tell them, grabbing Bailey's hand and pulling her along with me. Surprisingly, everyone goes their respective ways, leaving us alone. Even Cheyenne sticks with the group, shoving Jeremy aside when he tries to talk to her.

Bailey chuckles. "I don't know what's happening, but I'm sure as hell going to find out after here."

"You better spill the beans." I squeeze her hand softly. "Jeremy won't budge."

"You know I will." She winks as we talk toward a food stand.

She looks at all the food with wide eyes. Hot dogs, funnel cake, and cotton candy. But she definitely lingers on the cotton candy and looks back at me. So obviously, I ask for two, and she narrows her eyes at me.

"What?" I ask her with a raised eyebrow.

"Let me pay," she all but growls.

"No." I shake my head. "Don't insult me again. You know I'm *sensitive*."

This makes her laugh, and when I shove the cotton candy into her waiting hands, she takes it willingly. Her eyes twinkle as she gazes at me and takes a bite of it.

"You're a pain in my ass, you know that?" she asks, while smiling and looking *happy*. Like she's excited to be here. "But thank you for bringing me here."

"You really haven't been to one since you were a little kid?"

"I was seven." She nods slowly, taking another bite. I mirror her, the pink cotton candy's sweetness exploding on my taste buds. Damn, it had been a long time since I had some. "My parents took me, though I didn't appreciate those memories until I was an adult. I don't know why we never went back."

"What was your favorite part?"

"The games. Definitely the games." She grins. "Oh, and the prizes, obviously. My dad won a lot."

"No rides?" I ask her, looking around until I find the one I'm looking for. "How about the Ferris wheel?"

"Never been on one." Bailey shrugs, her cheeks turning a deep shade of pink.

"Excuse me?" I gape. "There's no way you're leaving here without going up there." I point to the ride. "I would never forgive myself."

It's also the perfect excuse to kiss her and make it memorable for her.

"How about you show me what you got over there." She points at a game of hoops. "And then we can go on the Ferris wheel."

"Are you playing too?" I grin. "Because I'll beat you if you are."

"Did you play basketball growing up?" She rolls her eyes.

"Only for fun." I grab her hand and go to the nearest trash can, where we dispose of the cotton candy sticks. "You go first, I'll go after."

Bailey narrows her eyes at me. "So you can make fun of me?"

"No, baby." I wink. "So I don't look like an asshole when I win."

This makes her laugh, and she throws her head back as she does it. She's beautiful. Breathtaking. Happiness looks good on her, and I'm glad I brought her here now.

She grabs my hand, interlacing our fingers as we make our way to the hoops game. My breath catches in my throat when her thumb brushes over my knuckles, and I stare down at her. Only she's not watching me; she's excited about the game, eyes on the prize. I don't think she even noticed she just did that.

Bailey starts the first round, and she misses every single shot. She's fucking atrocious. But she laughs every time she doesn't put one into the hoop, and I laugh with her. I can see her dimples the entire time, and I feel an ache in my chest that won't go away. What the hell is that about?

"Okay, big boy." Bailey rolls her eyes as I grab the ball. "Your turn."

I grin, taking the ball from her. "Watch and learn, B."

I then proceed to sink every ball into the hoop, and she looks at me with a gaping mouth. We're gathering a bit of a crowd, and she doesn't even look uncomfortable. I have three shots left, and I put them all in as well.

"What the hell, Theo." She groans. "Maybe you should've been a basketball player instead."

I chuckle. "Nah, I'm too rough for basketball." I wink. "I like to beat people up for a living."

Her laugh is loud and uninhibited, and she throws her head back. Her cheeks are flushed a deep pink as she looks back at me, and she bites her bottom lip momentarily as she stares. I look away first because if not, I'll do something crazy like steal more kisses here.

It's time to pick a prize, and there are so many that my head spins. However, she seems to know exactly what she wants and points at it immediately. "The triceratops, please." She beams at the lady behind the counter, who is nodding with a smile. Bailey grabs the triceratops Squishmallow and turns around, grinning at me.

"What the hell, Bailey." I raise an eyebrow. "You made fun of me for my dinosaurs, and now you're getting one?"

"I didn't make fun of you." She rolls her eyes playfully as I pull her toward the Ferris wheel. "I just stated a fact. You probably do know all the species known to mankind."

"You're not wrong." I chuckle. "But why did you get it?"

"It reminded me of you." She shrugs nonchalantly, but a blush creeps to her cheeks. "Stop staring at me," Bailey groans. "It's not a big deal."

"If you say so." I wink. "All I hear is that I'm memorable."

"You know you are," she mutters, but it's cute.

We finally make it to the Ferris wheel and wait in line for what seems like forever. There are a lot of people here, and I can see our friends ahead of us. But instead of cutting the line like I want to, I stay behind for privacy with Bailey. I'm enjoying having her all to myself.

It's our turn now, and we get on the ride. Bailey's eyes are wide as she looks around and grips my hand hard. It makes me chuckle, and I raise an eyebrow at her.

"Don't tell me you're scared of heights," I joke, even though she looks like she is, and now I wonder if this was a bad idea.

"No!" she shrieks as we begin to move. "I'm scared of rides."

"It's okay, Bailey," I soothe. "This one goes slow. You'll forget all about it when we get to the top."

"If you say so," she mumbles.

Bailey still looks everywhere as we go up, and when we get to the top, her jaw drops. I look around too, now taking in the view of the city. It's beautiful, and it's not every day you can see the Seattle skyline from this angle.

"Wow," she breathes, and when I look at her, her eyes glisten. "This is incredible."

"You are," I murmur, and she looks at me with wide eyes. "You're so fucking beautiful, Bailey."

She smiles shyly and scoots closer, and I take the opportunity to wrap her up in my arms. She tilts her head back as I look down at her, and her eyes fall to my lips. I lick them slowly, seeing if her gaze tracks it, and when I see she doesn't stop looking, I lean in for a kiss.

Her lips are soft against mine, and the kiss is slow and languid, nothing like the one we shared when she first arrived. She sucks on my bottom lip gently, and I groan, tightening my arms. When her tongue thrusts into my mouth, I suck on it, then tangle it up with mine. Fuck, I could do this all day.

I could do this for the rest of my life.

I pull back and rest my forehead against hers, our noses brushing. We share breath for a moment, and then she leans in and presses her lips against mine again. It's sweet, fuck. My heart aches as she does it. And I know I'm well and truly fucked, because what I feel for Bailey is already surpassing a simple friends-with-benefits arrangement. She makes my heart beat faster and my hands shake. She makes my chest tighten, and she steals my breath with every look. I don't think I can live without this girl anymore. And that's why I hold her a little closer, hoping she lets me keep her a little longer. Because one thing is clear as day—

Bailey Thomas belongs in my arms.

Bailey

CHAPTER TWENTY

"Morning," a soft voice calls out, startling me awake.

I'm in Theo's bed, and I briefly recall how I got here. He all but begged me to come home with him, and I relented. As soon as we made it to his place, I thought he was going to ask me to have sex. Strong arms wrapped me up in a cocoon and carried me bridal style all the way to this bed. Instead, he proceeded to warm me up—make me hot as hell is more like it—by cuddling me all night. Until I didn't feel him anymore, which is when I assumed he had left the room to make breakfast. I can smell bacon, and as I open my eyes and sit up in bed, I can see him walking toward me with a tray.

"Figured you might wake up hungry."

As if on cue, my stomach growls and I blush furiously. "You guessed right."

We left his friends late last night, probably at two in the morning, but I was asleep by three at the latest. I'm genuinely surprised since I haven't fallen asleep before daytime in so long that I can't even remember what it was like to sleep in the dark. But it was nice, especially with Theo wrapped around me like a weighted blanket. I shouldn't like that at all. In fact, I shouldn't even be sleeping in bed with him. It's too intimate. I'm not even sure why I agreed to his terms—sleepovers being one of them.

The truth is that as much as I want to deny it, I like him a lot. Even with all of my trust issues, I know him enough to feel somewhat safe around him. He doesn't seem like the kind of guy who would treat me the same way Robert did, and I think that's the only reason I wanted to be friends with benefits. That and the fact that I feel lonely. I don't want to fall in love, just have some company and the occasional good fuck—I'm only human.

The worst part is that going places with him, sleepovers, and spending time with him all seem like the most natural thing in the world. There's nothing awkward about it, nothing that makes me second guess my choices, and that is worrisome. I just don't want him to develop feelings for me because it's easy between us. After all, the only way this can end is with a broken heart. For both of us.

"Hope you like it, B," Theo says, smiling down at me as he sets the tray on my lap.

The delicious aroma of the bacon and omelet reaches my nose, and my mouth waters. "It looks amazing, Theo. Are you going to eat with me?" I smile back.

"I'm hungry for something else," he says softly, his voice strained. I glance into his eyes and they are heated, flaring.

"Oh, yeah?"

Theo nods slowly, and I set the tray aside on the bedside table. I raise one eyebrow, daring him, taunting him. Throwing the blankets aside, I flash him my pussy, which is easy considering the shirt I'm wearing. I bet he didn't even realize I was naked underneath, but now he does, and the way he bites his full bottom lip and sucks it into his mouth makes the need to clench my thighs almost excruciating. But not as excruciating as the need to have his mouth on me, all over me.

"Take it off, Bailey," he whispers. "I want to see that pretty little body."

Slowly, I pull my shirt over my head and drop it to the ground right next to the bed. It's my turn to bite my lip, so hard I almost draw blood from how nervous I feel.

"So perfect, baby," he breathes. "Made just for me, and me alone."

I clench my thighs at that, seeking relief. His grin is mischievous as he leans forward with his hands on the bed. One moment I'm sitting on the bed, and the next, my ass is on the edge. Theo sinks to his knees, gazing at me in a way that makes me want to close my legs again, so I attempt it. He slaps my thighs apart and I turn my head to the side, self-conscious of him being so close. I haven't done this in years because Robert wasn't exactly a giver. Theo, on the other hand, all he does is give.

"Look at me, baby." I do, leaning up on my elbows and looking down at him. His warm breath coasts over my slit, and he gives a tentative lick, both of us groaning at the same time. "Do you see what you do to me? You're driving me fucking insane."

Theo licks my inner thigh, taking his time with me, then bites it. Really hard. I'm sure there's going to be a bruise later, but it feels so damn good I still whisper, "Theo, please. *More*."

"More?" He murmurs against my pussy again, this time sucking my clit into his mouth, teasing me. Letting go just as quickly, he slaps my pussy. "I'll give you whatever you want."

"I don't want you to be gentle," I tell him, my hips rising toward his face, seeking relief.

"I won't be." He smirks. "Now watch me make you come, and if you close your eyes, I'll fucking stop. And you don't want that."

Like a starved man, he descends on my pussy and licks up my slit, swirling his tongue over my clit over and over. I know

I'm soaked, and the sounds of sex fill the room as his tongue keeps toying with me, enough to make me feel good but not enough to give me what I need.

"*Theo*." I want to come. I start to tremble underneath him, which makes him grip my thighs in a bruising grip and push them up towards my chest.

"This is how I want you, Bailey," he groans against my slit. "Open for me, wanting me, *needing* me." I moan when he sucks my clit into his mouth. "How bad do you want this? How bad do you want *me*?"

"So fucking bad." I breathe, thrusting my hips up, and he chuckles.

"Hold on to me," he demands.

Theo lowers his face back to me, swiping his tongue over my slit, making me shudder and shake. As I tremble underneath him, he sucks my clit into his mouth, then releases it. Once, twice, three times. Teasing, taunting, riling me up. My moans and gasps echo in my ears, and he groans from deep within his chest again. My fingers slide up the back of his head and hold onto his hair, and he smiles against my pussy, looking into my eyes. His own eyes dilate as his tongue peeks out, and with his fingers, he parts my pussy lips to reveal my clit to me.

Then he *spits*.

Right on it.

"So pretty," he murmurs, then sucks my clit into his mouth, hard, over and over, bringing me to the edge.

My hips jerk and thrust up, and when he shoves two fingers into my soaking pussy, I cry out. My legs close around his head as I rub myself all over his tongue, feeling the stubble as friction, although he doesn't seem to mind. In fact, it only makes him even crazier.

His fingers dig into my inner thighs again, trying to part me, and when I don't relent he bites my clit softly. My legs immediately fall open, and instead of thrusting his fingers back into my pussy, he uses one to thrust it into my ass.

My back arches, bowing off the bed, and I scream. "*Fuck*!"

Theo thrusts his finger in and out slowly, sucking on my clit, and I feel the familiar tingling all the way down to my toes as I get closer to climax. My nails dig into his skull, tangling in his hair, and I grip him so hard I can see tears in the corner of his eyes. But I don't care as I tighten my fingers even more.

"Yes, Theo." I moan, "Right there. Please don't stop. You're doing so fucking good." I groan when he thrusts another finger into my ass, and just like that, my body goes from trembling to full-body shakes.

He doesn't relent, sucking my clit harder, alternating between flicking and sucking it back between his lips. It's the most glorious feeling, one that I've never experienced. When he begins flicking his tongue again, I ride his face shamelessly. With his free hand, he begins to help me rock my hips while he thrusts into my tight hole. I scream, unable to contain myself, as he pushes me right over the edge of a freaking precipice. I can see myself falling, but there's no way to stop it, and when my body stops shaking and begins to relax, he kisses my clit and licks me clean.

Theo crawls up my body, spreading my legs to settle against them, his hard dick right on my pussy. I'm sure his gray sweatpants are soaked by now, but he still rubs himself against me. It takes me back to that bathroom with his dick inside of me, and it makes me want it so much more all over again.

"Did you like that, baby?" he asks against the shell of my ear, eliciting goosebumps and shivers. "Me on my knees for you?"

"Yes," I reply with a smirk. "Now, you'll have to let me return the favor."

"I will." He nods. "Just not today. We're gonna pace ourselves."

"Are you sure?" I frown.

"Positive." He smiles against my skin, kissing my cheek, then the corner of my mouth.

"If that's what you want."

"What I want is for you to get dressed and eat your breakfast." Theo stands up and takes a step back. "We're gonna go for a walk."

"Where?"

"Do you have to work tonight?"

"No," I reply slowly. "I'm all yours…"

"Yes, you are," he says, handing me my food once more.

I sit on the bed and eat my breakfast—a vegetable and cheese omelet that surprisingly tastes incredible. So he can play hockey, cook, *and* be funny. What else can the man do? It's kind of annoying how perfect he is. Surely, there's something that will make me cringe. There has to be.

Grabbing my overnight bag, I get dressed quickly, aware of Theo watching me. He looks edible as ever, with his brown hair a tousled mess, his lips still red and swollen from his time between my legs, and his chiseled abs, chest, and shoulders on full display from being shirtless. I kind of want to jump him all over again, not to mention the best orgasm I've ever had is a pretty strong incentive as well.

"You ready?" he asks me, now wearing jeans and a sweatshirt. It's pretty damn cold outside, and thankfully I brought everything I need to brave the weather.

"Yes," I sigh. "But it's so cold outside."

"We can just go by real quick and see the Christmas lights before they take them down," he says. "We don't have to make a day of it."

We're standing outside in the freezing cold a few hours later, staring at Christmas lights. They're very pretty. He didn't mention we were going to the botanical gardens, though now I'm glad since it's been on my bucket list since I got here. I just haven't had the time to come because of work. And Cheyenne said she'd come if she had to, but she's been here many times. So I didn't want to put her through that.

The trees are all covered in twinkly lights, and they're on even though it's not nighttime yet. It's late afternoon. Yeah, so we slept in a lot. But I really needed it because I've been working myself dead.

We walk through the botanical gardens side by side, our jackets brushing against each other with every step, our hands bumping too. It's fucking cold, and I can see my breath fogging in front of my face with every exhale, but I don't complain.

Soon enough, it's finally dark—at five p.m.—and the lights are brighter than ever. I grin as I look up at Theo, and his eyes crinkle in the corners as he returns the smile. He's so freaking beautiful it hurts—inside and out. How did I get lucky enough to know him?

There's a couple making out in front of the trees across from us, and I smirk. "That's a lot of PDA."

"Yeah, I don't think I could do that."

I roll my eyes, knowing that you do shit like that when you're in love. "Not even if it was me?" I tease, then regret it. *You're giving mixed signals, Bailey. Cut it out.*

"Hell no," he replies with a smile. "I can't imagine shoving my tongue down your throat in public."

"I bet you could for the right girl," I reply, sad all of a sudden at knowing it can never be me.

Even still, he replies, "You're the only girl for me." He grins, a twinkle in his eyes. "*My* girl." His hand reaches for mine, but I move it out of the way at the last second, pulling back.

"I don't think I'd be able to either," I deflect, and he rears back like I slapped him.

"Then it's a good thing we're just *friends* with benefits, right?"

I smile, even though I don't feel like doing it. "Yeah. Good thing."

Just like that, the magic is over, and we turn around, heading back to his place. The walk back is awkward, the air charged as the silence swallows us. I can't think of anything to say that will make it better, so I zip my lips until we get back.

He opens the door, and the warmth of the heater envelops me in a tight hug. I can barely feel my hands, and I rub them together in an attempt to warm them up. "Do you have hot chocolate?"

"Yeah, in the pantry, bottom shelf," he replies neutrally.

"Oh, thank God." I grin, trying to lighten the mood. "I can't reach the top one."

"You're just the right size, though."

"I have a special hot chocolate. I'll make it for you," I sing-song. "And then we can make cinnamon rolls together."

"Cinnamon rolls?"

I look in the pantry, finding everything I need. "Yes, Theo. Catch up."

"Alright."

Theo sits at the kitchen island as I make the hot chocolate the way the packets say, heating up the milk in the microwave and then mixing it together. Taking out the whipped cream, I put it on top and then sprinkle the whipped cream with chocolate chips, then call it a day.

"This is your special recipe?" He frowns, his brows coming close together.

"Yes…"

"Bailey, I hate to break it to you, but everything is already pre-made."

"Whatever," I huff. "It doesn't have to be made from scratch for it to be special."

"Let me guess, the cinnamon rolls come from a can that you find in the dairy aisle at the grocery store."

"Actually, no," I say with an eye roll. "Jokes on you because you're actually going to help me make them."

"Well, that sounds like a lot of fun, actually."

After a half hour of mixing, and making the icing, we finally have the dough ready. We leave it on the counter to rise for an hour and a half, then make our way back to the living room to watch *The Summer I Turned Pretty* Season Two. And this is the moment I realize just how perfect Theodore Anderson is.

And how much it hurts that he can't be mine.

Why am I so damn scared?

And why do I mess everything up?

CHAPTER TWENTY-ONE

I stare at Bailey as her hands wade in the water of the steaming hot tub. We're sitting across from each other after a quick dip in the pool right above my condo and I'm honestly staying away so I don't jump her bones. I know I said she'd be begging me by the time I fuck her, but at this rate, I might end up begging *her*—on my knees yet again. It's not a bad place to be though, and I'd gladly kneel and worship her if it means I get to keep her.

We're still keeping up this charade of friends with benefits, and I say that because even I know she wants more; she just won't allow herself to have it. However, I'm willing to give her the time she needs to assimilate to the situation. Eventually, though, she will realize she's made a mistake and finally give me a chance—a *real* one. At least, I hope so. Either way, nothing will stop me from trying.

"Why are you staring at me?" she asks me, raising one perfectly shaped eyebrow. Seriously, it feels like everything about her is flawless.

"I thought you said you like to swim," I tease Bailey. Okay, so maybe there was some swimming, but I would like to rile her up.

"I said I *like* to swim, not that I'm a swimmer." She rolls her pretty green eyes at me. "It's not the same thing. Besides, I also like sitting in the hot tub like a lazy bitch."

I snort. "And I like sitting with you, just to watch you," I reply. "Though don't think for one second that I actually enjoy being inside Satan's asshole."

"It's not my fault you already run as hot as literal hell."

She has a point: I run as hot as a furnace. Always have, and it's the first thing women comment on when cuddling. Bailey is the first one to not point it out—until now. I guess that's saying something. She's *nice*.

"*Aw*, if you keep being sweet like that, I might start thinking you like me."

"Never." She grins, shaking her head. "You're boring, I could never like you."

I press a hand to my wounded heart. Does she believe I'm boring? Is she serious, or is it a joke? I can't even tell. "You can't be serious. I'm funny as fuck."

"You watch Jurassic Park for fun, Theo," Bailey replies in a teasing tone, even though the comment still gets to me regardless.

I glance down at the water, staring at my hands. It's not that I'm a sensitive man—okay, maybe a little—but if she really doesn't like me, then—

"You know I'm just kidding, right?" Bailey slides closer to me, placing a hand tentatively on my forearm, then squeezing the corded muscles.

And just because I want to give her a hard time, I ask in my most serious tone, "Are you, though?"

"Oh my God, Theo." She splashes as she gets on my lap. "If I didn't like you…" She reaches between us, undoing my swim trunks. "Would I do *this*?" My dick immediately thickens underneath the fabric, begging to come out.

Bailey puts me out of my misery and pulls my hard dick out, letting it bob between us and staring down at it like it's edible.

"If you don't stop looking at it like that, it's going to end up down your throat, baby." I groan, just imagining her lips wrapped around me makes me even harder.

Rather than a comeback, she grins and gets off me. "On your knees for me, Theo." I peer around at the empty space, surprised there's no one here at the indoor pool. It's probably going to be short-lived, and I'm calculating just how fast I can come before being interrupted, and man, that would suck. I've already had a case of blue balls for weeks—not that I'm complaining. "Now," she breathes. "Before someone comes in and ruins it for us."

I do as she says, getting on my knees on the bench, the tiny tiles digging into me painfully. But I ignore it because she stands in front of me with wonder in her wide eyes, and all sense of self-preservation goes out the window. It's not lost on me that she has me on my knees for her again instead of the other way around, but she needs control—and damn it, I want to give it to her.

Her hand wraps around my dick and she jerks it slowly, then takes it into her mouth. The way her tongue swirls around the head makes me weak in the knees, and I grab onto the ledge to keep myself upright. She keeps licking at the sensitive spot under the head, and when she sucks and hollows her cheeks for me, I groan.

"Such a pretty little mouth, baby," I praise. "Suck me harder. You feel like *heaven*."

Bailey moans around my dick, making my balls clench, then begins to bob her head up and down. She's slow at first, finding her rhythm. Soon enough though, she gets faster, and my toes curl in pleasure.

Her hands wrap around my ass cheeks, nails digging in, and she begins to push me into her mouth. Doe eyes meet mine, begging me for something, and she nods once. I don't even know what that means, but I bury my fingers in her hair and pop her off.

"What do you want, Bailey?"

She breathes hard, chest heaving, then a grin curls her lips. "Fuck my mouth."

I smirk, looking down at her as she sucks me right back into her mouth, and I begin to buck my hips. Now it's my turn to find a rhythm, one in which I slowly draw out my pleasure, and right as I feel the tingles run down my spine and my balls rise, I begin to thrust in and out of her mouth faster. I meet resistance, her throat constricting around my length, and the sound of her gagging makes my dick harden to the point of pain.

"God, *yes*," I groan.

Bailey moans, bobbing her head to take me in deeper, and I close my eyes to chase the feeling. Her full, plump lips slide over my dick and wrap around the head; then she sucks me back into her mouth. I grip her hair tighter in my grip and open my eyes, watching her own eyes water as I do, and I begin to fuck her throat. Surprisingly, not only does she take it, but she also hollows her cheeks to make the suction even better.

Moaning, I grab the back of her head with both hands and fuck her mouth faster. "That's it, baby," I tell her as she gags. "Choke on my dick. Show me how much you love what I'm doing to you."

Tears gather in her eyes and trail down her cheeks, the most beautiful sight I've ever seen. Sweat trickles down my spine as she continues digging her nails into my ass and I pick up the pace. She's surely going to draw blood, but I can't find any fucks to give right now.

"Fuck, baby," I moan. "That feels so good."

Bailey reaches a hand up tentatively, cupping my balls and squeezing them gently. It sends a zap of pleasure down my spine, combined with the way the head of my dick is repeatedly hitting the back of her throat. "Tug them," I grunt. "Don't be scared, rough me up a little."

Except if there's something I've learned about Bailey, it's that she's a pleaser, too. She might give off the impression that she's just a taker if you don't know her, but here she is, ready to make me fall apart, giving me control, letting go.

My balls rise and my dick throbs, and when the familiar tingling sensation returns, I increase the pace even more, chasing the orgasm. "Swallow my dick, baby," I beg her as my cum shoots down her throat in hot spurts. "Take every drop."

Bailey swallows every last drop, giving my dick one more deep suck, then releases me. My semi-hard dick hangs between us, slightly bobbing, and she gazes into my eyes. Her green ones dilate, showing nothing but need for me, and I'm about ready to give her the world.

"That's my girl," I whisper, gripping her chin with my thumb and forefinger, lifting her face toward mine.

Quickly and with a splash, I sit back down on the bench and pull her between my legs, taking her lips with mine and diving my tongue so deep into her mouth that I can taste my cum. It only serves to turn me on all over again, and when her chest is heaving, and I'm entirely breathless, I pull away and try to compose myself.

"I want to go home now." She smiles at me, her dimples making an appearance.

I frown, "I thought you were spending the night."

"I am." It's her turn to frown, but then she recovers and puts on another beautiful smile. It's contagious, and soon enough, I'm smiling, too. "I meant the condo."

"Then let's go, B."

We get out of the hot tub, her going straight for the towels and me adjusting myself back in my swim trunks. After drying ourselves and gathering our belongings, we go back to my place. The one I wish was *ours* instead.

"Want a Blue Moon?" I ask her as she closes the front door behind us. "Then you can sit on my lap and tell me about your day?"

"Shouldn't you have asked me that before your dick was in my mouth?"

A low chuckle bursts through my lips. *This girl.* "I would've, but you seemed so eager that I didn't want to deny you, baby," I reply with a wink, and she rolls her eyes.

After opening two Blue Moons and putting an orange slice in each, we both sit on the couch together. She's practically on top of me, with her legs draped over my lap and a content look on her face.

"Tell me something, Bailey."

"Like what?" she asks and takes another sip of the beer, smiling at me. It's my favorite thing about her. She never stops smiling at me now. Well—one of my favorite things. Such a change from when we first met.

"Anything." I shrug nonchalantly when, instead, all I want to say is *everything*. Tell me everything about you so I can memorize your entire being. So I can understand you better. So I can love you the way no one else has.

"Let's see." Bailey pretends to think. "Last night sucked, I didn't get to drink coffee at work because we were slammed, and I think I peed one time in fourteen hours."

"Sounds miserable." I wince.

"But I'm here now." With a wink, she downs the rest of her beer. "What else do you want to know?"

"Everything about you."

"That's a lot, Theo." She chuckles and I join her, even though I'm not joking. "Okay. I like to *swim*."

I snicker and she rolls her eyes. "I know that."

"Road trips over airplanes." She gets a dreamy look on her face. "My dream travel destination is Banff."

"I can make that happen," I promise her. "What else?"

"Breakfast tacos over dinner tacos."

I frown, "Blasphemy."

"Oh?" Her nose wrinkles. "And what's the right answer, then?"

"Dinner tacos are superior." I nod slowly, trying to get her to understand. "Al Pastor, specifically."

"I can agree with them being good." She huffs, "However, bacon, egg, and cheese tacos? Can't beat that."

You can most definitely beat that, but I don't want to ruin the moment by arguing about tacos. "You ever been on Tinder?" I ask her, instantly regretting it when she turns her narrowed eyes on me.

"No," she replies. "You?"

"Briefly." I smile weakly. "It was a fucking disaster."

"Oh, please." She chuckles, "Tell me more."

"Not much to tell." There's actually too much to tell because every date I went on was a farce—on their end, not mine. "They only wanted me only because I'm Theo Anderson, star defenseman for the Seattle Sailors. Not for me. I'm just a walking wallet, Bailey."

"Is that really how you see yourself?"

"Not with you." I smile.

"Of course not—I'm your *friend*."

"Not *just* friends." I grin, but the little word is starting to hurt every time I hear it. "But anyway, if you didn't have to work the night shift, would you like to be awake during the day?"

"Absolutely not." She shakes her head. I'm a night owl through and through, but if I didn't work the night shift anymore, I'd have more time with my friends."

Cheyenne.

Me.

"If I could change my schedule for you, Bailey, I would," I reply, knowing she's about to ask me the same question. "I'd be awake at whatever time you are. But I love the sun, okay, my little vampire?"

We both laugh at that. "Whatever, dude." She rolls her eyes. "You're just jealous of my superior survival skills. I don't even need vitamin D or Serotonin to thrive."

"Lies." I chuckle. "You're getting daily doses of Serotonin just by hanging out with me."

"Okay, maybe a little," she relents, then yawns. "I don't know what it is about this couch, but it makes me so tired."

"It's magic." I wink, "I bought it on purpose, for the nights when I want to fall asleep to the TV."

"So you sleep on the couch when you have a perfect bed in your room?"

I shrug, "Sometimes."

Gathering the beer bottles, I put them on the floor next to the couch and get up. Then, I scoop Bailey up and carry her like a baby. I go past the living room and kitchen and then through the hallway all the way to the end.

"Are you gonna put me to bed, Theo?" Bailey teases. "I can walk here on my own."

"I know, but you shouldn't have to," I reply. "Even if you're not my girlfriend, I'll still treat you like my queen."

"You're spoiling me." Bailey pouts.

"I sure hope so."

I lay her down on the bed, facing my side with her head on my pillow, and settle in right next to her. It's dark in the room, but a sliver of moonlight enters through the curtains and bathes her in an ethereal glow. Her green eyes widen as I lick my lips, and they follow the trail of my tongue.

Bailey's hand tentatively reaches out to brush the hair away from my forehead. "You're so beautiful," she whispers with awe in her voice, fingertips skimming the skin of my face as if she's scared I might bite her. "The most beautiful."

I smile softly at her, yet don't dare move. I can only hold my breath while she stares at me as if she's hypnotized.

"And so good, Theo." My throat clogs and my eyes sting. "You're the sweetest thing to ever walk this earth."

"Then keep me," I blurt, regretting the words instantly.

Rather than having the reaction I thought she would, she moves closer until her nose brushes against mine and our lips touch. Then she gives me the softest kiss to ever grace my lips, the kind where I barely feel the brush of her lips, and she buries her face in the crook of my neck.

Bailey's breathing becomes heavy instantly, and before I even realize what is happening, she's fast asleep. It's hard for me to go to bed however, especially after the day we've had. I never expected to get a blow job at the damn pool, and definitely not for her to let me take control of the situation.

I've been more than willing to let her take the reins, although I can't deny that I want to be in charge too, from time to time. Either way, this is all fucking with my head. I want to be able to be her friend—with benefits—but how do I stop myself from having feelings, as she said? Because if we were speaking about her clause…we would've never started this arrangement to begin with. I just don't have the guts to tell her how I feel because I know she's not ready.

"Fuck." I whisper, "What are you doing to me, pretty girl?" I stroke the back of her head, my fingers getting lost in her hair. "I'm so far in love with you I see no way out."

She stirs in my arms, and I wrap her tighter against me—that is, until I feel tears coating my skin. Just as I'm about to try to figure out what's happening though, she whimpers, the slight sound driving a wedge into my heart.

"Robert…" she cries out. "Stop, *please, no*."

Robert.

That motherfucker.

Heat envelops me, but it's not the cozy kind; no, this one is fucking rage. That piece of shit hurt my girl, he did something to her that she will never get over, and it's affecting her in more ways than one. I wish more than anything that I could take her pain away, that I could give her a clean slate. But I can't, not really. I can't wipe her memory of him—I can only try to replace all the bad with good. And damn it, I will achieve it if it's the last thing I do.

"*Baby*," I whisper as I shake her. "It's just a dream. I'm here. *Theo* is here."

Bailey stirs as I wake her, "Theo?"

"Yes, Bailey," I reassure her, a knot forming in my throat. "I'm here."

Her leg wedges between mine, and she glues herself to my front, leaving no space between us. My lips brush against hers, and when I take her bottom lip into my mouth I can taste her salty tears.

"Sorry." She grimaces.

"For what?"

"Crying on you, I guess." She motions to my chest, and I shake my head.

"It's okay," I reply, leaning into her, our faces close together.

Bailey's eyelashes meet my cheeks as my nose brushes against hers, and she flutters them, making me chuckle. "Butterfly kisses," she whispers.

I brush my nose against hers again, nudging, and she tilts her head to meet me for a deeper kiss. One in which I thrust my tongue into her mouth and nip her bottom lip. It's all too much and not enough. Loving Bailey is like nose brushes and butterfly kisses, but it's also heartache and doubts.

And sometimes it really sucks.

CHAPTER TWENTY-TWO

T he energy in the arena is electric. Fans are standing up all throughout and waving shirts over their heads, yelling and screaming, as well as chanting 'let's go *Sailors*, let's go' as Matthew sinks one into the net. The buzzer is painfully loud as it sounds off, but even I'm so excited that I jump to my feet alongside everyone else and bounce.

"Holy shit!" I yell at Cheyenne, grabbing her cold hand in mine and squeezing it.

"Told ya." She winks. "Knew you'd love hockey."

I can't even deny the game is fun and relatively easy to learn with Cheyenne's help; even so, I can't pretend I'm not here for a certain someone. Yeah, I might enjoy watching, but it's *who* I'm watching that matters too. And that someone has already scored two goals tonight, putting the Seattle Sailors at four goals while the opposing team still sits at zero. There's only a few more minutes left of the third period, and everyone is on the edge of their seats, waiting to see what Theo's next move is.

"What do you think is going to happen?" I ask Alicia, who's standing to my left side.

"Honestly?" She smirks, flipping her blonde hair to the side. "Theo is a beast. Everyone is expecting him to score again."

"How much do you want to bet he'll flop?" Chey asks us with a broad grin, and I narrow my eyes at her.

"Shut up, trouble," I reply. "Don't be hateful just because Jer gets on your nerves."

"Getting on my nerves is putting it lightly," she mutters.

I focus my attention back on the game and watch Theo. He looks incredible, zooming past everyone, a rocket ship on skates. There's something so hot and satisfying about seeing him in his element, and I just cannot tear my eyes away. Not that I'm trying really, but still. It's hard.

Theo gains speed on the ice, blocking the net and helping out Oliver. He gets control of the puck, stealing it from the opposing team and flying down the ice with it. He passes it to Jeremy—which is hard as fuck to keep up with since it's happening so fast—and Jeremy passes it back. If I blinked I wouldn't have been able to see it—that's how quickly he rears back and releases a hell of a—

"Slapshot!!" Cheyenne squeals.

"Oh my *God*," I mumble, my eyes still transfixed on Theo, unable to look away.

The buzzer goes off again, and suddenly everyone begins to toss their hats onto the ice. Soon enough no one can skate—that's how many hats are on there, it's kind of obnoxious. Die-hard hockey fans. But if I had a damn hat, I'd be throwing it too. Maybe next time.

"Hat trick!" Alicia and Alejandra squeal, grabbing my hands and Cheyenne's until we're all jumping up and down like middle school girls who just got their first kiss.

Cheyenne briefly explained what that meant before we got here, and that's the only reason I know it's a big deal. I look at him, ready to give him a huge smile, when he turns around and points right at *me*. My blood turns to ice in my veins, and it's as if a bucket of freezing water has been dumped over my head when the Jumbotron focuses on my face. And since that's not bad enough and the universe must actually hate my guts, Theo comes barreling down toward me and slaps the glass in front of me, pressing his lips to his glove and blowing me a kiss.

Right. In. Front. Of. Everyone.

Fuck. *Me.*

I shake my head rapidly while my face heats, and he frowns. But when I look up and see that my face is still focused on the massive screen, I want to run away instead of explaining why this is a problem. He should know this was supposed to be between us, never mind the fact that I'm wearing his jersey—number ninety-eight.

I clearly made a huge mistake. Maybe doing this was telling him I was fine with us being public about this? I don't know what I did to communicate that, but I don't have time to wrack my brain when the entire Sailors Fandom is staring right at me.

Cheyenne pinches me, and when I look back at Theo, he seems slightly hurt. Although none of this would've happened if he hadn't just put me on display like this, I still have a nagging feeling of guilt. This is the only reason I'm propelled forward until I blow him a kiss back, and it's definitely the only reason I'm pressing one hand to the glass and my forehead to it as well.

Theo's smile makes my whole body warm and freeze up simultaneously. Then, when he returns the gesture, pressing a gloved hand up to mine and his forehead to mine, I shake a little. Not subtly either, but more like full-body shakes. It's as if I'm dying of hypothermia or something. God, I need to get out of here.

I peer up to find the ice finally cleared out, which means it's time for Theo to go back to his team and for me to go back to the girls. "What the fuck was that?" I ask Cheyenne with a biting tone, wondering if she knew he'd pull a stunt like this.

"What do you mean?" she asks with a slight furrow to her brows, confusion pulling them in.

"Why did he do that?" I huff. "The last thing I need is to have more attention on me and—"

Cheyenne laughs, "Oh, that?" Mischief dances in her eyes, and mine narrow in return. What the fuck is so funny? "He dedicated his goal to you. They do it all the time if the right person is in the stands."

"And you failed to mention this, because?"

"I don't know." Chey shrugs nonchalantly. "I figured you knew."

"When I know absolutely nothing about hockey?"

"It's a sport like any other."

We both know that's a damn lie. "I don't watch *any* sports, Cheyenne."

But she just smirks and grabs my hand, squeezing it softly. "Just be happy, Bai. You're okay."

"I'm not okay, though," I mutter. "What if Robert saw?"

"*Robert?*" she bites out. "Why would he see?"

"Oh, I don't know, Chey?" I almost sob. "Maybe because I'm on national fucking television!"

"Okay." She nods. "Take a deep breath. The game has one minute left, and then we can leave. I promise. But stay for Theo." She stares me dead in the eyes. "You came for *him*."

I take a deep breath and wait for the buzzer to confirm the game is over, then gather my purse and walk out of the seating area. Cheyenne grabs one of my hands, and Alejandra grabs the other, and they pull me until we're standing in front of the locker room. I roll my eyes at them, huffing with exasperation at being intercepted. Cheyenne knows I want to leave, yet she won't let me.

"You're not running away, Bai," she growls at me, squeezing my hand painfully. Alejandra lets go of my other one and walks over to Alicia, who is hanging back a little bit. "Don't be stupid."

"Why not?" I ask with a shaky voice. "He knows I didn't sign up for this."

"Above all, he's your friend." Her eyes plead with me. "Don't fuck him over."

I nod slowly, because she's right.

We stand in silence for a while, and just as I'm about to tell her that I want to wait in the car, a hand wraps around my bicep and drags me inside the locker room, where a dressed Theo presses me against the wall, out of sight from outsiders.

"What the fuck was that, Bailey?" Theo growls, caging me in with his arms, pressing closer against me. "Why were you about to leave me?"

I cringe and close my eyes, breathing in deeply. "I'm sorry," I whisper. "I told you I needed to keep this casual—hence, *friends* with benefits."

"Fuck that." One of his hands cups my cheek, and I open my eyes to see his blue ones brimming with emotion. "I can dedicate my goal to you and still be *friends*."

"Did you not see the camera right on my face, Theodore?" I snap. "Maybe you don't remember much about that night at the hospital with Robert, but let me make this very clear for you. I cannot afford to be put in situations where my location is obvious to him. I was just on National Television, and I bet you anything now he knows how to get to you and me as well."

Theo's eyes rapidly shift as he stares at me and his chest heaves. "Fuck, fuck, *fuck*," he mutters. "I'm so sorry, B. I wasn't thinking...it was just the high of the game. I just wanted to dedicate my goal to you. It was a big deal to me, but it's silly. You're right."

"It's not silly, Theo," I reply, sighing, and his eyes snap back up to mine. The blue of them is getting smaller and smaller as they dilate. "I should've said something before the game, but I didn't know how any of it worked."

"I guess now you know, and so do I. I won't be making the same mistake again," he assures me. "I'm sorry."

"As long as you're not claiming me for the world to see."

Something changes in his demeanor. "You are my girl,

though, Bailey." Theo's hands trail down my body until his fingers dig into my hips, then he cups my ass and squeezes. "Relationship or not—" He pulls me into him, away from the wall, until my front is plastered to his front. Our lips brush, and he nips at my bottom one. "You're fucking *mine*."

I gasp when he bites me again. "Yours?"

"So mine." He smiles against my lips and I kiss him softly. "*Only mine*."

I know I shouldn't like how that sounds, but I do. More than anything, I wish I could give him a chance…a real one. Only trust is hard to come by for me, and I don't know if I'm ready to give him my heart.

"Let's go?" I ask him with a breathy voice, and he nods once.

I walk out of the locker room first, and thankfully, the reporters have cleared out. Cheyenne is still waiting for me, and when I nod, she smiles and walks away. Theo grabs my hand and I follow behind him, trying to make sense of the maze he is pulling me through. Before I can question where he's taking me, we're standing outside right next to his vehicle. He opens my door for me and then joins me in the car.

The drive to his condo is quiet, yet the silence is charged with something else. The air is thick, and I find it hard to breathe when he rests his hand over my inner thigh and squeezes tightly, like he's trying to restrain himself. I feel it too, and I'm tired of waiting for him to give me what I want. If he doesn't fuck me soon—

We pull up to his parking spot, and he rests his head against the seat, his nostrils flaring. But then he gets out of the car and comes around to my side, opening the door. With a hand wrapped around my bicep, he drags me to his front door and unlocks it in a rush. As soon as we're inside, he pushes me against the door and cages me in again.

Heat rushes down my spine as he grabs my ass with both hands and squeezes. His forehead falls to mine, and his nostrils flare. Theo's lips brush against my own, and I reach up and cup his cheeks.

"Do you feel this between us, Bailey?" he whispers, and goosebumps break out on my arms. "I can't fucking breathe when I'm around you. I want you so damn bad."

"So what are you waiting for, then?" I taunt, knowing he's been the ever-respectful gentleman, but if we're going to seal this deal of friends with benefits, he needs to— "Fuck me."

Instead of protesting the way I thought he would, he picks me up carries me through the condo, then throws me on the bed. Theo makes quick work of my shoes and pants, lowering them in one swoop along with my lace panties—okay, so sex might have been on my agenda regardless of the outcome today —then throws them over the side of the king-sized bed.

His fingers dig into my thighs as he spreads them wide, and his mouth descends on me. I groan at the way his tongue twirls around my clit expertly, knowing exactly when to flick, when to swirl, when to suck. He already knows me so damn well it's unfair, and the worst part is that he knows it too. My hips buck off the bed when he sucks my clit between his lips, my fingers finding purchase on the back of his head where the wavy strands of his hair are in disarray.

"Oh, damn." I hiss, *"Theo."*

He smirks, removing his clothes and giving me a full glimpse of golden skin and abs for days. "Now show me that pretty pussy." His blue eyes take me in as I widen my legs for him. "God, I'm gonna fuck you so good."

Fuck.

Theo gets on his knees and crawls toward me, putting his hands on my hips and flipping me over in the blink of an eye. My face gets buried in the sheets and I shove them away, pulling my pillow toward me a little instead. I lift the jersey up to expose myself to him, and he squeezes my hips.

"You're dripping for me, Bailey," Theo groans as two of his

fingers bury themselves in my pussy, curling deliciously as he works me. "Are you ready for me?"

"Yes," I breathe, pushing back on him so his fingers go even deeper. A broken moan floats past my lips as he pulls them out, replacing them with the head of his dick.

"When I fuck you, I'm not going to be gentle, baby," Theo groans as he pushes in an inch, "You're not gonna break on me, anyway."

And then he buries himself to the hilt with a single thrust.

The breath whooshes out of my lungs as he pulls back and snaps his hips forward again, making my body jolt on the bed until my face is buried into the mattress once more. I groan when his hand snakes around and finds my clit, rubbing it in a way that has my toes curling already, and he's barely even gotten started.

Theo pushes me down on the bed until the only thing separating me from the mattress is his hand between my legs, and I push my hips back and forth to get him to start moving.

"Baby," Theo whispers against my ear. "You feel fucking amazing...just like I knew you would. But this? Damn, this is better than any memory."

His hips set a languid pace, one in which the thrusts are long and slow, and it has my eyes rolling to the back of my head when his two fingers continue to rub my clit at the same pace. He's driving me absolutely insane, and I need relief right *now*.

"*More*," I beg him.

"So impatient, baby." He bites the space between my neck and shoulder.

I moan as he hits a spot inside of me impossibly slow, over and over, like a little button begging to be pushed. When my pussy clenches, he rewards me with a moan of his own, and I fist the sheets between my fingers and push back against him.

"Greedy," Theo murmurs against my ear. "Fuck me back, baby. You know you want to."

So I do.

I fuck him back, shifting my hips back and forth faster, moaning into the blankets. But he doesn't let me for long. Instead, he firmly plants a hand on my upper back and fucks me hard and fast. His fingers speed up to the new rhythm, and his hips slap against me so hard my ass is beginning to get sore, but the pleasure he's bringing me makes that insignificant.

My toes curl and my eyes roll to the back of my head, leaving me a panting mess. My sounds echo as Theo makes good on his promise to fuck me, and when he wraps my hair around his fist twice, he yanks my head back.

"If you need to scream, bite the pillow, B."

I bury my face into the pillow, moaning, groaning, and panting. Making noises I never thought I'd be capable of making. But damn is he making me feel good.

My toes and fingers begin to tingle, and so does my spine, all at the same time. He's still rubbing up on that little spot inside of me that's lighting a fire deep within my core, and the way he's rubbing my clit has me seeing stars. But it's when he bites my shoulder again that he pushes me off the edge, and I fall off a precipice so high I can't see the way down.

But right now? I don't even care.

"Yes, Theo," I moan. "Right there, baby. *Oh my God*, yes." I shift my face and bite the pillow, screaming into it as my orgasm crashes into me.

Theo groans. "I'm right…" Thrust. "There…" Thrust. "*Fuck*." Thrust.

His movements become uncoordinated as he comes inside of me, and the little moans leaving his lips are something of fairy tales because there's no way the warm fuzzy feeling coming to my chest stems from sex alone.

No, this feeling is dangerous; if I'm not careful, it could ruin everything. Because there's no way, after all the shit I've talked, that I'm in love with him.

There's no fucking way.

Right?

Except that's exactly what it feels like.

"Baby," Theo breathes. "You're amazing. I l—"

Love you.

No.

"Are you a cuddler, Theo Anderson?" I ask him instead, hoping I'm mistaken and he wasn't about to say those three little words. "Cuddle me."

I look back at his soft smile and my heart threatens to stop in my chest, "I'll do whatever you want me to do, Bailey."

And just like that my heart melts a little more, and it's a dangerous game we're playing now because I don't know how I'll come out of it unscathed.

Theo

CHAPTER TWENTY-THREE

I t has been a few days since the hockey game—since Bailey almost left me behind. She pretended that's not what she was going to do, but I knew. I could feel it. Her eyes told me everything I needed to know, and I could see her flight instincts kicking in when the jumbotron focused on her face.

I'm pretty sure the only one who kept her there was Cheyenne, and for that, I owe her. Maybe I'll get Jeremy to take her out and I'll pay for their dinner. He may tell me nothing is going on between them, but it's pretty apparent that's a lie.

I was surprised to see Bailey standing outside the locker room, waiting for me. But when I took her home, and she demanded I fuck her...I couldn't hold back anymore. I've been trying to prolong the inevitable. Hoping that it keeps her around for a little longer, as if having sex with me will make her tire of me faster. It might be irrational, but it feels like she will eventually lose interest once she gets what she wants from me.

To make matters worse, I almost told her I loved her. I had to stop myself before I ruined everything. However, if her facial expression had been any indication, she knew exactly how that sentence would've ended had I had the guts to finish it.

Which is why I'm so surprised that she pretended nothing

ever happened, and even spent the night. We've had the best time too, spending as much time together as possible before I have to leave for an away game next week. And now here we are, at a planetarium, because I want to take her to experience new things, and she said she had never been to one.

We have already toured most of the exhibits at the Museum of Science, including the planet's exhibit, and are now entering the indoor butterfly garden. Bailey looks like a little girl, and her eyes light up like she has discovered magic for the first time. The sight makes my chest tighten, and I rub at the ache with my hand.

Butterflies make a home of Bailey's hair, perching themselves on her head, and she giggles. But when a giant Monarch butterfly lands on her small, straight nose, Bailey's eyes begin to water. Her bottom lip trembles and she stays very still. They stare at each other for a long moment, and when Bailey's first tear falls, the butterfly spooks and flies away.

I come to her side and put a hand on her shoulder as she frantically wipes under her eyes. "I've heard butterflies represent rebirth," I tell her softly, and she looks up at me with glistening eyes. "New beginnings can be beautiful too, Bailey."

She nods slowly. "They're scary, though."

"You can do scary things." I smile with encouragement, pulling her into my side by her waist, making the butterflies begin to fly in circles around us. Some begin to land on me, too. "You can do whatever you set your mind to."

She gives me a small smile, her dimples making an appearance, and I return it. "If you say so."

After another half hour at the butterfly garden, I all but drag her across the building to the laser dome. I was excited to bring her to the museum because I knew she had never experienced anything like it, but the reason for my own excitement was seeing her face during this experience.

A couple of days ago, I heard her singing Paramore songs in

the shower, and this is perfect because I booked us tickets to the Paramore laser show. I think she's going to love it.

We enter a room full of people, chairs on either side of us already occupied. Some are lying back and enjoying the laser show on the dome ceiling, and I see others lying on the turf-covered ground. The music hasn't started yet, so I direct her to an empty spot on the turf so we can get comfortable.

Once we're comfortable and lying side by side, we look at each other. Bailey smiles shyly as her hand brushes mine, and I grab it and interlace our fingers, holding it to my chest. My heart is beating erratically, and even though the first song is starting to play, all I can hear is the beating of my heart.

Bailey's eyes twinkle when *All I Wanted* begins to play, and she smiles. We break eye contact and stare up at the ceiling instead. The lasers dance around, duplicating and jumping all over the place until it feels like my eyes will cross. They're beautiful, though. They are bright yellow and black in color that goes with the cover picture for the song on Apple Music. I may or may not have been listening to the songs she likes.

When I look to the side, she's already staring at me. She's biting her bottom lip, and her hand tightens in mine. "What do you think?"

"It's beautiful," she beams, and my heart stutters in my chest. "Perfect."

I smile back, mainly since there's no way I can stop myself. This girl has no idea what she does to me. It's unfair. "Do you love it?"

Do you love me yet?

"Yes, I do," Bailey smirks. "How did you know?"

My smile widens because that's all I can do. I hope she can't tell what I'm thinking. She'd run away so fast if she did. "You sing pretty loudly in the shower."

She laughs at this, and I join her. Only her attention shifts quickly, and she goes back to staring at the lasers and listening to the music. Song after song, she stares up and then at me. My breath is shallow every time her eyes land on my face, and I don't know how I'm going to survive her. But I sure as hell want to try.

Her hand tightens in mine, and with a small smile, I wonder what it would be like if she were truly mine. Would it be the same? It already feels like she's mine. I just don't know if she thinks that way, too.

Though I intend to find out either way.

CHAPTER TWENTY-FOUR

Oliver's house is enormous, with its open floor plan and picturesque views of Mount Rainier. There are no walls at all, only floor-to-ceiling windows surrounding the entire perimeter of the home, and while it's unsettling, it's also beautiful. I don't understand why he'd need such a big home for just him and his partner, but I can't deny I'd kill to have a house like this. Maybe in the future, when Theo and I—

No.

You're not ready, Bailey.

I shake my head to clear my thoughts and look up at Theo, who is sporting a closed-off expression while staring down at me. I raise an eyebrow, and he smiles. His straight white teeth are on full display. Sometimes, I forget just how pretty he is with his floppy brown hair, beautiful blue eyes, and chiseled jaw. His full lips purse at me and I grin, squeezing his hand in mine. Just as I'm about to pull away though, he intertwines our fingers.

"Hey everyone," Theo announces as we get further into the house, going through the foyer and past an entry table and mirror, then stopping when we arrive at the living room where they are sitting around on the couches. If I thought his house was big from the outside, it's got nothing on the inside with its spacious living room and state-of-the-art kitchen visible from here. The dark hardwood floors give it a masculine vibe, but one that's subtle. "I brought company."

All heads turn toward us, and I notice it's all the boys plus Alicia and Alejandra. They seem to be best of friends, sitting together and talking animatedly with each other. A pang of jealousy runs through me at the thought of never having anything like that with such a close-knit group.

Don't be stupid, Bailey.

You're not with Theo.

Just friends with a *lot* of benefits.

Like dates and sleepovers and couples shit.

"No grumpy third wheel?" Jeremy asks with a pout, interrupting my thoughts.

I snort, "Not today, Jer."

"What could she possibly be doing if not spending New Year's Eve with us?"

"She's on a date," I deadpan, not beating around the bush.

The guy she's going out with teaches hockey at the arena where she works, so she sees him every day. They've apparently hit it off, and she looked happy to skip out on this party—a little too happy to not see Jeremy. She even mentioned him in passing, saying she didn't want to fight on New Year's.

Jeremy's face contorts and turns red, his jaw dropping. "Who is she going out with?"

"I don't know his name." I shrug. "She just said he teaches hockey at her arena."

"Of course he does," Jer mumbles.

"Alright…" Theo furrows his brows but continues to pull me toward the empty far side of the enormous four-piece sectional—even bigger than the one at his place, but then again, this house is huge. "Where's—" Before he can finish the sentence, the front door opens, and in strolls a group of what has to be at least twenty more people. "Everyone."

Suddenly, my palms sweat, and the overwhelming need to hide is intense. Something about large crowds scares me, and I attribute that to Robert. I never used to be this way, but ever since I left him, it seems like he's just going to pop up anywhere I go.

"I have to—" I take a deep breath, trying to calm down the hammering of my heart, loud in my ears. Letting out the breath slowly, I look up at Theo. "I need to go upstairs. Where's the bathroom?"

"There's one down here, B." Theo frowns, looking around.

"Upstairs." I all but growl.

Theo looks at Oliver, and they seem to have some unspoken conversation because they nod, and the next thing I know, he's dragging me up the stairs. My sweaty hand slips out of his grasp as we ascend the narrow staircase, and my heels are so loud they're giving me even more anxiety. I should just take them off, but I don't want to stop and be forced to interact with the rest of the team and their girls who just arrived. I know logically my ex won't be part of this crowd, but it still doesn't stop me from forgetting how to breathe properly.

He opens a bedroom door, which I'm assuming is a guest room, and shoves me in without turning on the light. I glance around for the bathroom—which there is one in here, thank God—but just as I'm about to head to it, he stops me with a hand wrapped around my elbow.

"Talk to me," Theo demands.

"I—" Deep breath in, slow breath out. "Can't."

The thundering in my ears hasn't diminished, the sweat coating my hands hasn't dissipated, and the need to pop a pill right now is overwhelming. I usually save my anxiety medication for special occasions, but this feels like one. Especially if I want to make it back downstairs before the party is over. His friends are going to fucking hate me if I keep him to myself this whole time—or worse—if we leave early. As in right now.

"Baby," he whispers, pulling me into his arms. He rubs circles up and down my back with soothing hands over my sweater dress. "I'm right here. You're okay."

My breath shudders in and out, and my chest clenches tightly, stealing even more breath from my lungs. It seems that even with my breathing exercises, it's not enough. It's not enough. I *need* my Xanax. "I can't bre—" My chest begins to heave, and then Theo takes me to the bed, sitting me on the edge of it.

"Breathe with me, baby," he demands, and I open my eyes. He puts a hand on my chest and mine on his. "In and out."

I do as he says, focusing on the way he breathes in and out, his heartbeat steady under my hand instead of rapid firing like mine. But the most magical thing happens while I sit here and listen to him, feel him. My heart rate goes down, my breathing slows, and I can take in air again. I don't even feel like I need my pill anymore, and that's saying something. Even with the coping mechanisms I've learned in therapy, most of the time, it's still not enough. Except here comes Theo, who flips my world upside down while simultaneously putting me back together. Every single piece of me that he touches, he mends.

"That's it, B," Theo praises. "You're doing so good."

I gasp in a final breath and grimace. "Thank you."

With my breathing back to normal, he lets his hand drop from my chest. "Do you want to go back down, or would you like to stay here instead?"

"Here," I blurt, cursing myself for being so boring sometimes. "I'm sorry. I know you came here to spend time with your friends. I don't need you to babysit me."

"Babysit you?" His brows furrow, and thankfully, the curtains are wide open, letting me see his beautiful face with the moonlit glow. "You're not a child, Bailey. I came here with you and I'm staying with you. I see my friends almost every day. One night of disappearing from the party won't kill them."

I nod, "Okay."

"Do you want to go home?"

It's my turn to furrow my brows. "No. I don't want them to hate me."

"No one could ever hate you." He smiles softly, trailing his finger down the slope of my jaw to my chin and then tugging my bottom lip. "You're *you*."

"Can you just lie down with me for a little bit?" I ask him, nibbling on my bottom lip. "I mean, you don't have to...I can just take my pill and everything will be better."

"What pill?" he asks cautiously.

"Xanax," I reply. "I take it when this happens. It's not very often, but I usually can't calm myself without it."

"If you need to take it, then do that," he whispers, grabbing my hand and tugging me toward the headboard. I lie down, and he does, too, facing me. "But I'll stay here with you as long as you need." His nose brushes against mine, his lips hovering just an inch away. "Only if you want me to."

I turn my face to get even closer, and right before I let my lips mold against his, I whisper. "Yes, please."

My chest feels tight again as his lips meet mine sweetly, slowly, but it's not anxiety I'm feeling. No, it's something much more scary. *Love.* This man is everything I've ever needed. But yet, at the same time, is also forbidden by my own doing. And I'm tired of it but don't know how to stop. If things were different, I'd jump in head-first, uncaring of the consequences and without fear. But the me that has gone through hell is hesitant. That part of me screams to slow down, that it's impossible to feel love for someone this quickly, even after how well we've come to know each other.

Theo's tongue probes my lips and I open for him, letting him tangle his tongue with mine. I suck his into my mouth, and he moans.

Pulling away, he says, "However long you want me to." And my heart flutters at his words.

"A friend with benefits wouldn't comfort me this way, Theo."

Theo chuckles, coming back for another quick, soft kiss. "You know damn well we're so much more than that," he whispers.

This time, I'm the one who makes the move and grabs the back of his head, bringing his lips back to mine. The moment our tongues touch is like electricity coursing through my body, lighting up every inch of me, and I need to release the energy back to him. I dig my fingers into his shirt, tugging it, hinting at him to come with me. And he takes the hint, getting on top of me as I spread my legs.

One hand cups my cheek while the other trails warm fingers up my hip, moving my dress up slowly. "Do you want this?" he murmurs against my mouth. "Do you want *me*?"

"Yes," I whisper, opening my eyes and looking into his blue ones. They're dilated due to the darkness, and he looks so angelic under the moonlight's glow. "I want you."

"If I bury my fingers inside of you, will you be as wet as I imagine you are?"

"Wetter."

His fingers come to the edge of my panties, but rather than ripping them or taking them off, he just shoves them to the side. He groans when he makes contact with my pussy. "So fucking wet, baby."

Thrusting in and out of me, he curls his fingers deep inside me. I moan at the feeling of his thumb rubbing against my clit, and he takes in a sharp breath when I shove his hand away. "Inside of me," I pant. "Now."

Theo doesn't waste any time. Instead, he unbuttons his slacks and slides his underwear and pants down to his knees, then shoves my underwear to the side again. The head of his dick positions against my entrance, and he enters me inch by excruciating inch. It seems he was serious about being nice, yet all thoughts die a short death in my brain as he stares into my eyes and grins at me. One of his hands grips my hip, and he bottoms out inside of me. We gasp in unison and his forehead falls to mine, his breaths coming out in short bursts. The way he makes me feel makes my chest ache all over again.

He pulls back slowly, all the way to the tip, then just as slowly fills me again. I gasp when he hits that spot inside me, and he speeds up slightly, knowing I need more. Rubbing himself on my clit, he shifts his hips, and I see fucking stars. I close my eyes as my vision explodes into white dots.

"That feels so good, Theo," I whisper. "*More.*"

"Open your eyes, Bailey." He whispers back as I moan, "I want you to look at me when you come."

I wrap my legs around his waist, the angle allowing him to hit deeper, and he gasps. Every sound from his lips takes me closer to the edge, but it's more than that. Those sounds touch my soul, will forever remain in my brain, and will always give me a shot of dopamine. One I didn't even know I needed.

Opening my eyes, I look at his face. At the way his lips are parted and how he lets out yet another gasp when he bottoms out once more. The way his brows are furrowed as if he's in pain, his blue eyes wide. I commit every single detail to memory, hoping I never forget this moment. Because it's right now that I realize, more than ever, that I don't think I can live without this. *Him.*

"*Bailey,*" he moans, and butterflies invade my chest instead of my stomach. The way my heart clenches is everything I need to know about how I feel. One single word has my entire body going haywire. "Tell me you're mine." He pulls back and thrusts back in. "Even if you don't mean it. Lie to me, baby. Please."

I groan at the way his dick keeps swiping against my G-spot, making me clench around him. Then he grabs my chin and pulls my face toward him, forcing me to make eye contact. "I'm yours, Theo."

"Mine," he whispers, speeding up. His hips slap against me, and he moans. "Touch yourself."

Sitting back on his haunches, Theo drags me by the hips and begins to pound into me. My fingers find my clit instantly, and I start to rub it to the pace he's fucking me. Hard and fast.

My legs start to tremble, my back bowing off the bed as the sensations take over my body. I bite my cheek in order not to scream as I feel the orgasm inching its way closer, and my fingers speed up even more.

I'm right there—

"God, baby," He moans. "You drive me crazy."

"Come for me, Theo," I moan as he fucks me even faster. "I'm coming."

My entire body is on fire, eyes blurry as I look up at his face, and then they refocus as I lose my breath. Because staring back at me is the most beautiful sight to behold. Theo falling apart for *me*.

My body trembles as Theo moans, and with a final groan, I come apart. He's right there with me as I immediately feel him spilling inside of me and his hips stutter. When he finally slows down and presses his forehead against mine, I feel at peace. What an odd fucking feeling after living on edge for the last almost eight months.

"How I feel about you transcends everything," Theo whispers.

I search his eyes rapidly and smile, but don't say anything. If I'm not careful, those three little words will slip right out. And I can't let them. Not when I don't know what to do about it. He deserves better than that.

Theo pulls out slowly, and I cup my hand around myself to avoid making a mess and run to the bathroom. After taking care of business, I meet him back in the bedroom, where he's already dressed and put together like nothing ever happened, save for his tousled hair.

"You have bedhead," I say, biting my bottom lip. "Want me to fix it for you?"

"Nah." He grins. "Let them know you're all mine."

I laugh. "You're so annoying."

"You love it."

I love *you*.

Digging into my purse, I take my Xanax, swallowing it dry. He offers me his hand, and I grab hold of it like it's my lifeline. Then, we walk to the door.

"You ready?" he asks as he opens the door.

"Ready," I reply with a smile.

And then we head back to the party.

Only something has changed in the last thirty minutes. When we walked in here, I felt empty, and now I don't. But I realize it's because Theo is holding onto my heart with his bare hands.

Theo

CHAPTER TWENTY-FIVE

I t's been a few hours since we arrived at the cabin in the mountains, and we're already snuggled up on the couch like old people. Not that I'm mad about it. My days of partying are over either way. I just never thought I'd be on a weekend getaway with Bailey, or that she would actually agree.

She didn't even fight me on it, she just said yes. I'll admit things slightly changed between us after the New Year's Eve Party. She turned softer toward me, more relaxed even. I don't know if it's because I almost professed my love for her, or if it was helping her through her panic attack, or maybe even the way I fucked her, but she's _different_. That's the only way I can explain it.

"Maybe we should go outside for a little while before the sun goes down," I tell her, and she pauses the TV. "We still have a few hours left."

"And do what?" she asks, grabbing my hand and holding it between both of hers. It's little gestures like this one that make my heart clench in my chest. I don't know if she returns my feelings or if she loves me, but when she acts this way, it makes me feel delusional.

"I may have already brought some things to pass the time before I picked you up."

"You drove here before getting me?" Her outrage is evident by her gaping mouth. "Are you crazy? It's like a two-hour drive."

"It was worth it." I roll my eyes, "I didn't want to spoil anything for you."

"I like spoilers." She pouts, and the way her bottom lip dramatically sticks out is comical. I smirk as she exaggerates the gesture even more. "Where are we, anyway? Why won't you answer that question?"

"It's my secret spot," I offer. "This cabin is my mom and dad's. It was my gift to them when I got signed. As you can probably tell, we're in the mountains, so that partly answers your question. I just can't tell you where we are because no one is supposed to know about it." Not unless you are part of the family. "Unless you want to be my wife."

Bailey chokes, then hits her chest. Freaking drama queen. "*Oh.*" I chuckle at how flustered she is, but it makes me wonder what it would be like to be married to her. To wake up every single morning with her by my side, make cinnamon rolls in the morning, drink wine, and watch *The Summer I Turned Pretty* or whatever other show she's obsessed with while eating chocolate cake. I could do that for the rest of my life. In fact, I'd gladly do it. "I definitely don't need to know, then."

Damn.

She's a savage.

I just laugh it off, not wanting to dwell on it right now when we have so many other fun things we could be doing. I don't want to spend my time crying; I want to enjoy it with her. Because I'm convinced that, sooner or later, if I spend enough time with her, making her laugh and treating her how she deserves...she'll have no choice but to fall in love with me.

I shrug. "Exactly." Getting up from the couch, I pull her up with me and smack her ass as I walk backward to get dressed in something other than sweatpants. "Now go put a snowsuit on."

"The one you bought me?" She wrinkles her nose. "We're not going snowboarding or some crazy shit, right? Because I hate to break it to you, but I would suck at that."

"Nah, baby." I grin. "We're staying right here."

"Then why put on a snowsuit?"

I laugh at her, and her face heats. Her wide green eyes flare in momentary annoyance at me, but I can tell she's over it quickly because she softens for me again. "Did you not see all that snow when we came in?"

"I'm not blind, Theo," she huffs. "Except why do you want me to go out there where it's cold as fuck?"

"To have some fun, Bailey," I tut. "Have you ever heard of it? Fun? Because I think I need to show you how to do it."

"Fine." Bailey stomps past me and into the bedroom, where I put our stuff. "But only so you leave me alone after this."

"I'll never leave you alone, my little sour patch kid," I call after her, and I can hear her laughing even though she pretended to be mad just a second ago.

After we both have our snowsuits on, I go to the mudroom and gather the supplies I brought with me, along with a snow shovel. As I grab the snow brick makers, the pang in my chest almost brings me to my knees. It's a pain so fresh you'd think I'm reliving her death all over again—my sister's—even though she's been dead for years. But that's the thing: grief is funny. Most days, I feel just fine, but when something reminds me of her, it's as if the pain renews itself in the cruelest of ways.

What I have planned with Bailey is something my sister and I used to do all the time when we were little, back when we went to the Canadian Rockies every single Christmas break. And I guess I want to share that with Bailey too, as well as a piece of my childhood, who I am at my core. I think she'd enjoy it, even if she's not one with the outdoors.

Once I've gathered all the supplies, I wait for Bailey by the front door. It only takes her two minutes to join me, and when she does, she raises a perfectly manicured eyebrow at me as she glances between the snow shovel and my face. Curiosity must get the best of her, though. Seeing as she's staring at the snow brick makers with a little glint in her eye, and now I don't know if this is a surprise at all. Maybe she's done this before, and this won't be our special thing anymore. I don't know, maybe—

"What are those for?" she asks, curiosity dripping from her voice. Suddenly, I'm not worried anymore.

"You'll see." I smile, "You ready?"

"As ready as I'll ever be to freeze my ass off."

I have to give it to her; it really is cold as fuck out here. To be exact, it's seven degrees Fahrenheit. However, we're bundled up with our base layers, a snowsuit, wool socks, snow gloves, and a balaclava with even a beanie over it. I guess you could say we're a little dramatic, but I didn't want her to feel embarrassed for getting cold easily, even if I'm cooking myself in all this shit.

We exit the cabin and go to the back where the yard is supposed to be, but instead, there are just mountains of snow. It's perfect to build a foundation with the shovel, and then we will build the walls together once that's done. I put all the supplies on the snow and turn toward Bailey, who's just standing there watching me closely. Even with the balaclava, I can see the way her cheeks are red underneath it, and she's shifting from foot to foot. I need to get her moving, working, so she doesn't feel as cold.

"Okay, so now, will you tell me what we're doing?" She takes a step toward me, then another. Once she makes it to where I'm standing, she wraps her arms around my waist and looks up at me. It feels so intimate that my body immediately warms to her touch, even at the low temperature.

"We," I gesture toward the supplies, trying to keep my grin from splitting my face. "Are making a snow castle."

Bailey looks confused for a moment, and just when I think

she's going to call me stupid and reject the idea, she says, "I don't know how to do that. Will you at least show me?"

My heart skips a beat, "Of course, baby. That was the plan all along." I pull away from her embrace and bend down to pick up the shovel. "My sister and I used to do this when she was—" I gulp, "alive."

"This was your thing with her?" she asks with furrowed brows. "We don't have to do this. I don't want to steal your special moments with her."

"That's why I'm doing this, Bailey." I grin at her, fighting the tears that want to make their way out of my eyes. I don't know why I feel so emotional. It's just a fucking snow castle. "Because you're special to me. She would approve of this."

I pause for a moment to take her in, watching her stance widen and her eyes squint as she smiles, but when she doesn't say anything back, I just continue.

"Now," I dig my shovel into the snow, "I'm going to build the foundation. See that snow? I'm gonna make walls with it."

"Oh, this is good, Bob the Builder," she jabs. "I didn't know hockey players could also be handy."

I gasp. "Are you making fun of me?" It's actually funny, though untrue. "My dad taught me a lot, and I actually *am* handy, thank you."

"I was just making fun of you." She grimaces. "But maybe it was a bad joke?"

"No, baby," I tell her reassuringly. "I didn't take it seriously; I'm just messing around with you."

Lifting the shovel, I pick it up and throw the snow over my shoulder, then do that over and over until I have some walls built. They're thigh-deep for me, perfect to build on top of them. If I made the walls too low then the bricks probably wouldn't hold. But I have my secret ingredient to keep them frozen for longer—cold water. So I head back to the house, leaving Bailey standing there looking at my masterpiece to get a pail of cold water. When I return and set it down next to her, her brows climb all the way to her hairline.

"Alright, Bailey girl." I hand her a snow brick maker, "It's your turn to help."

"Is this just like building a sandcastle?" she asks skeptically.

"Yep, except this is wet and way colder," I joke, though it's definitely the truth. Filling the brick maker with the snow, I pat it down until it's packed in and show it to her. "Here," I lift it up and take it to the foundation wall, where I set the brick maker on top, and the perfectly shaped brick lands on the wall. "That's how you do it."

Bailey grins, shaking her head. "That's easy enough."

We get to work after that, stacking the bricks until we've shaped the structure into an almost castle, but it's taking way longer than I remember it ever taking. Maybe it has something to do with when I was thirteen, time didn't hold any meaning, or maybe there were more hands on deck.

My dad would sometimes join us when we didn't mind it, but I know he felt special when we let him. Now, though? I don't mind the work. In fact, it's going to make it even sweeter when we finish and have a whole damn castle. What we're going to do in there, I don't know. Probably absolutely nothing if the way Bailey is shaking is any indication. I don't know how she hasn't turned into a popsicle yet.

It feels like hours have passed by the time we're done with the snow castle, and the sun is beginning to set. The chill in the air is even more potent, and now I'm even starting to shiver. I'd bet anything we're almost at negative temperatures if we're not already there. But even still, we plop down in the snow and admire our masterpiece for just a moment. It's definitely not perfect or shaped like a castle, but I wasn't expecting that since it's Bailey's first time, and I wanted to see where she would lead us.

"It's beautiful," I whisper with a smirk, and Bailey throws herself back in the snow and cackles.

"Stop, asshole." She grins at me, her eyes squinting in a way that makes my chest tighter. Mostly because it means she's giving me her most genuine smile. "I know it sucks."

"Actually," I reply, "It doesn't suck at all. Much better than my first time."

"That's because I had your help."

"Maybe," I shrug. "But I'd say you're a natural."

I don't see it when she does it; she's sneaky. Suddenly, a ball of snow lands right on my face, and I shriek. She gets up and begins to run around the side of the cabin, where she's trying to reach the front door before I catch her. But once on my feet, I'm too fast for her, and I grab her by the waist and haul her over my shoulder.

"Gotcha!" I yell with a grin. "Now, let's go get you warmed up."

"Let me down, Theo," she jokes, tapping my ass with her hand as I continue to walk us to the front door of the A-frame cabin, the exterior a black and dark brown that always reminds me of the one in Canada. "Or don't. I have a nice view."

"It's pretty up here, isn't it?"

"I was talking about your ass."

I snort, "Of course you were."

The day isn't over though, and now that the sun is setting I want to introduce her to another tradition. One that we had year after year ever since we built these castles. When I was fourteen years old, my mom taught us how to make her Maple Taffy recipe and told us how she wouldn't be around to make it for us forever. I'm glad I didn't fight her on it because it's moments like these that I'm grateful for the close-knit relationship I have with my parents. Even to this day.

I put Bailey down as we cross the threshold, and we immediately take off our snow boots. Hitting them against the door frame—something my mom despises but is not here to see —I get the snow off, put them inside, and then close the front door. Warmth greets us, yet it's not enough for Bailey. I can still see her shivering as she takes off the wet snowsuit and takes it over to the laundry room, so I busy myself by turning on the electric fireplace and then joining her.

"I have another surprise for you," I tell her as I take off my snowsuit and hang it up on one of the hooks behind the door right next to hers.

"*Another*?" She smiles at me, dimples popping on her cheeks —ones that drive me to the brink of insanity from how cute they are. "What else could you possibly have to show me?"

"Well, this one you eat." I grin.

"Okay, I can get down with that."

"It's going to be quick, too," I tell her, "I just need some more snow."

"You're going to eat fucking snow?"

"Hey, don't knock it 'till you try it." I laugh as we get to the kitchen, and I begin to pull out the maple syrup, a glass measuring cup, and other utensils. "Watch this for me." Pouring the maple syrup into the measuring cup, I put it in the microwave for a few minutes and step toward the front door. "Don't let it burn!"

In hindsight, going outside without shoes and only a glass bowl was probably a terrible idea. In fact, I know it is when my toes start burning as I walk a few feet into the yard. I push through, putting a small mountain of snow in the glass bowl, and then return to the house.

Fuck, now it really is cold.

"It's not burned," Bailey calls out as soon as I close the front door behind me.

"Thank you for watching it!"

I make it to the kitchen just in time for the microwave to announce that the heating is done. Putting the bowl of snow on the counter, I grab mittens and take the maple syrup out of the microwave. Technically, I should've boiled it on the stove, but this way is quicker. And I'm lazy, whatever. My mom doesn't have to find out this is what I've resorted to.

"So now, I pour the maple syrup over the snow like so." I show Bailey, pouring a few lines of syrup over the white powder and it immediately hardens. "Then you grab a stick," I motion to the wooden sticks next to me, "and you roll it until it's wrapped around it."

Bailey grabs a stick and does as I directed, then brings the Taffy to her mouth, moaning as she eats it. "Wow." She beams. "This is so good. Who knew you had it in you?"

"Oh, shut up," I mumble.

Cupping my cheek, she simply smiles. "Thank you so much for today, and for bringing me here."

Hauling her into me with both hands around her waist, I lean down and take her lips with mine. The kiss is soft, and I feel it all the way down to my toes. I pull away with effort and say, "Anything for you."

And that's the thing, though.

I actually mean it.

CHAPTER TWENTY-SIX

When Theo surprised me by bringing me to a cabin, the last thing on my mind was building a snow castle. The vulnerability he showed, however, and the things he shared with me, I'm so glad he trusted me enough to let me see that part of himself. It makes me feel special, and with the way my heart squeezes in my chest every time I look at him now—it's a dangerous way to live.

It's not that I don't want to let myself live this with him. It's that I don't think I have it in me to go through another relationship again. And I know it's my own fault, since I need to work through my shit and get past what Robert did to me. It would not be fair to profess my love for Theo and make promises I can't keep when I can't even trust that he'll keep my heart safe. And that's the catch—I will never trust anyone ever again. I know that Theo doesn't deserve it, and that makes it hurt even more. If it were up to me, this wouldn't have happened in the first place. It would've stayed strictly platonic, only friends with benefits.

Except Theo had to want more, of course. He demanded more from me, and I couldn't say no. Unfortunately, I have a weak spot for him, one that needs to be obliterated. People do really stupid shit for love, and I refuse to go down that rabbit hole.

So, I guess this is me making a promise to myself that if he ever returns my feelings—I'll let him go. He deserves the best, and I'm not it. I can't even come close to giving it to him. It's only fair that I let him find the love he deserves instead of tying him down to one filled with mistrust and pain. If you love someone, set them free—or however the fuck it goes.

It'll hurt me if I leave him, but I'll recover eventually. I'm still wracking my brain about how this will all end. At some point, it *will* end, and I need to be ready for it. One or both of us will inevitably, at some point in the future, be nursing a broken heart.

"What are you thinking about?" Theo asks me softly, breaking me out of my morbid thoughts. "You seem sad."

"Sad?" I clear my throat, because I know I am. "I feel okay."

Liar.

Theo slides forward until his front meets my back, and he tucks me into him snugly. It's been a while since we cuddled in bed this way, and it hurts even more knowing how intimate it feels now that I'm scared to lose him.

Please don't love me back.

"Liar," he calls me out, kissing my neck softly. I extend it, inviting him to continue, but he pulls back. "But I know just what we need."

"What?" I ask, skeptical.

"To go on a hike." I roll my eyes at him and scoff, "Hear me out. I know the cold isn't your thing. Hell, maybe even the overlook isn't your thing. However, there's this beautiful view of a trail that leads to the lake. I think we should—"

"Is there anyone else on this trail?" I ask him, an idea sparking. "Or will it be just us?"

"Us," Theo replies, his cheek coming to mine as he smiles. His scruff slightly scratches me, but I relish it. "Only us."

I perk up. "Perfect. Then let's get dressed."

An hour later, after we've packed snacks, water, and a picnic basket, we're on the trail. This time, for easier access, I'm wearing snow pants and a jacket rather than a snowsuit. If I'm going to hike four miles today, it will be worth it somehow.

The snow crunches under my boots, seemingly having melted from the mountain it was outside just last night. It's a much warmer day though, somehow being forty degrees Fahrenheit now, and the snow does not seem to want to stick around. Not that I want to complain, but this slush mixed with mud is not it for me. Don't get me wrong, there's still plenty of snow. It's just that what's left is getting dirty as hell.

Theo is ahead of me by a few feet, leading the way, and while I should probably be paying attention to the surroundings and pretty view, I'm focused on the way his ass looks in those hiking pants. Because, of course, he'd look good all the time. The man doesn't know the definition of an off day.

"Stop objectifying me." Theo laughs. "I can hear you thinking about my ass."

I choke on saliva. "Excuse me? It's a nice ass."

"I know." He shrugs, then looks back at me. "Come look at this instead, though."

I speed up to reach him, and he finally stops, allowing me to catch up. When I reach the top of the hill, I can see what he is talking about; this is only the halfway point. It's an overlook where we can see the entire town from up here. We can also see the lake, but I'm assuming where he wants to go, you can see it better if wanting to walk two more miles is any indication.

"Wow," I breathe, admiring the view. "This is so pretty."

I wait for him to go ahead of me so I can follow him down to the lake, and he peers over his shoulder at me with a smile that threatens to stop my heart. We hike the next two miles in silence, and it's relatively quick. The terrain is definitely rockier in this part of the trail, so I'm extra careful as I try not to fall on my face.

As we finally descend the last of the trail and into a beach area, my breath catches in my throat. It's so beautiful, with pine trees surrounding the perimeter and the bluest lake I've ever seen right in front of us. We walk to the shore and sit down just out of reach of the water, watching the small waves lap onto the rocky dirt. And this right now? It feels perfect.

Theo grabs the picnic basket and begins to take things out of it: fruits and peanuts, a little bowl of cheese and prosciutto, and a bottle of wine. It's cute, and even in the cold weather, I'm enjoying myself.

"So, Bailey," Theo starts, taking a chug of wine straight from the bottle, and I laugh. "Where do you see yourself in five years?"

"Is this an interview?" I joke, but he just smiles at me expectantly. "Ugh. Fine. I don't know."

"How do you not know?" He furrows his eyebrows. "Do you never think about the future?"

I shrug. "I try not to." It's true. I don't like to think about it. "My hope is to find a new specialty I'll be happy in. I just don't know what that is yet."

Theo passes me the bottle of wine, and I chug it too, relishing in the sweetness of it. White wine. My favorite. "What about marriage? Kids?"

I choke on the wine, coughing and sputtering. Once I've regained my bearings, I croak out, "Never thought about it, but I bet it's not in the cards for me. What about you?"

Theo looks pensive for a moment, then looks right into my eyes. "I could see myself doing the white picket fence and shit for the right person." Then he looks away and at the water lapping close to our boots. "Why can't you?"

"I think I'm just...damaged, Theo," I say softly, as if he won't hear me if I speak low enough. "It's just hard for me to trust people."

He sighs, "I mean, it makes sense." I nod, even though he isn't looking at me. "I just wish you trusted *me*."

A knot forms in my throat, and I clear it once to avoid

sounding like I'm dying when I speak next. "It's not personal, Theo." I chuckle under my breath and this time he looks at me. With tears in his eyes. Fuck. "It's just really hard for me."

"I understand," is all he says.

But I know he doesn't.

He couldn't possibly.

And now I'm just hurting him.

"I hope one day you let me in," he continues. "We could have something really special, Bailey. I think I'm—"

"I think," I interrupt before he can say something we will both regret. "We should go."

Theo looks stricken, but instead of arguing, he nods. We put everything back in the basket and head back to the cabin to gather all of our belongings. There's a silence between us that pains me, and I know it pains him too. If the look on his face is any indication...I know he's hurt. Deeply. I know that he's breaking his promise; to break it off if he has feelings for me.

I'm lost in my thoughts all the way back to his condo, and when we get there, I jump in the shower—alone. And I'm lost in my thoughts there, too. For as much as it hurts him, it hurts me as well. Regardless, I know what I have to do.

I have to break our hearts.

It's for the best.

CHAPTER TWENTY-SEVEN

I t's been a few hours since we got back to my condo after the lake. We couldn't stay another day since I have to leave for an away game tomorrow, but we made the most of our time at the cabin. Now, though? Bailey is acting weird as fuck. I made a mistake—almost professed my feelings for her. But she stopped me, and after thinking it through on the drive here, it was probably for the best. Everything was perfect up to the lake, and then once I screwed everything up, she started shutting down. I could sense it, shit, I could even see it. The way her entire demeanor transformed before my eyes. From happy—ecstatic, even—to somber within minutes.

How the hell do I fix it?

And now that we're lying in my bed for the last night together for the next week, I can't even make up for anything I could've done wrong. *I don't have enough time.*

Bailey sits up in bed, looking at me, then gets up and walks out of the room. My heart starts thundering in my chest, but I debate if I should follow her. For just one moment, I hesitate. Is this going to hurt? Will she leave me? What's wrong with her? I don't know the answers to any of these questions, so like the masochist I am, I get up from the bed and chase after her.

Maybe this is the wrong move, and I should give her the space she needs to gather her thoughts, but I can't stand the thought of having hurt her somehow and not knowing. That's why I get up from the bed and wait a minute before going out to the living area, giving her time to do—well, I don't know what.

"Bailey?" I call out from the hallway. "Are you okay?"

When I round the corner, Bailey is sitting at the kitchen island with a carton of ice cream between her hands and eating right out of it. My shoulders instantly drop in relief, and I join her on the bar stool right next to hers.

"Fine," Bailey mumbles, but it seems forced. "Just have the munchies."

Liar.

"Mind if I join you?" I ask her, and she immediately hands me the spoon. When she turns her face toward me though, my heart freezes in my chest. Bailey's face is red and blotchy, with tears trailing down her cheeks. "Baby?"

A sob rips from her throat. "Sorry." She swallows hard. "I'm fine."

"Don't lie to me, B," I beg her, then get off the bar stool and face her. "You can tell me anything."

"I don't want to." Bailey bites her bottom lip into her mouth as it trembles. "I don't want to hurt you, ever."

"Why would you hurt me?" I ask her, but I know deep in my bones what she's trying to say, and I won't let her. Goddamn it. I will *not* let her ruin this. "If you don't want to, don't do it."

"It's not that simple, Theo," Bailey whispers.

"I'm done with this," I tell her, and she sobs harder. I grab her from the chair and carry her over to the couch, bridal style, where I drape her over my lap, and she buries her face into the crook of my neck.

"Can we just cuddle and watch TV?" she asks me, and I nod because I can't deny her anything.

"Okay," I answer before grabbing the remote and searching for a movie. "Is this one good?" I ask her.

"It's whatever." I picked one called *Look Both Ways*, which is seemingly a comedy.

Bailey remains on my lap, watching the movie with me, and when I grab her hand she holds it tighter than usual. Like she's afraid to let go. Everything inside of me wants to reject the notion that she'd leave me, but something tells me she's about to hurt me so fucking bad I'll never recover. I don't understand what I did wrong. I've given her everything, all of me. Every single part I have to offer, and it's still apparently not good enough.

The irony of this movie isn't lost on me, though. And the longer I watch it, the more I think I should've never picked it. It's about what this girl's life would be like in two completely different scenarios. And both of them are happy. What if Bailey starts to think she can be happy without me? That's terrifying. The thought of losing her forever is heart-stopping. I don't think I could ever recover.

Even though the movie really is funny, neither of us laughs one damn time through the first half. I don't think there's anything that could take away the deep-seated fear within me other than her. I wouldn't think twice if she turned around right now and said that she made a mistake and wants us to be together. I wouldn't question her. I'd move on from this. Because this pain? I wouldn't wish it on anyone. And while she hasn't said it yet, I know it's coming. I can feel it deep within the marrow of my bones, the fucking *heartbreak*.

Bailey's sniffles draw my attention back to her, and she buries her face in the crook of my neck once more. My entire body tenses, poised for a fight, and when loud sobs begin to rip from her body, I hold my breath. My head starts to spin, and every sound she makes breaks my heart a little more, knowing she's battling with herself over whatever decision she's going to make. She's clearly in pain, but I know she's going to go through with it the moment she stops crying.

Just rip the Band-Aid off, Bailey.

"Theo—"

"No." Don't rip it off. I change my mind. *Don't fucking do this.* I shake my head, pushing her away so she can look at my face. "You listen to me. Don't fucking do this, baby. *Don't* you *dare* do this to us."

"I don't have a choice."

"And why is that?" I ask her, but I don't give her time to reply before saying, "Because you're scared of what we have? Because you know we're great together, and that fucking terrifies you? Well, you won't get off that easy, B. I'm right here. Don't do this to us. I *want* you."

"Wanting me isn't good—"

"I *love* you." My voice cracks with every word, feeling the rejection coming.

Instead, she's silent.

"No," she whispers, shaking her head. "You can't love me, Theo."

"But I do," I sniff, tears streaming down my face. "I love you *so* much."

"Don't say that!" she sobs, getting up from the couch and pacing in front of me. The rejection doesn't just sting; it stabs me deep within my battered and bruised heart.

I get up from the couch and stand before her, reaching out until my hands wrap around her shoulders. Tears stream down both of our faces and I shake my head. "Tell me you don't love me, Bailey. But if you say it, you should mean it."

Bailey takes a deep breath, "I'm sorry, Theo." She shakes her head, too. "I can't give you what you want. I'm—broken. There's something wrong with me, and I *can't* love you the way you deserve."

"Can't or don't?" I ask her. "Never mind. Don't answer that." I take a deep breath and walk away from her, running a hand through my hair. "I can decide what I deserve, Bailey. And what I deserve is you. In my life. Waking up next to me every day and forcing me to watch the *Summer I Turned* fucking *Pretty* because it makes you happy. Or feeding me molten chocolate lava cake because it's your favorite. Going with me on hikes because it makes *me* happy." I wipe tears from my face, "And I'm not going to just give up on you, baby, because you're special. What we have is special. We deserve a chance, please don't do this."

"I don't feel the same."

One sentence shouldn't shatter my heart the way it does, except I swear to God I can hear it breaking, echoing in my ears.

I don't feel the same. I don't feel the same. I don't feel the same.

"You, Bailey, are a *liar*," I say through gritted teeth. "You think I haven't noticed the way you look at me? Half fucking blind with love? Or the way you search for me in a room full of people? Like I'm the only one who exists for you? Well, you're it for me. Stop lying to us, to *yourself*. You love me too."

"I don't, Theo." However, I see the way her lip wobbles, how more tears stream down her face. If she didn't feel anything, she wouldn't be this distraught. It wouldn't hurt her as much as it does. "And I have to go now."

Without waiting for me to reply, Bailey goes to my bedroom to probably gather her belongings, but I don't go after her. I stay rooted to the spot, trying to figure out what to say or do to get her to stay. I'm not above begging. I'll get on my knees right fucking now. I don't give a fuck. But will that be enough? *Probably not.*

A few minutes later, she's back in the living room with her weekend bag and her shoes in hand. She sits on the couch to put them on slowly, like it takes effort, and that's when I see her hands trembling. She's not as unaffected as she pretends to be, which gives me a semblance of hope. *I love you, Bailey, please.*

"Baby," I whisper, and she peers up at me. "Please, please, don't go."

I walk to her place on the couch and get on my knees, sliding between her legs until I can hug her waist and put my head on her lap. Her hands automatically come to my hair, her fingers running through my strands, and I sob harder. I can't lose her; she's part of me now. It sounds so fucking dumb to say, but if she goes, she's taking a part of me with her. One I'll never get back. Which is why I can't let her walk away. Not yet. Not when I haven't had any time with her.

I haven't had enough time.

"Shhhhh," She cries. "Don't cry, please."

"You love me," I tell her, trying to convince her, or maybe myself. "You have to. I've given you everything."

"I know." Her fingers scratch at my scalp and I close my eyes. "I'm sorry."

"I don't want your apologies," I whisper. "I just want *you*."

"I'm so sorry, Theo." My heart fissures even more. "One day you're going to meet someone who makes you happy, someone who turns your world upside down. The sunshine in your life."

"I *already* have."

"Don't say that, Theo." Another sob rips from her. "This hurts me a lot."

"Then don't do it." I tighten my arms around her waist. "We can forget this happened. Let's go back to bed, and I'll never bring it up again. I swear, I'll forget about it."

"No." Her fingers halt in my hair and I almost sob again. "I can't do this to you."

"Please don't leave me, Bailey."

"Don't make this harder than it needs to be," she cries, pulling at my hair so I can look at her. "You deserve the best things in life, and that's just not me."

"I'll do anything."

Except she doesn't listen. Instead, she pushes me away and gets up from the couch, gathering her bag and walking toward the door. "I'm sorry," is all she offers my broken heart.

"Stay, Bailey," I call out, and she stops, turning around to gaze at me. *"Stay with me."*

"I can't."

And just like that, she walks out the door, leaving me to fall onto my hands and knees on my living room floor—alone. *Always* alone. I wish I could say that I can get over this and her in a few days, but that woman has marked me. She's written her name into my heart, carved it into my soul.

And I don't think I'll ever be able to erase her.

CHAPTER TWENTY-EIGHT

M y chest feels as if it's on fire as I run to the car with my bag hiked up on my shoulder. I never thought seeing a vehicle could make me feel equal parts relieved and yet repulsed with myself. What the hell did I just do?

Oh, yeah. I ruined the only good thing in my life. And the worst part is that I know this is the end of the line—there's no coming back from this. I could see it on his face when he begged me to go back to bed. There's no taking this back. The thing is, I really, really want to now. I wish I could turn around and knock on his door, tell him it was all a mistake, that I didn't know what I was saying, and go back to bed safely in his arms. I could bet my life that I'll never feel what I do for him with anyone else.

God, I'm so fucked up.

I knew Robert screwed me up as a whole, but I never realized just how much until now. The deep-seated trust issues are probably never going to go away, are they? I'll never be normal again, will I? I'm convinced this is the truth, so I need to hear from someone I know will support whatever decision I make. Even though I know it was the wrong one. She's always there for me. Always.

Cheyenne.

My feet slap the concrete as I run faster, the pain coming from the heels radiating up my legs, but my car is finally visible, so I slow down slightly. Looking down, I see the blood on the back of my feet from not wearing socks with my stupid Vans. Of course, this would happen to me; I might as well have just gone barefoot. Either way, I push through because I have to, ignoring the pain and closing the distance between myself and my piece of shit vehicle. You know what would be the cherry on top? If it didn't start.

I unlock the car door, and when my hand wraps around the handle, I hear the telltale sign of the elevator opening and then a choked "Bailey" coming from it. I cover my mouth to hide my sob and get in the car, reversing as fast as possible, forgoing my seatbelt and any measure of safety in my haste to get out. It doesn't even matter though, because if I died right fucking now it would be the perfect way to end my pain. Maybe I'll get lucky and get T-boned on the way out of the parking garage.

Don't think that way.

Theo wants you safe.

Fuck that. Theo doesn't want me safe anymore; he wants me gone. It doesn't even matter that he came after me. That when I look at my rearview mirror he's on his knees in the middle of the road, his face in his hands. I know that defeated feeling will only last so long before the hate sets in, as it should. Because I freaking deserve it. More than anything, I know that.

I can't handle it—not with everything I feel for him in return. So I speed up and leave him behind. I go faster until I can't see him at all, until the little picture in my rearview mirror is all but a figment of my imagination. At least that's what I'm telling myself to survive this. Because if I focus on how much I hurt him, even *I* am going to hate myself.

The fact remains that I do return his feelings, which is why I have to step back. It sounds really stupid, but I can't get hurt again. Not the way I already was, where my heart was ripped out from my chest and stabbed with a kitchen knife. I won't survive it if that pain is directed at me from Theo. And that false feeling of safety that crawls up my spine when we're together, I need to crush it. Because it's not fucking real. Nothing good in this life is. I can't even pretend to trust him or anyone else, and I'll always be looking over my shoulder, wondering if I'm safe from Robert. If he'll come back and disturb my life the way he already has. Fuck, he already knows where I work, which probably means he knows where I live. Even where my Theo lives.

Not yours anymore, stupid.

I don't have answers as to why I am the way I am. Why I hurt him and will continue to hurt any man who gets close to me. I think something died inside of me when Robert mutilated me. Some vital organ—my heart, I believe—just stopped functioning. The thing is though, I felt it start to beat again when Theo came into my life, so what the fuck is my excuse now? I'll never have a reason for the shit I just pulled tonight.

Thankfully, the drive to Cheyenne's is not that long, and before I know it, I'm pulling into the parking space next to hers. Ever since we moved here, I've had the remote to open the gate and keys to the apartment, which comes in really handy on nights like these, not that I frequently break up with people. Is it really a breakup if we were never a couple?

You know better, Bailey. You were so much more than that.

I run out of my car and up the concrete stairs to the second floor, ignoring the pain in my heels, and jam the key into the doorknob roughly. My palm meets the door as I push it open, and I slam it hard enough to hopefully wake Cheyenne. I just don't have it in me to call out to her. Oh, never mind, yes, the fuck I do.

"Chey!" I roar. "Cheyenne, please, I need you."

Sobs take over my body, controlling every limb, and I hear more than feel the crack of my knees as they meet the hardwood floor. The pain in my chest is unexplainable, and I imagine this is what it feels like to have a damn heart attack.

"What's wrong?" Chey asks, her sleepy voice coming from her bedroom door. "Babe?"

"I—I—" I sob harder, the knot in my throat not allowing me to talk. "Hate myself."

"Shhhhhh." Suddenly, her arms are wrapped around me, and I don't even notice when or how she got to my side so quickly, but it doesn't matter. "Don't say that. What happened?"

"I *left* him."

"You left who?" A male voice comes from Cheyenne's doorway, "*Who*, Bailey?"

I look up to find Jeremy in the doorway, in his boxer briefs, and I glance rapidly between the two of them. I thought they hated each other, that they couldn't even stand to be in the same room. I thought—

"I told you to stay in the room, Jer," Cheyenne growls. "Go back. *Now*."

"Hell no, *honeybun*," he tells Chey. "I'm going to my fucking friend, just like you are right now."

"Oh, fuck," I whisper, overwhelmed by everything that's going on. Maybe it was a terrible idea to come here. Now Jeremy is going to go to Theo and tell on me, say that I'm distraught and barged into Cheyenne's apartment, not myself. "Please, don't do that."

"You have some balls, Bailey," Jeremy growls as he goes back in the room. "Sadly for you they're not big enough to make me betray my friend."

"I'm not asking you to betray him!" I call after him, trying to get up from the ground and out of Cheyenne's embrace. She just holds me tighter. "Just don't tell him I'm here, crying, please."

Jeremy comes out dressed and with a bag in his hand. "I will tell him whatever I want, Bailey." He takes a deep breath and looks me in the eyes. "He's probably more devastated than you, anyway," he replies with disgust, "*You're* the one who broke his heart."

"Jeremy!" I wail when he goes to the door and opens it, but he stops. "*Please.*"

"You made a big fucking mistake, girl." He shakes his head as he looks ahead. "I hope you know what you just did."

Then, after he exits the apartment, he closes the door behind himself. And Cheyenne? She does not say a word, seeing as she knows what Jeremy said is true. *I think I made a mistake coming here.*

"What the fuck was he doing here?" I ask Cheyenne, needing to break the silence and, more than anything, direct the conversation away from me while I recover. Not that I ever will. He's totally right. "I thought you hated each other."

"We *do*," Cheyenne replies with a shrug, but I can tell she's lying now. Damn, how could I have been so blind? "Now tell me what happened with you, and stop trying to change the subject."

I wipe tears from my cheeks, but they just keep coming. It's useless. *I am.* "I—" My phone dings repeatedly, and like the masochist I am, I pull it out of my back pocket.

THEO

I fucking tried. Good luck with everything. I can't do this anymore.

My hands shake as I read the messages and almost drop my phone. But no matter how much it hurts, I can't give him hope. I won't do that to him or us, knowing I'm never going back.

BAILEY

I'm so, so, sorry Theo.

THEO

Just know if you don't come back today…
don't come back at all.

My stomach drops, knowing he's serious. This is also exactly what I wanted to accomplish. For him to never want to talk to me again, so I'm not tempted to beg on my fucking knees for another chance.

BAILEY

I won't. Feel free to turn off your location. You don't owe me anything.

Even if I recognize we both did it so I would feel safe, he no longer has to take care of me. I don't know why he wanted to in the first place.

Oh, yeah, because he fucking loves me. Great.

THEO

If that's what you want.

BAILEY

Goodbye, Theo.

And just like that, I let the phone clatter to the ground, my splattered heart going right with it.

Cheyenne looks at me for a beat, then grabs my hand and pulls me up, leaving my phone—and heart—behind on the ground. Settling on the couch should feel comfortable, but every part of me hurts, down to my fingertips. Is this what it truly feels like to have a broken heart? What the hell was I feeling for Robert? Because this pain…I've never felt it before. Not even when I was stabbed.

"It hurts, Chey." I gasp out, clutching at my chest. "Everything hurts."

"I know, babe." Cheyenne's face mirrors pity and sympathy,

and my heart clenches in my chest at the ugly emotions rearing their heads. "Just cry it out."

She pats her lap, and I go down with her, resting my wet face on her bare thighs. She doesn't seem to mind though, and at least I have that going for me, someone who genuinely cares about me enough to let tears and snot run down their skin for the sake of helping me feel better. Not that I ever will.

"Tell me what happened."

My sniffles and gasps are the only sound in the apartment as I attempt to get my emotions under control, unsuccessfully. The sound of my heart is so loud in my ears that I genuinely don't understand how it hasn't stopped beating. Surely, losing Theo would be enough cause to make it cease. But no, I'm *that* unlucky. I get to live with myself after this, regretting every ounce of pain I've caused him until the day I die.

"I—" Deep breaths, Bailey. Where is my fucking Xanax? I swear the tightening in my chest must mean another panic attack. "Left him. He said he was in love with me, so I had to go. I know it makes no sense, Chey, but I can't give him what he wants. What he needs. Fuck, what he *deserves*."

"And what is that?" Cheyenne sighs, running a hand through my hair. "What could you possibly not give him that someone else could?"

"Trust," I reply with finality. "*All* of my trust."

"It takes time to trust after what happened to you, Bai," she tells me softly. "You went through so much, and if you've explained it to him—I'm sure he understands."

"We were only supposed to be friends with benefits," I groan, running a hand down my face to wipe away as many tears as I can. "Falling in love with him wasn't supposed to happen."

"So when did it turn into more?" she asks me, her hand halting in my hair as her phone begins to ring. The call is rejected.

"I don't know!" A knot the size of Texas lodges itself in my throat, and I cough it out. "He wanted dates, and sleepovers, and—"

"I hate to break it to you, Bailey." Chey chuckles sadly. "But you were *never* friends with benefits. You were *dating* each other."

"No." I shake my head adamantly and get off her lap to face her. For whatever reason, the blue of her eyes is deeper today, and now I'm thinking of Theo's blue eyes instead because I can't ever stop thinking of him. God, when will I ever stop? Is it even possible now? "I was very clear."

"Were you also *very* clear with your heart before you fell in love with him?" she asks, her face serious. "Or was it only after?"

"I was clear, Chey!" I yell, then sob. My shoulders shake, and my abdomen clenches painfully with the force of it, and the tears just won't stop—

"Oh, babe," Cheyenne whispers. "It's okay. You're going to be okay."

"No, I'm not," I snap. "I've never felt this way before, Chey. And I've never hurt this way either. I'd rather let Robert stab me a million times over than live like this."

Cheyenne reaches out, pinching my chin and directing my gaze to hers. "Don't you dare ever fucking say that," she growls. "You don't get to leave me."

"What do I do?" I cry out, "How do I stop this pain?"

"The same way you stopped your pain with Robert," she affirms. "You move on." My stomach drops at the suggestion, and I tighten my fists until I feel the crescent marks on the palms of my hands. "You pick yourself up, go back to work, and lose yourself in it again. But if that's not what you *really* want, then you go back to his condo and get him back right fucking now."

"I can't, Chey." I laugh, "I fucked it up all the way. There's no turning back. He said so himself."

"He didn't mean it, Bai." She shakes her head like I'm stupid. "He loves you. He wants you back."

"If only it were that easy."

"It could be if you just get the hell out of this apartment and go to him. Tell him how much you love him, that you made a mistake, *that you weren't thinking*, Bai."

"Maybe I just need to think about this, Cheyenne," I snap. "What it would mean for me, for my carefully crafted fucking life, to have someone who cares about me to this degree." Taking a deep breath, I loosen my hands and turn to look at her once more. "What if he gets jealous, too? What if he hits—"

"He would *never* do that, and you know it," she snaps. "Don't taint him like that just because you're scared. Don't make him out to be a monster when you know he is *not*."

"You're right." I nod. "You're right."

Cheyenne is right because I know deep in my heart he'd never hurt me—not in a million years. No matter what happens, I know I have a safe place in Theo Anderson. I'm just the stupid one who let go of it, my safe harbor. And now I'll never get it back.

"Don't be stupid, Bai." Cheyenne bites her lip into her mouth. "Go get him back."

"I have to think about it, Chey." I shake my head, knowing how hurt he is. There's no way I can mend his broken heart right now. He needs a moment to himself, without me. "I really fucked up, and I need to figure out what I want for myself before involving him again."

"You're right. It wouldn't be fair to him to fuck this up again."

I yawn, then slap a hand over my mouth. My eyes feel heavy from all the crying though, and I'm a wreck. I just want this night to be over. "Can we go to bed?"

"Are you sure you wanna sleep where I just—"

"Don't say it." I sigh and roll my eyes, "I'm fine on the couch."

But because she's Cheyenne, she lies down on her side behind me and cuddles me. This is why she's my best friend. She's always here for me, no matter what. The person who lifts me up, who is my shoulder to cry on, who is my hand to hold.

"Let's sleep, Bai," she whispers. "Tomorrow will be even longer than tonight."

Goddamn, is she always right?

Theo

CHAPTER TWENTY-NINE

We're playing Vancouver again, and it's the perfect time to make that asshole pay for benching me. The boys may have said he got his teeth knocked out, but it's not enough for me. I'm fucking him up if it's the last thing I do. And that's why when the puck sails toward me, I ignore it.

Instead, I grab him by the jersey and slam him into the boards—hard. With only one minute on the clock and us being tied, I'm hoping the team pulls through, but it doesn't even matter right now as I rip the helmet off the guy who hit me upside the head with his hockey stick.

My gloves come off, but I keep the helmet on to protect my head. It's a cheap move, but all I feel is peace when my fist connects with his jaw and I hear it crack. I hit him again and again, and he clutches his face, pushing me away. I let him and watch him skate away with what's probably a broken jaw.

The sense of satisfaction I feel is unmatched. It's not lost on me that this is the first time I've felt anything close to happiness since Bailey walked away from me.

The horn blows, signaling that time has run out, and my teammates look at me with disappointment on their faces. We lost. And it's all my fault. My shoulders hunch with tension, but it's due to their defeated expressions. I don't feel guilty at all, and that's even more messed up, because I'm usually nicer than this. I usually wouldn't pull something this selfish, but lately, I haven't been caring about much. Not when I can't feel anything other than devastation.

Just not over this. Fuck hockey, it's just a damn game. Yeah, it might be my livelihood, but nothing will ever compare to the helpless feeling of watching someone rip your heart out of your chest cavity with their bare hands. Is this why she left me? To avoid feeling this again herself? If so, then I don't blame her. This sucks. But I would've never done that to her. I would've protected her heart with everything I had. Not that it matters now since I won't get the chance to.

Just thinking of going back to the empty life I led before her makes me want to throw up. I don't think I can do it; pretend she never existed. It's just not in my chemistry to forget about her. She's engrained herself into my very cells, taking them hostage like a fucking virus. And I don't want to get better. I'd do anything for the sickness. Being in love sucks. It might just be the worst thing that's ever happened to me because I've never felt it to this degree before, and it really hurts when it's over. I'm not sure how long it'll take me to recover, but if tonight was any indication, I probably shouldn't be on the first line.

We go back to the hotel room, and there's a silence between Jeremy and me that I don't like. But I don't know how to break it. I don't even know what to say. So I do the only logical thing —I stay silent. Until he decides to talk to me.

"It's okay, T." Jeremy sighs, his brown eyes closing. "You're gonna be okay. Trust me when I say she's not worth crying over."

I wipe my tears, chugging more Jameson straight from the bottle. "She is, and that's the problem. We connected, Jer. We really did, and it's not that simple anymore. I know this broke her too."

Jer frowns, "I have to tell you something."

"Yeah?" I ask him, taking another sip of the whiskey.

"I may or may not have seen her the other night."

I sit up from my slumped position on the bed, and the whiskey slightly shakes in the bottle, threatening to spill over. I could care less if I'm covered in it, though; it fits the vibe I'm emanating. "What the fuck did you just say?" I ask through gritted teeth, ready to break his.

"She went to Cheyenne's house while we were fuck—"

"Don't lead with that. As for being in Cheyenne's house, I'll take a rain check on that conversation, just know it's coming." I take a deep breath in through my nose, then exhale slowly. "What was *she* doing there? And why didn't you tell me this that night when you came over?"

"I—um." He runs a hand down his face. "She was distraught. Bailey was screaming when she came in, begging for Chey. She fell to her knees, crying her eyes out. So know you're not the only one hurting."

"Why the fuck," I growl, "didn't you tell me this?"

"That night was about you!" Jeremy stands up from his queen-sized bed and begins to pace back and forth in front of my bed, pissing me off further, if I'm being honest. There's a wildfire running through my veins, and he just keeps stoking it with every word coming out of his mouth. "Not her. I was fucking pissed, dude. That she'd do that to you. That she'd hurt you in that way. But let me just say that while I know she's hurting, I also know she has no intention of coming back. At least, that's what Cheyenne said to me this morning."

My heart drops, mainly because all hope has slithered and died with those stupid words. *No intention of coming back.* "I know," I whisper. "I told her not to."

"You did *what*?"

"To make the story short, I told her that if she wasn't going to stay, to not call me ever again. That we were done."

Jeremy grips his hair with both hands, which is a sign of the frustration I'm feeling, except triple it, and he's still nowhere close to what I'm actually going through. "Why the fuck would you do that if you don't mean it?"

"I do." I nod once. "If she can't stick by me, I don't need her."

"The fuck you don't." He shakes his head and pins me with a glare that makes his eyes seem even darker—black, even. "Look at you, T! You're a walking corpse. You're just as bad as when your sister died."

I flinch, mostly because he's not wrong, which just makes me feel guilty. "Listen, Jeremy." I sigh, "She doesn't trust me with her heart, and now *I* can't trust her with mine. She didn't just break it; she destroyed it."

He nods, because what else is there to say? He knows I'm right. Jeremy can see how broken I am. We've known each other for many years. He's been there for me since before my sister died years ago, and he's been my D-man since then, too. We've been inseparable since we were paired and put on the same line.

No one on this team knows me better than him. And right now, he knows there's no repairing me for a while, in fact, maybe ever. I thought that Bailey and I had a shot. Hell, I was hoping to be the end game. But clearly, we weren't ever on the same damn page. As soon as I professed my feelings, she bolted faster than a lightning strike.

"I don't blame you." He returns to his bed and sits on the edge of it again, snapping his fingers in a signal to hand over the bottle. I do, nearly falling off the damn bed in the process because I'm *sloshed* as hell. "Except what are you going to do if she does come back, begging you to be with her again?"

"We were never together." I shrug, my turn to signal for the bottle. I chug again, savoring the burn in my esophagus as it makes its way down. "And now? I don't want to be."

"You're kinda being heartless, T."

"Fuck that." I laugh, but it sounds bitter even to my ears. "She ripped my fucking heart out and stomped on it. If Bailey had cared about me even a little bit, she would've never done that."

"So what was the alternative?"

"Being with me, Jer!" I yell, getting up from the bed and stumbling immediately. I right myself, trying to keep my balance, but it's useless, and I fall back on the bed, sitting at the edge of it. "Letting me into her heart was the alternative. Only she didn't want that. And I'm not about to get played."

"I hope you know what you're doing, man."

"I do," I lie. "Let's go to bed, please. I'm fucking exhausted."

Jeremy turns off the lights, further giving me the space and time to think—time and space that I know I don't need right now. Although maybe it's necessary to drown in the pain, if only so I don't go back to her when she comes begging on her knees. I have a feeling she will when she realizes this is the biggest mistake of her life. It truly is, but maybe *my* biggest mistake was letting her in to begin with.

Bailey

CHAPTER THIRTY

I t has been two weeks since I broke up with Theo, and my world has never looked more bleak. The only person holding me together is Cheyenne—as always. She decided that I was working myself to the bone and demanded that I take time off so we could go on a trip together. Outside of Washington State. Where I don't have to worry about anything anymore. So, like the good friend that I am, I switched my shifts around and traded with other people so I could have the weekend off. I'm definitely going to regret it later, but I know I need it right now. I need to put myself first for once.

This trip is the perfect time to contemplate my choices and to think about what I want out of life. To *really* sit and think about it. And I know Cheyenne will demand I do it, and then she will help me through it too. I personally don't like to think much about the future. It scares me. But I need to make some serious decisions; unfortunately, they involve that.

I've realized that not only am I not happy with my life, but I've clearly made a mistake. I just don't know how to fix it. I feel like I'm too late. The truth is, I wouldn't forgive me either. I've been an asshole, and I doubted him. I didn't trust him. I all but tossed him aside. I didn't mean to. I wasn't thinking clearly, but it doesn't matter because I fucked up.

Since running from Robert, I've told myself I wouldn't let anyone else in—to protect myself. Mind, body, heart, and soul. It's not that I'm scared someone will break my heart again. I'm more scared that I will attract the same kind of man as him. I'm afraid that someone will slither into my life under the pretense that they're madly in love with me, just to turn around and start the vicious cycle of violence. I'll believe it for a while, that they're in love with me. But then, after the apologies, I will feel empty, and I will be. My cup was always running low with Robert; it was never half full, just dry. And his apologies? They were never real.

I know Theo is different though, logically at least. But it's hard to not only trust another man, but also trust myself enough to make coherent decisions. It took me years to get out of my relationship with Robert, and I only did it when I was left with no choice. So what the hell makes me think I could make responsible decisions for myself? The answer is that I don't trust myself to do it. I also don't know that I would leave a man with red flags, because clearly I'm color blind if I stayed with that asshole for that long. But Theo? He's green flags all around, and while I know that, I think it's even scarier than if he was a walking red flag.

Cheyenne grabs my cold hand, squeezing it and interlacing our fingers as we walk the trail at Rocky Mountain National Park. We decided to come to Estes Park, Colorado, for some views and rest, but resting is the one thing I'm not getting to do. She wants to explore, and of course, it involves the outdoors.

"Don't be a whore, Bai," she all but growls, tugging me closer to her side. "We're not leaving. The trail is less than a mile."

"But I don't want to keep walking anymore." I pout, and she rolls her eyes. To be fair, we've been on three different trails today, and this is the easiest one. I'm just tired. I want to go back to the hotel.

"Bear Lake Trail is the easiest one in the whole park."

"I want to sit." I pull away from her, jump on a giant boulder, and sit on it. My feet hang off it, close to the water, and I face forward as she sits beside me.

The views are picturesque, with the lake in front of us and all the pine trees around us. We're deep in the forest while at the same time being so close to civilization. It's beautiful, but as I sit here in silence, I realize I wish I could share it with *him*.

"I fucked up, didn't I?" I whisper, and Chey gets closer to me until she rests her head on my shoulder.

She hums. "You know you did." I nod slowly, and my eyes sting with unshed tears. "The question is: what are you going to do about it?"

"I don't know," I reply immediately. "I don't think he wants to see me again, and I don't blame him."

If only I had stayed when he begged, we could've saved each other so much pain. My biggest regret is knowing how he got on his knees for me and pleaded, but I didn't listen. I was too blind and scared to see what was right in front of me—the best thing that's ever happened to me.

I don't know how we got here, but I know the exact moment I fell in love with him. Watching *The Summer I Turned Pretty* and eating chocolate cake. I should've told him then and never kept him in the dark. I should've told him I was scared too, instead of disposing of him like trash. There's a lot I should've done differently, and none of it I can change now.

"There's only one way you can find out if he will see you or not." I sigh as she nudges me. "You have to talk to him."

"I'm scared."

But is this what I want? What I truly want? To live in fear for the rest of my life? Or can I put the fear aside for a moment and let myself experience life again? Let myself love again?

"Love is always terrifying," Cheyenne replies softly, and I

fist my hands on top of my knees. "And it's okay to be scared… but then you have to think about what you really want and conquer those fears. What do you want, Bailey?"

"I want to be brave," I whisper as tears trail down my face. "I want to be happy even if it hurts me."

Cheyenne nods.

"I want *him*."

Those words bring light into my life once more, but not only that, I do physically feel lighter. More free. Like what has happened with Robert still hasn't given him power over me. I have a man in my life who loves me, and I'm done being scared of loving him back. *I'm freaking done.*

It doesn't matter that Robert has ruined me in more ways than one, that I've been running from men since I ran from him. Because Theo took me in, grabbed a hold of my battered and bruised heart, and decided that he'd somehow put it back together. And he did.

"I have an idea, but you're going to have to be open-minded." Chey says, and I turn my face to look at her. She's grinning, and I narrow my eyes. "Say you'll have an open mind, Bai."

"I'll have an open mind." I roll my eyes but smile.

"You're going to go knock on his door, and you're going to beg on those pretty little knees for him to take you back."

I frown, "And if he doesn't?" She scoffs as if that's the most ridiculous thing she's ever heard. "What then? I embarrassed myself for no reason?"

"If he doesn't, then you offer a trial period." Cheyenne seems to be winging this, or maybe she's given it deep thought. I don't know. She's not even hesitating. But she sounds insane, as usual. "Seven days to prove to him that you're sorry."

"That sounds…like a good idea." I nod slowly. "But what would I do?"

"Oh, baby." She sighs. "You have so much to learn."

I chuckle and push her. "So what? You've groveled before?"

"Nope." We laugh together, because damn I don't see her on her knees for anyone. She's too much of a brat. "But men have groveled for me. And it's pretty satisfying, I won't lie. Now, you have to put your pride aside and do it."

"Ugh." I shake my head. "I think my pride is long gone, Chey."

"Good." She claps. "Then it won't be hard."

"I miss him."

"You guys were disgustingly in love." Cheyenne huffs, but she's smiling, her blue eyes crinkling. "It was so obvious. Of course, you miss him. But Bai, I hate to break it to you—there's stuff in your life you need to change before you can go back to him."

"Like what?" I frown.

"You need to be happy too. With yourself." I'm clearly confused, because she continues, "Have you considered cutting back your hours?"

I smile because I haven't told her what I did. In the past two weeks I've been away from Theo, I've done a lot of self-reflection. I realized I was not happy with my job, and while I haven't cut back on hours yet, I applied for a different position —a different specialty. I don't know how it's going to go, and I'm scared as hell, but I have to take a leap of faith and hope that it's amazing. Because it's definitely what I need right now. So, even though I've never spent time around children, I made a trip to the cancer ward and read them a story. I wanted to do something that reminded me of Theo, and surprisingly, I actually loved it. I think there's a soft spot in my heart after all, and for the first time in eight months, I felt like a good nurse again. Someone who cared about patients, someone not so cold anymore. So, I took the leap of faith that Cheyenne always mentions, and I applied. I have an interview on Monday, and I think I'm going to get the job.

"Yes," I reply. "I've applied for a different job. And I don't plan on working the way I have been since I moved here."

"That's huge, Bai," she squeals and wraps her arms around me, warming me slightly from the chill in the air. "Have they called you back yet?"

"I have an interview soon." I smile.

"Tell me all about it."

So I do. I tell her about the job, and then I tell her about all the other ways I'm going to change my life—for myself.

And for him.

Bailey

CHAPTER THIRTY-ONE

S tanding in front of Theo's door has never felt so daunting, and knocking on it has never made my heart race the way it is right now. I can hear it thundering in my ears, and I take a deep breath to try to steady myself. It's proving difficult, and my breath hitches in my throat when he opens the door slightly with narrowed eyes, only his face in view, hiding his body behind the door.

Is he naked?

With someone else?

Did he already move on?

Oh, shit.

"What are you doing here, Ms. Thomas?"

Since when are we on a last name basis? My eyes fill with tears as I clear my throat. Only there's no sympathy on his face; it's still hard as stone. Unwavering. His eyes are cold and detached. "I came to apologize."

He laughs. "You're two weeks too late."

"Please, Theo." I put my hand on the door and push slightly. "Let me in. Please."

Theo narrows his eyes again, but steps aside to let me in. Instead of acknowledging me, he turns and walks toward the couch. He's shirtless, and with his shoulders bunched up and his body tense, his muscles ripple in his back as he moves. And then he sits, legs spread wide like he's commanding the room. He gestures for me to get on with it, and I take a deep breath, walking toward him and stopping right in front of his bare feet.

"Theo, I'm sorry." I hold back tears, taking a deep breath. Emotion clogs my throat, and I speak past the lump in it. "I want you back."

"I knew you were going to do this." He chuckles. "I don't know why—but I just knew. That you were going to break my heart, and then realize that I'm good for you. Then you were going to regret it and come back. But none of it was real to you, Bailey. You just dumped me like trash. So you know what—no. You hurt me too much."

"Theo, please." This time, tears stream down my cheeks. He's being so cold, and it's so unlike him that it's like a punch to the gut. I get on my knees in front of him, my hands on his thighs right above his own, and when I feel his skin against mine, it's like a zap of electricity running through my body. But he pulls away too quickly, forcefully even. "You've changed my life. I see it; I always have. I was just too scared to take a leap of faith and—"

"And now you aren't?" He chuckles. "Bailey—"

"You loved me when I couldn't love myself, Theo. And for that, I'm grateful. It opened my eyes to the fact that I need to believe more in myself so I can believe more in you. I'm doing the work, baby. I've applied at the cancer ward—"

"You did *what*?"

Emotion flickers in his eyes, something like sadness.

"You opened my eyes." I take a deep breath. "You showed me I needed to change it. I went back to the cancer ward and spent time with those little kids. And it was life-changing. I wanted a new specialty, remember? Something that would make me happy? And I found it there that day. They gave me the job yesterday."

"Congratulations." Theo clears his throat. "That's great, Bailey."

"Please, Theo," I beg him, hugging his waist, my tears soaking his sweatpants. He doesn't touch me, but I can feel him breathing heavily against me. "Please forgive me."

"No, Bailey."

"Give me seven days." I pull away and look up at him. "Seven days, and I'll convince you that this is real. That's all I'm asking for."

"Seven days?" His brows furrow. "I don't know, Bailey—"

"Please?" I beg him, *"I love you."*

This is a crucial moment—the one where he makes his choice: Stay or leave, break my heart all over again, or put it back together.

Theo's eyebrows shoot up to his hairline, but he doesn't move. "Say it again."

"I. Love. You." His brows furrow, and his lips thin. "I love you so much." I smile, but it turns wobbly. "I'm so sorry I hurt you. I never should've left. When you told me to come back to bed, I should've—I'm sorry. I really am, baby. *Please* forgive me."

"And if I do?" he asks me quietly, tears brimming in his eyes. "If I forgive you, then what?"

"That's up to you." I glance down, fidgeting. "If you forgive me…we can be whatever you want."

"Anything?" There's hope in his voice, and I peer up at him again. "Whatever I want?"

"I'll do anything you want." My bottom lip trembles, and I clamp it down between my teeth, fresh tears spilling down my face. "You're everything to me, Theo."

"So start right now."

"Right now?" I ask him, stunned. "W-what do you want to do?"

"Whatever it is you were going to do to convince me."

I smile, "Go get dressed for the cold."

Fifteen minutes later, we're standing in front of my piece of shit car, and I hold my breath as he opens the driver's side door for me. Even when he's pissed off at me, he can't help but be a gentleman.

"I'm sorry about my car," I tell him, grimacing.

"What about it?" He frowns, clearly confused.

"It's not fancy like yours." My lips purse. "It's kind of a piece of shit."

"What did I tell you about me already?" He asks with a sigh. "I don't care about material things like you think I do. Sure, I drive a nice car, but I have an image to uphold. I don't splurge on unnecessary things. That's not how I was raised. And your car? It has never bothered me or embarrassed me. I don't feel any type of way about it."

I nod slowly, forcing myself to believe him and smile. "Get in, then."

The drive is silent as he stares out the window, not once looking at me. His body is tense, and the air in the car is thick and hard to breathe. The silence is killing me, but I don't fill it with nonsense. He clearly doesn't want to interact with me right now, not in this confined space. I can't say that I blame him. I know I've hurt him, that much is clear. He has purple bags under his beautiful blue eyes and looks like a shell of himself.

I did that.

Regret turns my stomach, but I don't have much time to think about it as I arrive at the skating rink. He looks over at me with confusion, and I give him a small smile, pulling into a parking space. Cheyenne said I could free skate whenever as long as I give the lady at the reception desk her name, and I'm going to take advantage of it right now. She has thankfully given me private lessons, and I've improved a lot in the last few weeks. I guess that's what happens when you're not working six days a week. You have time for self-care. Now, I wouldn't say skating is my favorite thing to do, but it's growing on me.

"What are we doing here?" he asks softly.

"I'm giving you lessons." I shrug, my cheeks heating.

"*You*," He laughs. "Are you giving *me* lessons? Bailey—"

"Oh, hush, Theo." I roll my eyes. "I know I suck, but it will be fun."

"Alright." He grins. "Let's see what you got."

After speaking with the receptionist and getting skates, we're finally on the ice. I'm no longer wobbly, and I stand on steady legs. When I glide, Theo's eyebrows rise. I skate toward him, stopping just in time before colliding with him, and he grins.

"*Wow*, you really did improve."

"I wouldn't say I'm the best." I shrug and wink. "Although I'm pretty close."

"Definitely close." His smile is wide as he looks at me, and for the first time since I got to him this morning, he seems happy. There's a twinkle in his eye that wasn't there before, and I turn around before he sees me getting emotional.

We skate side by side for a while, not close enough to touch, and yet I crave it. So I do the only logical thing—I close the distance between us and grab his hand, interlacing our fingers. He leaves them loose, but when I squeeze his hand, he returns it, tightening his fingers.

My heart stumbles in my chest, and it takes everything in me not to throw myself into his arms again and beg him to forgive me. But this is nice, this is fine. I can live with how things are right now as long as there is a light at the end of the tunnel.

Music begins to play from the speakers—Beautiful Things by Benson Boone—and I get in front of him and attempt to skate backwards by moving my butt from side to side. This makes him laugh, and he throws his head back as he does it. It's like music to my ears, and I want to wrap my arms around him and bury my face in the crook of his neck. I want to feel his body against me as it vibrates with his happiness. I want him to be mine again. Mine and only mine.

"Dance with me, Theo." I grin when he looks at me, and he shakes his head. "Please?" I pout.

"Fine." He sighs, and I give him my hands. He begins to skate backwards, probably to keep me from falling, and I chuckle. "But I'm leading."

We skate around in circles until I'm dizzy, and when he wraps his hands around my waist and pulls me in, my face resting against his chest as he glides backwards, I inhale deeply and smile. His scent has haunted my dreams for weeks, and now that I have him in my arms again, I *never* want to let him go.

So I don't. And he doesn't pull away, either.

My heart hasn't felt this full in a very long time.

CHAPTER THIRTY-TWO

Bailey made good on her promise.

She has taken me on three dates—once to the skating rink, once to eat street tacos because I love them, and then to watch _Elemental,_ a kid's movie. I won't lie, it's been hard for me to forgive her, but the more time I spend with her again…the more I miss her. She still makes me feel warm inside and gives me butterflies whenever those green eyes are on me. And that's hard, especially since I want to forget about what happened so badly, but I know she needs to work for it if she wants us to move on from that. I'm giving her those seven days she requested, yet I don't know if it will be enough.

After those dates though, I've been away for out-of-state games the whole week. During this time, she has communicated with me every day through text messages and video calls, even waking up earlier before work to speak with me. I can see the effort she's making, and it hurts my heart the way I'm treating her. A little cold. Not as bad as when she first came to my condo and begged for my forgiveness, but still unlike me. I wish I didn't have to, but I can't just forgive her this easily and move on from it. I have to have a shred of dignity, even if it kills me.

I gather my bag and descend the steps of the private plane, following my teammates. Once I reach the car, I exhale roughly and run a hand down my face. I'm supposed to be going to Bailey's place right now, but the last thing I want to do is spend time with her. I don't want to be around her and hold back from kissing her, touching her, feeling her body against mine. I'm weak for her, and I'm afraid I'll cave if I go there now. Except I'm too curious. I want to see her space, her plants, what makes her—well, her.

Before I know it, I'm pulling into a parking spot right next to her car. I turn off the engine and just sit here, contemplating leaving. But I made myself a promise to see this through. I need to give myself this chance. The last thing I want is to wonder *what if* for the rest of my life. And that's why I get out of the car and head up the steps, then knock on her door. My hands shake as she opens it, but the bright smile she gives me is blinding, and it immediately relaxes me.

"You coming in?" she asks after a long moment of me standing there and staring at her and the open door.

I clear my throat, "Yeah, sorry." I step in, and I'm immediately hit with the aroma of food. "That smells amazing." My stomach growls loudly and she laughs.

"Don't worry," she says with a chuckle. "It's almost done."

I glance around the place, and I can't believe she lives here. There's water damage and mold, and I know it can't be healthy to be exposed to it. But then again, she knows that yet I also know she's stubborn. But even with how fucked up it looks, she has made it her own. There's a small kitchen across from a queen-sized bed, the duvet a soft sage color that reminds me of her eyes. There's a long dresser that spans the length of the wall next to her bed, and the surface is filled with plants. She wasn't joking when she said she had a lot of them—it's basically a garden in here. But there's nowhere to sit, nowhere to eat. If she were with me, if she lived with me, she wouldn't lack anything.

But I shake those thoughts out of my head. I can't think about that yet.

Bailey frowns, "Do you hate it?"

I smile, "I could never hate anything that belongs to you." She smiles back, and my heart squeezes in my chest. "But where do I sit?"

"The bed, silly."

Bailey grabs my hand and pulls me toward the bed, and I sit down. She goes right back to cooking the pasta, and I just watch her. She's wearing sweatpants and a long T-shirt. *My* T-shirt. It says Seattle Sailors on the front and number ninety-eight on the back. Fuck, it looks good on her. It would look even better with nothing underneath, with her thighs spread wide open for me as I fuck her.

"So, how was your trip?" she asks me as she continues to stir the meat. She's trying to make conversation—*small talk.*

"Fine," I answer, then mentally slap myself when she turns around and raises an eyebrow at me. I can't just sit here and give her one-word answers. *It's awkward, Theo.* "It was uneventful. I slept the entire way."

"Of course you did," Bailey mumbles, going back to the food.

"How was your shift last night?" I ask her with a smile, but she's not looking at me.

"It was good. I'm just tired." She turns around and walks toward the bed, and it's now that I notice that she's not wearing a bra. I swallow hard and look up at her face, trying not to notice every little thing about her. Except I'm failing. As if she knows exactly what I'm thinking, she grins. "Those kids are giving me a run for my money."

I chuckle. "I bet they are."

"But it's worth it," she says. "I love it there."

"That's good, Bailey." And I mean it. I'm happy that she's happy. She definitely needed a change of pace, and I won't lie, it makes me feel warm all over that she chose those kids. "I'm happy for you."

"Did you guys win?"

"Nah." I shake my head. "We lost pretty bad. The other team had a shutout. We've been playing like shit for a few games now."

Guilt flashes in her eyes and I look away, not wanting to hurt her feelings. The truth is, I've been playing like shit ever since she walked out of my condo all those weeks ago.

"I'm sorry," she replies softly.

"So, this is a lot of plants. I guess you weren't lying." I smirk. "Do you really name all of them?"

"Yep." Her eyes light up as she points at them. "See those tags? They say their names so I don't forget them."

"Wow, that's dedication." I chuckle. "They're pretty, though."

"I got you one." She grins, going to her dresser and pushing one to the side. "It's a love fern."

"Bailey—" I laugh, "What the hell is a love fern? I'll kill it."

"Then you'll be killing our love for each other." She shrugs. "It's from a movie I like."

"Of course it is." I chuckle, and she's suddenly in front of me, standing between my spread legs. She looks down briefly at my crotch, and I know she can see something when a little twinkle appears in her eyes. I'm wearing gray sweatpants, and I know she loves them. "Bailey…" I warn, my nostrils flaring. I only have so much self-control.

"What?" The innocence in her voice is feigned, and she grins. "Food is done," she tells me as a timer goes off.

Bailey brings the food to us and we sit on the bed, sprinkling the pasta with parmesan cheese. I eat quickly, like a man starved, even though I ate about three hours ago. But I eat constantly, whether it's a snack or a meal. She looks at me and seems amused by how I'm devouring her food. Hopefully, she takes it as a compliment because the spaghetti is delicious, and eating next to her on a bed is not as bad as I thought it would be.

It took a lot to bring me here, and I don't take it for granted. Maybe I need to be a little softer for her. She's trying so hard. She hasn't even brought Cheyenne here. Her best friend doesn't even know where Bailey lives. Yet here I am in her space, eating dinner on her bed as she wonders if I'm judging her and her living conditions. If she can afford it or not. And I'm definitely not judging her. I just think she could have it better. She could be with me, and I'd give her the world. If only she had let me.

When we're done eating, I gather our dishes and wash them. It's the least I can do since she fed me, and she doesn't have a dishwasher. So I put away her leftovers in Tupperware and finish washing the pot and pan. Before I start to pull away from the sink, as I dry my hands, I can feel her body heat behind me. She plasters herself to my back, and I can feel her hard nipples grazing me.

Bailey rests her head against my back, wrapping her arms around my waist. I close my eyes, hating her proximity. Because I want her so fucking badly it hurts. I attempt to take deep breaths to calm the erratic beating of my heart, but it's useless. And as her hands go underneath my shirt and she palms my pecs, my nostrils flare. It's taking all of my self-control to not shove her toward the bed and fuck her.

"W-what are you doing?" My voice is hoarse as she lightly rakes her fingernails down my torso, all the way to the waistband of my sweats.

"Please, Theo," she whispers. "Give me a chance. Just one more."

My eyes open once more, and they sting. Fuck, I don't know if I can take much more of this. I *need* her.

I turn around to face her, and she takes a step back. But when she sees my unshed tears, she steps closer and cups my face with both hands. I avert my gaze, refusing to show her my pain, except she squeezes me once with a request to look at her.

And I do. Her eyes are brimming with tears again, and my heart aches. It fucking *hurts*.

"Can I kiss you?" She asks me softly. "Just once. If you're not going to give me a chance, at least give that much to me…please?"

My hand cups her jaw, and then I slide it to the back of her neck. Bailey tilts her face up for me, and I bend down to capture her lips with mine. The first press of her lips against mine sends sparks flying inside of me, and I groan when she parts her lips for me. She takes my bottom lip between hers and sucks hard, and I feel it all the way down to my dick.

Fuck.

I bend down and pick her up, my hands on her ass, as I carry her and drop her on the bed. She looks up at me as I crawl across the bed and over to her, settling between her spread thighs. And then I devour her mouth properly, grinding myself against her pussy, feeling pure bliss envelop me.

I kiss her for what feels like hours.

And because seemingly I love pain, I also hold her all night.

Theo

CHAPTER THIRTY-THREE

T he hospital is cold as we enter the kid's cancer ward. It's always cold in here, and it reminds me of when my sister used to be in a similar place. I wish things could be better for these children, that they had more than they do here. Some never leave their rooms since they are too sick to get out of bed, and others are alone and don't have anyone to leave the room with. The nurses are busy and can only do so much. It makes me sad to come here, but Bailey and I want to do something nice for them today.

We enter through the double doors that protect this floor from strangers and stop by the nurse's station. The nurse from a few months ago gives me a warm smile, and I smile back and nod. Bailey grabs my hand and pulls me into the station, and my feet falter when she squeezes me. All eyes are on us as we walk toward them, but the moment Bailey clears her throat, they all smile. I have no idea what's happening, but they seem to know something I don't.

"Hey," Bailey says to the ladies. "This is Theo. My boyfriend."

I choke, coughing for a moment, and straighten my spine.

What did she just say? Did she really introduce me as her boyfriend?

"Hi," I rasp out, and they chuckle.

"This is Haley, Anne, Felicia, and Sarah." Bailey points at each individual person as she introduces us, and I give them all my biggest smile. Maybe they won't mind if I come visit, considering my girlfriend—apparently—works here.

"Nice to meet all of you," I reply, since it's easier than speaking to each of them.

They look at me with smiles on their faces, and Bailey then pulls me toward the recreation center. She must have called ahead because there are kids already sitting there in a circle of chairs. There's recliners everywhere, IV pumps, and chemotherapy infusions running. I smile at them as we make our way around the kids and to the front of the room, where there are two chairs and books stacked on either side of them.

Some of the kids recognize me from the last time I was here, and when their eyes light up, and they say my name, tears burn the back of my eyes. Fuck. I get so emotional every time I come here, and it only makes me miss Courtney more. But I push through the pain because, at the end of the day, these kids deserve to have someone here for them. To care for them and about them. And even though I couldn't do that for my sister very often when we were younger, I can do it now. She would want me to. I think she'd be proud of me.

Bailey and I spend hours with the kids; it's her day off, after all, and she looks happy. Happier than I've seen her—probably ever. It suits her. She reads a book about snails to the kids, and I read one about penguins. They laugh every single page at the voices I'm reenacting, and it makes me smile. I want them to feel joy. I want them to feel less lonely than they are. It's probably unrealistic considering their situation, but I'm gonna try like hell to make it happen.

Right before it's time for us to leave, she sings the kids a lullaby—and she's atrocious. However, no one complains or says anything mean, instead they look at her like she's just hung the moon. There's a three-year-old with neuroblastoma that just breaks my heart. She's wearing a face mask so she doesn't get sicker. But Bailey? She treats her like that little girl is the most special person on this earth. And it makes me emotional, because I know she'd be an amazing mother. I want those things with her. I want everything with her.

We say goodbye to the kids, and they're all sad to see us go. I'm sad, too, but I know if Bailey and I can work things out, I'll be coming here more often, especially during her shifts, since she'll be too tired on her days off. We walk out of the hospital hand in hand, and I open the car door for her. We're returning to my condo for the first time since she came back to me, and I'm nervous.

Will it be awkward? Will we be able to go back to how things used to be? Is she going to want to spend the night? And if she wants to, will I let her?

The drive back is filled with talk of the kids from the cancer ward. Everything feels normal between us, and it's scary. It's not that I don't want things to go back to the way they used to be, it's just that I'm scared she'll break my heart again. I think it's a valid fear, but I'm tired of it. I *want* to be able to trust her.

At the end of the day, she has done everything she said she would. She has spent more than a week proving to me that this is real...that I matter to her and that she loves me. And I never said it back. She introduced me as her boyfriend, for fuck's sake. It was everything I'd ever wanted.

I pull up to my parking space and sigh. She looks at me curiously, but I get out of the car before she can ask me what's wrong. I open her door and she grabs my hand, making my stomach flip. I'm still not used to her initiating public displays of affection. I don't think she would've done this a month ago, but here we are.

As soon as we arrive at the condo, I sit on the couch and bury my face in my hands. I feel her presence in front of me, and when she puts her hand on my shoulder, I relax slightly.

"We need to talk," I say softly, removing my hands from my face.

Bailey kneels in front of me, tears in her pretty green eyes. She shakes her head at me as one tear trails down her face. "Please, Theo. At least let me say what I need to say before you break my heart."

I brush my thumb over her cheek, capturing the wetness, and nod.

"I know I hurt you. But I have to tell you that I want you in my life, and I'll do whatever it takes to make it happen. I want you to be mine. I love you, Theo. And I'm going to love you without guarantees. I'm going to choose you right now, even if I don't know what's going to happen in the future. I'm going to choose you every single day. I'm ready to try life with you. *Please*, Theo."

My heart begins to pound in my chest, my blood whooshing in my ears, and I feel my eyes sting. She wants me, *really* wants me. And after all this time…that's all I've ever wanted. So, without hesitation, I grab her hand and put it on my chest, right over my heart.

"You feel this? It only beats for you, Bailey. Every second I spent away from you…it felt like I was dying a slow death. Like I was suffocating, and I couldn't breathe anymore until you came back. I don't just love you. You're the air in my lungs, baby. I need you to survive. So yes, Bailey. I forgive you."

Bailey gives me a shaky smile, and I pull her up to me, letting her onto my lap. She cups my face with both hands, leaning in and capturing my lips with hers. The kiss is slow, and I can feel the emotions pouring from her. She pulls away, kissing my jaw, then my neck. She lingers, sucking on my skin, marking me. It feels possessive, as if she wants everyone to know I'm hers, and I grin.

"Baby," I breathe as she gets on her knees between my legs. "What are you doing?"

"Taking care of you."

Bailey removes her shirt, throws it behind her, and then unbuttons my jeans. I help her out by lifting for her so she can take them off, and she giggles as she struggles to get them under my ass. I take a long look at her as she comes back to me and does the same with my boxer briefs. And once I'm bare in front of her from the waist down, I relax back on the couch. My dick is hard now, standing at attention, and I grin when she looks at it and licks her lips. She's wearing a red and lacy bra—completely see-through—and my mouth goes dry as I stare at her nipples through the fabric. As if she knows exactly what she's doing to me, she takes it off and reveals her breasts to me. They're full and perky, her nipples small and rosy, and I groan.

"So take care of me, Bailey." I smirk. "Show me how sorry you are."

Bailey's hand comes to my length, stroking slowly as she wraps her lips around the head of my dick, licking my precum. I moan when she takes me to the back of her throat and swallows, and when her throat constricts from her gag, I fist her hair.

Fuck, she's so pretty on her knees for me.

"Come here," I tell her, but she gets up instead. She finishes taking off her clothes, stripping off her pants and underwear, and standing in front of me completely bare. My breath hitches, and I let it out slowly. "You're so beautiful."

She walks back toward me, straddling me, and I grip her perfect ass in my hands as she grinds against my dick. She lets out a breathy little moan, and I feel her wetness against my cock. It's driving me crazy, and I don't want to wait anymore. I get up from the couch and carry her; all the while, she's kissing and biting on my neck until I take her to my bed and drop her on it.

I stare at her for a long moment as she spreads her legs,

revealing her glistening pussy to me. I remember how tight she is, how she grips me like a damn fist every time I'm inside of her, and my balls tighten. My nostrils flare as I take her in, dark hair fanned over my bed like a damn halo, chest heaving as she fists the sheets, her full lips parted for me like she wants my dick in her mouth. I bet she'd let me again, but I want her pussy too bad to consider it.

"Come here, Theo," she whispers, her hand trailing down her abdomen all the way to her pussy. "Let me show you how much I love you, how bad I want you. Let me show you how I can't live without you."

My breathing picks up and my blood whooshes in my ears at those words, and I walk slowly toward her until my thighs meet the edge of the bed. Bailey is a work of art, and I want to be inside of her as long as possible, but if she keeps looking at me with those siren eyes, I'm not going to last very long. As I climb onto the bed and settle between her thighs, I forget about all my thoughts. All that matters is her. All I see is her. All I feel is her.

I thrust two fingers into her pussy and she cries out, rocking her hips toward me, taking them to the hilt. I curl them, hitting that sweet spot inside of her, as I circle her clit with my thumb. Her sweet moans fill my ears, and I grit my teeth as I pull my digits out and suck them into my mouth. She looks at me with uncontained lust and love, and all my feelings rush to the surface.

Fuck, I love her.

"Ready, baby?" I ask as I crawl up to her, putting my arms on either side of her head. She nods, gripping my shaft, and I groan. "Put me in."

Bailey does as she's told, holding me against her entrance, and I push in slowly. Inch by inch, I fill her up, and we both moan in unison when I bottom out. I thrust in and out slowly at first, then pick up the speed until my balls are slapping against her, the sound of skin on skin loud in the confines of my bedroom.

Her lips are parted, her eyes closed, as I grind against her clit and she whimpers. The sound makes a wave of heat rush down my spine, making my balls tighten and my dick thicken even more. I'm so close to coming it hurts, the heat of her pussy gripping me and making my eyes roll to the back of my head. But I breathe through the urge and continue to grind against her until she screams, her legs wrapping around my waist tightly as she comes.

"God, Theo," she moans. "I love you so much."

"Such a good girl," I whisper against her lips, sucking the bottom one into my mouth. "*My* girl."

I speed up, thrusting faster, focusing on the feeling of Bailey's wet pussy wrapped around me. The tingling feeling rushing down my spine doesn't take very long, and suddenly I'm filling her with my cum. I pull back and watch my dick going in and out of her, biting my lip as I pull out. I focus on the way my cum drips out of her, and my breathing speeds up all over again.

"You're so damn beautiful, Bailey," I rasp. "I love you."

Our eyes meet again, and she bites her lip. "I want forever, baby. Do you want that with me?"

"Always," I tell her, and I mean it.

"Will you be my boyfriend?" she asks me, and my heart skips a beat. It's one thing for her to introduce me that way, but the fact that she's asking me fills me with butterflies all over again.

I grin. "I'm so much more than that."

She grins and I get up from the bed, grabbing a wet rag to clean her. After wiping her gently, she looks at me with so much adoration my legs threaten to give up on me. But I just pick her up and take her to the bathroom, setting her down so I can run her a bath.

"Are you coming in with me?" she asks softly, and I nod because I would give her anything.

"If that's what you want."

She smiles and climbs in, and I settle in behind her. We just sit there and soak in the burning hot water, talking about the future now that we have one.

It's everything I thought it would be.

CHAPTER THIRTY-FOUR

Morning skate is early today, but I'm not complaining since I'll be done just in time to get Bailey from the hospital and take her out for breakfast. I skate up to Oliver—our goalie—and shred the ice with my blades, raining ice onto his face just for fun. He glares at me because it's an asshole move, so I just grin and shrug. It's all playful, and he knows it.

Ever since Bailey and I got back together a few weeks ago, I've been in a better mood. My boys can tell too, considering they tell me every chance they get.

Did Theo get his dick wet this morning? Did the pretty nurse come back?

I could go on and on about the bullshit they spew, but I'd be here all day. I have been open and honest about what happened though, without giving too many details. Just as simple as things didn't work out between us, being that she didn't want a relationship back then, and now she does. The only one who knows the full extent of the situation is Jeremy—as always.

We single-file off the ice and go back to the locker room, taking off our gear and getting ready to shower. I'm pushing it on time a little bit, so I take the quickest one of my life and return to my locker, where I begin to get dressed. Jeremy is standing next to me in his gear still, which tells me I'm clearly in a rush, but it's almost seven in the morning, and I need to get to the hospital.

"Someone's in a hurry." Jeremy grins, and I roll my eyes. "You gonna go see her?"

"Yeah." I nod once, pulling up my jeans. "You gonna go see Chey?"

Jeremy's face darkens and he shakes his head. "Nah, man. That's done." He purses his lips.

"That's it?" I furrow my brows. "You don't want her anymore?"

"She doesn't want *me*," he replies with a grimace. "Not after I went to your place the night you broke up with Bailey. Apparently, she expected me to stay with her or some shit. But I'm loyal to you, T."

"And she's loyal to Bailey." I shrug. "We have to understand that."

"It's just too messy for me," he tells me as he takes off his gear and I put on my shirt. "Remind me never to date one of your girl's best friends again."

"Noted." I roll my eyes.

"Tell her I said hi," Jeremy says as he walks away, not waiting for my reply.

My mood is chipper as I get in my car and drive the short distance to the hospital. The one thing I have going for me is that it's just a few minutes away, so I won't be too late. I mean, I'm already running late…but Bailey usually takes a while giving report to the next nurse anyway. She doesn't know I'm coming this morning. It's supposed to be a surprise, but a bad feeling is settling in my stomach, and now I wonder if I should've given her a heads up.

I park at a spot in front of the ER and race up to her floor, a smile on my face as I ring the doorbell at the cancer ward. They open up for me, and I stay in the lobby area for a few minutes until I get tired of waiting.

"Could you tell Bailey I'm here, please?" I ask Sarah, and she frowns, which also makes me frown.

"She already left..." she replies, and I tilt my head to the side. "She's been gone for over ten minutes."

I've only been here for eight of those.

Fuck.

My stomach drops and I nod, pulling out my phone to check the location she never turned off. I see that her car is on the highway, so I run back to mine and chase after her. I call her three times except she doesn't answer, which is unlike her as it is. What the fuck is going on?

Bailey is not going toward her studio or my place, which is weird, so I follow as fast as I can—which isn't fast enough, considering she won't answer her phone.

But it's all I can do for now.

I just have a bad feeling about this.

CHAPTER THIRTY-FIVE

The air is frigid this morning, cutting across my skin and raising goosebumps in its wake. As always, not putting on a jacket was a bad idea. But just like every other time, I don't seem to have learned my lesson. It's okay, though, since my car is not too far from the exit door.

A chill runs down my spine—the reason is unknown—but it encourages me to speed up my steps and close the distance between me and my vehicle a little faster. The next thing I know, I'm running to it, glancing around frantically like a demon is after me, trying to claw its way into my body. I know I really need to stop being so fucking paranoid, but it's hard when you've had a monster after you for months. No matter how long I work here, exiting the hospital doesn't get any easier.

My steps crunch on the gravel, and my ankle almost twists as I slow down for some stupid reason. I take a deep breath, gripping my door handle to find some kind of cloth lodged into it. I can't open my door without taking it out, and another chill runs down my spine as the freezing barrel of a gun finds its way to my temple.

"Miss me, Bailey?" Robert's warm breath coasts down the

back of my neck, and more goosebumps prick my skin. These are painful though, along with the ominous feeling running through every inch of my body.

"Not even a little bit," I growl, trying to move out of his hold.

His hand grips my hip, "Don't do anything stupid, Bailey." Robert chuckles. "There's a fucking gun to your head."

"So kill me," I shrug, feeling nothing but deep-rooted fear. My hands shake, and my fingers are already numb from the cold. The tips prickle painfully, and I clench my fists. Yeah, a mere long-sleeved shirt under my scrubs was definitely a bad idea.

"Why would I do that?" He kisses the back of my head and I cringe. "When I could have so much more fun with you."

"What do you want, Rob?" I ask him, trying to stall as much as possible. And secretly hoping someone rescues me. Someone getting out of work could see the gun to my head and call the cops. Anyone.

The gun moves against my temple as if he's flexing his wrist, and he growls. "Just. You."

Trying to stall, I ask him, "Haven't we had enough? Haven't you done enough? It's time to let go."

"It'll *never* be enough, Bailey." Fear crawls down my spine, and I swear if I could give it a sound right now, it would be nails running down a chalkboard. *Please don't let him—* "Open the fucking door."

"What is that?"

"That," he chuckles, "is your ticket into the car—*unharmed*. I'm not afraid to shoot you, Bells. Or does the scar on your side not remind you of what I'm capable of?"

"Are you asking me to drug myself?"

"I'm not asking." He laughs, the gun on my temple flexing once more, but I don't dare move. I know he would shoot me without blinking. "I'm *telling*."

"Where are you taking me?" I ask him, my knees feeling

weak. If he takes me out of Washington State, I'm well and truly fucked.

"You'll find out, eventually." His possessive grip on my hip tightens even more, and the barrel of the gun digs into my temple until it bites the skin. "Now sniff the fucking tissue, or I'll force you to."

My hand trembles as it reaches out to grab it, and my traitorous fingers wrap around it. I bring it to my nose and inhale deeply, the disgusting sour smell making my head spin immediately.

"Keys," Robert growls. "*Now.*"

I hand them to him, all the while trying to keep myself upright and praying that he doesn't find my phone in the cargo pocket of my scrubs when he puts me in the car. However, I don't have a lot of time to worry about it as my body gets colder than it already was, and I go limp. My eyes fall closed, and no matter how hard I try, I can't open them.

Unfortunately, somehow, I'm still aware of everything that's happening. I bet this was on purpose, too. He wants me scared and helpless, and goddamnit, he's achieving it. I promised myself that the last time he fucked me up would be the final time, yet something tells me that promise is about to be obliterated.

Robert throws my body in the backseat like a sack of potatoes, and I feel my head bounce hard. My body and my mind are completely detached from each other. I seem to be an entity floating around in limbo even while I'm aware of the rumble of the car as he turns the key in the ignition, the sound of the gravel under the tires, and even the suede scratching at my cheek. It's all so intense, and I want to make it stop. Only I can't even move my limbs. He's given me some sort of paralytic, of that I am sure. I have no hope left in me to cling to. All I *can* do is wait it out and hope that it wears off by the time we get to wherever he's taking me.

"We could've been so good together, Bailey," Robert says on

a sigh, as if this pains him when we both know he's capable of worse. Or I guess I'm about to find out what worse means because my leaving him doesn't bode well with him. His ego is hurt that I was able to escape and evade him for months, so now he's going to make me pay in blood.

"But now you're tainted, aren't you? You let that hockey player fuck you. You let him parade you around!" I hear his fist land on the steering wheel, and if I could flinch, now would've been the time. "Not just that, but I spent a little time in jail when security caught me at the hospital, you fucking cunt." If I could flinch right now, I would.

Where are you taking me?

Will I live?

Please don't hurt me.

Tears sting the back of my eyes and I feel them fall, even though my eyes won't move still. It's as if I'm trapped in my own body. Maybe this is how it feels to get possessed, to lose all ability and autonomy over your body. Or perhaps this is how people feel when they're in a coma? Fuck, this is awful.

I want to beg and plead and make promises, but I know they'd fall on deaf ears. Even still, it wouldn't hurt to try. What if he still has a soft bone in his body for me? What if he cares a little bit? Maybe I can convince him we can get back together, that Theo meant nothing.

He means everything to me.

But he doesn't have to know it.

I can tell him that I may be tainted, but the love in my heart is still there. That we could give it another shot if he wanted. Clearly, he's here for a reason, and I refuse to believe it's only for punishment. He has to care, even if only a little.

Bile rises to the back of my throat, and I can't swallow it down. It's fucking choking me—*God*, I'm going to die choking on my own vomit. My body spasms, and Robert growls. I can only assume he's pulling over, though, because a moment later, he's grabbing the back of my head and tilting me forward. He opens my mouth, letting the contents spill out on the seat right next to my face.

"You nasty little bitch," he mutters, and then he's gone.

The car is moving again before I can make sense of what happened, and I can only be grateful that my phone is still in my pocket. If I can't get in contact with anyone, surely Theo will know where I am.

Please check my location, baby.

My body relaxes into the seat, and so does my bladder. I have no fucking control over myself right now, and while I would feel embarrassed in any other situation, right now, I can't even care. I am scared. Scared of what he's going to do to me, scared of pain, scared of dying. But mostly, I'm scared I'll never see Theo again.

"Did you just fucking piss yourself?" Robert laughs. "Bells, I knew I'd scare you, but this is just gold."

I hear myself whimper, the first sign that my vocal cords are working again, and now I wonder how long he's been driving. This indeed lasts at least an hour, depending on how much I sniffed. I couldn't even tell a dosage based on that, but I have a feeling we're farther from Seattle than I think. Robert seems completely oblivious when it comes to the sound though, and that's to my advantage. Maybe if I pretend to be paralyzed after my limbs wake up, he will make a stop somewhere, and I'd be able to make a break for it.

More time passes, I don't know how long, but before I can keep asking myself...the car stops. It sounds like a dirt road, with the little rocks jostling the car slightly, but I can't be sure. I can finally wiggle my toes in my shoes now, and my leg can move, at least one of them. I can't make any big movements however, since I don't want him to know that I can run away, so it's hard to know which part of my body is ready for me to make a run for it. In fact, my mind could be betraying me right now, and I'm not ready at all.

Don't make a fool of yourself, it'll only cause you so much more pain.

I hear his door close, and I rapidly open my eyes just to be blinded by the sun. He pulls my door open and before he can fully see, I shut my eyes once more. I know I have to be careful, basically play dead, and that's sure going to be hard with the way he's going to hurt me. I just know it's coming.

Robert grabs my ankles and pulls, utterly uncaring in how he handles me. My head hits the edge of the car, where you step to get in, then bounces off the rocks on the ground. I whimper when the small, sharp edges cut into my temple while I try to keep my face as neutral as possible. God, that fucking *hurts*.

He's really going to kill me.

Fuck, fuck, fuck.

Why can't he just let me go?!

This can't be happening. I was so strong, and now I'm just…weak again.

He grabs a hold of one ankle and tugs, taking me with him. I relax my body even as I get cut by all the little rocks on the path. Once I feel the shift in his body, as if he's facing away from me, I open my eyes. I see the back of his head, his oversized jacket because he's not used to the cold, and pine trees everywhere. I don't know where the hell I am. Although I see he's taking me down a trail, deep into the forest.

No.

I close my eyes again, contemplating my options. I'm underdressed, with no water or food and probably no cellphone signal. In other words, I'm fucked. There's nowhere to go that I'll make it out alive, but I think I'd rather take my chances with the elements than die at his hand. I'd prefer getting hypothermia than being his victim again.

Somehow, luck must be on my side, because he stops.

Letting go of me, Robert walks away. This is when I'm brave enough to open my eyes again, just to see him with his back turned to me, walking to a bench. I don't wait; I quietly get up, and before he can turn around, I sprint at full force away from him.

My shoes are extremely loud on the path, but I don't turn around to see where he is. I pump my legs as hard as possible, and I thank God that I'm not the shortest and have long legs. My chest begins to burn with exertion, reminding me further that I should be going to the damn gym. It sure would've been helpful right now. Maybe I'd even be able to fight back. However, I know I'm not going down without a fight, regardless.

I hear the telltale sign of him running after me, and before I can run away any faster, I'm on a beach. There's a lake that looks identical to the one I came to with Theo, and I bet if I go to the other side of it, I'd be able to get on the path that leads up the mountain. But I must be dense because when I look back, Robert is almost on me. I don't have enough time to make it across, so I run to the water instead. If I could just jump in and wait it out until he leaves, maybe I'll survive this after all.

That is, if I don't die from hypothermia first.

My scrub top is grabbed from behind, and I'm yanked backwards with one tug. I trip but throw my elbow back as fast and hard as I can, and thankfully, it connects with something, knocking the wind out of him. He lets go of me momentarily, and right before I can jump in the water, I trip yet again. My face joins the rocky sand, my head jostling once more, and he grabs a hold of my ankle, swiftly pulling me into him. Without thinking twice, I throw my opposite leg back and kick him right in the face. His grip loosens, and I crawl as fast as possible toward the water.

Once I'm waist-deep in the water, I stand, trying to get deeper, but I hear something that makes me turn around—the click of a gun. I freeze in place, and the sound of a shot rings out. I know it's going to hit me before it connects with my stomach, but I wasn't expecting the blinding pain that actually came with it.

The wind is knocked out of me, and I fall back into the water, swallowing it with my scream immediately. The faint whoosh of metal connecting with the water is loud in my ears, and I see more than hear the bubbles as it comes down beside me. My heart pounds like thunder in my ears, and I haul my body from the sticky mud at the bottom so I can take a breath.

The water is crimson, no longer gray, and I can't see the bottom anymore. I gasp for air as I break the surface, clutching at my stomach for dear life, knowing the bullet is in there with every shift of my body. I can feel it moving, and I know I don't have much time before I bleed out. Did it nick my artery? Fuck, fuck, fuck. I don't want to die. Not yet. I haven't had enough time with *him*.

There's a splash, and then Robert is in the water with me. I tread under the surface, willing my body to go faster, but I can feel the tugging in my abdomen. Feel the pain that accompanies it, and I can't help moving forward into the fetal position, swallowing even more water.

"Bells, I'm sorry." Robert actually appears regretful. "Please come with me. Stop swimming further in."

I can't touch the bottom anymore, and panic claws at my insides, making me tread water even faster. Helping me die even quicker. I'm bleeding out. *Help me.*

"No."

He swims toward me anyway, grabbing my arm, and I can feel myself growing weaker. I don't fight him anymore as I let him drag me back to shore. "*Please*. Please, don't let me die," I beg, but he just chuckles.

"Bailey, this has been a long time coming," Robert growls. "You don't get to fucking leave me." He drags me toward the shore by my arm, and once there, I crawl on my hands and knees, sitting up right next to the water that's lapping at the rocky sand. "You don't get to *escape* me anymore."

"I'll be with you," I blurt out, though it sounds like a lie even to my ears. I'm hitting the first stage of grief. *Denial.* "I'll do anything you want."

Within the next blink, he's on top of me.

"Prove it, Bells." Robert begins to rip at my scrub pants, and the more he jostles my body, the more pain I'm in. Hot and searing, yet my limbs feel cold and slightly numb. "*Prove it.*"

"Is shooting me not enough?" I yell. "Are you going to fucking rape me too?"

Robert shoves my legs open, and this time, I fight back. I kick him right in the chest. Except he's too strong for me as he shoves his pants down, and I'm appalled to see he has an erection. I'm bleeding out, and his dick is hard. *What. The. Fuck.*

In my fear-induced stupor, my legs go numb too. Or maybe that's because I'm bleeding out on this rocky sand with no one to save me. His hands grip my thighs again, but this time, I don't have it in me to fight. My body is heavy, anchored to the ground. I can't move. *I can't move.*

"Did the fight leave ya already?" he asks, shoving himself inside me. I only know because he's rocking my body with the motion, and I clutch at my stomach, coming back with hot, sticky liquid. I feel the waves lapping at my face, and the more he thrusts into me, the closer I get to the water. "That's good. Just let it happen, Bailey."

"Please…" *Bargaining.* "*Please* don't do this, Robert," I sob, my lower lip trembling. I'm not above begging anymore. I don't want to die. "Please!"

"Shut the fuck up!" He screams, slapping me across the face. My entire body jolts from him fucking me harder, but I don't feel it. All I feel is numb. Maybe that's mercy, maybe there is a God after all.

"Theo!" I scream loudly. "*Theo!*"

Fear snaps my spine as Robert's hands wrap around my throat, and my torn scrubs keep giving way to his depravity. My back bows off the rocky ground, the pebbles digging into my shoulder blades, and I try to scream, but all that comes out is a loud wheeze. I mouth the words again though, *Theo*, which only seems to piss him off even more.

"I said, shut the fuck up."

I hear him groan, getting closer to his release. I see blood on his dick, and I close my eyes and pray.

Please, God.

Please don't let this be the end.

I'll do anything.

Fire invades my chest as the air dissipates from my lungs, and when he lifts my head and slams it against the ground, I feel my skull crack. The adrenaline that hits me makes my heart thump harder in my chest, and I begin to claw at his hands. Only it's no use, and with another jostle, my head is underwater. I see the blood in front of my eyes, the now red water taunting me.

Why?

Why?

Why?

Terror nestles itself into my very bones, breaking them, or maybe that's Robert. I scream into the water, but nothing comes out. No bubbles. And this is when I know this is how I die. I feel my lungs give way, and involuntarily, my nose begins to breathe in water. I choke on it, trying to expel it from my lungs, but it's no use. My body's betrayal comes at a high cost.

Someone help me.

My lungs burn, and white spots begin to fill my vision, but then they turn, leaving me more scared than ever. My hands claw at Robert, but I let go, thrashing in the water. My hips drive up, and I can feel the bullet move inside of me again. Blinding, searing pain takes over, and this time, I just give up. I inhale another lungful of water, and I'm not delusional. I know this is the end of the road for me.

My eyes widen as images of Theo flit through my mind. Us at the skating rink dancing together, the way he held my hand as we stared up at the laser lights on the dome ceiling, the way he cupped my face as he kissed me. I see it all playing like a highlight reel in my head, and I take one more deep inhale full of water.

Everyone talks about the white light when you're dying, the one you see right before you drift away. But it's all bullshit. All I see is black—a hole so deep there's no digging myself out of it. The color engulfs my vision, starting from the edges and creeping its way across the entirety of it. And once I'm blinded, once I'm truly scared, it grips its talons into me and tears my eyes out.

CHAPTER THIRTY-SIX

Driving after Bailey has been the weirdest experience of my life. She's always miles ahead of me no matter how much I speed up. And the weirdest thing? She's headed right for the cabin we stayed at. So when she reaches the state park, I speed up, wanting to know what the fuck she's doing. The problem is that she's miles ahead of me, *still*, and I'm getting more nervous by the second.

What is she doing?

Why is she coming here?

Does she know I'm following her?

No, there's absolutely no way she can know unless she searched my location, which I highly doubt she did. How did she even remember how to get here? I didn't use a GPS when I brought her, and she couldn't have remembered every single street I drove through. No way in hell.

I finally pull up to where the location leads me, except she's not here. *She's not here.* But her car is, although empty. I wonder if she went to the lake—the trail leads right up to it.

I open my car door and immediately hear my name.

"Theo!" Desperate cries reach my ears. *"Theo!"*

My hands shake as I get out of the car and slam the door, trying to figure out where she's at. But there's no more sound, there's no more cries. She sounded desperate though, which makes me run faster than I ever have.

It still doesn't feel fast enough, though. This trail is two miles long, and each mile feels longer than the last. Finally, I reach the lake, yet I still don't see her. I don't see anyone. Except suddenly, I do. I run to the shore, where bright blue pants are on the ground, half of a naked woman with blood fucking everywhere, half submerged in the water.

Oh, God.

Bile rises to the back of my throat, and I turn my head and begin to throw up. With my hands on my knees, I try to breathe through my nose. However, it just won't stop coming. Wiping my mouth with the back of my hand, I run to the woman. Please don't be my girl. *Please.*

I take my phone out of my back pocket and dial 911. Giving the operator as many details as possible, I drop to the ground and drag the woman out of the water. Bloodshot eyes stare back at me, a mouth wide open, a shirt full of blood, and a gaping hole in the abdomen. Fuck.

It's her.

My Bailey.

I didn't get here fast enough, and I know exactly who did it.

A roar flies from my mouth, and tears begin to stream down my face. "No! Bailey, baby, wake up!"

"Do chest compressions, sir." The woman calmly reminds me, but it only makes me want to throw my phone across the fucking lake and into the water. How can she be so goddamn calm when my world is falling apart? If I thought Bailey broke my heart before, it's *nothing* compared to this. *"Now."*

The woman snaps me out of it, and I place my hands on Bailey's chest, beginning compressions. I don't know what the fuck I'm doing, but I've seen it done on TV. With every compression, water flies out of her mouth until I'm sure she's choking on it still, but I have to get her heart started again. *I have to.*

"The police are almost there, and so are the paramedics." the woman says. "They can see your car."

"Bailey," I whisper. "Hold on, baby, they're going to help you." Tears stream down my face. God, please don't take her. *"Stay with me,"* I beg. "Stay with me, baby."

Hope blossoms in my chest, hope that they can save her. Although it's gone just as quickly as it came when I look down at her blue lips and purple face, her eyes still open. I can't stand to look at them, lifeless, so I look at the water instead. My arms begin to burn, my chest too, but before I know it, I hear the crunching of the rocks under the soles of shoes. The moment I turn my face, I see the police and paramedics running toward us.

Please save her.

We're not done.

I need more time.

Please. Please. *Please.*

The paramedics come to me, and one of them asks, "Did you move her at all?"

"Yes." I nod. "Her face was underwater."

"*Fuck,*" one of them mutters.

"Okay," the man replies, his eyes glancing down at her.

And then it's chaos, absolute madness, as they get her on a gurney as fast as possible and begin to all but run back to the trail. I follow closely, not wanting to be stranded, and when they turn on their sirens and peel out of the lot, so do I. I follow them closely, not giving a fuck I'm going over one hundred miles an hour, not caring that I might get pulled over. I'm not stopping until I'm at that hospital.

I pull up to the nearest Emergency Room and park, then get out of my car and run to the receptionist's desk. The receptionist looks at me with wide eyes, and it's then that I notice the blood coating my palms and clothes. I just can't bring myself to care about what they think.

"Bailey," I gasp out, my chest heaving. "Bailey Thomas."

The woman looks at me in confusion.

"Gunshot wound to the abdomen and raped." I lower my voice.

"Jane Doe." She nods once. "Who are you?"

"Her husband."

"She's in surgery right now," she confirms my suspicions. "I can take you to a private waiting area while she's in surgery."

"She's alive?" My heart constricts in my chest, and the lady nods. "*Oh, God.*"

"She is."

"Take me to her," I say quickly. "Please."

The kind woman leads the way, taking me through the double doors that lead to the patient rooms and then into one of the waiting rooms. It's a small space with bright white walls and yellow seats. Two blue recliners that pull out into beds also take up most of the room, and I go directly to one of them and sit down, my elbows on my knees and my hands in my hair. I tug at the strands hard, needing to ground myself, and the nurse clears her throat.

"Someone will come in with updates from time to time." Camille—according to her name badge—says softly. "If you need anything, the bathroom is right across from this room and so is the nutrition room."

"Thank you." I nod once. Not that I'll need it. Basic human necessities are unimportant to me right now. The only things that matter are breathing and keeping a pulse so I can know Bailey is alright.

I take my phone out of my back pocket and begin to dial Jeremy's number, except when I see the crusted blood all over my hands and inside my fingernails is the instant that my hands start to tremble, and I drop my phone. "Fuck," I mutter, picking it up.

I dial Jeremy, and he picks up immediately. "Hey, T. What's up, man?"

I swear I try to speak, but all that comes out is a choked sob, and it rattles me from the inside out. "She—"

"What. Happened?"

"She was dead!" I yell. "We're in the hospital." I sob again, my shoulders shaking my entire body. "Bailey has been shot."

Jeremy sucks in a sharp breath. "We'll be right there," he replies, and I hear rustling keys in the background. "Hang tight, bro."

"Bring Cheyenne," I tell him, then hang up.

There's a knock at the door, and I immediately straighten. "Come in!" I say, wiping my tears as fast as possible, but it's useless since the nurse has already seen them. I bet there's blood smeared under my eyes now.

"Sir?" The petite blonde looks mousy and scared but still walks in and shuts the door behind her. "Are you here about Bailey?"

I exhale a sigh of relief. "Oh, good. You got her name right." I scrub a hand down my face, coming up wet. "It was Jane Doe when I first got here."

"She nods, "Yes, you told the receptionist her name and she changed it in the chart. I'm Layla, and I'm one of the operating room nurses taking care of your wife. Do you mind if I sit?"

"Please," I reply softly, trying to control my body. It's shaking so hard my teeth are rattling, and she gives me the most sympathetic expression while handing me tissues. "*Nooo* —I—is she okay?"

"She has a heartbeat," Layla says. "However, we're having a hard time dislodging the bullet without damaging vital organs," she replies with the nicest, softest voice I've ever heard in my life.

Just how many times has this poor girl had to give bad

news? I imagine it's almost every day. But she's not making me feel any better. In fact, all I feel is dead inside. Nearly as dead as the love of my life. "I'll come to update you before we move her to the ICU, but for now, it'll be a while before we're done."

"What's a while?"

"It's hard to say." She gives me a sad smile. "She's not stable, and we have to get the bullet out. She's lost a lot of blood."

"Did you do a rape kit?" I blurt out. That motherfucker needs to die.

"We did."

"Thank you," I reply.

Layla gets up from the chair across from mine and opens the door. Before she can get out, all of my friends stare at me from the other side. Cheyenne pushes past her and looks at me up and down, stopping in the middle of the room.

"No!" she wails, then drops to her knees. "No, oh my God, *no!*"

Cheyenne crawls to me and grabs my hands, inspecting them before continuing to sob. I hoist her up from under her armpits and bring her to my lap, and she immediately nestles herself into the crook of my neck, shaking in my arms. I don't know how long we cry together before she calms down, but eventually, she pulls away and stands up.

"I'm sorry," I whisper, my words coming out shaky. "I should've been there sooner. I checked her location—I fucking followed her. I just wasn't fast enough. I'm so, *so*, so sorry."

"Theo." Cheyenne cups my cheek, trying to remove the smears of blood from under my eye, "It's not your fault. *Thank you* for finding her. She wouldn't be in this hospital—" She chokes on a sob, "If it weren't for you."

Jeremy sits in the chair next to me, his eyes never straying from Cheyenne. "What have the doctors said so far?"

"The nurse who just left said Bailey is still in surgery." I don't want to talk to him about this. I need to speak with someone about Bailey being raped. I don't know if she would want that, but I know she trusts Cheyenne. And I need to trust someone. "That they still need to get the bullet out of her abdomen, and they will move her to the ICU when she's done. Oh, and if anyone asks, I'm her husband." I stare at Cheyenne. "And you're her sister. Understood?"

A chorus of yes' rings out in the room, and Chey nods her head slowly, questions in her blue eyes. "Is there anything else?"

I peer around the room at Matt, Oliver, and Noah. They're here for me, of that I have no doubt. Except for whatever reason, this feels too intimate, and I want them gone. There's just no way to say it nicely—

"Hey, guys," Jeremy says to them. "I think we should give them some, um, privacy."

The guys all nod and say their goodbyes. But before Jeremy can leave, Cheyenne walks after him and grabs his wrist. He turns around slowly and with wide eyes, and she pleads with her eyes. I don't know what kind of silent understanding they've come to, but he nods and sits in the chair furthest from us.

"Now." Cheyenne sighs, sitting next to me once more. "What are you not telling me?"

"Bailey was…" I tug at my hair and whisper, "raped."

Chey gasps, her eyes filling with tears immediately, and then she jumps up and screams at the top of her lungs. Jeremy gets up from the chair and runs to her, scooping her up in his arms and taking her to the chair he was sitting in. "That—" She hiccups and sobs, *"Motherfucker."*

I know, Chey. *I know.*

"They did a rape kit," I mutter, not looking at her. "I heard her scream my name, you know. I was right there, almost there. Until I wasn't."

"It's not your fault," she cries out. "Tell him, Jer. It's not his fault."

"It's not your fault," Jeremy whispers. "Stop being so hard on yourself."

"Hard on myself?" I yell, getting up from the chair and pacing. "She was fucking dead, Jeremy! Because I didn't run fast enough. I'm a fucking athlete!"

"She was going to die anyway," Cheyenne says, "He's wanted her dead for months, Theo. This had nothing to do with you."

"Okay," I whisper. "It wasn't my fault."

It wasn't my fault.

At least that's what I keep trying to convince myself of as we spend the next two hours in silence, not daring to guess what must be happening behind the closed doors of the operating room. My only hope is that she makes it and recovers—at least physically. Seeing as I have the awful feeling she will never be the same again.

I thought she had built a wall of ice between us. Only that will be nothing in comparison to when she wakes up. *If* she wakes up. That thought rattles me to my core, and a fresh set of tears stream down my face. I have to be strong for her. When she sees me, she has to know I am and will always be here, no matter what.

Now all that's left for me to do is talk to the police. They're apparently giving me some time, but I'm sure I'll be the first one to be questioned. I was, after all, covered in her blood and she was dead and raped and—

The door to the waiting area opens, and in comes Layla. She's not smiling; instead, her eyes look almost as dead as Bailey's. As soon as she closes the door, we all stand, and she sighs. I've never heard a sadder sigh in my entire life.

"She's in the ICU."

"We want to see her—" Cheyenne starts, but she's interrupted by the nurse.

"It's touch and go right now," she says softly. "She's not out of the woods yet, but if she makes it through the next two days, maybe she has a chance. The bullet nicked her artery when we moved her into the operating room. We had to repair that, and she lost a lot of blood. Don't be scared when you see her; I'm sure she won't look like your Bailey." She stares into my eyes as she says it, and my own well with tears again.

Your Bailey.

I wipe my face with the back of my blood-covered hand. Even after all these hours, I haven't cleaned up. I'm just not in the right mindset to do it.

"I'll take you to her now."

Those words shouldn't get me excited, but I just want her to know I'm here. I want to talk to her, even if she can't talk back. I want to kiss her—I just got her back, and this might be the last kiss. I shouldn't think like that...but there are so many possibilities. If she pulls through, she could retreat from me completely. Or, the worst possibility, she could die, and the future we talked about that night in the tub would never happen.

The nurse takes us through some hallways and an elevator, then through even more hallways. Finally, we stand in front of some glass sliding doors, room number 98—just like mine. My heart drops. I do not like coincidences. I don't believe in them.

We enter the room with the nurse, and she begins to explain all the wires, tubes, and bandages covering Bailey's entire person. But what really gets me is the tube down her throat. Can she not breathe on her own? Or is she asleep just as a safety measure?

What the hell is going on?

I don't have much time to ask questions though, because just as my mouth opens to utter the insane thoughts going through it, there's a flat line.

A fucking flat line.

No.

"Bailey! *Baby!*" I yell, "Don't do this!"

"No!" Cheyenne screams, grabbing onto Bailey's feet and sinking to her knees.

I go around to Bailey's side as a flood of people invade the tiny room, and the nurse yells at us to get out. But I don't go, instead I hold on to Bailey's hand and squeeze once.

"I love you, Bailey." I sob. "Don't go yet, please. *Stay with me.*"

Then everything is chaos.

Bailey

CHAPTER THIRTY-SEVEN

There's an incessant beeping in my ears, one that wasn't there when the darkness swallowed me whole. The air is cold, making a chill run down my spine and simultaneously causing a blinding pain to run its course through me. What the hell is going on?

Did the fight leave ya already?

That's good. Just let it happen, Bailey.

You don't get to fucking leave me.

I said, shut the fuck up.

No.

No.

No.

The beeping gets louder, faster, just like my heartbeat. Mine thunders in my ears, rattles in my chest, and jumps at my throat. I can't make any sense of where I am, and that's when I realize I'm alive and haven't opened my eyes. Only I'm scared to. What will I find here? Will I be alone? How fucked up am I? Did he destroy the outside of me just as he did the inside?

I force myself to open my eyes, and they feel dry, like they've been submerged in sand, and maybe they have. My face was underwater after all…that's how my soul left my body. *I'm a dead girl walking.*

Except I'm not walking; I'm in a hospital bed, and the lights are so bright I have to squint to see through them. As my eyes finally focus, the first thing I see is a glass sliding door and a nurses' station. How did I get here? Surely Robert was not the one who brought me.

My hand flexes involuntarily, and it's then I realize that I'm holding on to something. *Someone.* I look down to see a head of dark hair draped over my lap, a straight nose, and full lips. Long eyelashes and the most beautiful fucking face I've ever had the privilege of gazing upon.

Theo.

"Theo," I whisper. "You're here?"

"I'll always be here," he replies on a whisper, and my lower lip trembles. "You're everything to me."

My stomach drops, and I try to sit up, just to cry out when I'm hit with a lightning bolt of pain right to my abdomen. Oh, shit. Robert—

"He *shot* me?" I ask Theo, but I already know the answer. I remember everything down to my last miserable breath. Inhaling lungful's of water may have been worse than this pain, so I guess I'll make it through.

"Yes, B," Theo replies softly, then shakes someone on the other side of me. I glance over to see Cheyenne slumped in the chair with her head on the edge of the bed. Soft snores come from her, and when Theo nudges her again, she sits up swiftly.

"What ha—" Her eyes land on me and immediately well with tears. "Bai!"

She throws herself at me, engulfing me in a tight hug, and I whimper in pain. It feels like I have been run over, and then I look around and see the bags of blood, fluids, medications, and everything in between. God, he really messed me up. I'm lucky to be alive. I'm lucky to be *here*.

"I'm alive, Chey," I grunt as she continues to squeeze me. "Please let go now, I'm hurting."

Cheyenne immediately steps back, but with a smile on her face. "I honestly thought you were gone, you bitch." I chuckle, covering my abdomen when I feel a tug that I'm assuming are stitches, and immediately sober up. I don't want to tear them. "How could you do that to me? Die on me twice?"

Twice?

I flinch. "I'm sorry," I reply, shaking my head. Her eyes are full of panic now.

"I didn't mean it—"

"*Where* is he?" I growl. "Did they find him?"

"Not yet," Theo replies softly. "Although they're working on it. He was stupid enough to take your car, so he'll turn up soon enough."

"Did they do the rape kit?"

Cheyenne winces at that, "Yes."

"How did I get here?" I ask her. "Who brought me here?"

Cheyenne opens her mouth, closes it, and peers over at Theo. He shakes his head, but she still says, "Theo did."

I glance over at him, at his bloodshot eyes, the way his bottom lip quivers as he stares at me. His hands shake in mine, and I look down at our connection.

"How?"

"I checked your location, B." He shakes his head. "I'm sorry, I normally wouldn't do that, but I was worried—"

"I'm glad you did," I interrupt, because is he actually kidding me? Does he think I'm going to be angry with him for saving my life? "Thank you."

Theo nods, squeezing my hand lightly in his. Just as he's about to pull away, I grip him firmly. "I love you, Bailey. I promise I won't let anyone else hurt you again. I'm sorry this happened—that I wasn't fast enough—"

"Theo," I say soothingly, squeezing his hand once more. I

wish I could've squeezed it as I died— "It's not your fault. He would've found a way to do it. He wants me dead."

"He doesn't get to take you from me," Theo says reverently. "Not again."

"I called for you," I whisper. "When I was dying, you were the last person on my mind. All I wanted was you—then everything went black."

"I know, baby," he whispers back. "I *heard* you. I was right there. I'm so sorry I wasn't fast enough. I was running—"

"It's okay, Theo." I smile, but it's sad. "It already happened, don't beat yourself up over it. Stop living in the *what-ifs*. I don't want you to blame yourself—ever. He did this, *not* you. All you've ever done is put me back together."

"That's all I've ever wanted." Theo reaches out, his thumb brushing my chapped bottom lip. "Piece by jagged piece."

"Do you know if they gave me Plan B?" I ask him, and he rears back. "I'm sorry. I should've asked the nurse, not you."

"They haven't," he replies solemnly. "I can call her—"

"I'll do it later."

His face is grim, "I'll respect whatever decision you make."

"Stop right *there*," I tell him. "There's no decision to make, Theo."

He nods in understanding. "Okay."

There's a moment of silence I'm desperate to break, except I don't even know what to say. I was raped, and now I may be pregnant with someone else's baby? I didn't choose this, and is it being stolen from me? But no, there's still a chance I'm not pregnant. And it's been, what? A day? I can't have been asleep longer than that. "How long have I been here?"

"In the ICU?" He asks with furrowed brows.

"Yes."

"Eighteen hours," he answers slowly. "Why?"

"I do need you to get that nurse."

Theo leaves as soon as the words are out of my mouth, and I breathe out a sigh of relief. If there's something I can control, it will be this. I was helpless to his assault—I fought him as much as I could until I couldn't anymore. However, he still did what he set out to do. This, though? I won't let him fucking have it. He won't get another part of me.

He's taken enough.

Nurse Ali comes in with Theo, and she has one single pill in her hand as she wheels in the computer behind her. She scans the medication wrapper, then my wristband, and hands it to me. My hands shake at the implication of what could've already happened—that this may not even work. *Please don't fail me now, God.* I still, however, manage to swallow the pill and an entire cup of water later. So I'm feeling hopeful.

"Thank you," I whisper, playing with my bloody fingernails. "For taking care of me,"

"I wouldn't want to be anywhere else," she replies. When I glance up, I see that she has a soft smile on her face. "You're so strong. You're the strongest woman I know."

Tears prick the back of my eyes again, and I breathe in deeply to keep them from falling. I don't reply, because what is there to say? I feel weak. I feel the furthest I've ever been from strong. At least the last time, before I ran, I was able to pick myself up off the damn floor and drive myself to the hospital. I was strong then. Now? I feel useless. Lying in a hospital bed, waiting around for the cops to catch him.

"Stop," Theo growls, returning to my side and tilting my chin up with a thumb and forefinger. "You *are* strong." My bottom lip trembles and he sucks in a sharp breath. "You're so fucking strong, baby. Just look at you—*here*. You fought for your fucking life. You fought for me—*us*."

"I'll always fight for us."

I don't tell him that he's stuck with me now, that this is forever, because I didn't just hand over my heart to be crushed again once more. No, he doesn't get to do that to me.

We're end game.

CHAPTER THIRTY-EIGHT

Bailey was discharged not even thirty minutes ago, and we're already on our way to the morgue. They think they have Robert, however they need her to identify his body to be sure. I'm sure it's him though, if what they told me is any indication. They found the man in her car, and he refused to turn himself in, even shooting one of the police officers. Now, maybe someone else could've stolen her vehicle, but I highly doubt that. And usually, someone who refuses to turn themselves in is guilty—in my opinion.

While I'm glad he might be dead, I'm more worried about Bailey. Will she be glad, too? Or will she feel like justice wasn't served? More importantly, is she ready to face him, even in death? Or how will this affect her recovery? The closer we get to the location, the more questions run rampant through my mind. I don't want her to feel alone in her pain, even for one second. The fact of the matter is we're both hurting in some way. I could never pretend to understand what she's going through, and I won't try.

My pain is guilt. No matter how much she tells me not to feel it—I just can't help it. Every day, I wonder what could've been—had I gotten to her sooner.

Would I have been able to prevent her death?

What my life would be like without her by my side—because she'd be dead. I try not to think about that much, but it's hard. Her screams still echo in my ears, the ones I heard after I opened the car door, and then the worst part—silence. It's the silence that hurts me more than the anguish coming from her mouth, knowing what that silence brought her.

Death.

And I don't think either one of us will ever recover from that.

No matter how much she pretends to be okay or how she puts on a brave face for everyone or when I feign sleep every night in her hospital room, the bed shakes with her sobs. Every time, I would get up from my recliner and comfort her.

Except it still doesn't feel like I'm doing enough.

My leg bounces as I drive, and Bailey rests her small, warm hand over my thigh. I gaze down at her dainty fingers and briefly wonder what they'd look like with a *rock* on her ring finger. Then again, maybe not something so big; she's a subtle girl. She doesn't seem to be the one who likes flashy things. In fact, I know she's not. Low-key and heartfelt are her personality, and one day, I will give it to her. Give her everything. The entire world will be at her disposal. However, first things first—moving in. At least until she's ready to go back on her own and—

"What are you thinking about?" Bailey asks softly, her hand tightening around my thigh.

I look at the GPS to see how long we have until we get there. Five minutes. Maybe this isn't a conversation we should be having before identifying a dead body, the dead body of the man who ruined her life, yet in a way it also feels like closure. I need her to know I'm not taking her to her apartment. No, I'm bringing her *home.*

"Baby," I take a deep breath, bracing myself for a fight. "I'm not taking you to your studio."

"I know," she responds immediately.

"You do?" My brows furrow in confusion. Did I do something to make it that obvious? "And you're fine with it?"

Turning my face briefly toward her, I see her shrug. "I don't want to be there. I don't want to be alone anymore."

"I want you to move in," I blurt. "I know you could always be with Cheyenne, and perhaps I'm selfish—but I want you to be with *me*." She doesn't say anything, nodding slowly as if trying to analyze every word coming out of my mouth. "If you want, after you recover, we could look for an apartment for you again." No way in hell, but I'll never say that to her. I'll just convince her to not leave my side again in this lifetime.

"And if I say no?"

My stomach drops, but I refrain from grimacing. "No means no, Bailey." I shrug with a nonchalance I don't feel. I'm sure she knows that it would kill me, but for her, I'd do anything. "Whatever you choose, I'm here."

"I've been stuck in the hospital for three weeks, Theo," Bailey replies quietly, and when I peer over at her, she's ripping at her fingernails. It bothers me, the way she's always nervous now. Her anxiety heightens mine since I know how much she's hurting. It fucking kills me that he made it even worse. "I want to be with *you*."

My heart flutters in my chest, and I swear my stomach does a little flip-flop. "I swear to God, Bailey." My hand wraps around her small one over my lap. "Whatever you want in this life will be yours. From now until your last breath."

"I've already had one of those, Theo." She squeezes my hand. "I'm a dead girl walking."

My stomach drops. "But you won't have a last breath again until we're old and wrinkly, baby." At least, that's what I try to convince her of, being that the alternative is just too morbid to face. *She's going to live a long life. Robert is gone.*

"I hope so." She whispers.

I pull into the parking lot of the building, where my GPS has just directed me, and take the spot right in front of the doors that reads *visitors*. I've never been more grateful to get special parking, especially because if this is it—if he's dead—we can get out of here quickly if she wants.

Unbuckling my seatbelt, I allow my head to fall back onto the headrest and close my eyes. I inhale deeply, filling my lungs to the brim, and then exhale slowly. I don't know why I'm so nervous, or maybe this feeling is helplessness. Whatever it is, I don't like it.

However when I open my eyes again, Bailey is sitting beside me, calmly, more than she should be. Her eyes don't have tears, and her hands aren't trembling. She's sure of herself, unlike me. It sounds stupid to pull from her strength—when she should be depleted—but I do. I straighten in my seat and force myself to press the brake and push the button to turn off the car.

"Ready?" I whisper, not trusting my voice.

"More than ever."

I get out of the car and go around to open her door, and then we both walk into the building together. It looks like a police station; I only know this because my father is a cop. When we reach the reception desk, the lady hands me a clipboard to sign in. We both do, then hand it back and sit down to wait until we're called back.

It only takes a few minutes before we're called back, and we follow the lady down the hallway and to the back of the building. A set of double doors opens for us, and the space suddenly feels like a walk-in freezer, which I suppose it is. Bailey is dressed for the cold for once though, thankfully, since I made sure she had a jacket to leave the hospital.

But still, I ask, "Do you need my jacket?"

Bailey glances at me with a smirk. "I have my own."

I shrug, "You can have mine too."

"I'm fine, Theo."

We follow after the lady all the way to some gurney. The person on it is covered with a blanket, not even his feet showing. An older man with white hair and glasses is waiting for us next to the gurney, and his white lab coat reaches all the way to his knees.

"My name is Mr. Brown." He says, "And I've asked you here to help us identify the body. Now, before I remove the blanket, you need to know that he has been shot in the forehead." Mr. Brown stares right at Bailey. "Are you going to be okay with that?"

I don't want to put words in her mouth, but what's a gunshot to the forehead when she has to look at the scars he left on her stomach every day for the rest of her life? Thanks to this motherfucker, now she has a stab wound and gunshot wound from him.

"Yeah." She nods. "I'm fine."

"Alright, ma'am." He grips the edge of the blanket and begins to lift it up, then lowers it all the way down to his waist. "Could you help us identify this man?"

We both gaze down at the corpse of the man who killed her too, and my jaw tics. His face is ashen, his lips a light gray. Suddenly, a sense of satisfaction fills me. That is, until Bailey's bottom lip trembles and she starts to sob. Now, I don't want to be the one to tell someone how to feel after the death of someone they know, but after everything he's done, this is *not* how I expected her to react. Not even a little bit.

"Ma'am?"

"Robert Hull." She wails, moving back from the gurney. "This is the man who raped and killed me."

Mr. Brown nods once and begins to pull the blanket back over the body, but Bailey holds up her hand. "Yes?" he asks.

"Could you give us some privacy?" Her bottom lip continues to quiver, and I bet if it weren't for that, she wouldn't get away with shit. Though right now, I'm so surprised by her reaction that nothing else shocks me anymore.

"Of course," Mr. Brown says, walking past me to the door. I nod once at him and begin to follow him out.

"Not you," she calls out. "You stay, Theodore."

My spine straightens at my full name, and I back up again to where I initially stood—right behind her. I don't dare touch her, though I can feel her body heat. When I see her shoulders start to shake, I want to reach out and wrap my arms around her.

Only I don't.

Her sobs echo in the empty space, bouncing off the walls and metal lockers where I imagine even more dead people reside. She could be in there—she *would* be, if it weren't for me. It's hard to think about that though, especially when the man who put her there is lying dead in front of us. No, I don't want to think about her death—I want to enjoy *his*.

I reach out to rub her back with her next sob, but it quickly turns into a cackle. I won't lie; the quick emotional turn scares me a bit, so I step back. I won't say she's unhinged right now, but I can't blame her either way.

I stay behind her, offering comfort if she needs it, yet out of her way all the same. Because I don't know what the hell to expect or even what emotions I'm dealing with here.

Closing my eyes, I take a slow breath in, then let it out. Except when I open my eyes again, the last thing I expect to see is happening right before my eyes. Bailey is against the gurney, the edge of it against her stitches that are barely now healing, and with her small fist, she pulls his hair and exposes his throat to the room.

"I did it, motherfucker." She giggles, and the hairs on my arms stand on end. "I *escaped* you." A little growl comes from her, making her fucking vicious. She may have been a victim three weeks ago, but right now? She's a warrior. "And there's nothing you can do about it, ever again."

There's a pause, and she lets go of his hair, stepping back.

"I win." Bailey steps back again, until she runs into me and my front plasters to her back. "I'm *free*."

"Yes, you are, baby," I assure her, a grin taking over my face. She's so damn strong.

Bailey grabs my hand and begins to pull me toward the door, but before we exit, she says over her shoulder, "Oh, and *fuck you*."

I squeeze her hand once. "That's my girl," I murmur.

Then we get the fuck out of there.

A few hours later, after stopping by her studio for some of her belongings, we're back at my place. Bailey is perched on the couch with her ankles crossed over my coffee table and a blanket draped over her lap. A Kindle is nestled in her hands, and she doesn't even notice when I open the front door and get a delivery of molten lava cake—her favorite. She still doesn't even notice until I offer it to her. That's how engrossed she is in this book.

I give her a soft smile. "Cake, baby?"

She looks up at me with doe eyes and bites her bottom lip into her mouth. "You remembered?"

"I remember everything, Bailey." Everything about her, *us*.

"Fine," she squeaks, putting her Kindle device down and patting the spot right next to her on the couch. "But only if you help me eat it."

"Let me guess." I pretend to think. "You want some Belly love triangle?"

"Duh." She rolls her eyes.

"Well, I hate to break it to you," I reply as she takes the first bite of the cake, her eyes rolling to the back of her head. "I already finished the season."

"No fucking way!" She gasps, making me laugh. "You didn't do that. You don't even *like* it."

"Is that why you like to make me watch it?" I grin, letting a chuckle slip through. "I really did finish it, though."

"What happens then?"

"The most fucked up thing I've ever witnessed." I sigh. "Does bro code not exist anymore? What the fuck was that about?"

"Bro code isn't even a thing." Bailey smirks. "Clearly."

"But they're literally brothers, Bailey."

"My point exactly." We both laugh. "Apparently, bro code dies when a cute girl steps in."

"Not for me." I shake my head, knowing I'd never betray my brothers—my friends.

"Alright, but are you Team Jellyfish now, or what?"

"I don't know, B." I shake my head to rile her up, knowing damn well that's what she was trying to accomplish from the beginning. For us to root for the same couple. "Conrad really did love her. I think he was just going through something. I think *they* are end game."

"Fuck that!" Bailey squeals. "No way! Conrad is a fucking tool. Jeremiah is definitely end game."

"We won't find out until next season." I wink at her, taking a spoonful of the cake. "Right?"

"Awww." She pretends to wipe under her eyes. "Are you saying you'll be here long enough to watch it?"

"Baby, I'm not going anywhere," I tell her as my heart speeds up in my chest. "Ever."

"Forever is a long time, Theo." But she says it with a grin, and when she puts the plate on the coffee table and straddles my lap, my heart somersaults. "Is that how long you want me for?"

"*Yes*," I growl without hesitation, then gently press my lips to hers. I don't know how long she'll need before I can touch her again, so I keep my hands to myself. "Mine, baby. You're mine forever."

"Nothing will steal me away from you, Theo." She grins, pressing her nose to mine and brushing them against each other. "I love you."

"I love *you*." I cup her cheeks and pull away, trying to look into her eyes. "Will you move in with me?"

"Move in?" She gasps. "Permanently?"

"As soon as you're better." I nod once. "I never want you away from me again."

Bailey's eyes brim with tears and her nostrils flare in an attempt to prevent them from falling. "I'd love that."

"You're safe here, baby," I tell her. "Nothing will ever happen to you on my watch ever again."

I meant every word I said. However, nothing will happen to her again while I still have breath in my lungs. I'd rather cut my own heart out of my chest before witnessing her pain again.

CHAPTER THIRTY-NINE

Two Months Later...

I t's been two months since Theo brought me home from the hospital.

Two months of pain and sorrow, sleepless nights, and ugly crying. Yet also two months full of love, joy, laughter, and understanding.

He's been an angel through it all, always trying to make my life better and find ways to help me through this. Even though he doesn't have to put me back together, he always manages to find a way to do it. My jagged pieces were shattered and scattered on a rocky beach all those months ago, yet somehow, Theo has found some of those pieces and put the puzzle back together. I don't even know how he did it, but he has a way of achieving the impossible.

Theo is the most patient man I have ever met. He's been here for me through all the ups and downs and still has stayed strong, not expecting anything in return. He's taken care of me in every way possible. I haven't been able to work in months since the doctor said I couldn't, and my return to work date is in a week now. So, while I know that Theo is a millionaire, and it shouldn't bother me, I still hate the feeling of someone else financially supporting me. I'd rather let Cheyenne do it, but after everything he had already done for me, I couldn't deny him anything.

Now, here we are, at my tiny studio apartment, packing the things I need to vacate the space. Which is precisely—two bins full of clothes and shoes. Yeah, that's all I have to my name that actually matters. We don't need any of the kitchen stuff or my bed, and there's literally nothing else in here. Theo puts my bins in the back of his new F-150—one he got in case we do things together that require space, like camping, he said—and gets his friends to put everything else on the curb of the apartment complex for bulk trash pickup. I let them say their goodbyes as I walk back into the studio for one last look—a goodbye.

Although I came to this place under the worst circumstances imaginable, it was nothing compared to what awaited me. I'm grateful for the refuge this tiny home provided me when I had nowhere to go, and I'll never, ever forget about the strength I found here. On my own.

"Thank you," I whisper.

Footsteps alert me to Theo's arrival, and I wipe a stray tear from under my eye. "You ready, baby?"

I turn around and gaze into his bright blue orbs, "No." I shake my head. "This is goodbye."

"Yes, it is." Theo nods, stepping into me and pulling me into a tight hug. "But it doesn't have to be a bad thing."

"It's the end of a chapter," I reply, burying my face in the crook of his neck. I press my lips to his skin, instantly sending butterflies raging through my stomach. "And the start of a new one."

"An amazing one," he agrees.

"I know just the way to say goodbye, baby." I begin to unbutton his jeans, pushing them down along with his underwear, and fist his hardening dick in my hand. "You've been so patient." I beam, tugging his now hard dick up and down. "I'm grateful for it, really. However, I'm ready to take my life back. I'm ready for *you*."

Theo inhales sharply, "Bailey—"

"No." I shake my head, needing to get this off my chest. "I'm not made of glass, Theo." I chuckle. "I died, and now I'm alive again. I want to *live*, damn it, and I want to do it with *you*."

"You want me to make you feel alive, then?" Theo whispers, his hand gently wrapping around my throat. His fingers dig in, flexing when I don't reply. "Because, baby, all you have to do is get on those pretty knees and ask nicely."

I drop to my knees so fast they crack on the hardwood floor, but it doesn't even matter because right now, I don't feel the pain. All I'm aware of is him. His scent—pine—and the feel of his skin as I trace his dick with my lips. "*Please*," I whisper, begging him just like he said to. "I want you,"

"Then take me, Bailey," Theo growls. *"Make a mess of me."*

I groan and take him in my mouth, wrapping my lips around his dick and taking him all the way to the back of my throat. Letting go of him with a pop, I say, "On your back, big boy."

Theo takes his pants off all the way, leaving them behind as he goes right to where my bed used to be and lies on his back. I strip too, at least from the waist down, and when I take off my shoes I almost feel bad for making him lie down on the freezing hardwood floor.

Almost.

My knees come to either side of his hips as I straddle him, and I can feel my wetness coating the inside of my thighs. I direct his dick to my entrance and sink down on it slowly. A gasp escapes him, and his blue eyes dilate as I stare right into them.

Grinding my pussy over his pelvis, I seek my own pleasure as I circle my hips for him. Theo's hands land on my hips, his fingers digging in, and he begins to direct my pace.

"Fuck, *yes*," Theo moans. "Just like our first time, baby. Ride my dick."

I grind against him faster, feeling that little tingling sensation begin, and keep up the pace. My hands move to his chest, squeezing as I ride him, and I chase the feeling of euphoria with every pulse of my clit. My pussy clenches the closer I get to my orgasm, and he begins to top from the bottom.

"Oh, God, B," he groans. "Just like that, baby. You're doing so good...give me *more*." I smirk, changing my position until I'm leaning back slightly, and spit on my fingers. "What are you —ohhh, *fuck*."

Two of my fingers circle his hole, and I put a little pressure behind my touch until I let one slip in. At first, there's resistance, and he sucks in a sharp breath like it hurts. However I keep going, rubbing up as I thrust my finger in and out, and he begins to shake.

"Baby," he groans, his legs trembling. "What the hell are you doing to me—" Theo lets out a loud moan as I keep thrusting my finger in and out, all the while rubbing my clit against his pelvis. "Oh—fuck, fuck, *fuck*."

I speed up the movement of my hips until I feel my release within reach. When he grabs my hips and rubs me on his pelvis again, I shatter. Biting the inside of my cheek, I taste blood as I ride through my orgasm, still fingering his hole. Theo's back arches off the floor with another thrust of my finger, and when I rub that sweet spot one last time, his dick jerks inside of me as he comes.

With a loud exhale, Theo closes his eyes like he's in pain. "Holy shit," he pants. "What a way to say goodbye."

"Yeah?" I grin, removing my finger from inside of him, then bending down to meet his lips with mine. "You like it?"

"Loved it," he groans.

"Let's go home now," I tell him, getting off him and going to the bathroom to clean up.

After a twenty-minute drive and unloading the two bins from the truck, we're back at the condo, making dinner. I don't know when I'll make the time to unpack, but it doesn't matter. Even though today is about starting a new chapter, and unpacking would signify that, I learned quickly that I'm going to be the one to decide how this chapter starts out, and I want to do it with all our favorite people.

There's a knock at the door, signifying the arrival of Jeremy and Cheyenne—together, for *whatever* reason—and Theo opens it.

"Hey, Bai!" Cheyenne calls out from the entryway. "You in the kitchen?"

"Yeah!" I call out, "Come here, you whore."

She laughs at that, and when she reaches me, she slaps my ass hard. "Pot meet kettle."

"Not to use my pity card on this, but what the hell is going on with you and Jer?" I ask her, abandoning the lasagna I'm preparing. Her eyes widen, and her lips tighten, which tells me she's not saying one word.

"Nothing, really," she replies quietly. "Don't make it a thing, Bai. He and I were just fucking—but now it's over."

"Is that why you arrived together?"

"Coincidence." Chey shrugs, "We didn't ride together."

Footsteps announce the arrival of someone else, and Cheyenne and I immediately pretend to be busy with preparing the lasagna. She hands me three different types of cheese, and I begin layering them with the meat.

"So," Theo clears his throat, seeing right through my bullshit and smirking, "I guess it's just us tonight. Oliver and his girl are going to her sister's house to meet the new baby, and Matthew and Noah can't make it for whatever other reason I didn't pay attention to."

"Hmm." I nod. "That's okay. We have each other." I smile and gaze at Cheyenne. "Right, Chey?"

"Yep." Cheyenne pops the 'p'.

"Perfect," Theo replies, then walks right back out of the kitchen to join his friend on the couch.

Chey and I take a moment to stare at them, but when I turn my face to look at her, she has a pained expression. Jeremy and Chey make eye contact, and his face drops immediately, too. "Tell me, Chey," I whisper. What happened?"

"I set him up."

"Set him up, how?" I ask with confusion, my eyes narrowing to slits as I look at her. She doesn't look at me, though. Instead, she grabs the bags of cheese and puts them in the fridge for me.

I hadn't noticed just how unput together she is, which is unlike her. She's wearing baggy sweatpants and a sweatshirt that says 'Hockey Mom' even though she doesn't have any kids, and her hair is piled up on top of her head in the messiest bun I have ever seen. She's wearing Nike tennis shoes, and her eyes aren't only bloodshot but also have purple bags underneath, which she's not even attempting to cover with makeup. Something is very wrong.

"How, Chey?" I repeat.

"I told him we should see other people, except I didn't mean it," she whispers, looking back at the living room. Jeremy and her make eye contact once more, but he breaks it first. "And he agreed."

"Okay? So? Did he go out on a date?"

Cheyenne sighs, "I don't know, Bai—"

"Then stop fucking moping, and let's have a good night."

"Fine," she huffs, turning around to leave me in the kitchen all alone. Instead, I grab her wrist and tug her toward me until I've enveloped her in a tight hug. "Bai, what are you doing?"

My eyes sting from the sudden emotion clogging my throat. "I'm sorry, Cheyenne. I'm sorry for not listening to you every time you told me to leave Robert. I'm sorry I moved here and left you without telling you where my new home is. I'm sorry for being a bitch and taking you for granted. You're my best friend, and I never meant for this to happen. Please forgive me. I love you."

Cheyenne stiffens against me, pulling away from me with a stunned expression. Her eyebrows draw in as if confused, and then she smiles sadly at me. "I forgive you, Bai." She grabs my hand and squeezes it once. "All I heard was that you love me. How much?"

I roll my eyes. "So much."

"In that case, I'm gonna go sit down and wait for you to serve me my damn food." She grins, going to the living room while I pop the lasagna in the oven. "But I love you too!"

I take a moment to take in the scene before me: the love of my life sitting on the couch waiting for me, his eyes never straying from mine. My best friend, who has helped me through everything, continues to be here for me. Theo's best friend, who has supported him through the most challenging parts of his life, is also here for us. It can't get better than that. I know it can't.

Closing the oven, I take a deep breath and muster my brightest smile—except this time, it's not fake. This time, I don't have to force anything. It just happens naturally.

Because I'm really, truly happy now, and no one can take that away from me anymore.

Bailey

EPILOGUE

One year later...

Theo made good on his promise. He brought me to Banff, my dream travel destination. The problem? He all but dragged me out of bed to go on a fucking hike at four in the morning. It's called the Big Beehive. Of course, he'd do that, he loves hiking. But damn, it is four in the morning in the middle of April in Canada. Do the math; it's still freezing.

Not only are we hiking almost seven miles round trip—fuck my life—we are also gaining over twenty-five hundred feet of elevation. All of this *just* to watch the sunrise. I'm sure it'll be worth it, but right now, as he tells me to hurry up and catch up to him, all I want to do is let myself fall back down the hill, and maybe if I'm unconscious, he will take me back to the hotel.

I huff, using my hiking pole to help me up the hill a little better. My shins are sore already from the angle at which we're hiking, and my chest is burning, but we're almost there, according to Theo. I can literally see absolutely nothing, and if it weren't for both our headlamps and a massive flashlight, we'd be submerged in complete darkness. I guess I should thank my lucky stars that we haven't run into a bear or mountain lion yet.

"This sucks dick, Theo," I groan as I ignore the pain in my shins the higher we climb. I'm sure I'll have blisters on my heels by the end of this. "We couldn't hike something less…high?"

Theo chuckles, "Don't be such a baby." Okay, so maybe I'm being one, but can he blame me? I don't love hiking, so this better be worth it. Now that I think about it, what the hell else is there to do here? Hiking seems like the only option. Why was Banff my dream travel destination again? "It's almost over, Bailey. Just another quarter mile."

"I need a break," I whine. "Please?"

"You'll get a break when we get to the top, baby." I can't see his face, but I can hear the smile in his voice. "We're almost there."

I press my lips together in a tight line and don't reply, focusing on my steps and not the pain I feel with every one of them. Let's just hope the climb is worse than the descent, because if I struggle at all to get off this damn mountain, I might just let myself free-fall. Going downhill is less of an exertion, but I think it will be scarier for me to see how far down we have to go. And since he wants to see the sunrise, I doubt I'll have darkness as my friend to keep me from being scared.

Crap.

"Ready?" he asks me, reaching for my hand just as I see the top of some huge boulders. The sun is not quite out, but there's some light. "Close your eyes."

"You want me to close my eyes, Theo? These rocks are huge. What if I—"

Theo laughs, grabbing my hand and squeezing it once. "You're not going to fall, baby."

"Fine," I reply, closing my eyes.

With a tight grip on my hand, he guides me to the top. The back of my lids has turned orange, and I can tell the sun is rising even without opening my eyes. Now I wonder if I'm going to throw up from the altitude or if it's going to be the most beautiful thing I've ever seen in my life. Or maybe both, knowing me.

"Open those pretty green eyes, baby," he whispers in my ear. "Look at this beauty."

My eyes flutter open slowly, and I blink back from the sunlight. Gasping, I cover my mouth as I sweep my eyes over the sight in front of me. Theo stays behind me, and I seek comfort in knowing he's here if I'm scared. "*Wow,*" I murmur.

Rocky mountains span the entire space in front of us, and we get the best panoramic view of them. There's snow on the peaks, shining against the rising sun, and I let my hand fall as I peer down. The bluest, brightest lake I've ever seen is nestled between the mountains, and pine trees surround it as well. It's beautiful. Breathtaking.

"Theo—" I gasp again, "This is *beautiful.*"

When he doesn't reply, I turn around, just to find him on one knee holding a glistening diamond ring between his thumb and forefinger. Tears well in my eyes, dancing to the beat of my heart and spilling over. This can't be real—

"Bailey." Theo smiles, and when I gaze into his blue eyes, all I see is *love*—and tears. "From the moment I saw you, I knew you'd be the most important person in my life. I don't know what it was about you, maybe your stubbornness—" I chuckle, and he grins. "Or maybe that I knew in my bones you and I were made for each other. Baby, I love you more than anyone in this entire world, and if you give me the chance, I'll spend the rest of our lives proving it to you. I know I'm not perfect—and I never will be, but I'll try really hard to be for you." He pauses briefly and searches my eyes. "Will you marry me?"

Tears stream down both of our cheeks, and I reach down to wipe his. With a shaky smile, I reply, "It's *always* been you, Theo." I sniffle and grin. "It will always be you. So *yes,* a million times yes, I'll marry you."

Before I can blink, Theo is up and pulling me into the

tightest hug of my life, lifting me off my feet and burying his face in my hair. "I love you so much, my Bailey." He says against my neck. "Forever and ever."

Putting me down on my feet, Theo takes a step back, grabbing my hand. I hold my breath as he slips the ring on, a perfect fit. I've never been a flashy girl, and I think he got that memo because it's a dainty diamond solitaire—absolutely perfect and breathtaking.

"I love you, Theo." I sniffle, and he grins. "I guess this stupid hike was worth it after all."

"Did I do good, then?" He chuckles, taking my hand in his and looking at the ring on my finger. "I love how it looks on you."

"You did amazing," I reply honestly. "I love it so much."

And I do, but mostly, I just love him more.

After everything that happened with Robert, I never imagined I'd find love again. I thought I'd never find the strength to let go of my pain, to start over from scratch.

New beginnings are scary, but now I'm ready to face them head-on—with *him*.

What's Next?

Thank you from the BOTTOM of my heart for reading *Stay With Me*! Please don't forget to review if you enjoyed the book. Reviews are so important to indie authors like me. I am forever grateful for your support!

If you'd like to be part of the community and talk about the series, join the Facebook Group, Ruby's Darklings.

STALK ME:
My **website** is authorshaeruby.com
Sign up for my **newsletter** at authorshaeruby.com/newsletter
Follow me on **Facebook** at Facebook.com/authorshaeruby
Join my **Reader Group** at Facebook.com/groups/rubysdarkling

Afterword

This book changed me on a cellular level. It was healing as well as difficult to write, but I wouldn't change a thing. None of this would've been possible without the help of my incredible sensitivity reader, so Jay this is for you. This book is yours. You have my words and my heart. Love you 'til the end of time. When I thought I was going to fail, you picked me back up.

Thank you to my readers for giving me a chance. If you're new here, welcome. If you're not, thank you for sticking around!

So much love for you,
Shae Ruby

Also By SHAE RUBY

Acknowledgments

Just like with every other book, it takes a village of supportive people to get it from the first draft to a final manuscript. I would never be able to do this alone, and I'm so grateful to the following people for making all of this possible.

To my readers, first and foremost. Thank you for giving me a chance in the first place. None of this would be possible without you. The past almost two years have been a whirlwind, and I still can't believe how much my community has grown. Thank you for being here and sticking around.

To my husband, Conner. You blow me away. The faith you have in me means everything to me. I wouldn't want to spend my life with anyone else. I love you.

To my mother, I love you. Thank you for your endless support.

To N.J. Weeks, wow are you tired of talking to me every day yet? Because I couldn't have done this without you. I love you more than you know!

To my amazing, incredible, one of a kind, personal assistant and best friend, Erin, I would never be able to accomplish this without you. Thank you for being by my side.

To Julia from entirely bonkerz editing (@entirelybonkerz), as you know, I'm super grateful for you. You make my stories shine brighter. I wouldn't be able to publish without the love you give my work. Your guidance is irreplaceable. Thank you.

To Lunar Rose Editing Services, as always, I'm so grateful for you. Wow, look at how far we've come together!

To Quirky Circe, as always, I bow down to you, my queen. Thank you for making my books gorgeous!

To Jay, my amazing sensitivity reader, you know this book is YOURS. In every sense of the word. I love you so much. Thank you for always being by my side.

To my beta readers—Erin, Jennifer, Kylie, Ellie. Thank you so much for everything. You're all so important to me and I love you.

To my Street Team, you guys are AMAZING!! Thank you for all your help. Wow, I really couldn't do this without every single one of you.

Lastly, I want to thank my social media followers both on Instagram and TikTok, my Facebook page, and my Readers Group. None of this would be possible without you spreading the word about my books!

With love,
Shae Ruby

About the Author

Shae Ruby spends her time writing books that make you *feel*.

When not writing you can find her spending time outdoors or planning her next trip.

Music is her love language, as you can probably tell by her playlists.

Shae Ruby is represented by Lunar Literary Agency. For all subsidiary rights, please contact
Angie Ojeda-Hazen:
angie@lunarliteraryagency.com